the silence

Jim Kraus

BARBOUR
PUBLISHING

the silence

Published by Barbour Publishing, Inc., P.O. Box 719, Uhrichsville, OH 44683
www.barbourbooks.com

Our mission is to publish and distribute inspirational products offering exceptional value and biblical encouragement to the masses.

ecpa Member of the
Evangelical Christian
Publishers Association

Printed in the United States of America
5 4 3 2 1

To my son, Elliot.

No one understands how God spreads out the clouds
or how he sends thunder from where he lives.
Watch how God scatters his lightning around him,
lighting up the deepest parts of the sea.
This is the way God governs the nations;
this is how he gives us enough food.
God fills his hands with lightning
and commands it to strike its target.
His thunder announces the coming storm,
and even the cattle know it is near.

JOB 36:29–33

april 1

"Is this sodium-free?"

Tom Lyton looked up from his notebook. He pushed a stray lock of thick blond hair out of his face. "It's water."

Ira Werblin held up the water bottle to the light, angling it away from his eyes. "I know it's water, but is it sodium-free? The print's microscopic."

Tom peered at the label, his brown eyes narrowing. "Sodium-free, chlorine-free, mineral-free, trace elements-free. . .not a thing in it, and it cost you three bucks. They sure saw you coming."

Ira unscrewed the cap and took a long swallow. "Tom, if you don't care about your health, no one else will." Ira reached over and patted Tom's stomach. The leather couch creaked with the sound of money. "You need to be at the health club more often, old boy. You're not getting any younger. You'll never be able to find a little something on the side—nudge, nudge—if you don't look the part."

Tom offered a weak smile in return. He was no angel, but Werblin's obvious enjoyment of the illicit was crass and unsettling. Ten years ago, when Tom had first come to Los Angeles, he hadn't liked Werblin—and he didn't like him any better now. But business was business, and Tom had a script to write.

Ira, the producer of the made-for-television movie, and Tom, the movie's screenwriter, were in the second day of their preproduction meetings. The concept of the movie was simple. A survivalist group falls under the spell of a charismatic leader with an anti-government grudge. The group plots to assassinate the governor of

California. The hero infiltrates the group and foils the villain's plot with his bravery and high-tech gadgets.

"Listen, Ira, let's leave my personal fitness habits out of this. The only thing I want to talk about is this movie."

"Tommy-boy, you are too focused on this work thing. Life is short."

"I know, but so is my writing schedule."

"Calm. . .center. . .focus."

"Please, don't start with that."

"Well, Tommy-boy, you need to center yourself. It'll do you good. You'll be able to work faster."

"You already know I'm quick."

"Indeed, Tommy-boy, that you are." Ira leaned closer and whispered, "You and I both know this movie won't take you more than a couple of days to throw together."

"Listen, Ira, I do have some pride in my craft."

"Oh yes, the craftsman. . .the artist. Well, Tommy-boy, all I want. . .well, how should I put this so a cultured man like yourself will understand? What this movie needs—and what I want—is a lot of sex, violence, loud music, and explosions. I want the hero to win. Write the kind of movie that you used to write in the old days."

Ira took another long drink from his water bottle. "That shouldn't be too hard to do, should it?"

Tom scowled and was within a heartbeat of a caustic response when the office bungalow began to slowly rock and vibrate.

Ira stood up with a smile and yelled out, "Earthquake!" He jumped up on his desk, assumed a surfer's stance, and shouted, "Surf's up!"

Tom had run to the doorway, as would any California resident well versed in earthquake precautions. The quake was minor and lasted only a dozen seconds.

Ira laughed and jumped down from the desk. "Tom, don't be worried, my man. When your time's up, it's up. Standing under a doorway isn't going to protect you."

Tom looked outside. A few dozen people had run from the small offices and now stood around laughing. No one seemed the least bit upset or panicked.

Tom tried to calm the hurried beating of his heart. He stepped back inside, sat down, and looked at Ira, who was rearranging the top of his desk. Stacks of papers, treatments, script revisions, and proposals had been scattered by his desk surfing.

"Does it seem to you these small quakes are happening a lot more often this year?"

Ira looked up and shook his ponytail. "Nope. The nerds at Cal Tech said it's no big deal. About the same number this year as last. Heard it on CNN last night."

"I don't know. . .feels like there are more. Not that I keep track, but it feels like they're happening more often."

"You could be right. But I'm no judge. I've become so immune to them that I've stopped taking them seriously." Ira sat back at his desk and propped up his feet. "I guess that might be stupid, huh?"

Tom wanted to answer but held his tongue and merely shrugged instead.

The Reverend Jerry Moses, pastor of The Temple of God's Calling in Stonefort, Illinois, ran his hand through his thick black hair and smiled. "Now listen to me, Pawlis," he said slowly and clearly. "Earthquakes will be first, then some other things will happen in the skies, then Jesus comes back."

"So it isn't the other way around then. I thought for sure that it was the other way." Pawlis Smidgers, Stonefort's mayor, often stopped in the parsonage on Monday afternoons to chat.

"I would have asked you about this yesterday after the service," Pawlis explained, "but you looked real busy."

The reverend waited.

"So what you're saying," Pawlis continued, wanting to make

sure that he got the scenario correct, "is that the earthquakes come first, then Jesus returns."

Rev. Moses nodded.

"But you need to remember, Pawlis," Rev. Moses confided in a stage whisper, "although I spend a lot of my week studying through God's words, that doesn't mean that everything I say will happen is truly going to come to pass. It may not happen exactly like I say it will happen. I daresay that many folk in this fine town will be wondering why they're still here and others are gone. . . . Pawlis, you are a believing person, are you not?"

Pawlis thought for a second, then nodded fast.

"Then you have nothing to worry about. I tell you this—and this is the gospel—that God protects His own. He protects His chosen people."

"That's the truth."

"Indeed, Pawlis. God protects His chosen, for sure. You just make certain that you're ready and among the chosen. Then you tell others to get ready as well. Will you do that, Pawlis?"

Pawlis nodded again. "I plan on doing that as long as I'm around, Reverend. I plan on that for certain."

Megan Smith was on top of the world—she felt strong, powerful, in control.

Commodity orders flowed around her like a blizzard. Corn, soybean, hogs, oranges, wheat—everything bought and sold in a frenzy of buys and puts and holds and buying short and buying long. She loved the swirl and dance of trading futures, the bark and growl of the buy and sell. It was intoxicating and heady.

Megan, only a few years out of business school, had spent one long, frustrating year learning the complexities of the commodities game at Long, Drackem, and Boyd in New York City. Over the next six months, she began to acquire a rhythm, a sense of the market. It was as if she were born with an intuitive sense of where the markets were headed. Some traders had it, she told herself, and some did not. The successful ones did.

On the fast tract to partnership, Megan wrapped her hands about the throat of the corn market and began to squeeze out dollars. She traded for her firm's clients, acting on her gut feelings, and reaped them profits and then more profits. Her clients loved her and her uncanny sixth sense.

Her career had taken off like a rocket. Money poured into her accounts, hand over fist. Success in this business begat power, confidence, a sense of invincibility. And invincibility begat the ability to bend the rules, defending it as a right and a privilege of success. And additional success begat even more money. Megan began to hedge some trades with small dollars of her own—in violation of the company's policy as well as a Securities Commission guideline. She could not trade under her own name, so she used a few of the dollars in the "float," the corporate version of petty cash. Long, Drackem, and Boyd liked happy clients, and the float was used to smooth out any small losses that might upset the more sensitive client. The float had assets of nearly $250,000, and every senior account executive had access to the money on an as-needed basis. Megan slipped nearly $50,000 out of the account into a fictitious account under her mother's maiden name. Megan was sure her mother, who had been dead for ten years, wouldn't mind.

"Everyone does it," whispered one senior manager during a boozy, after-hours get-together. "It's like padding your expense account. A few dollars here and there—and no one minds. Just don't get reckless."

And Megan surprised herself at how little this bending of the rules bothered her. In any other job, in any other situation, Megan would have demurred. But not here and not now. *After all, everyone does it. It's almost expected.*

Her father's noble sensibilities would be so bruised if he knew. If he learned that his only daughter was hedging the law, he would be grieved. A career police officer, he had instructed her to obey the laws of men with as much fervor as one obeyed the laws of God.

So Megan did her best not to think of her father as she traded on her account. She hadn't thought of God for many years. God played a very small part in her life and her lifestyle. Of the two images—her father and God—it was her father's face that was more troubling.

She finished a large trade for her wealthiest client, a real-estate developer on Long Island. As she passed over the buy orders, she tacked another 10,000-unit order onto it, adding her mother's name to the slip, and pulling the funds from the float. By tomorrow, when she sold, she would replace the cash into the float, take the profits, and slip them into her mother's account. No one would be the wiser.

She pulled her fingers through her long auburn hair. It was a nervous gesture that belied the steeliness in her green eyes.

Perhaps I should stop, she thought as the floor runner took the orders. *But everyone does it.*

Few friendships developed at Long, Drackem, and Boyd. Only the few top traders would be rewarded with a partnership and begin to reap its obscene profits. Megan, like a shark, hunted that prize with grim determination.

And a shark has to keep swimming forward or it drowns, she thought, then punched up another client on the computer screen. *And all I'm doing is swimming forward,* she mused with a tentative smile. Just swimming forward.

<hr>

The sky was a deep, pellucid blue, so clear that one could see into the very stuff of the universe beyond. For April in southern Illinois, the day was perfect—cool, dry, fresh. The winter snows had melted weeks ago, and the first green shoots of spring edged their way toward the sun.

Peter Wilson gently embraced his six-year-old daughter,

Becca, as he jumped the swollen creek a mile from their home. She laughed as he jumped, her blond hair flying in the crisp air. As soon as they landed, she struggled out of his arms and began to run, shrieking with joy as her legs pumped. Even with her slightness, her feet left small, wet imprints in the earth. Her features, always close to laughter and a smile, were wrapped in joy this day.

"Becca, wait!" he called out, running after her, laughing.

Peter, tall, stocky, with thinning blond hair, possessed an easy manner and a quick and gentle smile. His blue eyes danced when he laughed, tilting his head back to the sky. Lines carved that laughter into the corners of his eyes. The wrinkles were an echo of his broad grin.

The two cleared the rise, and home and their old weathered barn came into view. A glint of metal—the storm door—flashed in the sun and flickered as it closed.

Peter glanced toward the west. The sun was low—he guessed the hour to be close to seven. Linda would be waiting for them, pacing about the small trailer.

They would have returned earlier, but he had wanted to show Becca a warren of rabbits he'd discovered a few days earlier. She loved all things in nature, and rabbits were one of her favorites. He didn't tell her that he would return in a few months, with shotgun in hand, and take a few of them for dinner. *Let her be a child,* he told himself, *for as long as she can. No sense telling her every truth there is in the world.*

Becca stopped, almost tumbling over, and knelt down. Peter was sure her knees would be muddy and wet. "Daddy, what's this?"

Peter bent over her shoulder, pushing the long grass aside. "It's a deer print. See, you can tell by the two halves—the split hoof—that a deer walked right past here."

"When?"

Peter examined the print more closely. "The earth is still wet—the lines are distinct—maybe last night, maybe early this morning. Deer feed at night mostly."

"Could I have seen him if I was awake?"

"Sure, if the sun was up. And speaking of the sun," he said as he stood up, eyeing the trailer, "we better get home before the sun goes down. I think your momma's waiting for us."

He took her hand, and she followed at his side. He watched her face. She had closed her eyes, letting her father lead her, letting whatever she was experiencing be uncolored by vision—at least for these few steps. It was a gesture born of such security and confidence and love that Peter's heart swelled to near bursting. He allowed her childlike trust to bubble to the surface and kept her hand tightly in his.

After a few minutes, he stopped, picked Becca up, lifted her to his back, and took off at a slow lope. His daughter perched on his back like a rider, her arms clasped around his neck, her thin legs held to his sides by his arms. Even with her light weight, he was gasping and red-faced by the time he arrived at the trailer.

Linda was behind the storm door, holding it open, her face tight and drawn. "Where have you been?"

The day suddenly grew chillier.

"I've been waiting dinner for nearly an hour. You know I have a meeting at church tonight—and choir practice. It's like you deliberately do this every time I need to get out of the house. You make a point of being late, and then I'm late and you don't care a whit about it."

"Linda—"

"Mommy, Mommy, we saw a deer print and some baby bunnies and a big turtle over by the pond and—"

"I don't care if you went to the St. Louis Zoo. You promised you would be home by five and it's now—" she looked down at her watch, her eyes turning to slits—"ten minutes till seven."

"Linda, I'm sorry. We just had such a good time, and the day was nice—"

"Save it for later. I already ate. Your dinner is in the oven. You feed Becca. I have to go." She brushed past both of them and jumped into their rust-battered Toyota.

"What time will you be home?" Peter called out as his daughter climbed the front steps.

Either Linda didn't hear or didn't bother to answer. She drove off, stones and mud clattering angrily against the car.

"Is Mommy mad at us?" Becca asked later as Peter slid her chair to the kitchen table.

"Well, sweets, we were late. What Mommy does at church is important to her. She was angry with us for making her late. I was wrong."

"What does Mommy do at church all the time?"

Peter reached over and tousled his daughter's hair. "A lot of things, sweets. Mommy does a lot of things."

"Does she like being at church?"

Peter stopped, tried to smile, then said, "Yes, sweets, she likes it."

"Likes it more than home?"

Peter looked down at his daughter, unable to answer her innocent question.

april 16

The noise began with a low rumble, imperceptible at first, like a large cat purring in a pool of sun on a comfortable couch. The sound crept into being, slowly growing louder, just nicking at the edge of perception.

After a moment a louder, more persistent vibration followed. It increased a note at a time, building into an ever-louder hum, until people stopped their activities, turned, and searched for its source.

Dogs cowered under beds, and cats scurried beneath tables. Some pets scrambled frantically, seeking escape. Songbirds took to wing silently, quickly. Trees, their leaves motionless in California's warm morning sun, began to shimmer—just a breath at first, then faster, till the leaves bared their paler undersides to the sun.

At the top of a ridge above Malibu Beach, north of Los Angeles, Tom Lyton walked at the edge of his property line. He stared out at the ocean. He had owned this piece of land with its spectacular, multimillion-dollar view for more than seven years and had gleefully watched it grow in value, adding several zeroes to his net worth—on paper.

A delicate cup in his hand contained a thick espresso. He stood, watching the glass-smooth Pacific catch the morning light. It was his favorite time of day, just before he had to deal with the meetings and traffic and confusion and anger of a new day in Hollywood. This day, normal in most respects, brought no usual sounds of birds or surf. *A muffled morning,* Tom thought. *Odd, even for this protected enclave.*

A handful of pebbles trickled down from a rock outcropping a few feet above. They bounced at his ankles, rattling their way down the steep face of the ridge.

Curious, Tom thought. He turned to see what bird or squirrel had loosened the stones. He peered to the north, craning his neck upward.

It was then that he knew. A grumble, low and throaty, emanated far beneath him. He felt it, sensed it through the soles of his carefully polished, hand-sewn Italian loafers. He looked down. The tassels on his shoes trembled and danced.

He dropped the cup at his feet, splashing espresso on his trouser cuffs, and began to sprint east, back through the grounds of his ridgetop estate, back to his home and family. As he ran, he heard the rock begin to shriek in the canyon below.

His screams were no match for the screeching of the rock.

Peter Wilson stood, almost hidden in the thick wisps of fog, listening. He had followed the deer, a crafty old buck, through five miles of brush. The brush was wild and scraggly, full of thorns. A few anemic trees pocked the landscape. The land, unused by farmers for decades, possessed a dreary, abandoned look.

He shouldered his rifle, an old .30 caliber Springfield. It had belonged to his father, gone twenty years this summer. Peter wanted this deer. The animal was not sport to Peter; it was food.

He had stopped in a clearing, held his breath for a moment, hoping to hear the velvet crash of the large buck through the brush. When he heard nothing, Peter turned slowly, noiselessly, in a circle.

He's here. I know he's here.

Peter leaned forward into the late-morning gloom. The woods fell silent—no call, no chirp, no rustle of feather.

That's weird, Peter reflected. *Where are the birds this morning?*

Just then he felt a start, a sudden movement. It was unlike any movement he had ever known. He stopped dead still, tried to quiet his breathing, and listened hard. The noise—a twisting, a grinding, a gnawing—filled the air.

Peter looked down at his feet. His left foot, planted firmly on the ground, inched forward. He watched, tilted his head, much like a dog when hearing a high-pitched whistle. His right foot slid backward an inch, then two. He was walking without moving his feet.

A narrow furrow appeared between his legs. It opened up, perhaps a foot deep, revealing roots and white, fleshy grubs and earthworms in the moist soil. Then, with the startling impact of a firecracker, the earth split in a violent spasm and tossed Peter to his knees. He grabbed his rifle and rolled to his side as the earth pitched and rolled and dipped. Grabbing at grass tussocks and roots, Peter hung on, like he had hung on to the safety bar on a roller-coaster ride when he was a child.

But this was no ride. The screams and cries came not from children on roller coasters and bumper cars; they came from the very soul of the earth itself. Trees toppled and rocks sank as the earth swallowed them whole. In front of Peter, the old buck he had been trailing bounded into the clearing before him. The animal's eyes were circled with white in absolute terror, his legs scrabbling to grip the trembling earth.

Peter thought for a fleeting moment of unslinging his weapon and taking the deer. His arm began to move when the earth grimaced and frowned, and another narrow but deep chasm opened. The deer tumbled in, only its neck and shoulders visible. Then the rift began to close, like the chewing maws of a huge beast.

Peter watched, frozen in horror and disbelief, as the animal, in mute agony, disappeared into the earth. Then he stood unsteadily, with the earth all around him rippling like a pool after a boulder falls in its waters. He looked east toward his home and began to run. On his lips were the first words of a prayer.

The Reverend Jerry Moses paced in his office. On his desk was the beginning of this Sunday's message. He had written the first several lines, scribbling harsh strokes across the legal pad. Now he stood at the window, hands clasped behind his back. He rocked on his heels back and forth, back and forth.

I have the opening, he thought, *but what do I say now?* He sighed as he walked toward his cluttered desk, sat down, and peered at the tablet.

He scowled as he caught his image in the glass top of the desk. *I need a haircut before Sunday, and that means a drive to Evansville. Maybe tomorrow.* He wouldn't let the town barber work on his thick black hair. *I'd come out looking like a farmer. . .like everyone else in town.*

He flipped through a book of sermon illustrations, then stood up and stepped to the office door. It opened out on the parking lot of the church. Other than his car, the lot was empty.

He opened the door, and a spring breeze rippled past. He smelled fertilizer in the air and quickly closed the aluminum door. He never liked the rich loam scent of the earth, the thickening aroma of spring.

Rev. Moses had arrived in Stonefort thirteen years earlier. At thirty-eight, he knew he would never be young again—nor called to stand before a megachurch. Yet he had built this church from a mere handful to a congregation of more than two hundred people.

That is something I can take pride in. Two hundred people in this small town is a lot of people.

The reverend sat back at his desk. On the far corner was a picture of his wife. The picture gave him an odd feeling. *I should get rid of it,* he thought, then realized he wouldn't. His wife was in the state hospital in Dixon. Severe depression and schizophrenia. Incurable, they said. No one mentioned her much anymore. She had been gone nearly six years now.

Next to her picture was one of his son, Matthew. *Good thing he's adopted,* Rev. Moses thought, *or he might be at risk of inheriting his mother's pain.* A tall, unsmiling twelve year old wearing a baseball uniform stood staring back.

Matthew lived with his aunt and uncle in Eldorado, only thirty miles to the northeast. They had other children, and Matthew enjoyed living with them. "A child needs a mother and brothers and sisters, and he doesn't have any," Rev. Moses had said. "He needs a proper home, and everyone knows my home and my heart are the church."

Each summer and for the holidays, the boy visited his father, but returned to his aunt and uncle during most of the school year. The reverend often felt ill at ease with the child, as if he were being judged. But he'd dismissed those feelings with the thought, *It's not fair that a child should have only a father—and one upon whom the church leans so heavily.*

Once again Rev. Moses took his pen, a giveaway from the local feed store, and clicked up and down. He hoped inspiration would strike soon.

Before he wrote another word, however, he heard a shrill scream—not a human shriek, but the wail of metal to metal or rock to rock. He stood and ran to the door. A wave of earth formed at the far north edge of the parking lot, rippling under the gravel and stone. His car lurched like a ship tossed in a storm. He grabbed at the door frame. The wave broke before it hit the church. Several trees at the edge of the field toppled over like flowers in a wind. The fire siren from the town hall began to wail. Five seconds later its wail stopped in midscreech.

Another wave rolled across the parking lot, this one coming from the west. His car pitched violently. The reverend screamed as his new Buick turned on its side. Then, as if in slow motion, it rolled onto its top, windows popping as the roof compacted to the body.

A huge chasm formed at the far edge of the lot and snaked

toward the church. Rev. Moses held up his hand and screamed, "Stop!"

And to his absolute and total amazement, the rift stopped advancing. Even its width began to narrow.

He looked up at the sky in disbelief. "Lord," he shouted, "if You want my work to continue, spare me! Spare this church! I will spread Thy Word!"

He fell to his knees and closed his eyes. *If this is the end, let me be the Lord's trumpet. Let me announce God's calling to the nation. Lord, hear my prayer.*

Megan Smith glanced up from her computer screen. The digital clock on her desk read 12:03. Panic had begun to rise in her throat. Her stomach churned, and she twisted the coiled mouse cable into a knot over her thumb and hand. The markets, specifically the corn markets, had opened strong today. Megan had suffered through a weeklong streak of bad luck, poor decisions, and rotten timing.

"I need to be right today," she whispered to herself. Long, Drackem, and Boyd would not tolerate losses.

"Chicago on line three, Smith. You better answer it," barked John Peck, a newly hired trader. He was aggressively snapping at her heels, closing in on her position.

Corn futures had taken off like a rocket, each day clicking up increases. She had bought short the day before and with each tick of the market had increased her share—and her earnings. Knowing when to sell out was the key. It was like catching a wave—timing was everything. Go too early, and tumble into the turbulent waters. Wait too long, and you miss the crest. Then the wave heads to shore, with the indecisive paddling furiously after it. Megan's genius had been in knowing the absolute crest of the commodity's wave. She would bail out a fraction before the wave broke, yielding profits and praise. But not this week. This week she had been lost in the foam and swirl as the waves broke over her head, threatening to drown her.

The phone crackled and snapped, static interfering with the satellite transmission. ". . .and then they headed south. . ." The voice trailed off again.

"Hello! What was that? You're breaking up!" Megan shouted into the phone, trying to be heard over the shriek of loud voices filling the office.

"I said that the futures are taking a nosedive! Why on earth are you holding on to them?" The voice belonged to Nate Green, one of her counterparts in the Chicago branch of Long, Drackem, and Boyd. He was as close to a friend as she had in this friendless business.

"What!?" Megan screamed. "It can't be! The prices are still on the uptick. I'm fine!"

"All I know is that the corn market is farther south than Mexico at the moment. You had better bail now while you can still get out under the margin call."

Megan cried and cursed. "This can't be happening." She scrutinized her screen, set to the Chicago commodities market. She scanned the figures. They looked fine to her. She was still winning. She checked the bottom left of the spreadsheet, its numbers glowing amber.

"Oh God," she cried again and reached out and hit the machine with the heel of her hand, an ineffectual but instinctual gesture. The number in the bottom right-hand corner of her screen—the time code—indicated that the numbers she was looking at were more than thirty minutes old. Occasionally, when trading went frantic, positions traded hands in a virtual hurricane of orders. When that happened, computers failed to keep pace. They could fall behind up to five minutes. That was serious but not crippling. But thirty minutes! That was unheard of. Such deviation could not happen.

Megan slammed the phone down, grabbed the keyboard, and clicked some keys to access the smaller commodity market in Des Moines—it did less volume but was always on time.

"Oh," she cried softly. The call from Chicago was right. The futures had dropped more than 40 percent, a monumental shift in prices.

"My account's all margined," she said under her breath. "I have to get out. I can't cover $500,000 in losses. I have to get out."

Selling her options—held in secret, held in violation of trading regulations—now, even at the lower prices, would cause a six-figure loss. If she managed to sell, if she could find a buyer, she might get off with being fired rather than facing prosecution for illegal margin trading with the firm's money.

She picked up the phone on her desk, punched in the speed-dial number for the Chicago office, and waited, every second booming in her mind like a Fourth of July firework. Her heart thudded fast in her chest.

On the ninth ring a voice answered, garbled and indistinct.

"Nate Green! I need to talk to Nate! Now!" she screamed.

As her last words reverberated around her miniscule gray-and-white cubicle, the phone went dead—no static, no rustle of wire transmission, no fading crackle and wheeze—just absolute silence. She stared down at it, puzzled, then checked around. Several other traders were doing the same with their phones.

Then the lights flickered. After a brief and panicked glimpse at the ceiling, Megan hurriedly checked her computer monitor to see if she had lost her work. For a fraction of a second, the amber numbers continued to hold. But in a wink, the computer crackled from someplace deep inside. The ceiling lights went black as her computer whimpered and whirred its way to its death.

The entire group was stunned. The unthinkable was happening on the most volatile day of trading in the last seven months. Everyone grabbed at their cell phones or pagers. Not a single one responded. For a second, silence filled the room in a deafening wave. Then all was pandemonium. Traders ran from office to office, trying phones, computer hookups, cellular lines, radio phones. The more athletic and well-conditioned traders ran to the street, thinking that the problem was confined to their building. They fanned out over lower Manhattan, just as many other traders and brokers left their buildings in search of the same goal.

Radios and televisions sat dark and mute. Those who stayed behind in the office sat in panicked silence, the air in the room heavy and thick and dark.

Megan sat by herself, crying softly. She was ruined, no doubt, and faced a fate worse than termination.

How could I be so stupid?

Tom Lyton sprinted toward his house as the ground convulsed in rippling breakers of stone and earth. He fell to his knees three times, rolling forward to his shoulder, bouncing back to his feet, just like the heroes in his movies did as they ran from danger. He reached the brick drive as another wave of earth knocked him down, and his slick loafers skidded on the smooth bricks. He lay there, waiting for the rolling and pitching to stop, looking south along the ridge. Next door, a quarter mile distant, stood what was left of the Mahons' multilevel glass and concrete home—a series of short concrete piers, toothed into the sky. The rest of the home, broken into quarters and eighths, tumbled down the steep pitch toward the sea.

One lot farther south, a sprawling copy of a Carolina plantation mansion cracked down the center. The slate roof collapsed inward as Tom watched. Pulsing arms of flame flailed through its basement windows. Through a rent in the foundation, Tom saw the basement transform into a yellow and blue inferno as the gas line ruptured and caught fire.

He spun about to his knees and faced his home. Whitney

Morris, the noted architect to the stars, claimed it was his finest work. The residence was built of natural stone, cedar, slate, and glass, a delicate honeycomb of porches, windows, patios, balconies, arches, and walls. It was not the largest home in the neighborhood, with only five bedrooms and five baths, but it was handmade, organic, as if growing from the ground itself. It was designed to merge with the vibrations and aura that the golden coast of California provided. It sat like part of the ridge, resting on five thick steel beams drilled into the rock and stone of the earth. Its most unique feature was a small room, no bigger than a hotel room, perched at the very top of the structure, looking like a single massive stone resting upon high ground. To the occupant it provided a panoramic and private view of much of southern California, from the mountains to the sea. It was in that room where Tom wrote his screenplays and movie treatments. It was the perch that made him rich and powerful.

Tom watched as that room tilted, shook slightly, then tumbled from the rooftop with a giant growl. Bits of his computer system crashed to the earth in a cascade of rubble. Books and unfinished screenplays tumbled lazily toward the sea.

Then the earth lurched upward again. With an angry metallic shriek, the first supporting beam split—jagged and gaping—and lost its grip on the hillside. Each remaining beam tried to shoulder the increased weight, but in turn twisted and bent, screaming just before rending in two.

In slow motion, the house rocked gently toward the sea, nodding first to the south, then slowly pirouetting to the west. At the last second, as Tom silently screamed to the heavens, the house stopped its forward movement.

At the shattered and splintered window of the dining room facing the ocean, Tom saw his wife's face. Lydia's eyes were white, huge circles of terror. In the midst of the screaming of the ground, they called to Tom. They called out for the safety of his arms.

He saw her mouth form his name. Before he could hear the words, the beams slipped again, and the house began to die. Almost in one complete piece, the structure leaned down into the hillside; then, with a crashing roar that seemed to fill the world with the cries of steel and stone, it began to plunge down the steep hill, gouging out huge chasms in the dirt, plowing up earth as it crumbled and crashed the hundred yards to the sea.

Tom stood there transfixed, his body limp, his eyes staring after the wreckage as it rumbled down the ridge to Highway 1 and the sea. It took but a few quick steps to reach the edge of the ridge as he watched the bits and pieces of his life being ground into wreckage. The house, its pipes and wiring hanging like entrails from beneath, shrieked and crashed down the hill, turning and twisting and flattening itself.

He saw Lydia disappear as the ceiling met the floor. She had no chance. His daughter, Kalli, who had turned a year old only a week ago, had been asleep in the downstairs bedroom as the quake started.

Tom leapt over the rocky edge of the hillside and slid feet first down the steep slope, lost in a huge cloud of dust and smoke. Debris—wood and piping and shingles and glass—clattered past him as if he were being tossed in a giant's deadly kaleidoscope.

At the bottom of the bone-rattling slide, he bounced off the wreckage of his house, knowing that his shoulder would be bruised for weeks. Frantic, he clawed at the ruins, pulling up shards of his life—a piece of carpet, a broken stick of furniture, shards of a plate, a child's flattened toy—while looking desperately for his family.

He tossed and yanked and dove at the edge of the wreckage for what seemed like hours. He stood on what was once the roof of his house and scrambled from side to side, peering over the edge, trying in a herculean manner to pull the tons of debris off and toss them aside. The rubble resisted his every effort and tore his hands bloody.

He called out to Lydia, hoping for some reply, some indication that she had somehow survived the tragedy. He called to Kalli and listened for a faint cry that would tell him she had been spared. No human sounds reached his ears.

Gasping, Tom fell to his knees. A thin wisp of smoke curled about him, the scent of wood and fabric burning. There had been a fire in the living-room fireplace that morning. Even though it was warm in California, a fire in the morning was a delicious extravagance that Tom loved. Now that fire was smoldering beneath him, licking at what was left of his life, burning what had not already been ground to dust.

Tom knew then that his wife and daughter were dead. No one could have survived as the house compacted all open spaces. The huge slabs of rock and concrete had compressed, then crushed everything he held dear in life. He collapsed on the rough ground and wept. He doubled over in agony, wishing it had been him instead of his loved ones who had been inside.

Finally, with a heaving gasp, Tom sat up and peered up the coast. A dozen fires erupted where once there had been homes. The highway had disappeared into the waves. He glanced toward the east. The hillside behind him had begun to smoke. That meant the brush had caught fire, and the hills would be in flames within the hour.

Looking up into the heavens, Tom cried out, "My God! What have You done?"

⚒

The world had gone silent. The earth had bellowed and roared for more than five minutes, and in the eerie aftermath, it appeared that the birds had lost their song, the insects had forgotten their calls, and the very wind ceased to recall that it should slip across the flatland through the trees as a whisper.

Peter Wilson made his way back to the gravel-and-mud road where he had left his battered Ford pickup. The truck lay on its side at the bottom of a muddy new ravine, pitched into the soft southern Illinois soil. The trench was filling with dark and brackish water.

He stood there for several minutes, gathering his breath and his thoughts. Shouldering his rifle, he examined the sky, now colored a coppery green.

Lord, if this be the day that You return—and somehow I missed Your coming—please take me home with You. I have tried to be the best Christian I could, but I'm sure I have failed You more than I have served You. I love You, Lord, with all the heart I can. Please, dear God, take me with You to heaven.

With those thoughts preeminent, Peter headed west, toward his home, more than ten miles distant through deserted country. As he traveled, images of the trailer he and Linda and their daughter, Becca, had shared for the past ten years began to flash before his eyes.

I'm also asking, Lord, if this is not the Second Coming, that my wife and daughter be safe. If it be in Your mercies, let me find them alive—or in Your arms.

Unbidden, images came to him—of twisted metal and torn insulation, of fire, of chaos, of blood, and screams that went unanswered. As the images danced before him, he started to jog. The images seemed to laugh and cant at him, with delirious laughter screeching among the dead aspens along the road. His feet moved faster and faster until he was at a full sprint.

Lord, it has been years since I ran my last cross-country race. Allow me to do it one last time.

As Peter ran, sharp stitches of pain radiated from his sides and his breath rattled in his chest. His rifle bounced and banged against his back, hitting against his thighs. If this were any other day, he would have paused and walked, waiting till his breathing slowed and his heart found a comfortable pace. But this was no such ordinary day.

Peter retraced the route of this hunting expedition but was forced to detour three miles along the South River. The bridge that had existed only hours before was gone, a tangled fist of steel beneath the deep waters, still fast from the spring rains. Peter was not a strong swimmer and would not risk a wet crossing, so he crossed a couple of miles downriver, using the county bridge near Crab Orchard. Huge holes and cracks pocked the surface of the roadway, and because of the metallic groans and creaks, Peter crossed quickly.

The rural countryside belied the immense damage of the quake. Trees were toppled in much the same way as they would be following a severe thunderstorm or tornado. But other evidence attested to the severity of the damage. Two bridges were destroyed or damaged. Billboards along County Road 45 had fallen or canted toward the earth. Snapped electrical lines lay in loose coils, hanging from tilting poles.

From the crest of the small ridge, Peter fought his way through a thickening of brambles a couple hundred yards from home. From there he saw his trailer, at the edge of the lonely one-lane dirt road. The old barn still stood, but may have shifted a degree or two from perpendicular. The trailer appeared to be fine. It had slipped from one of its foundation blocks, but there seemed to be no major damage.

Peter took a deep breath and continued his loping run across the field covered with brush and prairie grasses.

Lord, let them be alive, he prayed. *Let them be safe and alive.*

He began to shout, "Linda! Becca! Linda!"

With panic rising with every step, he shouted louder, through his gasps. There was no response. Turning at the edge of the old foundation, he shouted again. The front door inched open, and Becca screamed out, "Daddy!"

In an instant he scooped her up in his arms. For the first time in days, Peter felt a small sense of peace and comfort glow in his heart.

Tom wanted to stay at the house and try to save his family, but the logical side of his brain took over. He was powerless to move any of the rubble, and the force of the destruction made it impossible for anyone to survive—no matter how much he wished otherwise.

Yes, he wanted to stay. . .more than anything in his life, he wanted to stay. He wanted to lie on that warm stone until his heart ceased beating. He wanted to ebb into nothingness, just as the rest of his life had receded from him.

But he did not.

He knew that the pain would tear at his heart to near the point of death. But, in spite of that pain, Tom remained logical. His survival instincts took over. He was alive. Still alive. And he would find out what had happened.

His cell phone, clipped to his belt, was dead. Highway 1 along the coast was broken and ruptured—Tom could count at least ten breaks. His pager was mute, its built-in GPS silent. Even if he could call for help, how would anyone get to him?

It took Tom nearly thirty minutes to climb the hillside to the spot where his house had once stood. He could barely see through his tears. As he climbed, his bloodied hands lost their grip many times and he slid several yards down. He stopped, gulped in air, and scrambled back again and again until finally he made the crest, just in advance of a sweep of flame. Up and down the shore, multiple fires crackled and grinned amid the wreckage of million-dollar ocean-side homes.

Tom caught his breath and stiffly walked to the garage that remained untouched by the heaving of the ground. Tom had wanted to incorporate the garage into the design of the house, but Morris had protested, saying it would compromise the integrity of his creation. Tom had thought the architect eccentric and decided not to push the issue for fear the architect would walk off the job. But now he was glad he had relented and allowed the garage to be placed southeast of the house, across the brick drive.

He slipped in the side door of the garage and used the hand gearing to raise the massive door. He knew where he had to go now. He knew of only one person who might be able to explain all of this to him. Tom climbed into his new Mercedes. The car responded with a click each time he tried it and then stopped making any noise altogether. He slipped out and tried his wife's Mercedes. Nothing. He tried the four-wheel-drive Range Rover. Nothing. He tried his new, chrome-laden Harley-Davidson motorcycle. Nothing.

At the far end of his garage was what Lydia had called "Tom's feeble attempt to recapture his youth." He always smiled when she said that, for he knew it was true. He yanked the tarp off the restored 1962 Volkswagen Beetle. It was the same model and year as the car he'd driven when he'd made his way to Hollywood decades prior. The entire car had been rebuilt to original specifications, and it was painted exactly like his car of years ago. The keys were in the ignition.

He opened the door and slipped in. It was smaller than he remembered. . .or perhaps it was that he was now larger.

He turned the key, expecting the car to be dead. But the engine sputtered once, then popped to life. By the time he got to the winding hilltop road, he knew that the devastation that had just occurred wasn't the fault of a localized tremor. When he looked south, the whole of the Los Angeles basin was spread out before him.

It was not smog that obscured the view today; it was smoke and dust and fire. Tom could see the flames of at least three office towers at the north end of the basin. He scanned the basin for the newest tower, built by the same architect that did his home, but it was gone. He hoped it was simply obscured by the smoke and had not toppled over.

Tom's destination was only five miles away, along a road that snaked along the ocean's bluff, then tumbled down to the floor of the ravine and back up to an eastern ridge. On that ridge away from the sea, homes became almost affordable. The B-level players in the Hollywood game lived there.

Calvin Freemont lived on that ridge. Tom and Calvin had shared a screenwriting credit a few years ago—a small, independent film. The story was about a paroled murderer returning home to seek forgiveness. Tom had written much of the dialogue, but it was Calvin who had understood the meaning—and the implications—of forgiveness and grace.

"It's all in the Bible, Tom," Calvin had explained, laughing. "I'm just copying Scriptures, or at least what they say about forgiveness."

Tom had laughed in return. "Pretty shrewd way of avoiding royalty payments—using God as a cowriter and all. He doesn't demand His cut, does He?"

Calvin had smiled. "He doesn't demand it, Tom. He deserves it, and I give it to Him."

During their meetings, Calvin had shared what he knew of the Bible and what it meant in his life. Tom expressed no deep interest, but feigned attention. He had better things to do with his life than discuss crackpot religious views. The only things that had held his attention were the fantastic yarns that Calvin had spun about the end of the world. Hundreds of books in Calvin's study detailed every theory and reference about the subject.

"It'll end soon, Tom," Calvin would say, sweeping his hand about the room, encompassing everything. "This will all fade away. What are you going to do then?"

"I'm going to enjoy life and spend all my money now, Calvin. No sense in saving anything, is there?"

"You'll change your tune, Tom, when the end comes. You will. When your world explodes—if it ever explodes—you'll come running. Maybe not to me. But someone like me. Someone who told you beforehand that they had the answers. You'll be in a panic, and you'll remember I said I knew it was all going to happen. You'll be sure I'll have all the answers."

Tom had merely dismissed him with a wave of his hand.

Yet, despite Calvin's strange beliefs, Tom had enjoyed their time together, and even after finishing the screenplay, they had continued to have lunch on a regular basis—and not just for career advancement purposes.

Calvin had once explained that the Second Coming would happen in an instant. Earthquakes and wars would mark the beginning of the end.

"But there are earthquakes every day," Tom had argued. "Afterwards we rebuild and go about our business. I have yet to see God show up and tell us not to bother. And the world has been at war since man learned to pick up a club and whack his neighbor."

Calvin had smiled when Tom said this. It was not an amused, but more of a pained, smile. "Tom, when it happens, you'll know it. You'll listen then. And you'll be dying to find the answer."

The fancy clock on Megan's desk had stopped. She looked at her wristwatch, a dependable, hand-wound Timex—a high-school graduation gift from her father. It read 2:20 P.M.

The office door flung open. A gasping, red-faced John Peck slammed through to the reception desk. He was disheveled and sweating. "A guy over at Buck Associates said he knew what happened," John claimed. "He read about it in an old *Popular Science* magazine. Said he swore it was true."

All faces turned to John.

"A solar flare. A huge solar flare," John explained. "The guy said it could happen. Said flares come in cycles. If there was one ten—maybe twenty—times as powerful as the biggest one yet reported, then all of Hades would break loose." He gasped for air. "He said every communication satellite would be fried. Cellular phones would be gone. Computers would be shot. Everything electronic would be fried, scrambled by the flare's radio waves. Not even cars would work. Planes would drop from the sky. He said it would be like an atom bomb going off over the world. Only nobody dies—just yet."

John sat at the edge of the desk now, his frame suddenly gone hollow and small. "He said we'll have to start over again—from scratch." He threw himself into a chair, limp and drained. "I don't believe a word of it. The old goat was crazy. That's all. This can't be the end."

I don't know if this is the end of the world, Megan thought to herself, *but if it is, it came at a very opportune moment.*

John Peck's stunning announcement did explain a lot of what Megan had seen that afternoon. As she and the others waited for the power to come back on, she watched the street below and realized that something bigger than a simple blackout had happened. The normally congested Wall Street had literally become a large parking lot as every car rolled to a stop. Some had crashed into other cars, others into streetlights or storefronts, but none was moving. She had watched as the occupants lingered around their cars, all equally confused. Gradually they had locked their vehicles and walked off, Megan presumed, to their homes or to other forms of transportation. Facing such a loss, most people's initial impulse was to run to the known, the comfortable, the secure. For most, that meant running home.

Back in Megan's office place, one trader argued, "But we've lived through 9/11 and blackouts—and everyone worked together. No one panicked—really. Even 9/11 was calm. We pulled together. That's all this is."

A balding trader from the currency exchange shouted back, "9/11 was two planes. I've already seen four planes go down and crash. I saw them. And the blackout—well, my cell phone still worked. Cars still worked. This is something else—something big and horrible."

Another man shouted, "I heard someone say that LaGuardia is a hell of crashed planes. No terrorist could do all this."

"Yeah! What about the phones! They aren't working!"

"And the buses. They've stopped in the middle of the street!"

"There's an airplane burning in the East River!"

"It's not a terrorist attack—this is the end of the world!"

Adding to the confusion were traders, bankers, operators, and secretaries who poured out of the buildings in waves. They streamed away in all directions. Wall Street had few residents, so within several hours the streets had gone from mobbed to nearly deserted.

But Megan couldn't gather up the will to leave. As the office emptied, she stayed behind, curled into a ball, hiding out in the walnut-paneled conference room. She sat, her knees drawn up close to her chest, and stayed silent. She could see the flickerings from a score of fires.

As the sun worked its way across the sky, darkness began to fill the room. As a child, darkness had terrified her. Even to this day, the sun slipping toward the western horizon brought an edginess to her voice, a faster pace to her heart. What came to mind as this thickening of night fell over the city was the voice of her father. As a child, when she was frightened, her father would take her hand and recite a familiar Bible verse to her. He said that it would always be with her to calm her fears. All she needed to do was repeat it and God would be there.

It has been so long, she thought. *It has been so very, very long.*

The words she began to recite felt awkward and forced, but the mere sound brought a tiny hope of comfort. "The LORD is my shepherd; I have everything I need. . . ."[i]

Staying at the crest of the hill, staring down at the grave of his wife and child, was too terrifying to consider. Tom had to do something. Going, moving, doing were all preferable to standing still and allowing his heart to explode in agony.

Tom steered his little Volkswagen toward the bottom of the canyon road. Boulders had slipped from their ornamental locations and rolled into the street. Landscaping walls had given way, spilling ground cover and expensive topsoil into the roadway. Telephone poles lay like a child's game of Pick-Up Sticks. Parts of the hillside were on fire. Smoke and dust choked the air. Tom was forced to back up several times, then drive through lawns to bypass obstacles. He stopped the car only once, in the Jeagers' front lawn. Bruce Jeager was a vice president of production at Fox Studios; he'd given Tom work when he had first arrived on the coast.

Parts of the Jeagers' house had collapsed, but the garage and the maids' quarters still stood intact. The marble fountain in the middle of the circular drive had fallen, shattering into hundreds of sharp pieces.

Bess, Bruce's wife, sat like a tiny bundle against the garage door. There was blood on her hands and a smear of red on her forehead. She stood as Tom pulled up. Her eyes looked vacant.

"I can't get the garage door open," she called out, her voice flat and unemotional. Her usually perfect hair was left to flutter in the wind. Her dress was torn at the shoulder.

Tom set the brake and jumped out of the car. He hefted open the heavy garage door and jammed a broomstick in the track to hold it open. Bess jumped into her Jaguar and turned the key. Tom was not surprised when nothing happened. She jumped into her husband's Range Rover. The result was the same.

"The same happened to mine," Tom called out.

"What's wrong? Why won't they start?" Her voice edged to a shriek. "I have to get out of here!"

"Where's Bruce?"

Her voice was trembling now. "In the house."

"You should stay here with him."

"Why?"

"It's safer. Downtown L.A. looks like it's on fire. And Highway 1 stops a mile north of here."

"Stops?"

"It fell into the ocean."

"Oh."

She stared down at the blood on her hands. There was a small spot of blood on the thick gold necklace about her throat. She looked smaller now, as if the blood had caused her to shrink in on herself.

"Did you cut yourself, Bess?"

"No."

"No?"

"It's Bruce. . . ." Her eyes swam with tears.

"Is he hurt?"

She gazed up at Tom, her face twisted with pain. "He's dead."

Pointing toward the rubble that had been her house, she added, "He was in the den. The house fell on him."

Tom turned to take a step toward that spot.

"I saw his arm. I tried to pull him out. It was loose. . .you know. . .his arm was loose. . .from his body." Her hands shook with renewed vigor.

Tom put his hand to her shoulder to steady her. "Bess. . ." He wasn't sure what to say next to comfort her. No words would ease her loss—how well he knew—so he opted for a more practical course of action. "Bess, you stay here. You'll be safer here. Stay in the garage. I'll close the door. You can get out through the back entrance if you need to. But I'll come back for you. I have to see Calvin."

"Calvin?"

"Calvin Freemont."

"Why?"

"I just do. He said I would come running to see him on this sort of day—and he was right. Stay here and I'll be back as soon as I can."

He hugged her briefly. She felt so slight and brittle in his arms—a perfect example of a too-thin Hollywood wife.

"Stay here," he repeated as he lowered the door. "I'll be back." He sprinted to his car, hoping he could make good on his brave promise.

When he reached the bottom of the canyon road and rounded a sharp corner, Tom swung the wheel hard, swerving to the left. He narrowly missed a knot of ten or so people who stood, nearly immobile, in the middle of the road. He bounced onto the shoulder and through a dry and brittle thicket of weeds and brush. Gunning the engine, he spun the car back onto the pavement. He stopped and leaned out the window.

A tall, balding man in an expensive Italian suit lurched toward him. "Do you know what's happening?" he shouted.

"It's an earthquake; that's all I know. Is anybody hurt?" Tom winced when the words left his mouth. He had no medical training, nor was he willing to try and navigate a trip to the hospital fifteen miles to the south.

The tall man was within a few feet of the car. "Don't think so."

Tom had his foot on the gas, his hand on the wheel.

"How come your car's still running?"

Tom shrugged.

"Nothing works. I have a $250,000 Rolls, and it just sits there like a dead raccoon. I need to get to Bel-Air."

"Sorry," Tom replied. He wasn't sure why, but his foot tensed and he gripped the wheel more tightly.

"I mean I *need* to get to Bel-Air. My wife will kill me if she knows I've been out here. You know, old girlfriend and all that." The bald man actually winked, as if letting Tom in on his secret would change his mind.

"Sorry, but I'm not going that way."

"I need to get to Bel-Air," the man shouted and leaped at the car, his hands clamoring for a grip on the open window. As if anticipating the move, Tom gunned the engine, spinning the tires on the loose gravel.

The bald man held on for a few seconds, trying to keep pace with the car as it picked up speed. Tom swerved again, and the bald man lost his grip, stumbling along after him.

Tom looked in the rearview mirror and watched as the bald man picked up a rock the size of a softball and hurled it at him. The rock hit the rear of the car with a *thud.*

Tom floored the engine and shifted into third gear as he tore up the canyon road on the second ridge from the sea. There were fewer homes along the road that led to Calvin's house, and Tom only had to detour twice—both times for huge crevices splitting the road.

At last Tom pulled into the long, hidden driveway. Smoke had darkened the sky and swirled about in dense, thick patches. The hillside above him was charred and blackened. Tom skidded the car to a stop and jumped out, leaving the door open and the engine running. The left wing of Calvin's house, a sprawling ranch, was on fire.

"Calvin! Calvin!" Tom scrambled up the front steps. He almost tripped over a curled form lying outside the opened front door. Tom shut his eyes in fear that it was Calvin. The person's clothes were singed and smoking, and his skin—black, like Calvin's—was badly burned.

Tom knelt beside the form and placed a hand on the shoulder, turning it slightly. A deep, pained moan followed.

"Calvin?" Tom whispered. "Calvin? It's Tom. . .Tom Lyton. Can you hear me?"

Calvin coughed once, then actually tried to smile. "I hear you. I always knew you'd come. Didn't I tell you? I said you'd come to see me and I was right. And now you think. . .that I have all the answers, don't you?" Calvin began to cough again, and his arms twitched in angry spasms.

Tom left his friend and ran frantically into the house. Smoke made the rooms hazy, but the fire didn't seem to be in a rush. He grabbed a couple of pillows from the sofa, ran into the kitchen, and took a bag of ice from the freezer. He had to step carefully to avoid slipping on the scores of broken plates and dishes that littered the floor.

Hurrying back to Calvin, Tom laid the cushions under his injured friend's head. He slipped an ice cube to Calvin's mouth.

Calvin licked his lips and smiled. "Thanks, Tom." He coughed again. "I didn't want to die alone."

"Hey, hey, don't be stupid. There ain't nobody dying here nohow!" Tom said, repeating a line from their shared movie script.

Calvin managed another weak smile, then coughed. A thin line of water, mixed with blood, trickled down his cheek. "I'm ready, Tom. It's okay."

"You won't die. My car is still running. I can get you to a hospital."

Calvin placed his hand on Tom's arm. Tom glanced down. The flesh on Calvin's fingers was burnt; Tom thought he saw an exposed bone in his friend's forefinger. He looked away, holding back the rising bile in his throat.

"It's okay, my friend, it's okay. I won't make it beyond the driveway." Calvin's voice was barely above a whisper, but it was calm and without fear. "It's okay, Tom. . .it's okay."

"Calvin, what happened? How did you get hurt?"

"I ran back. . .I had to get—" Calvin coughed and grimaced.

The loudest sound around them was Calvin's labored breathing. It was louder than the crackling of the flames.

Tom leaned in a little closer. He licked his lips. Suddenly they were very dry. "Is this the end, Calvin? Is this the end of the world that you told me about?"

Calvin opened his eyes. His expression was calm and knowing, almost as if he had anticipated the question. "No. I'm still here. If it was the end, I'd be gone." His hand tightened on Tom's arm. His words labored to find purchase in his throat. "I believed, Tom. . .I still do. If this was. . .the Rapture. . .or God's judgment. . .I'd be with Christ now. . .in heaven."

"Are you sure?"

"I'm sure," he said, coughing. "God won't end the world until His children are safe. . .and I'm still here. It's in Romans 5:9. It says, 'Since we have been made right in God's sight by the blood of Christ, he will certainly save us from God's judgment.'[ii] If this was the judgment, I wouldn't be here." Calvin coughed again and his whole body trembled. "Others believe differently. I have a book for every theory. . . . Yet I'm pretty sure I'm right because it's what the Bible says. And I've been a child of God for a long time."

"So this is just an earthquake, Calvin? It's not the end of the world?"

Calvin blinked and swallowed. "Can I have another ice cube?" He sucked at it for a moment, then answered. "I'm. . .I'm not sure. . .really." His eyes darted about, as if assessing the damage. "This is bigger than a California quake. A lot bigger."

Tom nodded. "It looks like half of the buildings in L.A. fell. There's fire everywhere. I saw a plane fall into the ocean. There may have been another one that crashed north up the coast. Too much smog to be sure. Other than my old VW, I haven't seen one car that's running. Radio is gone. Not a station anywhere—not even shortwave. Not even on the battery-powered unit I had in my garage. I haven't tried TV, but I bet it's out too."

"It's bigger than an earthquake. . .but this isn't the very end. It's not. Maybe. . .maybe it's God's way of getting our attention. . . . I bet the whole country's in bad shape, not just L.A. Well. . .it isn't a bet. . .I know it is. My heart says we're in for a dark summer. I'd stake my life on that."

Tom watched Calvin wince from his painful joke. Tom hadn't considered that possibility. What if this wasn't localized? What if it was national, even global?

Calvin slumped off the pillows, toward the earth, and coughed again. After a long moment, he tried to push himself upright. Tom slipped his arm about Calvin's shoulders and helped him sit.

"The house is gone, isn't it?" Calvin asked.

"Not yet. It looks like the far wing is, but the rest is okay. Stone and brick don't burn well."

Calvin smiled. "This isn't the end. . .just earthquakes and wars before He comes again."

"He?"

"Jesus. . .He'll be back. He said He'd be back. . . . He said to watch for earthquakes."

Tom closed his eyes, trying to keep himself from retching. The smell of Calvin's burnt flesh tainted the air. Blisters pocked his face and chest.

"Tom. . .will you promise me something?" Calvin asked weakly.

"I'll try. But first I need to get you some help. There's a doctor over on the canyon road."

Calvin shook his head. Tom could see the burnt flesh crinkling about his neck. "Three things. . .once I'm gone—"

"Calvin, don't talk like that—"

Calvin lifted his hand to stop Tom's interruption. Tom knew that the tiniest movement must bring his injured friend horrible pain, so he leaned closer to listen.

"Once I'm gone. . .bury me in the garden. I know it doesn't matter, but I don't want to just lie here."

Tom swallowed hard. He knew, without a whisper of a doubt now, that Calvin was near death. "I'll do that."

"And say a prayer for me when you're done."

Tom looked into the eyes of his friend. "I don't know many prayers, but I'll try, Calvin, I'll try."

"And now for the big favor."

What could be harder than burying a friend? Tom thought, in agony.

"There's a Hummer in my garage. I hope it works. I think it will. In it are survival gear and gas cans and all that. I want you to take it. . .and this bag." He pointed to a heavy canvas bag lying near his feet.

Tom couldn't believe he hadn't noticed the bag before. He had been so intent on helping Calvin.

"The bag is full of gold Krugerrands. Maybe worth $100,000, maybe a lot more than that. . .now. That's what I went in to get."

"Why?"

"I was going to—" Calvin began coughing again and slumped over. Tom reached out and held him up. "My wife. . .I mean, my ex-wife. . .Deborah. . .she lives near Des Moines. . .with my daughter. I was going to take the gold to them. I want them to have it. I mean. . .they're not poor or anything. . .but I bet they could use it."

Daughter? Wife? Tom's thoughts spun. "I didn't know you were married."

"It was a long time ago. . .before I believed. Been ashamed and guilty for a long time."

Calvin shut his eyes. "Can you find a way to get the gold to them? You could take the Hummer. You could be there and back in a few days. . .a week, tops. I know you don't want your wife and baby to be alone for too long."

Smoke swirled about them, and Tom blinked, his eyes tearing. He would not tell Calvin about their fate. There was no time. "I'll try, but I don't know their address or names."

"It's all in the Hummer. There are books and maps and all sorts of stuff. I was almost ready to leave. Keep it all. But take the coins to them." Calvin struggled to hold his head up. "Do you promise? Please? Get this to them. Get this to my daughter."

Tom stared at his friend. He looked up into the smoke-filled sky. *My wife is dead. My child is dead. My house is gone. My world has collapsed.* He fought back tears. *There's nothing left in California to hold me.* And then he whispered, "I promise, Calvin. I'll get it to them."

"And the prayer. . .don't forget the prayer."

With those words, Calvin slumped forward, his head lolling against his chest. Tom laid him back and listened. There was no sound of breathing. He put his ear against Calvin's chest. There was no heartbeat. His friend was dead.

"I promise."

———

"Daddy!" Becca was crying hysterically as Peter held her close. She was barefoot and still in her pajamas. Her long blond hair was in tangles about her face.

"It's okay, sweets. Daddy's here. Everything is going to be okay. You're going to be fine. Daddy's here."

As he held her, his eyes darted about the tiny trailer. Was Linda lying injured in the bedroom? Had someone come and taken her?

Peter closed his eyes and offered a short prayer—thanking God that his daughter was safe and that his wife would be safe as well. He lowered Becca to the ground and knelt in front of her, his hands firm on her shoulders. He pushed the hair back from her face and gazed into her blue eyes.

"Where's Mommy, Becca? Do you know where she is?"

Becca shook her head slowly.

"Is she here?"

She shook her head again.

"Did she leave?"

Becca nodded.

Peter swallowed once and took a deep breath. "Becca, Daddy isn't angry at you. I'm not mad. You haven't done anything wrong. I just want to know where Mommy is."

The little girl sniffed once and wiped at her chest with her wrist. "She left."

"When did she leave?"

Becca sniffed again.

"Did she leave after the. . .after the ground shook?"

Becca nodded.

"Where did she say she was going?"

Her lip trembled. "She said she had to go see Rev. Jerry. She said I had to stay here and wait for you." Tears started to fall from her eyes and rolled down her cheeks like pearls. "And it took so long. You weren't here and I got scared."

Peter leaned forward and gathered Becca close to him, kissing her forehead.

Just at that moment, the earth lurched again. The trailer rocked for thirty seconds, and Peter heard a low rumble outside. Becca clutched at her father and cried out.

"It's okay, Becca. It's okay. Daddy's here."

Peter tried hard to sound brave and sure, though his heart was beating incredibly fast. He was afraid. . .and angry. In fact, angrier than he'd ever been in his life.

How could you have left your daughter here alone? You uncaring witch!

Six cars, all abandoned, blocked the narrow bridge into town. When Linda Wilson realized she could go no farther, she drove onto the side of the road and nosed into the greening brush. She got out of the battered and now scratched Toyota and looked behind her. The road was empty and still. She turned to the river and the rush and burble of water.

I never liked bridges.

Her palms grew clammy.

And now I have to walk across.

She walked toward the bridge, but then halted just before her foot touched the narrow metal walkway. The gridiron surface allowed one to see the water below with every step, beckoning and calling. Linda closed her eyes, her hand gripping the rail with a furious tightness.

I can do this, she repeated to herself. *I can.*

But her feet would not move.

She opened her eyes and stared at a distant point across the river. If she stood on tiptoe, she could make out the very top of the cross that rose above the Temple of God's Calling. She turned back once more and stared along the deserted road.

Nothing. Nobody.

Closing her eyes, she willed herself to make the first step.

I have to do this. I have to. Only Rev. Moses will know what is happening. I couldn't risk taking Becca in case something happened on the way. But I have to find out. I have to find the truth. I have to. I have to see him.

Linda opened her eyes, grimaced, and took her first step. Her shoes made a chinking sound on the metal surface. She took another step.

This isn't so hard.

She stepped again and smiled.

This isn't so hard after all. I can do this. I can. I will.

In less than a minute, she was on the west side of the river, striding with renewed purpose toward the Temple of God's Calling.

Tom put the shovel down and wiped the sweat from his forehead.

"You wanted a prayer. . .I'm sure I'm the wrong one to do this, but you made me promise."

He stood by the mound of fresh dirt. Though it was only about three o'clock in the afternoon, the smoke from the various fires made it seem closer to dusk. As he'd dug Calvin's grave, he had checked the progress of the brush fires multiple times. So far none had come within miles of this section of the canyon. Calvin's house smoldered, the fire having consumed about half of the building before running out of fuel, leaving behind blackened stone walls and chunks of charred wooden beams.

Now Tom bowed his head. It felt most unnatural.

"Dear God, I guess this is a prayer for Calvin. He was a good man. He seemed to know what religion was all about. He said he knew You. He was a wonderful friend."

Shots sounded nearby. Tom looked up. All through the afternoon there had been sporadic gunfire.

"God, I hope this is enough." Tom swallowed hard.

What am I supposed to say here? Why I am saying this?

He closed his eyes and added, "And take Calvin to heaven."

Tom looked up again. His eyes blurred with tears. He wasn't certain if it was the emotion or the smoke.

This religious stuff seems so crazy now. I'm alive, and Calvin—who said he believed—is the one who's dead. This doesn't make any sense. God, You sure picked a pretty absurd way to handle this.

Gazing into the smoke-laden heavens, Tom said, "Amen."

After finishing his grim task, Tom drove his VW out of the way and entered the darkened garage through the side door. Inside sat the immense Hummer, the army's standard four-wheel, all-terrain vehicle. No civilian truly needed its range and abilities—at least not for commuting in Los Angeles.

He sat in the cool of the garage in the front seat of the Hummer for a long time, catching his breath, chasing the demons from his thoughts. Time had become but a wisp. He closed his eyes and hoped against hope that what he had just seen and done was but an illusion. But after that long quiet, he opened his eyes—and found that nothing had changed. He sighed deeply and turned the ignition key.

Calvin was right—the motor did work. The military version, Tom surmised, included a less-sensitive ignition system. Packed into the cavernous interior were bags of camping gear, freeze-dried food, metal water jugs, spare gasoline cans, pumps, tools, a rubber raft, flares, a stove, kerosene; in fact, the vehicle was as well supplied as a small sporting-goods store. Tom placed the heavy bag of gold coins into the locked compartment under the driver's seat and slipped the flooring over the top. There was a stack of books on the passenger seat. At the top of the stack was an address book. He noted the underlined name of Deborah Freemont, then McClure written above it, with a new address in the same town of Panora, Iowa. Underneath that was a well-used Bible. Beside the stack of books were a pistol in a well-oiled holster and four boxes of shells. Tom didn't want to think about using them.

The only items Tom puzzled over were two fifty-pound bags of dry dog food. *Did Calvin have a dog? Or is this his weird idea of emergency rations?*

He consulted his watch—it read 9:05 but had stopped running hours earlier. By how gloomy the sky was, he guessed dusk was close at hand. It was hard to be certain, though, since smoke had clouded the normal path of the sun all day. Tom had promised to return to Bess Jeager hours ago. He also wanted to get back to what was left of his home. Maybe there was still something he could do for his family.

Tom pulled open the garage door and switched the headlights on, piercing the haze. In their glare, he saw something move near the spot where Calvin was buried. Without thinking, he picked up the pistol, checked the chamber, and stepped out into the smoky obscurity. Slowly Tom walked over toward the garden. If what he saw was some sort of wild animal, a scavenger, he would shoot it and leave. He should have dug the grave deeper, but it was difficult work.

As he moved closer, he heard a low growl. He stopped and raised the gun to the noise. He stepped to the side, and the light shown hard on the fresh dirt. At the foot of the grave lay evidence of fresh digging. Tom pulled the trigger back. He leaned forward to get a better aim. Then he heard a bark.

Lying at the foot of the grave, almost hidden by a bush, was a golden retriever, face and paws covered with thick dirt. It lowered its head and whined, its large eyes looking up at Tom in submission.

Tom figured the dog was Calvin's.

"You looking for Calvin, boy?"

The dog whined and thumped its tail in the dirt.

"You knew he was there, didn't you, boy? You smelled him there, didn't you?"

The dog managed a thin bark.

Tom walked over and knelt beside the dog, who raised his head to Tom's outstretched hand. He felt for a tag, found it, and read: "Revelations. If lost, call 1-800-555-1345. Reward."

"Revelations? What kind of name for a dog is that?"

The dog lifted its head higher.

"Revelations?" Tom said directly to the animal. The dog responded by wagging its tail and scrambling to its feet, whining softly.

Darkness was closing in. The horizon was now tinted red. Tom heard gunfire again—ten or so shots in quick succession. There were no sirens, no helicopters, no cars. Nothing man-made stirred, except the rumbling of the Hummer.

Tom stared down at the dog. The dog stared back up.

"Well, we've both said good-bye to Calvin. I guess it's time to go," Tom told the dog.

Then he turned and walked to the Hummer, the dog beside his every step. Neither of them looked back.

Peter heated water over a tiny fire just outside the trailer. The propane tank was full, but there was no telling when there might be another delivery. He thought he'd save the propane for cooking and heating.

Becca had fallen asleep quickly, and Peter jangled with an energy born out of fear and adrenaline. He sipped at the hot mug of instant coffee. He had left it black. There was only a half-gallon of fresh milk left, and that would be for Becca. It wasn't much, he thought, but it was something.

He sat on the front step of the trailer, now canted a few degrees from level. A foundation block had slipped, but Peter didn't have the energy to repair it this evening. Tomorrow would be soon enough.

He wondered where his wife might be. He considered giving chase, but his truck was mired in a ditch miles from here. Stonefort, if that was her destination, was eight miles away. He would not leave Becca and charge off into the darkness.

Peter was a realist; he saw things as they were. If the earthquake was as strong in St. Louis as it had been here, he reasoned, the next several weeks could be most ominous. Most of Stonefort's food and supplies came from St. Louis, some from nearby Evansville. But if the bridges on the interstate were damaged or gone, it might be weeks or months until normal commerce resumed. And if the bridges were down, how would they get to stores and work?

Peter wasn't in bad shape. He had a few months' supply of dried deer meat. The little den in the trailer, converted to a room for storage, was packed with hundreds of jars of preserved fruits and vegetables. He had three huge boxes of powdered milk, purchased recently at the Evansville Wal-Mart. He had more than four hundred pounds of flour and oats—payment for his fieldwork last year. He had his rifle and a few hundred shells—more than enough for months' worth of hunting.

It was curiously fortunate that he had no real job to get to—most of his income was derived through odd jobs, plowing fields, doing planting and seasonal work. He could still manage to do that sort of work—if it needed to be done.

He was less sure of Becca's future. Would her school be closed? Would her school bus locate a route with no damaged roads or bridges? Would he have to stay at home to care for her?

A couple gunshots rumbled up from the direction of the state road.

Might be the McCord place. . .or the Ambertons'. Hope there isn't any trouble.

He leaned to the open door and checked to see if his rifle was still where he had placed it, on the rack above the sofa.

Another several shots echoed from the direction of Evansville. They sounded distant. It was not unusual to hear gunshots in the dark. Many farmers spotted deer with searchlights, immobilizing the animals in the glare, then shooting. The shots might be from the guns of hunters.

Peter stood and stretched. He hoped to see headlights turn from the two-lane road, a half mile distant to the west. If he had seen headlights, it could only be Linda's old, rusted Toyota. But the road remained dark. In fact, he had seen only two cars pass during the last hour. That was unusual. State Road 41 wasn't a freeway, but it carried a lot of traffic.

In the dark, his eyes open only to the stars, Peter sat on the front step and sent his prayers to heaven.

———

Peter had fallen sound asleep while he was praying. He awoke with a start when someone shouted from the dirt road, no more than fifty yards away.

Peter's heart raced. He thought about jumping for his rifle.

The shouting continued. "Wilson! That you? Peter Wilson?"

Finally Peter understood. It was Herb McCord. McCord, his wife, and five children lived on a ramshackle farm a few miles south of Peter.

"That you, McCord?" Peter shouted back.

"What are you doing? Sleeping on your front steps?"

Peter ran his hand through his hair, smoothing it down. "It was dark. I was tired."

Herb spit toward the road. His teeth were stained from years of chewing tobacco. He carried an old Coleman lantern. "Well, boy, this ain't the time to be sleeping."

"Herb, what are you doing here?"

In the ten years Peter had lived in this trailer, Herb had never visited. They saw each other in town on occasion and in church. Each would wave to the other as they passed on the road, but they never actually went as far as a social call.

"Listen, boy," he barked, spitting again. "Where were you today?"

"I was hunting up by Crab Orchard. That's when the earthquake hit. Took me the rest of the day to get home."

"Earthquake? Blazes, boy, this wasn't no earthquake."

Peter shook his head again. "No earthquake? What was it then?"

Herb glanced suspiciously around the trailer, as if checking for eavesdroppers first. "It was the Chinese."

"Chinese?"

"Yep. Dropped some sort of bomb on us. Screwed everything up. Ain't any radio, any phone, any television. Nothing. It's the Chinese, for sure. The Russkies ain't smart enough anymore to do something like this. Nope, it's the Chinese."

"Chinese?"

"Yep, they're behind it. And I think you better be defending yourself before they try to take over."

"Chinese?"

A little voice from behind Peter and inside the trailer called out softly, "Who's Chinese, Daddy?"

Both men swiveled their attention toward the voice. Herb actually tightened his grip on the shotgun he carried.

"Becca," Peter called out, "no one is Chinese. Mr. McCord is just explaining what happened today."

Herb leaned to the side to see the little girl now standing in the living room. "It's the Chinese all right. Best take care of your young one too." Herb pivoted and began to step quickly toward his house and farm. "I'm heading back to the farm. You're welcome to join. Easier to fight off the Chinese from my barn than this flimsy old dump."

"You walked over here to tell me that?"

McCord nodded, then spit again. "Like I said, it's the Chinese and their bomb. My new Ford sits there like a broken cinder block. Nothing works except for that old John Deere I had stuck in my barn. Go figure." He swung his head back and forth, as if looking for an invading army. "You take care now, Wilson. If you decide to come over—do it in the daylight. And call out your name as you come. We don't want to shoot you, thinking you're a Chinaman."

"I'll do that, Herb. I'll be sure to do that if I come. And thanks for the warning."

Peter stepped inside the trailer and shut the door.

"Where's Mommy?"

"She must have stayed in Stonefort. They may have closed the bridge."

Becca nodded without comment.

"I'm sure she'll be back anytime."

She nodded again, and Peter scooped her up and carried her back to her bed. As he laid her down, Peter glanced out the window again, searching the two-lane road for any sight of Linda's battered and rusty Toyota. Before he turned back to Becca, he made sure he had a smile on his face.

———

After leaving Calvin's house and with Revelations sitting next to him, Tom zipped down the canyon road toward the Jeagers and what remained of his house. The fires in the surrounding canyons gave the early nightfall a hellish glow. Abandoned cars and trucks littered the roadway. Some were left with doors open and possessions strewn about on the pavement. In the forty-five minutes it took to drive back to his neighborhood, Tom saw no one. People had either vanished or were hiding.

Calvin did talk about this sort of thing—and he called it "the

Rapture" or "the Tribulation." He said that Christians would be taken up into the sky. But that was for Christians, wasn't it? I can't imagine that in Hollywood there would be many who would qualify for the honor. I know I wouldn't make it. My bet is that nobody was swept into the sky in L.A. and that everyone is hiding till morning.

Tom buzzed into the Jeagers' driveway and snapped off the headlights. Revelations whimpered and peered into the darkness, as if to ask if this was his new home.

"Stay here, boy. I need to check on an old friend, okay?"

The dog responded by wagging his tail and barking softly once.

"Good boy."

Tom grabbed a flashlight and made his way around to the back door. He called out, "Bess. . .Bess? It's me. Tom Lyton. I said I was coming back. Bess? Are you there?"

The glare of the flashlight caught a sparkling on the walk at the far end of the garage. It was broken glass. Tom's heart jumped in his chest. He snapped off the light and stopped. He wondered if he should retrieve the pistol from the car. Then he shook his head.

I'm just being paranoid. And I could wind up shooting someone with it.

Tom hesitated. A series of shots echoed along the canyon ridge, perhaps a mile away. The canyons caused strange echoes— one gunshot might sound like ten as it echoed and multiplied. Deciding that paranoia might keep him alive, Tom turned on his heel and hurried back to the car, where Revelations sat huffing in the darkness.

"Good boy," Tom said, opening the door and reaching for the pistol. "Don't bark."

In the redness of the night, he felt his way back to the rear door of the garage. He bent to listen. He heard nothing—no motors, no voices, no breathing, no footsteps.

"Bess?" He kept his voice at a low, urgent whisper. "Bess? Are you there?"

He waited. No response.

"Bess?" He called louder, his concern increasing. "Bess? It's Tom Lyton. Are you in here?"

The gun rested almost too comfortably in his right hand, the flashlight in his left. He nudged the door open with his foot and entered the garage. The beam swung about, flashing off expensive polished metal. In the far corner, behind the Jaguar, Tom saw a metallic sparkle. It was her Rolex—easily worth several thousand dollars.

Why would she leave it here?

He looked closer. There was a spot or two near the watch.

Is that blood? Or oil?

He walked the property with the flashlight, calling her name. There was no answer.

Where would she have gone? Why would she have gone?

He slumped by the garage door and tried to slow his thoughts. The dog got out of the car and laid down by his side.

Would she have gone with someone? Or did someone come get her? Do I wait for her?

Tom stood, wiped his face with his hands, and called for the dog to get back in the car.

⚊⚋⚊

When Tom reached what was left of his house, he winched open the garage door and pushed the Benz into the driveway. The car stopped rolling as it crunched into the boulders that the earthquake had moved to the far side of the driveway. Tom didn't even wince at the sound. He pulled the Hummer inside, switched off the motor, and closed the garage door, jamming a block of wood into the track to deter any would-be thieves. He slumped down in the Hummer's seat and let sleep free him from this horrible nightmare. With Revelations curled up next to him, Tom's only wish was that his sleep be dreamless.

april 17

When Peter awoke, shortly after midnight, the trailer was as quiet as a tomb. He snapped into a sitting position on his bed. There were no electrical motors running, no clicking or hissing of the furnace, no hiss of the water heater, no hum of alarm clocks or refrigerator. He felt beside him on the bed. It was empty. Linda had not come home.

He got out of bed and stepped into the hallway. He heard Becca rustle only a moment. Silence followed. Carefully he opened the front door, hoping it wouldn't squeal.

The moon was out, fat and yellow. It lit up the landscape like a beacon. The driveway remained empty. There were no lights along the main road, no whine of truck or car. There was no gentle glow from the lights of Stonefort. He heard the *whir* and shrieks of the bats who nested in the barn. They swooped and flapped, searching for insects in the dark.

"Linda," he said to the night, "you better come home soon. Your daughter needs you."

The sun was barely a dark smudge in the thick smoke and fog when Tom blinked several times, wiping at his eyes. He rose and stumbled to the garage door when he heard Revelations standing by the door, whining softly. The dog ran out, sniffing at everything. Tom grabbed the binoculars from the Hummer and ventured out to the edge of the ridge. He first focused on the rubble that had been his house. The house still smoldered—the interiors and furnishings burnt beyond recognition—leaving the rocks charred and black. Somewhere under the rubble lay his family. He could only look for a moment because the agony was too deep to bear.

He turned the glasses north, to the group of people milling about on the road. Perhaps twenty stood there, and Tom could now see six rifles and a few sidearms. The group was well dressed, mostly male and middle-aged. He may have seen a familiar face, but he couldn't place a name to it. They didn't appear to be guarding any property. Tom saw a bottle being passed around. He heard the animation of shared laughter.

Revelations made his way to where Tom crouched, sniffing enthusiastically. The dog saw the group below and barked loudly. Tom watched as one man unslung his rifle, pointed it up in the air, and squeezed off two shots.

Revelations ducked from the noise, just as Tom did.

"Down, boy," Tom hissed. "Down!"

The dog lay several feet away, head between his paws.

The group broke into laughter again. Another rifle was pointed upward, and more shots echoed into the sky, shattering the silence.

Shooting and laughing are not a comforting combination.

Whistling softly for the dog, Tom hurried back to the dim garage. His heart was pounding. It was most unsettling to hear gunfire in Malibu, of all places.

Who knows what those jackasses might do.

"Well, Rev, let's get some breakfast. I know it's early, but I'm ready for some. Are you?"

The dog looked up and began to wag his tail. *Breakfast* was a word that he understood.

"And maybe I'll read some of Calvin's books. Do you think they'll tell me what's happening?"

The dog barked quietly, as if to say they would.

The dark burgundy of dawn finally began to filter down the artificial canyons of lower Manhattan. Megan had spent the night by a window in her office building. There had been no vehicle traffic, save a scattering of old cars that picked their way through the maze of stalled vehicles.

Around midnight a group of young men, some well dressed, had smashed through the window of the high-priced electronics store at the street level of the building next door. They had swarmed in and, within minutes, exited with armfuls of cellular telephones, camcorders, and digital cameras. She could see their faces lit in the glow of a large fire north of her office.

The rest of the staff had cleared out immediately after the blackout and panic. No one had stopped to ask if she was staying or leaving with them.

"Well," she now said to herself, her voice loud in the deserted office, "I guess the corn market is closed today." She picked up a phone to check and heard only silence. The computers and lights remained dark.

Before leaving the office, she slipped out of her dress, pulled on some baggy sweats, and changed into her running shoes. Thank goodness she had them at the office. Often she worked out after a day's trading to relieve tension. Using her duffel bag, she packed up her purse, the photos of her father, and the one grainy black-and-white photo of her mother from her desk and made her way toward the outside world.

The stairway was black, so she felt her way down, touching the wall with her fingertips, stepping gingerly. The building was silent. She stopped at every floor and listened at the stair door.

The lobby stood empty, save for the papers strewn about the floor. Between the stair door and the front entrance were a dozen, maybe more, discarded briefcases on the floor. As she saw them lying amid the debris, she felt an overwhelming sadness. Only hours earlier each case had carried someone's dreams and ambitions. Now each was no more than useless garbage.

At the front doors she could see that the streets were littered with papers, boxes, cartons, shoes, newspapers, coats, discarded food containers, bottles—as if a volcano of trash had erupted and spewed its vile lava over the streets of the city.

Megan opened the front doors and stepped into the chilly air, traced with smoke. In the distance she heard the wail of sirens and what might be volleys of gunshots on her left, the West Side. There was a fiery glow to the north. Behind her, toward the Statue of Liberty, a scream erupted, faint and persistent. A few shadows streaked across the street a block away. If they saw her, they didn't slow down to investigate. No lights blinked on, no neon signs, no streetlights, no stoplights—all was dark.

Megan knew this was no ordinary crisis, no typical blackout. But she didn't allow herself to agonize over what was happening to the world. She knew that her only goal this moment was to get back to her apartment, thirty-five blocks to the north and east of where she now stood. Her thumb was poised on the cap of her pepper spray, a gift from her father, who had always been concerned for her safety in the often violent city.

It isn't much, she told herself as she held the spray canister at chest level, ready to use, *but it is all I have.*

Hugging the side of the buildings and darting at a fast run as she crossed streets, she began her journey home. The streets were virtually deserted for most of the distance from Megan's office to her apartment. No buses rumbled about, no cars zoomed along the street, and only a handful of pedestrians hustled along in the shadows. In the usually crowded and congested city of New York, the absence of all activity was profoundly disturbing. The silence was louder than any construction project or traffic jam.

As Megan hurried along the sidewalk, she always watched behind her and kept her ears alert to any footsteps or sound. A few solitary figures slipped about. A man and a woman, carrying a huge canvas bag between them, sprinted past her, running west, toward the Hudson River.

Three blocks from home, when she was beginning to feel weak with relief that she'd made it safely, she heard voices, shouts, and curses rush from behind her. Megan ducked into a deep, darkened doorway and tried to become smaller, less noticeable. She slipped behind a short wall in the entrance and knelt.

The sounds grew louder and angrier. The voices were those of young men. Some were the cursive tones of urban blacks, some the nasal harshness of urban whites. Megan ducked farther back into the darkness. An argument swirled about the street in front of where she hid. Shadows rippled across the bricks behind her.

Above the cacophony she heard a single shouted word—"Gun!" Then a *pop*, then another, and another.

Oh God, oh God, oh God.

A darker, booming report crackled out. Then another. Then a scream and the sound of scuffling.

Please protect me, God, Megan prayed. *Please God, please God, please God.*

There was the meaty sound of a fist against flesh. Another long scream exploded. A covey of running footsteps followed—the sound of sneakers taking flight. Then another angry volley. *Pop! Pop! Pop!*

For the next five long minutes, Megan cowered where she hid, hands covering her head, afraid to move or even breathe. Silence returned all around her. Gradually her breathing deepened and her heart began to slow to its normal pace.

She lifted her head and saw no shadows dancing on the wall behind her. Still kneeling, she craned her head, peeking at the street. She saw no movement, heard no sounds. She rose to a crouch and stepped forward. No one was in the street. She stood and stepped from the vestibule onto the sidewalk and promptly tripped over a body slumped against the wall. Blood pooled on the pavement.

Megan's hand rose to her mouth in an attempt to stifle the horror that rose in her throat. Even before she could focus on what lay at her feet, her eyes darted to the street. Two black men—boys actually—no older than sixteen or seventeen, lay faceup, eyes open and white to the dawn, spread-eagle on the pavement, dark circles of wetness ringing their bodies.

Megan swung her head from side to side, frantic. *Are the rest of them still here?* If they could kill so casually and leave their dead so indiscriminately, then who would be safe?

She stepped over the body at her feet, her heel slipping in the blood. Without looking back, she began to run, her shoe making crimson half-moons for nearly a block. She did not stop running until she was outside the door to her apartment on Fifth Avenue.

Her building's front door had been smashed. A thousand slivers glinted mutely in the dark. The hallway and stairwell were dark. Megan felt her way along the railings, counting the landings until she reached her floor. She cracked the door. A weak golden light from the window at the end of the hall brightened the hallway. She sprinted to her door and scrambled inside, securing the dead bolt and latch behind her. She slid a large wing chair in front of the door. It would provide only a second or two of extra security, but she felt better after doing it.

For perhaps fifteen minutes Megan sat in the darkness, letting her breath return to normal, willing her heart to stop its frantic pounding. Then she flipped the light switch. She didn't expect anything to happen, so she wasn't surprised when the room stayed dark. Megan opened the blinds for some light, even though she really didn't care to see the outside world. The apartment, with no running motors, no clicking thermostat, no rattling radiators, no dull thud of radios and stereos from above and beneath her, was still. She had never before heard it this quiet.

She slipped off her sneakers and padded to the kitchen. The refrigerator held two cases of bottled water, a gallon of milk, a few condiments, several containers of leftover Chinese take-out, and little else.

Not much to spoil, anyhow.

Megan poured some of the milk on a huge bowl of cereal. Not having eaten for nearly a day, she was famished. Eating breakfast was the most normal activity she had performed since noon the day before, and it felt comforting and sane. She sat in the dim light of her kitchen, eating slowly, not thinking of anything at all. She didn't want to remember anything she had seen last night. . .or this morning. She wanted no images retained.

From the faucet came a thin brown trickle when she turned the hot-water knob. So instead of washing the bowl, she wiped it with a paper towel.

She felt grimy and dirty, but a shower looked impossible. From the back of her hall closet, Megan extracted a camp stove. She jiggled it close to her ear. *At least half full of cooking gas.*

She poured out two quarts of bottled water into a large pot, pumped the gas chamber, and began to heat water for a very spartan bath. Within an hour, she had washed as best she could, even shampooed her long auburn hair. She changed into jeans and a sweatshirt.

Now what do I do?

She picked up the phone again, hoping that it would no longer be silent. It was. She tried her cell phone. It too was dead.

But now that the sun was fully up, the apartment began to feel less dreary and bleak.

Just then she heard a tapping at her door, and she froze.

Then came a faint whisper of her name. "Megan? Megan? Are you in there? It's Angela. From down the hall. Megan? Please say you're home. Please."

Megan slid the chair away, unlocked the dead bolt, and eased the door open. Angela slipped in like a shadow. Megan did not consider Angela a friend, but they had lived down the hall from each other for more than a year. Occasionally the two shared lunch or spent time in the laundry room chatting. Megan's work had left little time for a social life, but Angela's social life seemed to be her occupation. Megan had counted many different men on her arm at one time or another. Some of them she saw leave the apartment in the early morning as she went to work. Angela's and Megan's bedrooms shared a common wall, so Angela's late-night activities left little to Megan's imagination.

Angela's face was drawn, her eyes red and watery. "It's the end of the world, isn't it?" she wailed, nearly bursting into Megan's arms. "I'm all alone, and it's the end of the world."

Alarmed, Megan put her arms about the more petite girl to offer comfort. "It's all right, Angela. You're not alone. I'm here. You'll be fine. It's not the end of the world."

Other than the sound of Angela's sobs, the room was still. Megan drew Angela by the hand to the sofa and sat down, facing her. "It will be all right, Angela. I bet they'll have it all fixed in a week or two."

But Angela's face continued to show terror and fear and panic. "I don't think anybody can fix what's broken. I should have listened to my mother. She warned me. She said it was all coming to an end, and I never believed her. Now it's too late for me. I know it. It's too late."

She continued to wail and dove into Megan's arms again like a scared child waking from a nightmare.

Angela sobbed for another thirty minutes until Megan could finally calm her down. Then she sniffed one last time and wiped her eyes with her sleeve. She looked smaller than before, as if the tears had reduced her physically. Without makeup, her face looked so innocent, so demure. But her eyes told the real story, of a soul lost and desperately confused.

"This *is* the end of the world. The Tribulation has begun," Angela cried.

"Angela, it isn't that at all," Megan began in the calmest tone she could muster. "It's serious, I admit that. It looks very serious. But the world is not going to end. It's just like a big blackout. I'm sure everything will be back to normal soon."

"How do you know that?"

"Because. . .well, because God is too nice to do such a thing, isn't He? I mean, He's not out to get us or anything. He loves us, right?"

Angela leaned forward. "Do you know what the Bible says?"

"Well, I went to Sunday school. Sure. . .I know what the Bible says. . .I guess."

"I don't think you do, Megan. I don't think you do. My mother has made it her hobby to predict the end—both hers and the world's. Some of this fits, Megan. Some of it fits like a glove. It's like what it says in Luke, when there will be signs in the heavens. . . disturbances."

"Disturbances? I. . .I don't think. . .that's in the Bible. . .is it?" Megan felt herself losing ground.

"And one of the prophets says it will be 'a day of darkness and gloom, of clouds, blackness,'" Angela continued. [iii] "I've never seen dark come quicker and thicker than it did yesterday. Have you?"

By now Megan was thoroughly confused. If the truth were told, she had never paid much attention in church. She'd only gone because her parents made her.

"My mother talks about this all the time," Angela said. "She always said it would be soon."

"But do you believe that? I don't. It just sounds so. . .crazy."

Angela looked as if she were about to cry again. "I don't know. It *is* crazy. But how else do you explain it?" She sniffed loudly. "I don't know if I believe it—or at least all of it. But something evil happened yesterday. And I'm scared, Megan. I am really, really scared."

Just then a volley of gunshots sounded in the street below. Screaming followed, then another series of shots rang out. Both Angela and Megan dove for the floor, covering their heads with their arms.

Shots and screams and shouts echoed along the street below for what seemed like hours. Both Megan and Angela remained motionless the entire time. Running feet pounded down the hall outside Megan's door. There were the sounds of a scuffle and muffled shouts and curses. Both women crawled behind the couch, curling up tight and small.

Angela whispered first, after many minutes of stillness. "It's the gangs. They'll go for liquor and food first. Then gold or jewelry or sex."

Megan shook her head, not wanting to believe what she heard. "The police will be back. The National Guard. Somebody will fix this."

Angela shook her head. "Not this time. Not this time. That's not what my mom says is in the Bible."

The two women huddled by the couch the entire day, speaking only in whispers, nibbling at the little food that was available in Megan's apartment. When the first signs of dusk began to darken the sky again, soft footfalls sounded in the hall. Both women tensed. There was a slight tapping somewhere in the hallway.

"Angie? Angie?"

Angela jumped up and ran to the door, angling to the left and right as she squinted through the peephole. She grabbed at the lock.

"Angela!" Megan hissed. "What are you doing?"

"It's Mike! He came for me!"

"Mike? Who's Mike?"

Angela opened the door a crack and whispered. "Mike! Over here! It's me, Angie. I'm next door."

In a moment Mike, a very attractive boy with sharp Mediterranean features, was sitting on the floor between them. He was at least three or four years younger than Angela. She had embraced him when he came in and had not let him go.

"I was worried that you'd try to come find me," he said. "And that would have been real stupid."

Angela looked relieved, like she'd suddenly been rescued from a swift river current.

Mike took in the apartment. Despite the growing darkness, he nodded. "Nice place."

"Thanks," Megan replied.

"You been here the whole time. . .since it happened?" he asked.

"No," Megan said and related her night in the office and her harrowing trip home.

"That ain't bad at all. Above Forty-second Street, you can forget about it. There are fires and shootings and gangs. It's toast."

"How far did you come?"

"My place is at Forty-ninth and the river, sort of."

Megan consulted her watch. It was 6:30 in the evening. The sky now looked blacker than she had ever remembered. "Does anyone know what happened?"

"Nope," Mike said plainly. "I've heard lots of crazy things— aliens, Russians, even the CIA. I heard one guy talking about earthquakes out in California or Illinois or some state out west right before we went dead. Big quakes. Real big. Maybe they had something to do with it. And the planes—must have been ten or twenty of them crashed, like rocks falling out of the sky. Big explosions and fire, just like in the movies. This all would be way cool if it weren't so real. I mean, I was around for 9/11—and that was like a Sunday school picnic in comparison. I wish it were terrorists—that would be easier to handle. But it ain't."

A dread rose inside Megan's chest, a dense darkness that chilled her heart. "Where are the police? The National Guard?

Isn't the government doing anything?"

Mike laughed, the brave laugh of youth. "I ain't seen one cop the whole trip. There ain't nothing working. Only seen a few old cars running. Gas pumps don't work. I heard some of the subway tunnels are filled with water and everybody on board drowned. Someone said the Lincoln Tunnel is flooded too. I tried to get money out of the bank or the ATM, but nearly every one I tried had already been busted into. Ain't no banks open for sure. Most every food store has been looted already. It ain't no blackout."

Angela nestled in closer to the boy. He pulled her tight. "People shooting at each other for no reason. A lot of people are leaving. The George Washington Bridge was jammed. Hope the gangs don't start taking tolls."

Megan felt more and more dislocated, more and more confused. Her life seemed to teeter on the brink of some unfathomable chasm. "Why is this happening? We've had power failures before, haven't we? Why so much panic? Why the destruction?"

Mike rubbed at the stubble on his chin. "Hey, when the power goes out, the phones should still work. Power goes out and cars still run. Planes still fly. Not this time. A couple of planes crashed in the Hudson. . .that's when my neighborhood started to go nuts, when those planes crashed in the river in a ball of fire. That told me this was a whole lot bigger and nastier than just a fuse blowing somewhere. Something a whole lot more evil. This time everything is. . .gone. Everything."

"But what about the government, city hall?" Megan argued. "Aren't they around?"

"You think city hall is going to protect you? I bet most cops are home guarding their own places. At least they got guns. I mean, I got an uncle who's a cop. He might hang around for awhile—until all hell breaks loose. Then he's gonna head home for sure. He's got family, you know. Family comes first."

He swallowed once and raised his body into a crouching

position. He was ready to leave. "Listen, this place is about to explode. I got family out on Long Island—pretty far out on the island. I came to get Angie, and that's where we're heading. Anybody in this city ain't going to be alive for long. The gangs are heading south, and I ain't going to be the one to stand in their way."

He stood up and pulled Angela to her feet. "Angie, grab a bag full of stuff and let's go. Better find a pair of sneakers or boots or something. We got a long walk."

"You're leaving now?" Megan asked, incredulous. "In the dark?"

"At night nobody sees you and nobody waits in the shadows—'cause it's all shadows. In the day everybody sees everybody. Don't worry. We'll get there." He took a silver revolver from his pocket, showing only the handgrip and trigger. "We'll get there for sure."

Mike eyed Angela, hesitated, then asked Megan, "You want to come with us? Our house out there is plenty big. We could find room for you."

"No, but that's very nice of you to offer. I have family west of here."

Mike looked relieved. "Yeah, I guess it's important to get to your family."

Megan managed a weak smile and nodded in the dark.

After Mike and Angela left, Megan sat alone in the darkness. She opened her bedroom window a crack, and the sounds of the city rose up from the streets. There were no horns or traffic or planes. Those comforting sounds of civilization were replaced with shots and screams in the night.

Is this the end of the world? Is this the way it's all supposed to end?

Megan lit a couple candles, shut her blinds, and began to assemble her old and not recently used camping gear. Over the past year her life hadn't allowed time to camp or hike.

Now she assembled it all—a backpack, hiking boots, sleeping bag, cookstove, matches, camp knife, compass, insect repellent, pepper spray, and assorted other gear.

It might not be enough, but it's all I can carry.

She was in her bedroom looking for jeans and sweatshirts when she heard a soft tapping at her door. She took the knife with her and peered through the peephole. "Angela? I thought you left."

"We're on our way. I just wanted to give you this. I wanted to thank you for being my friend." Angela handed Megan a well-worn Bible. "It was my mother's. She underlined a whole bunch of stuff and wrote notes in the margins."

She wrote in a Bible?

"Maybe you'll be able to read it, find some answers."

"You don't want it? It was your mother's."

"She had a bunch of them, and I can only carry one."

Angela leaned forward and embraced Megan for a long farewell. "Take care."

Megan latched the door and returned slowly to the bedroom. She began to thumb through the pages. Big portions of the verses were underlined, and notes filled the margins, just as Angela had said.

Her eyes stopped at one spot. She turned the book toward the flickering candlelight. The section was from a portion of the New Testament. . .in Matthew. Megan knew some of the books of the Bible, but it had been a long, long time since she opened one.

The words were in red.

> *"And wars will break out near and far, but don't panic. Yes, these things must come, but the end won't follow immediately. The nations and kingdoms will proclaim war against each other, and there will be famines and earthquakes in many parts of the world. But all this will be only the beginning of the horrors to come. . . . Immediately after those horrible days end, the sun will be darkened, the moon will not give light, the stars will fall from the sky, and the powers of heaven will be shaken."[iv]*

"Are the powers of heaven shaking tonight? Is that what has happened?" Megan wondered as she stepped to the window and pulled the shade back an inch. She looked for the moon but could not see it. The New York sky was obscured by thick smoke and clouds.

In the grayness of dusk, the Reverend Jerry Moses stood, praying loudly, in the pulpit of the Temple of God's Calling. The veins in his head visibly pulsed as he called out the words. Before him were nearly one hundred of his congregation. Most were ashen faced and dressed in an odd assortment of clothing. Some members were in pajamas and overcoats. Some wore denim overalls and muddy boots. Some wore camouflage jumpsuits, with pistols and knives holstered at their waist. There were curlers and scarves. There were billed caps from seed companies and farm-implement dealers.

"We are gathered here in Your temple, O God, gathered here for Your protection."

He let the words echo for a long dramatic moment.

"You have spoken to us. Your judgment is upon us." Rev. Moses kept his eyes open as he prayed. "You are angry with the land and Thy people."

He glanced down at Linda Wilson, sitting demurely in the second row. She had shown up at the parsonage door yesterday afternoon, seeking comfort and an explanation of the day's events. Many others had come as well, but Linda stuck out in Rev. Moses's memory.

"We rejoice that we have been spared." His voice rose to a shout. "You have chosen us! You have chosen God's Temple! You have chosen all of us to be spared! You have spared me. It is Your sign that what is within this building is sacred. What is within this building is under the protection of Thy mighty hand."

Stonefort, not a large town to begin with, lay in ruins. Of the

127 structures within the city limits, 126 lay burned, collapsed, or torn asunder. The one building that stood whole and totally intact was the Temple of God's Calling. The only damage to the building was to its steeple. The rocking earth had caused it to tilt several degrees away from plumb.

"You have laid waste to the heathen and the rebellious. You have spared the saints and the holy. You have spared this building." He paused, carefully considering his next words. "You have spared this building and this church!" His words rang like thunder. "You have spared this humble servant, Your humble child, Jerry Moses, to carry Your message unhindered into the land of darkness."

He let silence reign in the room. He heard tears and sniffles, then a soft chorus of amens.

"You have anointed this church, this servant, this message. This is Your anointing upon us, O God. We have been chosen!" he screamed.

More silence followed, then an amen and another and another. . .until the entire room swelled with shouts and sobs and weeping and praise.

Tom unpacked every item from the Hummer and laid them out on the floor of the garage. A pair of citronella candles provided all the light he needed. Tom marveled at Calvin's foresight. Virtually everything that a man might need for long-term survival was packed into the vehicle. Among the materials were a tent, sleeping bag, stove, water purification systems, cooking gear, shovels, a rifle (in addition to the pistol), fishing gear, mosquito netting, two huge duffel bags of freeze-dried foods, maps, a compass, and a stack of books. The books fell into one of two categories—survival skills or prophecy.

Revelations sat in the corner, watching Tom lay out each piece of gear. When he finished his inventory, he spent an hour carefully reloading the gear. What he didn't think he'd need for awhile, he stored at the bottom. The sleeping bag, tent, food, and dog food were stored at the top. He stashed the loaded pistol in the pouch on the driver's door. The rifle lay against the passenger seat.

For the hundredth time, Tom lifted his wrist to check his watch. The Rolex had cost him over five thousand dollars and had stopped hours earlier. There was no stem to wind and he couldn't change the battery, yet he wasn't willing to discard it.

Tom yawned and arranged a sleeping bag on the garage floor. He slept fitfully for several hours, with doors locked and a loaded pistol inches from his hand.

Tom awoke hot, groggy, and unsure of his reality.

He opened the back door of the garage and slipped out. The moon hung fat in the sky, colored a dusky red by the ash and dust in the air. Tom picked his way to the far edge of the property. Revelations stayed at his side, matching him step for step.

On a good, clear day, rare for Southern California, Tom could see to the northern edge of downtown Los Angeles. If the night was clear, Tom could make out the lights of the office towers. Tonight all he could see was a scarlet glow masked by a thick pall of smoke and dust. The city burned, and the choking thickness of the smoke was pushing north and east.

His thoughts jangled. Somewhere below him lay his wife and daughter, crushed and buried in the remains of their home. His emotions had slipped into a muted autopilot, a sort of trance. He did not feel pain. He did not feel joy. He felt almost nothing. But once the immediacy of his situation was past, Tom knew then that the pain and tears would take up residence in his soul.

He sat at the edge of the ridge, looking past his ruined life and out to the vastness of the sea. He sent a few pebbles cascading down.

Maybe I could pray. . .or something?

He tried to. He tried the same sort of words that he had spoken at the foot of Calvin's hasty grave. But the words felt hollow and impotent. Calvin asked for the prayer and would have believed it. But Tom's wife, a lovely person who worshipped both body and beauty, had had no time for religion. Neither of them had.

I have lived too well for God to take notice of me now. I have committed too many sins in my life, he thought sadly.

The rubble was now only barely visible in the hellish glow of a thousand fires. The late-evening sky remained a deep burgundy from the fires up and down the coast. Tom whispered into the breeze, "Lydia. . .Kalli. . .I have to say good-bye now. The world has gone dark and mad. I don't want to say good-bye, but I have to go. I can't stay here. My heart hurts so much, Lydia. Our three years together were too short. Had I known, I would have spent more time with you, with Kalli. But now. . .you are down there. Our daughter is down there. But I made a promise to Calvin. I don't want to leave, but it hurts too much to think of staying." He wiped at his eyes. It was not the smoke that caused his tears. "I love you both with all my heart. That is the monument I will leave you. I loved you and will always love you."

Tom knelt in the gravel, lowered his head, and let the tears flow. Time slipped by without his recognizing its passage. His cheeks burned from his salty tears by the time he stopped.

Gunfire echoed again up the valley—some isolated shots, some concentrated volleys. A few fires still glowed nearby. The Jeagers' house had burned. The Mahons' house was consumed to its foundation. Tom gazed toward the west. The Pacific reflected the moon and the flames in equal measure. The moon was a diamond twinkling, the land a blood-red ruby.

Tom looked down the hill one last time at what remained of his house and said out loud: "God, I know this may be self-serving and that I've never really prayed since I was a kid. I've done a lot of things I'm not proud of. . .but Lydia and Kalli were innocent. They didn't know. My daughter was too young to know what sin is. I don't know how You decide these things—or if I should even be asking. . . ."

In agony, Tom stared up into the night sky. "God," he pleaded, "would You take them to heaven? That's all I'll ever ask of You. I promise. Take them to a better place." He fell to his knees again and wept.

Nearly a full hour passed until he rose and walked slowly to the garage. Revelations greeted him with a bark. Tom reached into the Hummer and pulled out a thick road atlas. With a flashlight in one hand, he opened the book to the map of California and spread it flat on the hood of the Hummer. The pencil-thin beam traced a route from Los Angeles north, past Modesto and Sacramento, past Redding, and into the Cascades. The light stopped and hovered on the small town of Hornbrook, just south of the Oregon border. Lydia's parents lived there, in a tiny cottage at the edge of the national forest.

"I have to tell them," he whispered in the dark. "They have to know—if they're still alive. I have to tell them what happened."

From there, the light, wavering slightly in Tom's hand, traveled back south, illuminating a route through the mountains and desert, stopping finally at Las Vegas.

"If this is a time for final good-byes, then I need to make one final stop before heading east." Tom looked down at the dog. "I need to stop in Vegas. This may be my only chance to see her—if she is still alive—and to settle that part of my past."

The dog loudly sniffed the night air as Tom switched the flashlight off.

"Well, boy," Tom said, his words dull and cold, his heart beating without life, "how would you like to go for a ride?"

april 18

Commotion outside woke Rev. Moses just after midnight. He stumbled from the couch in his study and made his way to the vestibule. He watched as Herve Slatters and two of his sons jockeyed a generator into position in the back lot of the church. It appeared to be at least thirty years old and was coated in dust and oil.

The reverend had his doubts about the machine's usefulness, but Herve had offered it to the church earlier that day, and Moses couldn't refuse it without hurting Herve's feelings. "Reverend, the church needs our generator more than we do," Herve had said. "You need it to keep preaching and ministering." The Reverend Moses knew that if anyone in town could perform an electrical miracle with this beat-up contraption, it would be Herve.

So Herve and his sons snaked cables as thick as a man's arm from the back end of the unit toward the church and through the storm door in the cellar. Herve climbed down after it and, ten minutes later, came out a little dirtier but smiling.

"Let her rip, boys. We got a connection."

Ternell, the oldest son, cranked the key in the ignition. The engine popped, chugged, then blasted into life, drenching Ternell in blue smoke.

Herve shouted to his other son, standing slack-jawed to his left, "Goodboy, set the throttle a hair lower. The engine sounds a little bit too vibratey."

Goodboy nodded, fiddled with the fuel-adjustment needle,

and the engine began to back away from its bone-clacking chatter. All the lights in the church winked on. The refrigerator cleared its throat, then began to hum.

"Well, I'll be!" Rev. Moses said, smoothing his hair with his hand. "The thing works, and I got lights." He turned around in the vestibule, marveling at the sight of electric lights, only less than a day gone dark. Then he stopped dead still for a long moment.

His face wore a smile as he turned around. "Herve," he called out, waving, "Herve, come here." Rev. Moses slipped his arm about the older man. Herve beamed with pride. "You're a godsend, Herve," Rev. Moses confided. "An absolute godsend."

As the two watched the generator for another minute, the reverend leaned closer to Herve. "Herve, do you think. . .no, that's too much to ask."

Herve looked hurt. "No, no, Rev. Moses, you just ask away. I'll see what I can do. It'll be an honor. I mean that. A real honor."

Rev. Moses leaned in even closer. "Do you think this motor would be enough to power the radio station? I mean, if the radio station isn't completely broken up by the quake and all."

Herve put his hand to his chin and stroked at his whiskery stubble. "Well, Rev. Moses, I don't know. But if any man here can do it, I can. I'll take the boys, and we'll find out. I know for a fact that the radio building isn't too bad off. It might be the only building on Main Street that isn't fully down." He stepped away, then turned back. "You do want the radio equipment here, don't you? If it's not broken up. You want to do the radio from the church. Right?"

Rev. Moses beamed like a child on Christmas morning. "Herve, you are one smart cookie. That's what I'd like to try to do. That's exactly the idea the Lord gave to me."

Herve wiped his chin with the back of his hand. "Then it's a real good thing that Old Man Baker hasn't spent a dime on that station in twenty-five years. If the tubes didn't break, we may be in business."

Rev. Moses chuckled and nodded. He stepped back into the house, then called back at Herve, almost as an afterthought, "You know anybody who might be able to get to Eldorado?"

Herve tensed his eyes up. "Eldorado? What for? Not much up there that anybody would need."

"I want to find out if my son is okay."

Herve's face brightened. "Oh yeah, your son." He scratched through his whiskers. "Well, I bet I can find someone to get there and find out. Don't you worry about it. I'll get word."

Megan took one last look around her apartment.

Is there anything else worth bringing? Anything I could use?

Everything electronic stayed, and that eliminated virtually all of her possessions. The TV, stereo, Walkman, camcorder, digital camera, computer, laptop, digital assistant—all were useless bits of plastic, glass, metal, wire, and silicon. She tried each one and they all remained inert, lifeless.

She placed all her available cash in a money belt her father had given her and tightened it under her blouse, against her skin. She used another belt around her jeans. Like her father, she trusted cash more than plastic. It wasn't unusual for Megan to hold several thousand dollars in her apartment, tucked beneath a plastic potted plant in the bedroom. She wondered if thieves would take the time to check if she wore a money belt. The backpack was full of camping gear. She carried three gallons of water—heavy for sure, but she was unwilling to trust the local supplies until well out of New York. She jammed extra jeans, socks, underwear, sweatshirts, and boots into the cavities of the backpack. She stuffed in all the canned and jarred food that she had in her kitchen—tuna, soup, vegetables, peanut butter—plus a manual can opener. It was a heavier load than she had ever carried before, but she knew it meant her survival.

It will get lighter as I go, she told herself.

She peered out the window. It was early morning and very dark, with the moonlight hidden behind the layer of smoke that hung over the whole city. She heard sporadic gunfire and screams coming from the north.

Slipping on her rain jacket, she hoisted the backpack to her shoulders and stepped out into the hall. *Should I say good-bye to anyone?* Besides Angela, there were only a few people she spoke with—and then only a nodded hello or good evening.

Should I leave a note or something? She paused. *But to whom? And why? If this is the end, who would care?*

Carefully, she made her way down the pitch-black steps. A gun barked out in the distance. *My camp knife and pepper spray are no match for that,* she thought.

As she took her first step into the street, she began to recite again the words that she remembered from her Sunday school days, " 'The LORD is my shepherd; I have everything I need. . . .' "ᵛ

Revelations whined with his nose against the Hummer's window until Tom reached over and rolled the window down most of the way.

"There's too much smoke for this, boy," he said, though the dog kept his nose poked into the air. The animal sneezed every few minutes but would not relinquish his position.

Tom took the back way from his home, down the fire lane to the canyon floor. The road was rutted and bumpy, but there were no abandoned cars to block the way. He turned south, skirting along Flores Canyon Road. It was another three miles to Topanga Canyon Road, where he'd turn north and head toward Simi Valley.

Cars and trucks littered the two-lane road, though most were pulled over toward the side. He slalomed along, having to drive off-road only for short periods.

If the roads remain this good, I might make it close to Santa Clarita and I-5 before the sun comes up.

Tom blinked his eyes from the smoke, tears welling at the corners.

That's if Santa Clarita still exists.

New York was silent as Megan began her journey. She skulked south, alone on the darkened Fifth Avenue. No stoplights flashed, no neon signs blinked, no storefronts were lit. The clouds glowed scarlet, alive from fires north of her, bathing the streets in a thin whisper of illumination. Two old cars raced past her, weaving between the abandoned buses, cars, and trucks. Each time, she ducked into a vestibule or behind parked cars. Several people ran past her as she walked, running to escape the darkness. A few carried bags or suitcases. No one spoke, no one stopped, no one dared risk making a connection.

She passed Ninth Street, then Houston, then on to Broome. She turned to the west. She was less than a quarter mile from the Holland Tunnel. If it was blocked or flooded, Megan would have to reverse her path and walk nearly ten miles north to the George Washington Bridge. There was no other way off Manhattan to the west. If cars didn't run, Megan knew the ferries wouldn't be sailing either.

In the darkness, Megan prayed over and over that the tunnel might be passable. A block from the entrance, her heart tightened in fear when she heard gunshots. The muzzle flashes lit up the front of the tunnel entrance. She ducked back in the alcove of a video store and covered her head with her hands, repeating the Twenty-third Psalm under her breath.

A young man, no more than twenty, ducked in the alcove and knelt beside her. He was sweaty and breathing hard. "Those people are crazy," he gasped.

Megan turned to face him. *He doesn't look dangerous, and he doesn't look desperate. . .yet.*

The young man leaned out into the street a couple inches, peering toward the mouth of the tunnel. "There's a bunch of gang-bangers out there who started yelling something about tolls for the tunnel."

"And they're shooting people who don't pay?" Megan's voice edged toward shrillness.

"Naw, not yet. They're just shooting for effect. But they'll get serious quick enough."

"You heading to New Jersey?" she asked.

"Yeah, I live over in Harrison. Been hiding out in the office. But then the fires started, and I headed south as fast as I could."

Megan didn't want to know more. She saw the pale flickering of perhaps a hundred faces huddled in the darkness in the deserted streets that ringed the entrance to the tunnel.

For the first time, the man really looked at Megan, his eyes sizing her up. His voice lowered slightly. "Where you headed?"

"West."

"West?"

"Family in Pennsylvania."

"You have money for the tunnel toll?"

"Money?"

"The clowns are asking for a hundred bucks a person to let them go past. I left the house with lunch money two days ago, and I'm up the creek all right. Haven't found a single ATM that hasn't been broken into. I don't want to head north to the Washington Bridge, that's for sure."

Megan stared over his shoulder toward the mouth of the tunnel. "A hundred?"

"Yeah, that's what they were shouting an hour ago."

Megan closed her eyes for a moment and offered a prayer. She felt a hum of impertinence course through her heart—asking God for protection after ignoring Him for the last twelve years. Yet she was lost. She was cornered. She needed to turn to someone.

"If I did have the hundred dollars," she whispered, "would you go with me through the tunnel? Could I trust you?"

"You have an extra hundred? You'd give it to me?"

Megan nodded. "But only if you go with me."

The young man smiled and extended his hand in greeting. "I'm Randall. Randall Noss. Yeah, I'll go with you. For a hundred bucks, I'd do anything right now."

Megan returned his handshake and told him her name. She then turned and fiddled with the bottom buttons of her blouse. Her skin prickled at the chill. She extracted four fifty-dollar bills from the money belt and handed them to Randall, then tucked her blouse back into the waist of her jeans.

"We go together, right? That's what you said."

Randall stood up and leaned out toward the street. "Sure, we go together."

Megan heard muted shouts, but the gunfire had ceased.

"And if anybody asks," Randall said, "you tell them you're my wife. They'll be less likely to do anything to you if they think we're really together."

Megan nodded.

Randall stepped into the street, holding the four bills tightly. He turned back and whispered, "Let me take the backpack."

Megan, reluctant to part with all her possessions, hesitated.

"Come on, Megan. I'm not gonna steal your stuff. Just let me carry it. A husband wouldn't let his wife carry this heavy pack."

She slipped it off, and Randall hefted it onto his back.

"What do you have in here? Gold?"

"Water."

He adjusted the straps and started walking. Thirty or so young men stood in a ragged line just west of the tollbooths. Megan saw the cold steel of a handgun flash in the red glow of a trash-can fire. Cars were abandoned where they had stopped. The roadway was jammed, bumper to bumper, with dead automobiles.

Randall walked up to the group with long, bold steps, Megan only a step behind. "The toll still a hundred a head?"

No one answered at first. Then a tall teenager holding a small silver revolver stepped forward. "Yeah, it's still a hundred. Special tonight. Goes up to two bills tomorrow." He raised the revolver and pointed it at Randall's chest. "We got a blue-light special tonight."

The crowd behind him laughed.

"You got the cash?" the tall teenager demanded.

"I got it," Randall answered. "Enough for me and my wife. We have to get home. She's pregnant, and we need to get to the doctor in Newark."

The crowd of tunnel guards was silent for a minute.

The teen eyed them both, like a crow eyes a dead squirrel in the gutter. He spit, then snatched the bills. "Yeah, git out o' here. And don't come back."

Randall reached back and took Megan's hand. He pulled her to match his quick steps. "Come on, honey. We have to keep moving."

And in a few hurried steps, they entered the absolute darkness of the tunnel.

"You have a flashlight in here?" Randall asked as he walked farther in.

"Side pocket."

He found the flashlight and followed its weak beam through the brackish, evil-smelling water that got as high as midthigh. After what seemed like an eternity to Megan, Randall snapped off the flashlight. A faint glimmer lay ahead.

"We're close to the other side," Randall said.

Megan hated the water, imagining "things" brushing against her legs with each step.

The west entrance was deserted. Randall looked about, then at Megan. "You want to tag along? I'm going west for a couple of miles. You're welcome to come along as far as Harrison."

Megan peered about in the dim light. She turned back toward Manhattan. A thick pall of smoke hovered over everything north of Fifty-fifth Street. Tongues of fire flickered at various other spots southward. She consulted her watch. It was 3:00 A.M. "I guess I will," she whispered, "if you don't mind."

"Hey, you paid the toll. It's the least I can do."

They set off to the west. A half mile later, Randall stopped and turned to Megan. "What's that you're whispering? You've been whispering since I met you."

Megan blushed at being discovered. She was embarrassed to admit what it was. "Uh. . .well. . .it's sort of the. . .it's sort of the Twenty-third Psalm. You know, from the Bible."

Randall smiled. "Yeah, I know the Bible." He hitched her pack high on his shoulders, then looked back at the glowing skyline of the city they had just left. "Let's get going. I don't want to be out here when the sun comes up."

april 19

Riley Weston sat stone still, his intertwined fingers resting on a notebook. As a top-level operative with the CIA, he had been to more presidential briefings than he could remember. This was the first, however, that took place on one of the classified levels far below the Pentagon. The elevator hadn't numbered the floors as they descended, but Riley's clearance told him that they were on the twentieth.

After everyone left the meeting room, Riley reached into his breast pocket and pulled out a cigar. He would not light it, knowing that the flame would set off a myriad of sensors and the Pentagon's entire internal fire department.

It would be enough to chew at the end as he reviewed and revised his notes. He took out his pen, a standard, government-issue ballpoint, and began to tick off the highlights he had written down. Government reports went on too long, he had always insisted.

> Solar flare—eruption on the surface of the sun—
>   happens all the time
> No warning—plumes of high-energy radiation
> Bigger the flare—the more X-rays and destructive radio
>   pulses
> Biggest flare—like an atom bomb set off in atmosphere
> Huge pulse of electromagnetic energy—tidal wave in space
> Burns up silicon chips

Civil Defense system—computerized—and all gone
Civilian broadcasting—a few small stations
Working radios—old units—five to ten million
Energy—computerized delivery systems destroyed
Power grid—maybe back in six months—maybe
    two years
Portable generators—a few million old units without
    electronics
Cars, trucks—only pre-1971 will work
Good mechanic could retrofit engines
3 percent of cars, trucks still run
Thousands and thousands dead in plane crashes
Affected entire world—worse in China and Africa
Earthquakes—West Coast, Chicago, and south—8.9
    on Richter scale
Japan devastated
Air Force One serviceable in a week—head to Italy
    for VP
Rioting in big cities—casualties could be huge
Money system destroyed—3 percent in hard currency
Military—25 percent AWOL—rest may be loyal
We can't launch, nor can anyone else

Riley didn't smile or frown. He was a professional. No matter how bleak the situation, he would approach it dispassionately and analytically. He took a separate notebook and began a to-do list for himself.

Loyalty checks on base commanders
Ascertain weaponry levels, secure armories
Request Humvee and ride-along operatives
Big cities—let burn out before sending troops
Small towns—ascertain loyalty of any new chieftains

Riley clicked his pen closed as he heard the door swing open. He didn't turn around.

"I thought you'd still be here."

Riley recognized the voice—President Garrett—the man Riley once guarded when he was still a senator from Missouri.

"You're the only one I trust to give me the unvarnished truth here, Riley." The president's thick southern rumble was softer today. "What's your real take on what's going on?"

"I admit that things are pretty bad out there," Riley said. "Really bad in some places. But the generals painted too bleak a picture." He swiveled toward the president.

President Garrett's eyes narrowed.

"We have contingency plans, sir," Riley insisted. "We can restore the federal government's power. It will take a few months, but we'll be back in charge. We're cleverer than the generals give us credit for. People will find ways to adapt. Big cities are going to have it tough. No question. Lots of casualties and no way to get order back for awhile—until we can get enough loyal troops together. Small towns will figure it out on their own. Suffering for sure—but we'll make it."

The president chose his words carefully. "What's your plan? I know you're not going to stay inside the beltway."

Riley continued in his dry, nearly menacing drawl. "Situation is this—a thousand new fiefdoms will be springing up—most will be okay. Some won't be so nice. Any fringe group that tries to take power is absolutely leader-dependent. Cut off the head and you don't have to worry about the rest of the snake, Mr. President."

"And that's your plan? To go after all the local militia heads?"

"Just the ones who are dangerous—to the health and well-being of the nation, sir." Riley took the cigar out of his mouth. "We have the operatives. We have the capabilities. If the military can get to 50 percent staffing and 20 percent weapon-ready, we can be back in control. . .by the Fourth of July, sir."

President Garrett remained quiet. No one else at the meeting had shared Riley's optimism about the quick return of a properly functioning government, but he knew it was what the president wanted to hear.

The president sighed again and nodded. "You may proceed with your contingency plans. But do me a favor—keep me apprised of your operations."

"Oh, I will, sir. I will."

After the brief meeting alone with the president, Riley sat at the conference table, skimming the report no one else seemed to have the patience to read. Of special note to Riley were the predictions of the impact of a solar flare on the general population. These he reread carefully.

> *At Extreme Risk: Urban areas of a density greater than 500 people per square mile and greater than one million aggregate population (i.e., New York, Los Angeles, Chicago).*
>
> *Population: Within six weeks, population majority (60 to 70 percent) will try to exit urban area in search of food and/or safety. Many will fail and return or perish in attempt. Local government will have no communications structure in place to prevent panic.*
>
> *Commerce: Banking and monetary activity will cease (for some period). Barter and thievery/looting will be only mechanisms for trade.*
>
> *Public Welfare: Coupled with sanitation problems, hospitals and medical delivery systems will fail. Potential for aggressive introduction of cholera, dysentery, and other forms of virulent contamination is high.*
>
> *Viability: Because of authority fragmentation, remaining police may only patrol individual neighborhoods. Many*

will exit city. Centralized authority within civilian police will be lost due to communication failure. Fire protection, sanitation, infrastructure will collapse. Following loss of governmental control, gangs and/or armed citizen groups will fill leadership vacuum. Many areas will fall under gang control.

At High Risk: *Urban areas of a density between 250 and 500 people per square mile and under one million aggregate population (i.e., Des Moines, Charlotte, Chattanooga).*

Population: *Smaller population with greater access to land will hold most of population to current residence.*

Commerce: *Banking and monetary activity will cease (for some period). Barter and thievery/looting will be only mechanisms for trade. Using animal power, distribution of foodstuffs may be achievable in limited amounts.*

Public Welfare: *Some limited social viability will be possible. Smaller scale allows greater flexibility. Medical and sanitation still problematic, with virulent contamination a risk.*

Viability: *Local authority will quickly revert to a dictatorial/marshal-law status, guaranteeing peace and civility over individual rights and due process. Anticipate entrenched political figures to assume leadership. Police/National Guard will offer loyalty to local political leadership. Communication via personal contact will permit authority to deliver news on a somewhat timely basis.*

At Risk: *Rural areas of a density lower than 250 people per square mile and under 250,000 aggregate population (i.e., farmland, rural areas more than 200 miles distant from cities of 500,000 population).*

Population: *Groups, mainly family and culture related, will band together for support and protection. Small pockets of viability will form.*

Commerce: *Banking and monetary activity will cease (for some period). Barter and thievery/looting will be only mechanisms for trade. Farmers and crop-growers will have renewable resources to trade.*

Public Welfare: *Limited risk. Few large-scale projects—no hospitals, sewage treatment facilities, etc.*

Viability: *Owing to access to farmland, livestock, and wild game, these areas will remain most viable for a long period. To remain secure from outside aggression, they will quickly resort to highly aggressive defensive postures (i.e., barricading roads, blockades, refusing entry to outsiders). Owing to smaller populations, these areas will be at risk from any organized attempt on their resources. Terrain and small population will permit fluidity in structure.*

Riley heard the door open again. This time he turned right away. It was Todd Blackridge, a senior aide to the president. He returned to the report to finish the last few lines:

Based on all demographic interpretations, risk analysis, chaos management, and computer modeling, the United States would need between seven and twelve years to recover fully from such an event. (Please review statistical analysis in Appendix 32-D for further detailing of probabilities.)

As Riley closed the report, Blackridge whispered, "You think you can do it?"

"Do what?" Riley asked.

"Bring it all back?"

Riley nodded. "We have five hundred operatives all over the country. I've been able to reach 90 percent of them already." He leaned close to the presidential advisor. "Our equipment is a lot better than the standard government issue, my friend. We're tracking the militias. Truth is, we're running the militia in most areas. We'll let the rest of them function for now—a militia commander with absolute authority in an area is better than no authority at all. If one fouls up too much, well, we make sure he is unable to make any more mistakes."

Riley winked as he opened his jacket to expose his shoulder holster. "We'll get control back. Don't you worry. We'll have your boss back on the throne in no time. And things will come back sooner than we thought," he continued. "Regardless of who is saying what. Americans are resourceful. We don't sit around waiting for things to fix themselves."

Riley held out a thin sheet of paper with several lines of dense type. Todd Blackridge squinted but was too far away to read the document. "A report on some preacher in Illinois. He's on the radio already. Says he's God's chosen man to lead us out of our ruination. Says God spared him and his church. A modern-day savior, he says."

Riley made a deliberate show of folding the paper and slipping it into his pocket. "I may handle this one myself. Have family in Illinois. Be nice to visit them on my way."

may 15

Megan glanced over her shoulder with a practiced move. Since leaving New York almost four weeks ago, she had performed the same motion at least a thousand times. There was no one behind her—no one that she could see. The woods remained quiet and still. She shrugged off her backpack and lowered it silently to the ground. Other than the feathery rustle of a few birds, she was alone.

She sat with her back to a large pine and faced west into the setting sun. Spring had warmed the earth slowly this year. Megan wondered if she would ever feel warm again. She unsnapped the back flap of the pack and pulled out a tin of kippers. Farther down in the pack were two small packages of saltines. Dinner was over in three minutes. She wanted to set up the stove and boil water for coffee, but she had used the last of the instant granules four days earlier.

Within another few minutes, she had buried the can and cellophane and removed her sleeping bag from the pack. She didn't zip herself in, but merely draped it over her body and tucked it under her. She would not let herself be slowed by the zipper in case a fast escape was required.

She hunched herself into a small, tight bundle, pulled her wool cap farther down over her head, and waited for the darkness. She closed her eyes and waited for the memories and images to stop dancing before her eyes. She waited until sleep would free her. The last four weeks had been a dream to her—a bizarre, surrealistic, waking dream. It was like seeing a familiar face in a movie—a most dangerous and troubling movie.

Megan had stayed just one night with Randall Noss and his family on their winterized porch, until darkness early in the morning on April nineteenth. Without telling anyone, she had slipped back into the night and headed west.

It had taken her these four weeks to cross New Jersey and to get a handful of miles from the Delaware River, which separated New Jersey from Pennsylvania. A sign on the interstate told her that Stroudsburg lay five miles west, across the river. She had skirted along the main roads, hiding in brambly pockets of thicket and brush that lay along the interstates.

For nearly two weeks, at the beginning of her journey, she had camped out in a deserted house, hidden from view of the road because it was down a skinny, tree-lined dirt lane. The pantry had been stocked, and those supplies helped keep Megan rooted there until the cupboard ran bare. Those two weeks, Megan seemed to live in a nearly catatonic state—as if her emotions had been scared and needed time to regenerate. She slept fitfully, not noting if it were day or night. And instead of moving, she cowered on the faded couch in the living room and watched the progress of the sun or moon through a slit in the curtains. It was all that she could accomplish.

When she managed to resume traveling, during the nights, she saw bonfires raging, sometimes on the roadway, sometimes in neighborhoods. Around the fires, scores of people gathered. Occasionally, from her hiding places, she would watch as bottles were passed among them. She would cower in the dense thickets as gunfire exploded. Sometimes she would hear either the coarse laughter or painful screams of a woman as a group of men, drunk and liberated, took their grunting pleasure with her.

I don't understand how quickly it all crashed about us, how quickly civility disappeared. Where are the police? The military? Who is going to stop this violence?

She passed burned-out hulks of looted shopping centers, jumbles of cars, trash and possessions, strewn like a river along the roadway.

Where is God in all this? she continued to wonder. *Where is God?*

⟞⟜⟞

Tom had not smiled for what felt like years. Revelations lay curled on the passenger-side floor of the vehicle, searching for a breath of coolness. Five miles north of Lone Pine, the heat still shimmered off the black asphalt. The owner's manual stated that air-conditioning increased gas consumption by 20 percent on hot days. Tom knew he could not depend on gas supplies, so he had switched it off three weeks ago and had not used it since.

The road was deserted, as most roads were. No clear-thinking person would be out on foot in such desolation. And this portion of California, not populous to begin with, seemed all the more deserted now. On his left, Tom passed a weather-beaten sign proclaiming a trail to Death Valley National Park. Tom stopped and checked the map again. South of Lone Pine, the road offered two choices. One route led to Beatty, Nevada. To the south lay Death Valley Creek and then Death Valley Junction, twenty miles farther. Though both towns showed only the tiniest of black dots on the map, he thought there would be a better chance of finding gasoline and dog food in Death Valley Junction. After all, this part of the desert had been a prime tourist attraction before the Silence—what Tom and others now called this catastrophic event—had struck.

As the sun began to dip below the horizon, Tom scanned the roadside for a safe camping spot. To drive at night with headlights on invited detection. He most often drove at dawn and at dusk, sometimes on back roads and mining trails.

A dry wash crossed the road, and Tom stopped. In a few minutes he had the Hummer parked in a large depression, hidden from the road. He spread a couple tarps over the vehicle, and it all but disappeared.

In the elbow of a cluster of man-sized boulders, he built a small fire and began to cook his dinner—freeze-dried beef stroganoff with wild mushrooms. Revelations had run free for the last several minutes and now nosed at Tom, sniffing in the air, wagging his tail, practicing his puppy-dog-eyed, hungry look.

"Yes, I know what you want, you old mooch," Tom said, ruffling the dog's head. "Okay, okay. I'll share it with you. I'll do up a batch of stroganoff à la kibbles."

Revelations seemed to nod and wag his tail in joyous agreement.

After dinner, Tom rolled out his sleeping bag, lit the lantern, and placed it above him on a little rock ledge. He opened a duffel bag and pulled out a book bound in gilded burgundy leather. He thumbed through the pages. It had been one of those blank gift books, the kind Tom had received many of and never used. It had lain in the trunk of his car for two years—no need for it in the age of laptops.

So much had changed in a few short weeks.

Tom opened the first page and sipped his instant coffee. Revelations lay at his feet, snoring quietly. He began to read what he had written so far.

April 18, near Lebec, CA

Driving is difficult—roads jammed with deserted cars. Rains came briefly yesterday. Smoke from L.A. seems to be less—everything burnt? Or are fires out? I don't need to know, and there's no one who is reliable enough to ask.

Hardly anything works. Curious—I've seen three other Hummers—each driven like Satan himself was on its tail. Also old cars, bikes, some motorcycles, one tractor-trailer, but little else mechanized. I still don't know what's going on.

I'm as tired as I've ever been in my life after only a few hours of driving. Parked above Route 5, a mile off the main road—hidden in brush. Rest was hard to come by. Stayed awake most of the night guarding. Good thing Rev is here. Barked a couple of times—hikers with backpacks who posed no problem—but I was ready.

April 19, near Mendota

Heading north along Interstate 5. I often stray off the highway and use off-road trails and access roads that parallel main roads marked on map. Much less conspicuous, and I feel safer. Traveling a lot slower—often no more than 25 or 30 mph. Only a few travelers—nearly all on foot—heading back to family. No one has any answers. One fellow claimed it was God's wrath and another said solar flares. Both seem plausible. Tired to the bone by midafternoon. Stopped after only a few hours' slow driving. I know I need to get to Hornbrook, but tiredness sweeps over me in waves. Iowa seems as far as the moon.

Picked up Calvin's Bible. Wish I had him to talk to. Funny, though, I would swear that part of Calvin is in this dog. Afraid I'm imagining this—or losing my tenuous grip with reality, such as it is. Nothing else to do so I leaf through the Bible and Rev lays his head in my lap and noses at the pages. I play along and turn back till he stops at the section titled Isaiah. Passage underlined: " 'Don't be afraid, for I am with you. Do not be dismayed, for I am your God. I will strengthen you. I will help you. I will uphold you with my victorious right hand.' "[vi] Dog whimpers once, then goes to sleep. After I read the section, I felt a little better. Maybe the dog knew I needed that. My heart wants to believe, yet in the midst of all this chaos, who could believe in a benevolent God? A good God does not make sense. If God is still here, why all this destruction? Was God that angry? Did we sin that much?

April 20, Red Bluff

Thought about Lydia and Kalli this morning as I drove. Could not stop the tears. Cried for over an hour. My soul feels empty. My heart is a dead, cold spot in my chest. I'm thankful that I have this mission. Otherwise I'd be one of the walking dead. Or huddled over the wreckage of our home, starving and alone.

Yet what happened this afternoon made my problems seem small and God appear impotent and distant. Stopped on old farm road on ridge above interstate. Hid car in thick brush, left Rev with orders to bark if approached. He stood as if he understood. Amazing creature—but still think I'm personifying his actions.

Took pistol and binoculars. Wanted to talk to someone about conditions north toward Sacramento. Was a few hundred yards from freeway when I saw a band of eight walkers headed south. Heard roar of dirt bikes. Ducked under cover—watched with binoculars as twenty bikers stormed out of fields and tore into the walkers. I saw pistols and short, angry-looking rifles. Gunfire erupted—it looked and sounded like a war movie. I could only watch as bikers—all in camouflage outfits—fired indiscriminately into the walkers, and a handful fell, clutching and screaming. Bikers took food, valuables.

I tried to turn invisible. My pistol and six rounds aren't much of a deterrent.

In movies, people who are shot suffer quietly. In reality, there are screams and shrieks from the wounded. My ears may never forget the sounds of agony. I will have nightmares remembering the crimson arc that blood makes when a bullet hits flesh. The rest of the group tended to their wounded—and I slipped away. I had nothing to offer and did not want to become a target. And I wondered. Was civilization that thin a veneer? Are we all animals just waiting to be loosed?

Sobering thought—what would I be doing now if Calvin had not been there? What would I be doing without his supplies and his vehicle? Would I be killing for crusts of bread? I know I couldn't make my own. There but for the grace of God, I guess.

Stayed on I-5 except where it looked dangerous—or I felt threatened. Though Hummer is a great equalizer, I pay more attention to intuition and the whining of the dog. Sounds crazy, but I think he knows. Maybe he smells danger. Ten times I veer off the road and bounce up and down dry washes, covered in dust, trying to stay hidden. Drove as fast as I could past Sacramento. Made good time—Red Bluff by nightfall. Too tired to write more.

April 21, Yreka

The air feels cleaner driving through Klamath Forest. Now just east of Yreka. The pristine beauty of the tall pines and redwoods almost made me forget what happened. Stopped several times as I drove through deep green canyons. Came upon a tiny meadow and clear lake. Revelations loved splashing in the water. I stayed there for the afternoon, watching sun and clouds till darkness overtook the sky. Could not bear to travel farther. If Lydia's parents are still alive, the news I carry in my heart will crush them.

April 22–May 12, Hornbrook

Lydia's parents saw me as I drove up. I watched their faces. For a brief moment, they were happy. As they saw that I traveled alone, they knew, without a word being spoken. Her mother, in slow motion it seemed, walked toward me. Her arms were open and empty, and her face had become an anguished mask of tears. She embraced me with a fierceness born out of a soul-numbing loss. My father-in-law stood behind his wife a few paces and stared at the ground as tears rolled down his cheeks. He turned from me as I caught his eye. Lydia had always said he's embarrassed to show any emotion, but even a practiced stoic like him cannot bear to keep such a depth of pain hidden.

We cried for days. I did not open this journal again until the 11th of May. Nearly three weeks slipped by as we wallowed in our grief—for a wife and daughter, for a child and grandchild, for a way of life that is lost forever. Most mornings found us all stone-faced, watching the sun rise, then watching it fall, without saying or doing much. After two weeks passed in a zombie-like silence, Mr. Creshon and I went hunting. We may have spoken several sentences as we hiked but not much more. He took two deer, and I had my first lesson in gutting and skinning a still-warm animal.

A month ago I would have lost my lunch. Now I see the deer, bloodied and eviscerated, lying before me, as lunch and dinner.

Mr. Creshon confirmed some of what I had heard. He taught physics in high school. He claimed the only explanation for the Silence is a solar flare—a huge one—that would destroy all silicon chips, computers, etc. In our wired world, so much depends on computers; and without them, it would all break down quickly. He said flares like this have happened before—on a smaller scale. The earthquakes were just a second stroke of bad luck, but he said that man's descent into brutality was to be expected.

As May's warmth began, I knew I must leave. As wonderful as Lydia's parents can be, my promise to Calvin rattled at the edge of my thoughts all day long. I will not be settled until I fulfill that promise. I don't know if I'll find anyone alive in Panora, but I must go. If I stay here, I'll eventually drown in grief and hopelessness. Leaving was difficult, but my face, too, was troubling to them, for in my eyes they saw a reflection of their daughter and grandchild. With me gone, they can concentrate on surviving rather than grieving.

May 13, Auburn

Revelations seemed excited about going. He barked and frolicked as I loaded the Hummer. Good-byes were hard, yet necessary. I doubt whether I'll see Lydia's parents again, but part of my heart feels better that we've grieved together.

I traced a route past Sacramento, then Reno, and on to Las Vegas. Maybe I am on a quixotic journey, but it's a journey I must make.

Interstate 80 west of Sacramento proved impassable—a long bridge gone. I thought about splashing across, but the river looked too deep, even for a Hummer. And since Vegas lies south, there are a dozen possible routes through the mountains. Camped just east of Auburn. Reading the Bible again. Still confused. Am I one of the lost? Or is God simply hiding from the world for awhile? My soul remains dead.

May 14, Angel's Camp

I'd imagined that the quakes had left the mountains untouched. I was wrong. The road east of Placerville was out—miles of asphalt had slipped into the valley below. A mile-long stretch of road past Jackson was gone. The road to Arnold was gone. I may have been able to go cross-country, but that would be a long, arduous, and really bumpy trip. Each closed road requires long miles of backtracking over winding and twisting roads. Even the dog looks carsick after hours of this kind of driving. There are a few more roads that cross into the Nevada desert from California. My worst-case scenario is to head south to Interstate 15. That seems like a *long, long way. Stayed outside of Angel's Camp.*

May 15, Lone Pine
   A gut-wrenching road and trail through Yosemite was passable. Slow, but I made it through. Route 395 southward was intact, hardly an abandoned car or truck in sight. Made wonderful time after torturous crawl through Yosemite. Camping a few miles north of Lone Pine. If all goes well, I could drive into Las Vegas by tomorrow night. I'm deciding what route would be best—Death Valley Junction or Beatty, Nevada? Better chance of gas in Death Valley Junction, I bet.

The fire popped and crackled as it burnt itself down to a miniscule pile of embers. Tom closed his journal and clipped his pen onto the cover. He stirred the fire down, shoveling dirt over it to avoid attracting any attention to himself as he tried to sleep. He turned off the lantern and gathered the sleeping bag around him. Revelations climbed on the nylon cover by his feet.

Tom looked up into the sky. The stars shone bright and large. "Lord, I hope You are up there. I don't know what I'm supposed to believe or supposed to do. This Bible doesn't come with instructions."

Revelations rolled on his side and began to scratch his ear with his back foot.

"Lord, if You're listening, could You give me some sort of sign? I do well with signs. I do well with directions. I really do. . . . Amen."

Despite his words, despite the fact that he felt as if he were just "covering his bases," he quietly began to search for such a sign from above.

may 16

The rolling hills in southern Illinois had first greened, then fleshed out the land with their delicate yet dense spring colors. The calls of birds and insects and animals, once nearly drowned out by the hum of civilization and society and its machinery, had returned and filled the skies with a chattering cacophony of burrs, tweets, and chirps. The sound was loud enough to wake a man from a deep slumber.

Peter Wilson was up before dawn woke the rest of the world. The chorus in the fields and the woods had just begun. He took his bucket to the stream at the edge of the field and scooped up the cool, clean water. He stopped and pulled a shock of early cattails from the bank of the stream. He planned on frying the soft tubers, mixing them with the goose eggs he had found the day before.

Becca deserves a treat, he thought. *She has been through a lot and endures everything without complaint.*

He stood and took a deep, cleansing breath. *If I could only say as much for others.*

Peter knelt and splashed handfuls of the chilled water on his face. He shook his head like a dog, sending a spray about the bank. He'd repeated this ritual every day for the past four weeks and every day had hoped and prayed this would be the day when the pieces came back together and when the world felt whole and right again.

He squinted into the first rays of sunrise. Even though his

heart wanted the world to be the way it once was, his head told him that the earth and his world would never be that way again.

Linda had not returned home since the quake. She had sent word to Peter through a messenger that the Reverend Moses needed her—needed her to help with his ministry, with his new radio outreach, with the choir, with the ripples of people making their way to Stonefort. A steadily growing group of pilgrims had begun to make their way to the small town—all informed by word of mouth—to see where the battle with the Silence had begun. After all, the Lord had stopped the jaws of the earthquake and spared an anointed church.

The Reverend Moses spoke to the faithful and the lost, powered by Herve Slatters's wheezing diesel generator and the liberated radio equipment from Stonefort's radio station.

Peter stopped and stared blankly, his mind reliving his one and only trip to Stonefort five days after the quake. . . .

After a day's tinkering, Peter's old rusty motorcycle had started up with a flash of oily blue smoke. He and Becca, wearing a battered, too-large helmet, puttered into town. The main bridge over the river had lost much of its decking, yet the metal grid sidewalk held as they zipped across it.

The town was in shambles. The village now consisted of piles of rubble and debris. Broken toilets, insulation, aluminum siding, shattered windows, and other pieces of housing cluttered streets and front lawns. Foundations of cement and cinder block grinned up in toothy smiles from the moist spring earth. Telephone poles lay like Pick-Up Sticks across streets. A wall remained here, a jagged roof tilted to the ground there. The fountain in the town square had fallen to its side, cracked into jagged shards of cement. Tents, lean-tos, and makeshift shelters of wood, canvas, and plastic pocked the landscape. Smoke from dozens of fires curled into the warming spring air.

Standing in front of the church, Peter had been dumbstruck by what he saw. In the middle of a freshly dug hole was a huge square of concrete. Herve and Ternell Slatters were busy wrenching big sections of steel and iron together. Four posts were already anchored and some cross-bracing was in place. They were building a radio tower.

Behind the church gaped a violent chasm, the one the Reverend Moses had ordered to halt. A knot of people stood by it, staring in awe as if at a shrine.

Peter, Becca, and that knot of people had watched one of the first radio broadcasts done from the very pulpit of the church. Shades were drawn and the church interior became dim, musty, almost medieval. Linda stood behind the pulpit and sang in her controlled and pure alto voice without any accompaniment a song so sweet and clean that it nearly broke Peter's heart: "I once was lost, but now I'm found. . . ."

Her eyes were closed, both hands entwined around a microphone stand. Her head was tilted back, her dark hair shining like polished obsidian in the glare of a single spotlight. As she finished the last verse, she dropped her head to her chest and slumped down, growing smaller as the last notes of the hymn echoed through the sanctuary. She stepped back a couple feet from the microphone.

The Reverend Moses slipped out of the shadows and took the pulpit. "Thank you, Sister Linda. Such a beautiful voice for the Lord. Such a beautiful song for the time. And, dear friends, remember that God loves you. He does. It may be dark now, but the light is coming. We are building a bigger tower to reach the entire world. Pray for us. And for today, this is good-bye. This is Rev. Moses speaking. . .from Stonefort. Tomorrow, my children. God has promised us a tomorrow. Listen for the Chosen Voice of God, from the Temple of God's Calling."

A cold silence followed as the broadcast ended.

"Mommy?" Becca whispered, though not as a greeting.

Rev. Moses appeared startled.

"Linda," Peter called out softly. "Linda, are you ready to—"

She turned her head, looking like a deer caught in the bright lights of a speeding pickup. "Peter. . .Becca. . ."

Rev. Moses broke the deafening silence. "Ah, Peter. How good to see you again. Marvelous what Herve has accomplished, is it not? We have already had a visitor from St. Louis—he heard our broadcast and had to visit the miracle himself. Isn't that marvelous? And after only a few days of broadcasting. People are hungry for the truth—especially in times like this."

"Linda," Peter spoke, his words edged with iciness, "I think you should come home. It's been five days."

Linda's eyes widened. She looked past Peter to Becca's face, then spun about, her eyes fixed on Rev. Moses. He was wearing a deep scarlet vestment that flowed behind him like a cape as he descended the stairs of the platform. The robe had belonged to the town's Lutheran pastor, who was among the many still missing. Slowly, Rev. Moses spread his arms, and the robe fluttered like wings about his arms. The slight tracing of a smile edged his mouth. "Peter, my son, let us not be hasty. In times such as these, we all must make sacrifices."

Peter didn't look at the reverend, only at his wife. "Linda, Becca needs you. I need you. You should come home."

"Peter. . ." Her voice limped into quietness.

Rev. Moses took another step. "Peter, she is needed here. . .at least for now. Her voice is a clarion call for the lost. They hear such beauty and truth in it. It is a balm to all those who have lost so much."

Peter chose to ignore the Reverend Moses's entreaties. "Linda?"

She scanned the room, her eyes like a frightened bird's, trapped by the shadow of a hawk.

"My son," Rev. Moses soothed, "she should remain here, at least until the tower is completed. Perhaps only another week.

Then the words of the Chosen Voice of God from the Temple of God's Calling, well, then those words will be stronger, and she will be able to step aside. In just a week, Peter. That is all I ask you to bear. Seven short days."

Rev. Moses inclined his head toward Linda. Peter thought he saw a smile creep across the man's face—a slow smile of pleasure.

"Peter, we must be vigilant. We do not have much time. This is simply the first card played in the last hand of the final game. We must be about spreading the Word. God has called His disciples to do that. He has spared this church. . .anointed it to spread His message. We have to follow God's command, Peter. Linda has to follow that same command—and she must follow what God has laid on my heart for this church. We do not have much time, Peter. Perhaps a mere forty-four weeks are left before Jesus comes again and takes His anointed church to heaven. Forty-four weeks, Peter. That's a biblical number."

Peter listened without comprehending. The Reverend Moses's eyes appeared to dance with energy. Peter turned to his wife. Linda seemed to hang on the reverend's every word.

"Peter, I just can't," she said timidly. "Not just yet, but soon. The church needs me. The truth has to be broadcast. It must. Who else will tell the lost of the coming of Jesus? We have to do that; don't you see the urgency? We have to spread the word of His coming. We have to. It's the end of time, Peter, and we have to tell others. All that has been spoken of is being fulfilled. Peter, Becca. . .not today. I must stay here. The truth of the Second Coming must be broadcast. You must understand."

Smiling, Rev. Moses clasped his hands together. "Peter, you can join us. We could find room for all three of you."

"Linda, please," Peter called out softly one last time. "Come home."

She lowered her head and averted her eyes. "I have to stay. You could stay."

"I can't," he replied and walked with a slow, steady pace down the aisle and out into the bright spring sunshine.

Megan awakened with a start because the sun was already up. She leapt to her feet, ready to run as fast as her legs would allow. She spun about, but didn't see anything or hear any unexpected sound.

Dropping to her knees, she gathered up her sleeping bag and stuffed it into her backpack. Since she had begun traveling again, she felt a new urgency and a renewed purpose. She had to get home. She knew that now. As if scales had fallen from her eyes, she now saw the goal of her journey.

She carried only two pages from a Rand McNally road atlas with her. She examined the Pennsylvania map for the hundredth time. She had followed the path of Interstate 80 as it wound westward from Newark and Harrison. She planned to cross the deep and swift-flowing Delaware River near Stroudsburg and follow I-80 west again. Erie—and her father and home—lay 375 miles west of Stroudsburg.

I might make it in three weeks if I really pushed, she told herself. *Maybe two weeks if I can find food and water. That's if I can walk nine hours a day. And if there's nothing blocking the way. That part of Pennsylvania is pretty empty, so I should be able to move more freely and make better time.*

Today her path paralleled the road, yet she remained hidden by the pines and oaks. The air smelled sweet and fresh in the woods, and she felt protected, hidden.

By noon she stood in the shadows of the woods on the bluffs overlooking the ramps to the Stroudsburg Bridge. She lay on the matting of pine needles and ate her last can of kippers for lunch, quieting her growling stomach. A few tiny cans of chili and half a box of crackers were all that remained in her pack. She snapped it closed, not wanting to think about such matters just now.

Besides her stash of hundred-dollar bills, which she imagined were now worthless, she had little else worth trading for food now, save her own flesh. And she hoped that starvation would be more honorable and desirable than to degrade herself in such a manner.

Holding her binoculars, her one item of great trading value she had left, she focused in on the east end of the bridge. Her heart sank. There were at least twenty men in various degrees of military camouflage and uniform, most with rifles slung over their shoulders. Two round structures, built from hundreds of sandbags, hedged the pavement. A few slits were visible, and Megan saw the glint of the protruding rifle barrels. She also spied several boats with armed men patrolling the river.

She lay there, watching, for a full thirty minutes. No one approached the bridge. No one crossed it. The guards milled about, smoking and talking.

They are keeping people out of Pennsylvania—or at least out of Stroudsburg.

Megan lowered the binoculars. "God," she whispered, her voice hushed by the fragrant matting of pine needles, "are You listening? Or am I right in believing that You have forgotten me? Have I been saying this childhood prayer over and over for the last month for nothing, saying it to no one? Have You been listening?"

Wearily she closed her eyes. "I want to see my father, God. I want to see my daddy. Just one last time." Her voice quieted to a hush. Tears dripped from her eyes, splashed onto her cheeks, and then fell to the forest floor like rain.

Silence filled the woods. Even the wind fell still. A bird fluttered to the air from behind her, calling out a bright song.

"Excuse me, miss."

Megan spun about, knocking her binoculars over the edge of the bluff. She scrambled to her feet, grabbing for the camp knife she wore at her belt in a panicked rush to defend herself. She stood there, knees bent, knife in hand. Her breath came in angry, raw gasps as the weapon wavered in her outstretched right hand.

Is this my time to die? she wondered.

Then her vision cleared. Before her stood a frail-looking man, his face a mask of shock. He wore the formerly white collar of a priest.

With a curious state of dispassionate awareness, Megan watched the color drain out of the priest's face. She watched his hands flutter, one touching the cross around his neck, one held out toward her, palm out, bidding her stop.

"Miss. . ." His voice trembled with surprise, yet Megan knew he was not afraid of her, just surprised. "Miss," he repeated, turning his outstretched hand around, as if offering an invitation, "please do not be frightened. I am just a priest who—"

"Who are you? What do you want?" Megan struggled to keep her voice from shaking.

"I don't want anything, miss. I just want to help. That's all. I saw you a few minutes ago. I was down there on that trail." He pointed down the hill, south of where he stood. "I'm Father William."

The priest, in a tattered and dirty cassock, stood only a couple inches over five feet, with a narrow, pinched face and a trembling smile. Wispy gray hair floated about his head like fog, and his gray eyes were lit with concern, not intimidation. Megan fought the urge to smile and resisted the urge to lower her knife.

He certainly doesn't look very dangerous.

"Well, Father William, what are you doing in the woods?"

"Well, Miss. . . ?"

"It's Megan. Megan Smith."

"Well, Miss Megan Smith," Father William began, his voice even, almost happy, "I'm on my way back to Stroudsburg. I was in Hackettstown visiting a parish that doesn't have its own priest. You'd be surprised how many parishes these days have to make do with nuns and laypeople. There just aren't that many folks interested in taking the vows anymore. Such a pity, if you ask me. It's a most rewarding life, filled with exciting challenges. Take me, for instance. I'm just in a small diocese, but the Lord has given me a wonderful life and allowed me to do many exciting things. To be a servant is such a noble calling. Such a rewarding life indeed."

Megan could not respond. Her thoughts whirled.

For over a month, I haven't spoken to another soul. And now this odd little man is chattering away like we're at a church social. How I have missed such a simple thing as conversation.

She closed her eyes and willed her tears not to come.

"Megan, I know what you're feeling. At least I think I know. I have seen a thousand people since the Silence that find simple, normal conversation overwhelming."

Megan opened her eyes. Tears turned her vision to a blurred watercolor. Without knowing why, she fell to her knees and let her head fall into her hands. The tears began to flow. It was the first time she had cried since walking through that long and dark tunnel, leaving New York behind.

Kneeling beside her, Father William placed a tender, tentative arm about her shoulder. "Megan, it's okay to cry. Everyone has lost a great deal. It's okay to cry."

He murmured words of comfort for nearly an hour while Megan's shoulders heaved and shook as she cried. A month's worth of loneliness and terror washed out with her tears.

Finally Megan looked up, her face streaked, her eyes red. "Why did you stop?" she sniffled, her voice raspy and thin. "Why did you stop to come to me?"

Father William's face flushed. "I think. . .I think. . ." He looked around, as if attempting to determine if anyone might overhear his words. "I think I heard your prayer, Megan. I think I heard your words to God."

Her brows arched in surprise.

"You want to see your father again, and I think I can help you." She fell into his arms and wailed.

"I think our Lord wants me to help you get home. I think that is what He has told me to do."

She stared at the priest blankly.

"Since the Silence," he murmured, his words like a prayer, "God's voice has gotten louder. Or maybe without the constant drone of our modern world, His words are more easily heard."

A chilly, whispering wind curled about the foundation of the trailer in the early afternoon, so Peter lit the furnace. The propane gas would last another two, perhaps three months now that summer was approaching. Yet he knew that winter followed close enough. He began to draw out a plan to cut into the side of the trailer and build a fireplace for heat and cooking. He also figured on digging a cold cellar to store perishables. But he had no skills at sewing and didn't know how he would clothe Becca and himself.

Do I really need to worry about this? Could it be as bad as what I imagine? Things will come back. They have to. Linda will come back, and the world will return to normal.

Becca's voice broke the quiet. "Daddy, is Mommy going to stay with Rev. Moses forever?"

"No, sweets, just for a little longer. She thinks it's important to help him with the radio show, I guess."

Becca's face tightened. "Should we stay with her?"

"No," Peter answered firmly. "No. Our home is here."

She shouldn't be facing this at her age, Peter thought. *She should never have to face this.*

"Do you like Rev. Moses, Daddy?"

"Like him? Sure, I guess he's a nice enough man."

"Does Mommy like him more than you like him?"

"Well, I guess she does. But I like him fine."

"If Mommy wanted me to stay with her at the church, would you let me?"

Peter's heart thumped wildly in his chest. "Do you want to stay with Mom?"

Becca closed her book and held it in her lap, her hands crossed on the cover. "I like it better here with you, Daddy. I don't like church. I get bored."

His heart slowed a bit.

"But what if she says I have to stay with her at church, Daddy? What would you do? Would you live there too?"

"Well, sweets, I don't think you have to worry about this just now. Mom will be back soon; then everything will be back to normal."

"Promise?"

"I promise."

<hr />

Father William stood, his hands on his hips, and looked to the west, as if deep in thought. He turned back to Megan and frowned momentarily, then tried to smile.

"Well, Miss Smith, I think it is time for us to walk to Stroudsburg. We must decide on how we are going to do it."

Megan zipped her backpack closed and stood.

"I've spent a lot of time thinking about this, and I'm struggling with a plan. As you know, anything these days can be dangerous. But my plan poses more of an ethical dilemma, I'm afraid. I'm still a man of God, Miss Smith. I don't like being in these situations."

Megan tried to sound brave. "Father, I wouldn't want you to do something that compromised your faith."

"Miss Smith—Megan, I can be an honest priest and follow the Scriptures to the letter. If I did that, you would have to fend for yourself. You may get across the bridge. You may not. I'm sure I don't have to tell you of the dangers a woman faces these days."

Megan winced. Hurtful and twisted images were never far away.

"I'm sure any woman could barter her way across the river. That often seems to be the price of admission these days." Father William focused on the ground. "I have seen things, Miss Smith, sights that I had prayed the Lord would protect me from all my days. Yet since the Silence, I have experienced the coarse nature of both men and women—coarse and blatant and terribly crude. In broad daylight. In plain view. Without shame. With anyone and with everyone. I am so often heartsick."

Megan nodded, unwilling to risk her voice.

The priest spoke as if addressing a courtroom. "Yet in this new world, am I unbound by God's existing laws to protect the weak? To keep others from harm? To honor His commandments?"

Megan only stared. She didn't know how—or if—she should participate in the priest's one-sided theological and ethical discourse.

"I ask myself every day which commandment is greatest. To love God. That's too easily chosen. It seems to have little real-life application—now."

Father William began to walk about the quiet woods. Megan wished she could have heard him preach. There was a warmth in his voice that was compelling and soothing.

"I love God. I honor God," he continued. "But what do I do when I walk up to those guards on the bridge? They will allow me passage, for I am a man of God. They have allowed me passage before. But what of you? Do I leave you on your own, all the while knowing what will happen to you. . .to your virtue. . .if I do so?"

Megan would not speak. It was oddly comforting to know that this innocent priest saw her as a woman of virtue and purity. Megan prayed he wouldn't ask further questions of her or her past life.

"Or do I walk up to those guns and leers and lie to them—bold-faced and knowing? Do I break a commandment in order to protect you?" He stopped pacing. "You know the answer, Miss Smith. You know what I must do."

"I do?" Her voice was as fragile as a wren.

"You do. And I will ask you to remember my sin in your prayers." He faced her directly. "I must do what I must do to get you across to safety. I heard your prayer. I do not know how, but I did. You will walk with me to the bridge," he said with great finality.

"And I will introduce you as the daughter of one of my parishioners from Nazareth, a small town southwest of here. I will say that you have walked from New York and that you are under my authority for the rest of your journey. I will say I have pledged to bring you home to your mother. What is your mother's name?"

"Elizabeth, but she died when I was a teenager."

"Elizabeth. . .a pretty name. Well, then, Miss Megan Smith, shall we go? It is time to cross the river."

Father William had been correct. She never would have made it on her own. As she walked across the bridge, Megan couldn't help thinking about the guns and the leering, lustful expressions on the men's faces. She knew she couldn't have crossed the bridge without surrendering herself physically to ragtag soldiers.

The guards blustered and postured, shouted and scowled, but the diminutive gray-haired priest would not waver. He insisted that Megan was the daughter of one of his parishioners and that he had the authority of God Himself to get her home.

Reluctantly the men guarding the bridge allowed them passage. They colorfully ordered Father William to never again bring a stranger across the river. But if he was intimidated by their taunts and orders, he gave no outward sign.

Megan and the priest did not speak for nearly an hour after crossing the river. They marched along, the priest leading the way, taking fast steps westward on Interstate 80. His shorter legs moved faster and faster. Megan was forced to walk quickly and often nearly jog to keep pace.

The sun was just beginning its tilting toward the west when Father William first slowed down. It took him perhaps a quarter mile to fully stop, and when he did, he placed both hands on his sides and bent over double. Megan caught up and saw that he was gasping for air.

"Father," she cried, kneeling at his side, "are you all right? Do you need a doctor?" She glanced wildly around the deserted countryside, realizing any help would be a long way off.

The priest waved her back. He wheezed, "I'm. . .fine. I just. . . never have been. . .so scared." He gulped in a breath of air. "I have never walked so far so fast before in my life."

Megan tossed off her backpack and pulled out a water bottle. She cracked the protective seal and handed it to him without giving her dwindling fresh water supply a second thought.

He swallowed some of the precious water, then sat down on the pavement and leaned back. A thick sheen of sweat glistened on his forehead. His stained collar was soaked through. "The men on that bridge were evil. I knew it. The entire time we argued, I saw more and more blackness hovering about them. It was a blackness I could see. . .almost touch."

Megan poured some water on a handkerchief and wiped it across his forehead.

"Are you a believer, Megan?"

She didn't stop wiping his face. She didn't answer him.

He reached up and took her hand. "Megan? Do you really believe?"

All at once she felt empty and frightened—perhaps even more frightened than she had been on the bridge. "I. . .I have a Bible. With me."

The priest's hard grip on her hand softened. She did not want to look into his eyes.

"As a priest, I was expected to believe. And I did. . .at least at first."

Megan sat back on her heels and listened. The roadway, though pocked with abandoned cars and trucks, was quiet. A crow cawed in the distance. The wind began to rustle the fresh sprouts of leaf and bud.

"I knew the words. I administered the sacraments," the priest said. "But many times I went through the motions without much passion or awe. It was an honorable career, not much more. I had stopped really loving our Lord, stopped really thinking of Him." He took another drink, then offered the bottle to Megan. "But in all my years of service to God, I have never felt evil before. I have never encountered the enemy before. Not until today."

He peered behind him, as if checking to see if the blackness had followed him. Then he continued to explain. "If you're playing a game and have no chance of winning, do you think the opponent cares? Do you think a seven-foot basketball player concerns himself with a three-foot player? No, there would be no threat." Father William squeezed his eyes shut. "I have never been a threat, so I have never seen evil."

He took Megan's hand again. "And now I have, Megan. The evil ones are out there, and they're feasting on this Silence."

"They tried to stop us. No, that's not true. They tried to stop you," Megan said and shuddered. Her very bones shivered. She could not think of any reason, other than their passions, they would have for wanting her.

"I have crossed that bridge many times before today. Each time it was a simple wave to the guards and a 'How's the padre doing today?' I never saw blackness before." He turned back and faced the east. "This was the first time they were threatened."

He grabbed Megan's hand and pulled her up. "I'm not a mystic. I'm just a simple old priest. But I saw the blackness and felt the cold. It must have been because of you, Megan. You're a threat to them."

Keeping her hand in his, the priest began to walk. "You have to get home—and fast. I think that's what God is telling me." He urged her to keep pace with him. "That's what God wants."

Megan felt like a child, shuffling her feet in futile resistance. "But, Father, I'm not sure I'm a believer. You asked. And I'm not sure anymore. I'm not sure I ever was."

The priest's steps did not falter or slow. "Well, that simply means that we'll have a topic of conversation along the way."

Father William maintained a jogger's pace for the next several hours. Megan pushed hard to stay even with him. She was soaked with sweat, and her muscles ached with a slow, screaming pain by the time the priest slowed.

I-80 was deserted. There was a depressing sameness to the littering of cars and trucks along the road. Every vehicle had been looted, stripped, or destroyed. Megan couldn't help but think that she had stepped into a Mad Max movie.

After he tucked Becca into bed, Peter stepped outside. The wind chilled him deeply this evening. He yearned for a cigarette. He had given up the habit fourteen years ago, but he had never fully forgotten the taste and the ritual of smoking.

I wonder if anyone in town has cigarettes. Maybe I could trade some dried venison for them. I'd love to have one to smoke right now.

He sat on the front step and pulled his jacket tight around him. The chill helped focus his thoughts.

How do I protect my daughter? If Linda wanted her, who would stop her from taking Becca? I'm pretty sure Rev. Moses would side with her, and I bet he's carrying more weight in this town today than he ever dreamed of.

Peter questioned again if it really was the end of the world.

Could Rev. Moses be one of the prophets of the end times? Has God really blessed that church? Is there something I should be doing to bring others to the truth? Should I be taking God's Word to others?

Peter knew he believed. He knew he was saved. He knew he would go to heaven at his death. But he had never been vocal about sharing that belief with others; it simply wasn't his style. He was shy—that's what he told himself before.

But now—is there something I should be doing now? Is Rev.

Moses doing the right thing? Do we warn others that this is the beginning of the end?

Peter focused his attention on the sky.

What about those who are lost, Lord? What do I do for them?

He stood, put his hands in his pockets, and breathed out, making a cloud ring in the grayness of the dusk. He smiled, for it too reminded him of smoking.

Maybe I'll go into town and barter for a carton of Marlboros. I can still taste them after all these years.

He turned and went back into the trailer.

But tonight I think I'll read a little from the Bible to see if I can figure any of this out. I may not be as smart as some, but the truth is still the truth, isn't it?

The door clicked shut behind him. The gas lantern filled the room with a vapory, shrill light. As he opened his Bible to the New Testament, he heard Becca rustle in her room.

I'll find out for you, sweets, he promised. *I'll find the truth for you.*

<hr/>

The priest finally stopped when darkness started slipping up on them. He wiped at his brow, then looked about. Megan could see no houses from where they stood, no signs of people or habitation. She was certain that there were people living along the sides of the road, but they were hidden from view.

"We'll stop here tonight," Father William said. "We can stay in that Greyhound over there." The bus, its door left open as a sad invitation, sat to the left of the road, dusty and abandoned. "We can build a fire, and I have one good tea bag left. That will provide us something."

Megan stepped into the bus. In the darkening gray of evening, she couldn't make out much. She was certain, though, that nothing of value—and no food for sure—was left behind when the occupants deserted it. She had one small can of chili left in her pack—and she would share that with Father William.

The priest gathered wood from the brush along the road and returned with an armful of firewood, which he carefully arranged in a neat, square stack. Using sheets of old newspaper he found in the bus as kindling, he lit the fire and coaxed it along until the flames leapt heavenward.

Megan opened the can of chili and began to warm it on the flames. Father William found water in a nearby stream, and by the time night engulfed the area, they had eaten their tiny meal together. Megan watched as Father William said a prayer under his breath and made the sign of the cross. No words were exchanged as they ate, neither having the energy to speak. Both seemed lost in thought and the swirl of images that were as dark as the night itself.

The fire soon reduced itself to a soft, orange glow.

"Where is everyone?" Megan asked into the inky blackness.

Father William turned to her. "I wondered about that as well. Seemed like everything was so crowded a month ago. . .was it only a month? Seems like years. But it was crowded, wasn't it?"

Megan nodded.

"I think I know what happened." He swallowed the last of his tea and sighed. "They gave up. When they ran out of food or time or hope—they simply stopped where they were. Not many people can carry a month's worth of food with them."

"Just like that?"

"You have someplace to go, Megan. You're heading to see your father. That's a very powerful goal. I think a lot of folks don't have that. They have no place to run. They'll make the best of it wherever that is. Maybe they'll steal food or what they need to live on. Maybe they'll barter themselves for it. I know you have seen it happen too."

Megan shuddered. "Any person will do that?"

"That and worse, Megan. The will to live is very strong—and that's good. But that will is often a lot more powerful than a person's moral core. People who want to keep breathing and eating will do anything."

The priest touched the cross around his neck. "Yet maybe if a person can't steal or trade, he'll just lay down where he fell and fade away. A month isn't that long, Megan. Two months. . .three months. . .then maybe more will fall. If things don't come back to normal by then, you'll see people just slip away because they're too tired to fight. They'll figure that fading into the darkness will be better than the pain they're in."

"Just like that? They'll give up?"

"I've seen some people I thought were so strong give up when they had much more at stake than that—like children or a family. Fighting's hard, Megan. Fighting for what's right is even harder. I see that more now than I have ever seen it in my life as a priest."

He stood up and paced away from the fire. When the night swallowed him, she only heard his disembodied voice. "Megan, you can't give up. You need to continue your journey, to go home."

He reappeared by the fire, the orange glow illuminating his face. Megan saw the first glistening of tears on his cheeks. "You have to make it home, Megan. I'm not one to get a 'word' from God, but I've never been more sure. It's like Almighty God nudged me in the ribs and whispered that you need to keep going—you have to get home."

Megan stared at him, awed by the depth of his emotions. "But *I* haven't heard anything, Father. Shouldn't God be talking to me if that's what He wants? Wouldn't that be more logical?"

Father William returned to her side and knelt beside her. "Well, yes, that would be more logical." His eyes sought hers. "Maybe for now I'm the one who needs to hear it. Maybe you'll hear it when you need to."

"But what if I never hear it?"

"You will. You will."

He waited until the echo of his words drifted into silence, into the night. "I know a man in White Haven, west of here. If anyone can help you—us—get to your father, he can."

Megan's heart hurt. She heard the priest's words, heard the power of his conviction, heard the truth of what he had heard. But she felt nothing. She felt no power, no presence, no reality that was beyond what she could touch or taste or feel.

"But what of your congregation? Won't they need you too?"

The priest's head slumped to his chest. "I know. My heart is heavy when I think of that. But I am being called to help you. I know that. There are other priests in my diocese to carry on. The Lord will install someone to shepherd His flock."

"Are you sure, Father William? Are you sure?"

He embraced her, like a father embraces a child he loves, for a protective moment.

Her heart hurt more that moment than it had since the Silence began. She became aware in a blinding instant of what had been lost. It was the connection with another person, the protection and provision that only another person could provide.

Silence filled the darkness and began to edge into Megan's heart.

Father William spoke softly. "I am sure, Megan, I am sure."

———

Riley Weston gnawed on an unlit cigar that seemed to be permanently clenched between his teeth. For the past three weeks, Riley and his three operatives had crisscrossed Virginia, Pennsylvania, and were now heading west again. A dark metal box resting on the Hummer's center console began to warble slightly. Riley, in the passenger seat, instantly snapped to attention and flipped the box open, grabbing at the lethal-looking phone resting in the padded interior.

"Riley here." He nodded, listened, then nodded again. "Message received."

Replacing the phone in its cradle, Riley tapped a button, and the familiar high-pitched squeal and garble of an incoming fax filled the vehicle. From beneath the phone, a coil of paper emerged, until a final squeal marked the end of the transmission.

Riley tore off the long sheet of paper and began to read. When he finished, he carefully folded the fax and slipped it into his breast pocket.

"Good news? Bad news?" asked Mark Macaluso. "Which?"

"Good news; it's all good news."

The three agents leaned in closer.

"Remember our termination in Columbus? Well, our man has assumed power. He'll hold down the fort with the local militia until Uncle Sam is back in power." Riley's thick smile seemed inappropriate. "Pentagon says they're making progress in taking control of New York City. Troops are working their way through the Bronx. What's left of Chicago seems quiet."

The three agents all nodded, their eyes hidden behind dark sunglasses.

"And our friend in Stonefort just boosted his signal again," Riley said. "That's why he was so clear last night."

Save for the rumble of the tires, there was quiet in the car for several miles.

"Riley," Macaluso asked from the backseat, "you believe anything that Moses says? Or is he just wrapping his kind of crazy in God's coat?"

"It's not important if I believe it," Riley replied, shifting the cigar from one side of his mouth to the other. "It's whether other fools believe it. So far it looks like a lot of them do."

"And that Rapture stuff. . .and the final battle and all that? Is that just a bunch of hooey?"

Riley began to pat his pockets, looking for his chrome lighter. "Naw, I don't think it's hooey at all." He found the lighter, snapped it open, lit the end of the cigar, and began to puff. A thick cloud of smoke rose in the Hummer. "A lot of people could have disappeared, just like Moses is saying," he replied, exhaling. "And if what we're doing now doesn't seem like the final battle, I don't know what would."

"So, why are we doing any of this if this is the end?"

"I didn't say it was the end exactly," Riley said, puffing. "But I figure even if just part of what he says is true, then somebody best be taking charge of what's left. And I want to be on the side that's in charge." He puffed again. "Don't you?"

After a brief pause, the other agents nodded ever so slightly.

may 17

What is the truth?"

Silence.

"What is the truth?"

Nearly five hundred people had jammed into the sanctuary designed to hold two hundred and fifty. Behind Rev. Moses, a second diesel generator chugged on as persistently as a spring breeze. Herve Slatters's two sons had guided the machinery through town behind a team of mules. Where they found it, they did not say, but the unit now provided lights and sound for the evening service. The bigger generator continued to supply the power for the radio broadcast.

Rev. Moses leaned forward on the pulpit, the sweat on his forehead glistening in the spotlight. He could see several rows deep into the church. Every man, woman, and child was transfixed in rapt attention. He knew he had them.

First he glanced at the radio microphone that had been indelicately bolted to the side of the pulpit. Herve Slatters was handy, but he had no sense of aesthetics. Rev. Moses narrowed his eyes at the bright spotlight. He knew he was sweating, but to this audience, sweat meant hard work; and for that alone, he was worthy of great admiration. He waited as the silence grew in intensity.

Then, at the top of his lungs, he screamed, *"This is the truth!"* As he shouted, he windmilled the leather-bound Bible in a long arc and with the speed of a major-league pitcher slammed the Bible flat against the pulpit. The crash was louder than a cannon in a cathedral.

Everyone visibly jumped in their seats, some clutching at their throats, others clasping their Bibles to their chests. Tension crackled and sizzled through the dark warmth of the church.

Rev. Moses felt the crowd's anxiety slowly slip away like a vapor. He bent forward, his face bathed in the harsh light. His mouth was only inches from the microphone.

How many people are listening to me right now—electrified by my message? he wondered.

In a caressing whisper, he soothed, "This is the truth. The Bible. . .God's truth."

Silence again reigned. He could hear the first few rows breathing—rhythmically, hypnotically, in and out.

"This book is God's mystery and His plan and His secret. Let me show them to you, my friends. Let me show them to you."

Linda Wilson didn't remember another word of the rest of the message. She sat behind Rev. Moses, hidden in the shadows of the choir loft, cloaked in a robe the color of a deep forest pool, clasping her hands in her lap. She stared into the darkness at her feet. When Rev. Moses was finished, she knew he would call her name, and she would rise, walk to the pulpit, and sing.

There would be no accompaniment. Her voice would fill the church and the radio waves with clarity and purity. Linda's solo had ended every one of Rev. Moses's broadcasts since they had gone on the air, less than two days after the earthquake.

It was the sound of hope and truth and light, he had told her. "Millions are waiting to hear your sweet, innocent voice and feel better. They know that God is still in His heaven every time you sing. It is because of you that I am able to bless so many listeners. Your voice. . .your voice and all that it means is more important than my feeble words."

Her heart had swelled at his statement, and since then her life had felt as if it were a dream.

"We are blessed, Sister Linda," Rev. Moses had told her, "for this church was blessed as it was spared from Satan's destruction. We are under the obligation of God to tell others about the nature and the time of His coming again. The church is His bride. The Bible tells us that." He had placed his hand under her chin and lifted her face to see her eyes. "You and I are the church, sweet sister Linda. We have been chosen. We must tell others. You must continue to help me."

But now, as Rev. Moses gave his sermon, something sweet and indistinct tugged at Linda's heart. As she blinked her eyes, she saw a blond baby held close to her breast. . .and felt a twinge of guilt.

Then the reverend began his closing comments. When he announced it was time for her solo, Linda shook the image of the blond baby from her head. She was needed at the Temple of God's Calling. . .and by Rev. Moses.

"Hot! Boy, is it hot!" Tom exclaimed.

He eyed the dog, whose tongue was lolling out and whose head rested against the side of the door. The hot air flowing through the open windows made Tom feel hotter and stickier. And while the dog couldn't speak, he made it apparent that the heat was getting to him as well.

"I thought the desert was a dry heat, old Rev," Tom said. "This sure doesn't feel dry to me."

Revelations, looking limp as a boned animal could look, panted a little harder. Tom desperately wanted to switch on the air-conditioning, but he knew that would be wasting fuel on comfort.

How much I took for granted before all this.

"We have water," he told the dog, "and we can find shade if we need to. We won't die from the heat, boy, but we can be 100 percent uncomfortable."

When Revelations seemed to offer a weak smile in return,

Tom patted the dog's head.

This desert route was indeed abandoned and desolate today. Tom figured it had not been a very busy stretch even before the Silence. Only a few houses dotted the landscape. Some had probably been deserted for years; others appeared tidy and lived-in.

From a mile away, Death Valley Junction appeared as a lonely cluster of houses and weather-beaten buildings, lit red and gold by the setting sun. Tom checked the automatic door locks once again. He rolled up the windows, leaving only a crack for air. Revelations whimpered a bit, then circled twice about the passenger seat and curled up in resignation.

The Hummer rattled noisily on the rough pavement, the big, knobby tires growling as he slowed a few hundred yards from perhaps Death Valley Junction's only gas station. Tom lifted the binoculars to his eyes and scanned the landscape. Cars were scattered about the roadside. Two dogs trotted across the roadway, unconcerned about possible traffic. He focused on the gas station. He saw two faces at the window.

Tom steered the car off the road toward the gas pumps. Several ropes of multicolored plastic flags flapped weakly in the warm evening breeze. Tom cradled the revolver in his hand, hidden below the window. He rolled his window down and called, "Do you have gas to sell?"

Both men—old, gray, and weathered—creaked out of the station, leaning forward as if they could not believe their eyes. Neither man spoke, but Tom read the surprise on their faces.

"Do you have any gas?" he asked again.

The shorter of the old-timers spoke first. "That a Hummer, son?"

Tom nodded.

"Nice car for the end of the world, I bet," said the other.

"It gets me where I want to go," Tom said, keeping his voice calm and casual.

"Good gas mileage?"

"It's not bad. Haven't really checked it close."

"How's the ride?"

"Well, she runs a bit noisy and doesn't stop all that fast, and sometimes it feels like you're in a boat—but it's still okay."

The men nodded, taking only a step or two closer to the Hummer.

"That a golden retriever?"

Revelations was standing on the seat now, responding to new voices. His tail was in fast motion, and he was grinning his dog-wide smile.

"He like riding in the car like that? My old Jack Russell terrier always looked about ready to throw up."

What are we doing here? Talking cars and dogs like nothing is out of the ordinary?

Tom was surprised by the small talk he had taken for granted, even avoided, before everything went nuts.

The old men turned to each other and nodded. "That was a good old dog, Ervin. Whatever happened to that'un?"

"Harlon, you remember that fellow that used to come in here all the time? A rancher up north of here? Sold her to him. Dog was plum crazy over herding things. Liked critters in small groups. Wanted me in a small group mosta the time."

Both began to laugh, the taller man holding his chest and wheezing as he fought for breath.

"Uh, excuse me for asking again," Tom said, his voice paced and even, but carrying a hint of demand. "But do you have any gas here?"

Tom had quickly ruled out any danger from the old men and had already lowered the hammer on the pistol. He slipped it back into the pouch on the door while he waited for their answer.

The shorter man nodded. "We have gas. Nobody buying it, except for Clancey and his motorcycles. That seems like the only machines that have been working."

"Them and Adgel's old, beat-up blue truck."

Nods were exchanged between the two of them again.

"And Sammy's tractor—you know the one that's been over by the old school all these years."

"And that old generator over behind the police station. That still works."

Tom cleared his throat. It was wonderful to hear conversation again, but the longer he stayed in the open, the more likely *something* would occur. "Can *I* buy some of your gas?"

"You got money? Sorry to say, I can't take any of them plastic charge cards," Ervin said. "Can't figure out how to get through to the place that checks if the card has money or not. Have to be cash on the barrelhead, son. Hope that's not a hardship."

"No, that will be okay. Cash is fine." Tom stepped out into the desert heat, Revelations bounding out after him, running in wide circles and sniffing the air with a passion. "I have five gas cans—each holds five gallons. And the main tank is half full—so that will be about another twenty gallons. I guess forty-five gallons all together. Maybe fifty."

Harlon rubbed at his chin. "The pump pricing don't work right now. Ervin, how much you figure fifty gallons of gas cost?"

Ervin looked befuddled. "Let's see now. Gas was going for $1.37 a gallon or something like that before. Now if you takes that times forty-five—"

"Fifty," Harlon interjected.

"Yeah, fifty. . .that be. . ."

Tom knew a confused man when he heard one. "Tell you what. You fill everything up to the top, and I'll spot you two hundred dollars even for the deal—a hundred apiece. That sound fair?"

Ervin and Harlon almost fell over each other getting to the hand pump and swinging the nozzle to the first of the five-gallon cans. "Be fair for sure, mister. Be more than fair."

While the men were busy filling the tanks, Tom noticed two

policemen exit a squat, square building a block away. There was a tall antenna behind it. He felt his muscles tense. He had done nothing wrong, but he couldn't be sure how the locals would treat outsiders at this time.

"How are the police handling all that happened?" Tom asked, trying to remain casual.

"You mean since the electricity went out and all?"

"And the earthquakes," Tom added.

Both men looked up. "We heard that there were quakes farther west, but not much happened here. A rattle or two—we must have been lucky," Ervin said.

"And there's only a handful of people in this town on a good day, so the police haven't had much to do since then—no one chasing any speeders you know," Harlon said with a smile. "You're the first car we had all day. A couple of bikers passed yesterday—and a few days before that an old beat-up semi rolled through. Must have been forty years old, if it was a day. Remember that rig? So owing to the slow traffic, things are pretty slow for police work, I'd say."

The policemen, their shirts soaked through from sweat, sauntered toward the station. Both wore aviator-style sunglasses. One was short, stocky, and about forty-five years old. The other, tall and gangly, was no more than twenty-five. A wisp of a mustache grew at his lip.

"Howdy," the older one said. "I'm Chief Wiggum—and no laughing allowed."

Tom smiled, recognizing the name of the bumbling police chief on *The Simpsons*. "I wouldn't think of it. In fact, I worked on a couple of those shows awhile back."

"Really?" The chief's voice was deep and paced as slow as butter melting on a hot day. "I didn't watch it much. But the name always got a laugh."

The younger policeman stood several paces behind Chief

Wiggum. He was not smiling. "Where you from?"

"I'm Tom Lyton. I'm from Los Angeles. Malibu, actually, up the coast a bit."

"Where you headed?"

"Des Moines."

The young policeman whistled. "Des Moines, Iowa?"

Tom nodded. "I'm making a short stop in Las Vegas to look up an old—" Tom squinted as if the next word he needed to say was painful—"I need to look up an old friend."

The policeman smiled as if he understood. "Des Moines," he whispered. "That's a pretty fair piece of road between here and there."

Tom nodded again. "It's a favor to a friend. He wanted me to say good-bye to his wife. He died in the quake. Mainly been heading east. Ran into a few detours along the way. Takes longer than it used to."

Chief Wiggum slipped his thumbs behind his belt buckle and rocked on his heels. It was a very practiced move, Tom thought.

No one volunteered any further information for several moments. Ervin screwed the final cap back on the last gas container. Tom nodded and pulled out four fifties from his wallet and handed two to each man.

"Two hundred bucks for gas?" Chief Wiggum said. "Ervin, that's high—even for you." The chief turned back to Tom. "He was a pirate before all this happened—and still is a pirate, I guess."

Tom waved it off. "It's okay, Chief. This gives me enough to get maybe halfway to Iowa without stopping. That's worth a lot."

Chief Wiggum shook his head in resignation. "This old world sure has gone crazy." He paused, then added, "You know where that's from?"

Tom smiled. "The Three Stooges. When the Stooges were pretending to be plumbers and had water squirting out of the stove and lightbulbs. The black cook said it."

Both police smiled. "You're a smart one, Mr. Tom Lyton of Malibu."

When no one spoke, the world fell back into silence, save for the gentle rustlings of the plastic flags. Tom motioned for the dog. Revelations dutifully sniffed each man standing in the growing dimness, then bounded into the car. Tom followed him in and closed the door.

"Listen," Wiggum said, "was it as bad as we heard on the coast? Somebody said all of L.A. burnt to the ground."

Tom knew his eyes would reveal his own deep sadness as he replied. "It was. It was very bad. I guess it still is. My wife and daughter died when my house fell off a ridge. There were fires everywhere. I don't see how much could be left standing."

"Can anyone explain why nothing works? I mean a quake doesn't stop a car. Why does this Hummer work and some old tractors, and not much else?" Wiggum appeared close to tears.

Tom shrugged. "I don't know for sure. My father-in-law said it was solar flares. Nothing else made sense."

"Wasn't the Chinese or the Russians or some terrorist?"

"Didn't see anything like that at all," Tom said. "Just the fires and the quakes. If it was, I'd think we'd have seen some enemy soldiers by now." He leaned over and switched the ignition. The engine jumped to life.

Tom noticed the radio light was on. *No sense wasting power on something that doesn't work.* He reached over and hit one of the buttons. He was not sure which one controlled the power, and he hit the SCAN button rather than the OFF button. The radio automatically scanned the entire radio band for stations, stopping only when a signal was received. There was static and hisses and curious, ethereal whines. But then the radio scanner stopped. Quickly every man drew near the open window.

Through a scramble of noise came the following words: "This is Stonefort calling. You're listening to the Chosen Voice of God, from the Temple of God's Calling." The radio crackled and static spit out of the speakers. Everyone leaned closer to hear.

Then a smooth, deep voice took over. "I'm Rev. Moses from Stonefort, Illinois. This is the day of the Lord. Listen to His voice through His humble messenger."

Tom was shocked, and he could see the others were as well. All save Chief Wiggum, whose face was lined with tears. "The world has come back," he whispered. "It's back."

may 18

Dawn poured through the trailer's tiny kitchen window. Peter had nodded off in the tattered reclining chair facing the mute and lifeless television. He awoke with a start and clutched at the Bible that rested in his lap. He caught it just before it tumbled to the ground. None of the myriad bits of torn paper that he used as bookmarks escaped. He did not want to spend another long night searching for the verses by the lantern's light—verses on prophecy and the end times and the Second Coming.

He stood and ran his hand over his face, clearing the sleep from his eyes. As he stretched, the bones in his back popped and creaked almost loudly enough to wake his daughter.

He stumbled to the kitchen and filled a kettle with water. Without thinking, he lit the burner on the stove. The water was almost boiling when he remembered that he was saving the gas for more important uses—not just a cup of coffee.

Well, it's already hot, and I still have part of a jar of instant left. May as well use the water now.

He sat out on the front steps and sipped his coffee. He winced a little. Powdered milk only dented its blackness. At dawn the world outside his door was beautiful. Steam rose off the creek at the edge of the field. Birds called out in song. The sun lit the grasses and the trees with the rich umber of morning. Squirrels called from the woods north of the trailer. All of nature appeared to have found its place again. Perhaps nature had never been far from normal.

He finished his coffee, tiptoed back into the trailer, and checked on Becca. She was still sound asleep, never much of an early riser.

Peter stepped back outside and gathered wood for a fire. He would heat water for her bath this morning and maybe wash out some clothes.

When the fire burned hot, Peter stood back from the smoke and gazed out at the landscape again. The smoke obscured much of his vision; the outline of the far stand of trees was hazy and indistinct.

It's just like my world, Peter thought. *Filled with smoke.*

Almost everything that had once existed still did, but was less clear now, less sharp. Linda still existed, as did Stonefort and Rev. Moses. But in Peter's mind, their images had begun to fade and tatter.

If I only knew what to make of what the Bible says about all this, he thought as he poured a bucket of stream water into the old cast-iron kettle. *Maybe I just need to keep reading. Maybe God will speak to me and show me what I need to know. Or do I simply follow the example of Jesus and trust that God is in control of all this? I know what a Christian should do—love, witness, share. And I haven't been doing a good job of it before now. Maybe that's all I need to know, all I can do.*

The wind stiffened, swirling the smoke toward the west. Tom dipped his arm in the water, checking to make sure it wasn't too cold. It was nearly time for Becca's bath. When she was fully awake, baths became bigger battles.

One thing at a time, I guess.

━━◍━━

Becca was clean and fed by the time Peter took the remaining warm water and poured it over his head and shoulders. He nicked his face in several places as he shaved. He had only a few disposable razors left and wanted to extend their usefulness as long as possible.

He was buttoning his shirt when he noticed a figure heading

toward him, walking along the main road that led to Stonefort. He grabbed his binoculars. The visitor was indeed a stranger—a full red beard, a baseball cap that almost covered his eyes. On his back was a ragged, very full pack. He carried a long walking stick. And he was smiling.

Since the quake, unknown travelers were not just unexpected—they were threats. Peter eyed his rifle, hanging by the front door. Becca was inside reading. Peter debated whether he should take his weapon, just in case, or greet the stranger in a more Christian manner.

He chose friendliness over pragmatism and prayed it was not a foolish choice. When the stranger was a hundred yards distant, Peter waved and called out a hello.

The stranger waved back and returned a cheerful hello.

Becca stuck her head out the door. "Who's here, Daddy?"

"Go back inside, Becca. Now! I will tell you when it's okay to come out." His clenched whisper was harsh, but he did not want to risk his daughter's safety. Peter heard the latch click shut behind her, then called out, "Where you headed, stranger?"

The man stopped, slipped off his pack, laid his staff on the ground, and slowly turned around, his arms outspread, slowly talking as he did. "Stonefort. I'm heading to Stonefort. I wouldn't have stopped, but I saw the smoke from your fire and figured you might want to share breakfast. I've got a tin of condensed milk here. I was kinda hoping you had some coffee to go with it."

"How come you turned around like that? And took off your pack?"

The stranger seemed puzzled. He looked back toward his pile of possessions. "Well, up until right now, every time I said hello to anyone, they most always had a gun pointed at me. I did that to show I wasn't carrying a weapon. I don't see the use for carrying such things. I'm a believer. I believe God will protect and provide. So far He has."

Peter smiled and stepped toward him. "And He's going to provide today as well. I'm a believer too. I'll be happy to share some coffee with you."

The stranger picked up his pack and stick and extended his hand to Peter. "My name is Elijah." He waited a few seconds and added, as if he had practiced the line before, "My mother was a devout woman, and she loved those Old Testament names. Bad as Elijah is, my brother had it even worse—she named him Malachi."

Peter shook Elijah's hand. "I'm Peter, and my daughter, Becca, is inside peering at you from a window. Welcome."

As the water heated on the fire, Peter brought out some dried venison, a few slices of homemade bread, and a Mason jar of last year's tomato preserves.

"I know it's not the typical breakfast, Elijah, but it's what we have."

Elijah's smile split his beard in two. "Peter, I have been living on scraps and green fruit for nearly a week. This is like a banquet for the queen of England. It looks wonderful." He breathed in deeply. "And it smells like the scent of heaven." He took his portion, lowered his head, closed his eyes, and prayed.

Becca stared at the stranger intently as he mumbled his prolonged blessing.

When Elijah looked up from his prayer, he began to eat slowly and with great enthusiasm, relishing every bite.

"So you're headed to Stonefort?" Peter asked. "Can I ask why? Stonefort isn't much of a destination. Never has been. Most of us who live here been looking for a way out—and sorry to say, most of us never found the exit."

Elijah gnawed at the venison strip. He nodded as he chewed, smiling, holding out one finger to indicate that he was not evading the question, just waiting to swallow. "I just started out on my way south," he said as he gulped. "I've spent my whole life in

Milwaukee, and it's just too cold in the winter. And next winter isn't going to be easy for anybody staying up there."

"It's that bad?"

Elijah's smile vanished. "It's worse. Much worse."

A cloud seemed to pass over the stranger's features, a darkness, a sadness. "A few days ago I heard this preacher from Stonefort on the radio. Spent the night in a church a few days back, and they had an ancient radio and some sort of generator or battery. I guess those old sets have finally come in handy. Anyhow, this preacher was saying how his church was spared and how he was having visions of what God wanted the world to do. I can't say I'm that sort of believer, but Stonefort was sort of on my way south. And if God is using that preacher to tell us what to do, then I figured I should at least stop long enough to find out the truth."

Peter nodded. "Rev. Moses."

Elijah brightened. "That's the man. You know him?"

Peter nodded again. "I know him well enough. I can take you there later if you'd like. Introduce you."

Elijah nodded with polite eagerness.

Silence hung over them while Peter grabbed a ladle and scooped out two more cups of hot water. He carefully measured out two tablespoons of coffee and stirred them in, adding into his a long pour of the condensed milk. It smelled heavenly.

"What happened up north?" Peter finally asked. "Rumors are that Chicago is pretty well gone. Did you pass through there? Is it as bad as we heard? All sorts of news spreading like wildfire about what's gone and what isn't. None of us knows what to believe anymore."

Elijah sipped his coffee, deep in thought. "Well, Peter, there is one thing you can believe in, and that's the Almighty. Everything else is colored by who did the seeing. I can tell you what I saw, but I can't tell you if it's the gospel truth or not."

"I understand."

"Chicago *is* gone—least as far as I could see. I skirted well to the west of it. A lot of people there are acting real crazy. So I hurried as best I could—didn't stop walking for three days straight, night and day—till I hit the farmland south of Kankakee."

"So what's left?"

"Well, for a start, you know the Sears Tower? It isn't there anymore, or at least most of it isn't. Now it sits in the skyline all jagged looking. The Hancock Center isn't there either. I was way far west and couldn't see much through the smoke—maybe some of it's still there, but I couldn't tell for certain. Empty cars and trucks all over the road. A few running here and there, but none of them stopping to chat, if you know what I mean. A bunch of bridges gone. Had to swim three rivers—don't know their names."

Peter stared ahead, trying to absorb the details. "What about the people who live there? What are they doing?"

Elijah took a long swallow of his coffee. "My, my, this does taste mighty fine. It isn't brewed—but it does taste fine." He peered up over his mug. "I'm not avoiding your question, Peter, but the plain answer is I don't know. I saw a lot of people doing the same thing I'm doing—heading somewhere, maybe nowhere, looking for. . . well, looking for that something that disappeared on us, I guess."

"But what about food and medicine and stuff like that?"

"Peter, I wish I knew. I suppose that the grocery stores and warehouses would have had enough to hold a city from going hungry for awhile, if most of it wasn't stolen. And then there are farms nearby. I don't know about medicine. Didn't stop to ask. Nobody stops to ask. Saw more horrible things than a man should see. Life doesn't seem to mean a lot to some folks, I guess."

Elijah leaned back and drained the last of his drink. "Mighty fine. I've been thinking about a cup of coffee for nearly four weeks. Tastes every bit as good as I remembered it did. I truly have to thank you, Peter. And you too, Becca, for having a nice daddy like you got."

Becca giggled.

"But you're asking a bigger question than just what happened. I know that. I've been asking it all these weeks myself."

Peter looked puzzled.

"You're asking when everything will get back to normal, aren't you? When all this craziness will end?"

Peter stared out across the field. "I guess I am."

"Everybody is."

"Do you know the answer?"

Elijah's gaze fixed on the western horizon. "Peter, if I were a betting man—which I am not—I'd bet on things never getting back to normal."

Rev. Moses stood and cleared his throat. Immediately the eight people around his kitchen table quieted and looked up with eager faces.

"I'm so glad that you could all join me today. Herve, Pawlis, Madge, Ronny, Burness, Charles, Linden, and Linda—your presence is truly appreciated. And Herve, thanks for making that trip to my in-laws'. Nice to know that they've got food and supplies for all the young ones, including Matthew. Most appreciated.

"I have called you together because there are things we must now do, things we must accomplish. There are matters of protection and supply. I invited you because you are the most capable citizens and believers. Herve, what you're doing with the radio program is amazing. Pawlis, I'm amazed that you found tents for all our visitors. Fantastic! Just fantastic."

They all smiled as Rev. Moses went on about their accomplishments and abilities. He noted that Linda glowed when he spoke of her sweet voice and critical role in the ministry.

"But now," he continued, "we must consider an even wider world. Others will be coming to Stonefort to see this miracle and to hear the truth. I am certain of it. Just yesterday we had a visitor who traveled all the way from Florida. Can you imagine it? He heard us on the radio, heard about what's going on, and came to us on a rickety little motorbike."

Herve whistled. "Florida? That's amazing!"

"Others will be coming, and we can be sure that they will not all be our friends."

There was an audible gasp.

"It's true. There will be those who want to see this voice silenced. They will want to do the church harm." Rev. Moses stared hard at Pawlis, the mayor. "It will be your job, Pawlis, to provide protection. Protection for me. . .and the radio and the church. Where God works, there are many enemies."

Pawlis nodded and began to write in his yellow legal pad.

"Many others will be coming," the reverend said. "Maybe hundreds at first, but then maybe thousands. All coming to see the miracle of the temple that has been spared. They will come because we are no longer silent. They can hear the voice of truth. They will come."

Heads bobbed up and down around the table.

Rev. Moses was beginning to preach, his cadence stretching, his voice edging up and down. "People will come to Stonefort, a fort built on the stone truth of God. When they come, we can begin to plant and farm and rebuild. This can be"—he paused for dramatic effect—"this can be the new Eden! We can restore the world and all that God intended. We will build the new Eden."

Herve nodded with devout vigor. The rest of the people had the dazed look of being swept up by something mighty, something bigger and more powerful than themselves.

"We can create the new Eden!" Rev. Moses boldly proclaimed again. He looked deep and long into each face. "Have we heard any other word from the Lord? Has anyone else filled the air with God's truth? Is not God favoring and blessing and anointing this small church. . .and my message?"

All nodded, obedient and mute.

"Then you must follow me. Together we can build the new Eden."

He lowered his head in the quiet that swept about him. When he looked up, his eyes addressed Linda. "And we will populate this new Eden with God's faithful. We must be fruitful. We must multiply God's truth."

may 22

Dust collected in every corner of the Hummer. The Hummer and Tom's entire body were covered with a thin sheen of fine, chalky grit. Every time he moved, he felt it crunch with tiny, coarse abrasions. His food tasted like fine, chalky grit. His water tasted of fine, chalky grit. He was as miserable as he had ever been in his life.

The radio remained silent, adding to his misery. So great was the power of its crackling and static-filled speakers that Tom had stayed in Death Valley Junction for over four days, hoping that the quirk of atmosphere or geography that had carried the radio broadcast would repeat itself. Virtually every resident of Death Valley Junction gathered at the Hummer each afternoon as Tom searched and searched the radio band for a repeat of Rev. Moses's broadcast. Only static filled the disappointed air.

When Tom finally left Death Valley Junction, he headed south. The shortest route to Las Vegas was directly east, but Chief Wiggum had warned him against it.

"We've heard all sorts of rumors," he had cautioned. "They say a band of gypsy bikers is patrolling Routes 373 and 178. Clancey said they'd kill you as soon as look at you. I know that way would be shorter, but I would head south to Baker and I-15. You don't want to risk your life over a few miles, do you?"

Tom glumly agreed and remained on back roads, heading first to Shoshone, then down to Baker in the blazing desert heat. From the small town of Baker, Tom planned to take I-15 east into Las

Vegas. The drive should be no more than two or three hours at the very most.

A few miles east of Baker, Revelations began to whimper and bark; then he jumped from the front seat to the backseat. He whined louder and louder. The dog had never acted like this before.

At first Tom was startled; then he got angry. He knew the dog didn't need to stop. Tom kept driving, hoping Revelations would settle down. Instead, the dog actually nipped his right hand, drawing blood, in his serious attempt to get Tom's attention. Tom flew into a rage. He was tired, dirty, and hungry, and he had no patience for this. He cuffed the dog sharply on the head. Revelations whimpered but did not stop whining, nor did he back down from his aggressive stance.

Finally Tom slammed on the brakes hard enough so the dog tumbled from the front seat into a furry heap. "Is this what you want, you blasted animal? To stop here?" he shouted.

The dog clambered back to the seat and stared at Tom unrepentantly.

"Is it?" Tom's angry shout rang in the hot air.

The dog wagged his tail.

Tom was still furious. He yanked open the glove box and ripped the map open. He traced his route with a shaking finger. "Blast it to the moon and back!" Tom shouted again. "There isn't any other way to get to Las Vegas than this interstate! You stupid mutt! Look, there isn't any other way!"

Tom bent closer to the map and looked again. Snaking south from where he now sat was an unimproved trail. From there he could cut over to Kelso or catch Highway 40 to Needles or follow back roads to Nipton and Lake Mojave.

"Why would I take a hundred-mile detour, you crazy dog?" Tom knew what this detour would mean. Hours of rutted, kidney-jarring bouncing and rocking and lurching—to go a few miles.

"Is this the blasted road?" he shouted, pointing to it as if the dog could read.

Revelations still wagged his tail.

Tom breathed deeply, trying to regain his composure. With great care and deliberation, he folded the map and slipped it behind the visor. He took another breath as he shifted into reverse.

"I must be crazy from this dirt and heat. I'm taking directions from a dog," Tom muttered. He was sure that Revelations had a smug look as he stared out the open window.

And, only an hour later, Tom discovered that Revelations was right. As Tom rumbled down that trail, he came upon a cluster of tents. He stopped only long enough to ask if the trail was still open to Kelso.

None of the six raggedy campers knew for certain. They were all heading west—away from Las Vegas. One young man, barely out of his teens, wiry, with a face burned to an unhealthy crimson shade, stepped forward. He kept his distance, yet leaned toward Tom's open window. "You're not with the Death Head squads?"

"Death Head squads?"

"You know, the DH squads, man. The elimination men. You know."

"No, I don't," Tom replied, confused. "But I'm not with them, whoever they are."

The young man nodded and tried to smile. "Okay, man, then the karma I'm feeling about you is right on. You stay away from the Death Head, man. There's a whole bunch of 'em just east of here. They hide in the dry washes and pick off single travelers. I hear they got Stinger missiles. Yeah, dude, Stingers. You would be a prime bonus with that Hummer, man. You keep driving south. You'll miss 'em that way. Get to Vegas from the south, man. I hear that's the safest way—if you have to get to Vegas, that is."

Tom, grateful for the warning, waved a thank-you and bounced his way south. He had not asked for more information on the Death

Head squads—nor how the young man knew about them. Too much information was often as bad as too little.

The next time Tom looked at the dog, he could have sworn the animal smiled at him. "Sorry, Rev. You were right, and I was wrong." Tom was sure that the dog nodded in acceptance. He spent the next several miles wondering how things got so weird between him and this dog.

Tom spent the night outside the deserted town of Kelso. He drove down the main street at a slow cruise and saw no trace of anyone. Two or three miles farther, he set up camp behind a deserted highway maintenance shed, well hidden from the highway.

may 23

The next morning Tom and Revelations crossed the Colorado River into Arizona. As soon as the dog saw the glistening water of Lake Mojave, he began to whimper and quiver—he was, after all, a retriever. So Tom pulled off the road near the lake. He owed at least that much to Revelations for saving his life from the Death Head squads.

Across the lake he could see the town of Searchlight. Nothing moved in the shimmering heat. The land was flat and featureless. The water lay glistening only a short twenty-yard run from the Hummer. Revelations was whimpering louder now, almost shaking in frenzied anticipation.

Tom closed his eyes. He kept his eyes closed and waited, hoping he would receive some sort of sign. His wait was interrupted by the touch of a dog's cold nose pressed hard against his cheek. Revelations would not be denied.

Tom wanted to stop as well. He could finally wash the grit and dirt from his body.

"Well, Rev, old boy, I'm not completely settled on this spot. But I want to get into that water as much as you do. I haven't had a good bath in a long, long time. If I'm going to see her, I know I need a bath."

Tom opened the door, and both rider and driver ran as fast as they could, leaping and diving into the warm waters of Lake Mojave.

At that same moment, two low-ranking members of the United

Militia of Arizona were on patrol. Their assigned area was the land between the southern stretches of Route 93 to Lake Mojave. Ernie Hertzog and Mike Stotler, childhood friends from Kingman, rattled north past Mount Tipton.

Mike peered in the rearview mirror, watching the foreboding hills recede into the horizon.

"Watcha looking at?" Ernie asked, peeling the cellophane off his third piece of beef jerky.

"That mountain behind us—that's Mount Tipton, isn't it?"

Ernie turned around and squinted at the reds and blacks of the jagged crags and deep ravines that lined the mountain's face. "I guess. Never been too good at geography." Ernie turned back and stared out at the road ahead.

"Gives me the willies every time we pass it," Mike concluded.

For a mile there was no sound save the rattling hum of Mike's 1959 Ford pickup. Dented, rusted, dirty, and slow, it was one of the few vehicles in the United Militia of Arizona's motor pool that would start with any consistency after the Silence.

Mike and Ernie had been loyal members of the UMA for eight years. They spent weekends in weapons training and stockpiling one of a score of munitions and supply depots hidden deep in the bowels of the desert. The depots were well hidden and well guarded. They had spent those eight years preparing for Armageddon, and now it had happened, much to the delight of the entire militia group. They had planned and trained and worked silently to bring about the downfall of the federal government—and their wildest dreams had now come true. They were in charge.

Tendrils of the earthquakes that had leveled the West Coast had damaged Kingman as well. Perhaps half the structures in town had suffered significant damage. One building had completely resisted the shakes of the sliding land. That building was the squat, gray, provincial headquarters of the UMA. Even the hundred-foot shortwave antenna behind the massive cinder-block, cement-and-steel structure remained standing.

During the past weeks, Ernie, Mike, and the rest of the UMA had taken their orders from General Rolfen Devilber. He would address the men in long, rambling speeches, usually beginning or ending with, "God has proven us right. We have prepared for this day for years, and now God has ordained us to be in charge. We have been chosen, because of our foresight, to be the absolute rulers of the new Jerusalem."

Mike and Ernie never fully understood what he meant. Yet they were proud of what they had done—laid in provisions and weapons enough to last a thousand days at full rations for the whole UMA.

At present the UMA had assumed all jurisdiction in Kingman and everything in northwestern Arizona—and parts of Nevada when their own state militia was lax about guarding its borders. Armed UMA soldiers had quickly taken over the work of the police force and had maintained law and order with an iron fist. They dispensed justice swiftly and without mercy. UMA patrols became familiar sights, slowly cruising the streets in an odd assortment of military surplus vehicles, vintage restored cars, and old tractors. Other smaller, weaker militia bands were neatly absorbed into the UMA.

Mike and Ernie enjoyed being the big dogs for once. To be in control felt, in Ernie's words, "better than a banana split with whipped cream and a cherry."

Ernie crinkled off the cellophane from his fourth piece of spiced beef jerky and gnawed off a cheek-bulging mouthful.

"At the rate you're going, that jerky'll be gone in a week," Mike said.

"Baloney."

"It's true. I bet they're not making any more of it."

"Sure they will. The factory is in—" Ernie squinted at the

label—"Tulsa. No earthquake in Tulsa."

"Yeah, but how are they going to get the jerky from there to here? You see any trucks? You see any railroads? You see any planes in the air this past month? You're not going to have any more of it after this case is gone."

Ernie's chewing slowed. "You think? You really think?"

Just as Mike was about to answer him, he saw a flickering reflection off the shoulder of the road—perhaps a mile away.

Mike slammed on his brakes and spun off to the side of the road, grabbing for the binoculars on the seat beside him. They had patrolled this highway for four weeks and had yet to pass a single person or operational vehicle of any sort. Now it finally looked like they'd see some action.

"Whatcha stopping for? We're not done with patrol."

Mike pointed down the road.

"Where? I don't see a blasted thing," Ernie answered.

Fiddling with the focus knob on his binoculars, Mike leaned forward. "Well, I'll be blasted to kingdom come. It's a Hummer!"

"A Hummer?"

"You know, that big, fancy jeep the army's been using."

Ernie squinted into the waves of heat rippling off the road, then smiled. "We could sure use one of those."

Mike was silent. He watched the man walk around the Hummer, followed by a large dog. "We sure in blazes could." He laid the glasses down, put the truck in reverse, and backed up a quarter mile until a small ridge hid them from view. "We better get back to HQ. Bet the general will be interested in knowing there's a Hummer parked on the side of the road."

A sudden twinge twisted Tom's heart as he realized that he felt guilty about feeling good.

More than a month had passed since the quake, the death of his family, and the start of his journey. For virtually every one of those days, Tom had sensed a darkness about him, a sense of deep and painful foreboding. His nightly dreams overflowed with images of blackness and destruction. Daylight was filled with anxious, over-the-shoulder glances. His heart stayed clouded with grief and pain and loss.

But the last two days had lifted that veil of worry from his mind. He and the dog had camped along the shore of Lake Mojave and luxuriated in the peaceful warm waters. He hid the Hummer deep in a thicket of brush and scrub pines. He removed only a few items from the vehicle—sleeping bag, campstove, fishing gear. If he was to remain stationary for a few days, he wanted to arouse no one's suspicion. He set his camp fifty feet from the sandy shore of the lake.

This sliver of time, this lake, offered a measure of peace and solitude. The sparsely populated area stood empty and alone—and safe. The destruction, the Silence, and its aftermath seemed far away. . .almost as if it had never happened.

Panora, Iowa, never completely left his thoughts. Yet stronger than that promise to Calvin was a gut-tightening foreboding. . . foreboding brought on by a name and a face in Las Vegas that kept him camped here at the water's edge.

Tom had spent most of the first full day lying in the warm, calf-deep water at the lake's edge. Revelations lay beside him. For the first hours all Tom could manage was to play with the dog. At least fifty times Tom tossed a stick into the water for Revelations to retrieve. This simple act was repeated until the dog looked and acted justified—for he was finally doing his "retriever" duty of retrieving things.

Tom consulted his watch again for the two-thousandth time. It had read 9:05 for the last month. The watch was useless, but it provided him a tenuous connection to his old life.

Glancing up, he guessed it was nearing four in the afternoon. He stood up from the water and fetched his fishing rod from the shore. He cast out deeply into the blue water. The dog started to leap in after it, attempting to retrieve his lure from the deep water.

"Hold! Revelations, hold!"

The dog turned back toward Tom, whimpering slightly, its face tensed.

"Sit!"

The dog turned back once again toward the ripples where the lure had splashed and whimpered. Tom smiled, knowing the dog's instinctual desire. Revelations desperately wanted to retrieve the lure. For Tom, the dog had come to represent all he had lost—friends, companions, and therapists. Revelations provided Tom's only connection to the living, breathing world.

"Rev, old boy," Tom said as he slowly wound the fishing lure in, "this is called fishing. Retrievers don't fish. They hunt. You know that in your bones. So just sit there and wait until I catch dinner."

The dog whimpered once more and continued to stare at the ripples the line made as it cut through the still water.

An hour later, holding a full line of panfish and bass, Tom waded up to the shore. Revelations resolutely remained in the water, hoping Tom would return to toss that stick again.

But as the scent of frying fish grew stronger, the dog padded out of the water, shook itself with a mighty series of wiggles, and sauntered up closer to the campfire.

"Now you come back when dinner's almost done," Tom said with a chuckle. "Where were you when I was cleaning these fish? That's when I could have used you."

By the time the western edge of the lake had nearly swallowed the sun, the fish dinner was gone—both man and dog were full—and the air had grown calm. On the shore, bullfrogs croaked, and crickets and cicadas joined in their nightly serenade.

The dog circled a few times on the tan ground tarp and curled into a loose, furry ball. Tom slipped three arm-sized pieces of wood onto his campfire. He didn't need the warmth, but the crackling light provided him a sense of comfort and security. From the rucksack beside him, he withdrew his wallet. Made from expensive Italian leather, it held credit cards, currency, and a small sheaf of pictures.

He only glanced at the photos of his wife and child, because he knew more than a glance would have set tears welling in his eyes. Despite his expectations to the contrary, his heart had not hardened, nor had the memories grown less hurtful over the past month-plus. From the last compartment of his wallet, he extracted a tattered and creased photograph. He had not looked at it for a long time.

The photograph was grainy. Over the years its colors had faded to hazy tans and golds and browns. The shot was taken on a valley road, looking west over the indistinct, smoggy haze of Los Angeles. In the background, at the side of the road, was a battered blue Volkswagen Beetle, pocked with rust. In the foreground stood two people. Tom wiped at the photo as if to clear the haze and the years.

The young man on the right was Tom, two decades earlier. He was wearing bell-bottom jeans, carefully cut and frayed at the cuffs, and a tight brown pullover. His hair was shaggy and hung well past his shoulders.

Beside him stood a woman. *No more than a girl,* Tom thought. *If I was twenty-one then, that would have made Norah just eighteen.* Petite and dark and hauntingly beautiful, Norah Westbrook had long hair carefully parted in the center. It cascaded past her shoulders in a series of glossy angles. She was wearing round, wireless glasses and a tie-dyed T-shirt and jeans.

"Do you want to see what I looked like when I was young and very, very stupid, Rev?" Tom turned the picture and held it in front of the dog's face. The dog sniffed it politely.

"We were so very young," he said softly. Revelations looked at Tom, then lowered his head to his paws. He kept his eyes open and focused on Tom.

"Do you want to know about her?" Tom caught himself waiting for the dog's reply, which didn't come. "Well, you're going to hear anyhow. I was going to take Hollywood by storm. I had my degree in English literature, my published stories in the school magazine, and my one sale to the *New Yorker*. And I had my typewriter, an old Royal. Norah followed me to the sun"—Tom replaced the wallet in his rucksack with a slow tenderness—"and I left her before she knew what hit her."

As he gazed up into the growing darkness above him, it seemed as if he could hear the noise of the stars as they traced their paths across the heavens.

"I remember that tiny efficiency we lived in by the beach like it was yesterday. It was no bigger than my closet at home." His voice caught a moment as he realized again for the thousandth time that home no longer existed. "I wrote and pestered the studios and wrote and hung out at the right restaurants and wrote and networked all over Los Angeles. At the end of that second year, I landed a writing job. I wouldn't win any Pulitzer for the schlock I wrote for that variety show, but it was a stepping-stone."

Revelations lifted up his head and pressed against Tom's hand. "And I was a clever fool," Tom said, stroking the dog. "I played that job like a violin. Then a couple of years later came *Kojak,* and the money started to get healthy."

He scratched behind the animal's long ears. "I left her before it started, Revelations. I left her for a California girl, a blond with a body. I left her with nothing." He sighed, and his voice grew soft, almost liquid. "It was easy, Rev. We were in love. . .and then I wasn't anymore."

Tom took a deep breath. "It was a year—no, two years after that—when I landed my first movie script. Ever see *The Long Good-bye?* No? It got good reviews and did bad at the box office. But the money became really serious after that. . . . Norah got married. That's what I heard. Then divorced and remarried, I think. She lives in Las Vegas, or at least used to."

A private detective in Hollywood had found her address only a year ago, and Tom had paid the man's fee without a smile. "He said that the rest of the story wasn't very pretty. I didn't ask. I didn't want to know. I feel responsible for what happened, how she turned out."

Revelations kept his eyes on Tom, watching him speak into the darkness.

"My life is full of loose ends, boy."

Tom stood and stretched. The dog raised his head to follow Tom's movements. Tom turned toward the water. Night left it black and silent.

In the fire's light, he picked up Calvin's address book and read out loud the address underlined in red: "Deborah McClure, two miles north of the junction of 4 and 44, Panora, Iowa."

He turned back to the dog.

"I promised Calvin I would get his gold there, and I will. A promise is a promise. But first I have to go to Vegas, Revelations. I think I'll try to tie up this one loose end."

The dog whimpered once, then peered into the darkness, as if he had seen movement.

"That's what the Bible talks about, isn't it? Making peace with others? Asking forgiveness? Repenting?"

The dog simply stared at Tom.

"And it's not like I have a lot of time to decide. I do it now, or I never do it. I might not get another chance at this. And she could have moved—or been killed since the Silence." Tom turned again to the lake. "I wish this stuff was easy." The black surface of the lake embraced the wavering reflection of the moon. "But it isn't. It really isn't."

It would take Tom almost three days to work up enough courage to drive north again.

It had taken Megan and Father William nearly eight days to hike the forty miles from Stroudsburg to White Haven. After the first day of furious walking, Father William's feet erupted in blisters and his muscles spasmed for hours. After two days' rest, he could barely manage walking, let alone hurrying. So Megan, arm around his side, supported the priest every step that following day. Thunderstorms and lightning held them back for another two full days. The next day they walked about eight hours, but then spent part of the next day backtracking because they had walked past the exit on Interstate 80, and Father William hadn't realized his mistake until evening. He had spent the rest of the following day apologizing for his error every hundred yards.

The two of them, tired and dirty, had finally arrived at twilight the previous day, the twenty-fourth of May, at Henry Tallent's rambling, weedy farm. Megan was certain that the place was deserted, but Father William assured her that it appeared better kept than usual. Henry came to the door with a menacing shotgun. When he recognized Father William, he dropped it with a rusty clatter and grabbed Father William in a great, wheeling-about-the-room hug. They spent all of that day and the night at Henry's, and he had stuffed them with as much food as they could eat.

Father William had seen Henry through the death of his wife a few years prior and had been the rock that anchored Henry as he fought off the pain and loneliness. There was no one, Henry claimed, with more wisdom and compassion than Father William. No other clergyman ever sought Henry out or stood beside him with as much love as did Father William.

The Silence had left Henry untouched. He was not much a part of the world before, and now, isolated on a dirt road a mile from the end of pavement, Henry simply lived on. He raised his own food and tended to his own business. He had no use for the world either before the Silence or after.

This very morning, after a farmer's breakfast, Father William had explained their predicament to the loyal Henry. "We need to get to Erie, and that's a long, long walk."

Without a word, Henry had risen from the table and escorted them to the gray, weathered barn. He had fiddled with the padlock and creaked the door open. Sunlight poured in on over twenty tractors, trucks, and motorcycles that had been crammed into the dusty space—some covered by tarps, some with doors winged open and silent, some with hoods propped up. All had a thick veneer of dust and barn debris sprinkled on them.

"Not all of 'em work, Father William," Henry had explained. "But a few of 'em do."

Henry had walked over to a small red car near the front and pried the door open. He had wiped the dust off the driver's seat with his red bandanna, then slipped behind the wheel. The engine had coughed, growled, coughed, then started, clattering in a nervous staccato.

"This one be a runner, all right. She'll get ya to Erie and back."

Father William had swept the dust and hay from the hood, searching for a name. "What kind of car is this? I've never seen one before."

"It's a German car called a Goliath. Ain't many of 'em on the road. Them Germans sure make some fine automobiles."

By midafternoon, Father William and Megan had discovered that the Goliath was a Goliath in name only. It refused to operate at any speed above thirty miles an hour. Even slight inclines caused it great distress. Any real hill almost did the car in as it wheezed its way slowly upward. At the crest of most hills, they stopped and watched the steam pour from the radiator, then had to wait until the engine cooled.

"I guess it's faster than walking," Megan had offered, "but it's less comfortable—and a lot less certain."

After the first hour, Megan had dumped a quart of oil into the engine in response to the blinking oil light on the dashboard. It was a pattern they would repeat often. To keep the engine from overheating, they had to run the car with its heater on.

The backseat was jammed with three full cases of oil, several five-gallon cans of gasoline, assorted wrenches and tires and belts and spark plugs. Henry evidently hadn't realized one thing: Neither Megan nor Father William had the slightest idea of what made a car work.

"Come on, come on," Megan now entreated the car. "You can make it; I know you can."

Every few seconds she lurched forward, doing her ineffective best to maintain the car's momentum. A thick oily cloud settled on the road behind them.

Father William's head was tilted out the window, trying to catch a breeze that wasn't hot. "I know it's not Christian to think ill of anyone who helps a pilgrim," Father William gasped, "but right now, I'm not thinking pleasant thoughts about our old friend Henry."

"It may be wrong for you," Megan coughed out over the grumbling engine, "but I sure can think bad things, and I am. . . loudly and often."

At the end of their first day of driving, the Goliath sputtered and coughed just east of Milan. They had traveled no more than a hundred miles.

Megan and the priest tumbled out of the car in a sweaty urgency. The day was cool, but the interior of the car was tropical.

"I will never buy another import as long as I live." Megan gulped, her forehead creased with sweat and the oil that permeated the car's interior as well.

may 26

On their second day of driving the Goliath, nearing noon, Megan and Father William reached the Susquehanna River. The bridge over the river at Lewisburg had been barricaded and was guarded by more than fifty uniformed men with rifles. Father William quickly stopped. Several rifles were trained on him as he switched the engine off.

"You a priest?" demanded a tall man, wearing a camouflage beret, a pistol strapped to his belt.

Father William nodded.

"Let me see some ID."

The priest offered his driver's license, social security card, diocese identity card, blood donor card, Knights of Columbus membership card, and a laminated photo of the current pope for good measure.

The tall man stared at each for a long time, comparing Father William's face to the photo on the cards in his hand.

"Who's she?" he asked, pointing at Megan.

"The daughter of a parishioner." Father William had carefully prepared his speech. "Her mother, God rest her soul, died in a. . . disturbance right after the Silence. I promised her, as I gave her the last rites, that I would get her daughter safely to family in Erie. And a promise made before God and a dying mother is not one to be ignored. So I'm taking her to Erie."

"That so?"

Megan had kept her eyes cast downward. Even though these

men seemed organized and controlled, Father William was certain that she too felt the dark, leering sense of danger.

"You look like an honest man, Padre."

A heartbeat of tension released from Father William's chest.

"You are an honest man, aren't you?" the guard insisted. "You don't want us to have to chase you down for lying to us, do you? You wouldn't want to make us shoot you, would you?"

Father William's eyes widened just a bit, though he tried to hide it.

"And it's too stupid a story to be made up," the tall guard said with a harsh laugh. "I guess you can go through."

Another uniformed man came to the other side of the car and tied a long red-and-white pennant to the Goliath's antenna.

"That stays on your car till the roadblock twenty miles west of here," the tall man ordered. "They'll take it off for you. Just don't stop or get off this road. No shortcuts or quick trips into town. We don't have anything you're looking for. And if any of us sees a car without this flag. . .well, the orders are to shoot on sight. We don't want to be shooting any clergymen, now, do we?"

Father William shook his head vigorously. He set his hand to the ignition, then leaned out the open window. "Son, can I ask you a question?"

The tall man turned and nodded.

"Do you have to guard the whole town? Are there that many people trying to get in?"

As the guard crouched down by the side of the car, Father William heard the man's knee joints pop. "We're guarding enough of it, Padre. We got most of the farms around here under guard. We got a few bakeries and dairies and food warehouses guarded. We may have been hurt by all this, but we're not going to roll over and die, by God. We're going to take care of our own. Strangers can watch out for themselves, and God help them if they try to take what's ours."

"Is it that bad all over?" the priest queried, sadness in his tone.

The tall man stared at the ground. "I think it's worse in other parts. We'll make it 'cause we're family here. For those that don't have family. . .well, I pity them."

Father William turned the key, and the Goliath barked into life.

The guard stood up and stepped back. "Hey, did you hear that the president was on the radio last night? A few of our shortwave people heard it."

Both Father William and Megan looked startled.

"He said everything will be back to normal in three or four weeks." The tall man spit on the ground. "You know, I didn't vote for him when he ran 'cause I didn't trust him then, and I sure don't trust him now. A bunch of BS with smoke and mirrors."

"He was on the radio?" Father William asked, still in shock.

"Yeah, well, don't think it's all that much of a surprise. There's a preacher fellow in Illinois that beat him by a couple of weeks. Fellow by the name of Rev. Moses. Now there's a man I think I could trust."

<hr>

Father William reached back into the car and retrieved the map. Megan thought he'd have had it memorized by now, as often as he checked it. He inclined his head close to the map. Then he squinted into the warmth of the afternoon. "We have about forty-five miles to go, maybe fifty."

Megan nodded. She was familiar with these roads.

Father William eyed the car, which was hissing like a kettle left on the stove to boil. "We won't make it by nightfall."

Megan nodded again.

Father William surveyed the narrow, two-lane country road that wound through the thick forest and brush. They were nearing Titusville, sight of America's first oil well. Then he turned his stare eastward. "I say we make camp here for tonight. It seems as safe as any other place."

"Agreed," Megan said. She trusted his judgment more than she trusted her own.

"There's a stream at the bottom of the hill," she said, getting two empty plastic jugs and an old towel from the car. "I'll get fresh water for us and the beast. And I may wash off a bit. . .so I could use some privacy."

Even though the old world had gone, the core of who Father William was and his sensibilities had not. Such an innocent comment brought a red flush to his face.

She set off with a wave, leaving him alone to spread the tarp and set up the canvas tent Henry had provided for them.

Within minutes the camp was up and a fire started.

I should have gone camping before, Father William thought to himself. *I think I would have enjoyed it then.*

He set the blackened kettle—another loan from Henry—at the edge of the flames. All day he had looked forward, with great anticipation, to his evening pot of tea. It provided such a sliver of normalcy, but without that tiniest of anchors, he'd have felt totally adrift and lost.

Several satisfying minutes later, steam from the mug curled up, and he blew on the hot brew. He leaned back against a tree trunk and closed his eyes briefly.

"Father William? Father William?" Megan knelt next to the priest and softly called his name.

He blinked his eyes open.

"I didn't want to wake you," she said, "but you were about to spill your tea in your lap."

He shook his head, clearing his dreams and thoughts.

"I'll start dinner," she said. "Why don't you go down to the stream? There's a deep pool of clear water on the left side of the road. It's cold, but it feels good."

He flushed red again, then nodded and got up. He walked slowly down the hill to the stream.

Megan busied herself with dinner. Henry had given them a sack of potatoes, carrots, zucchini, squash, and five pounds of stone-ground flour. They had slowly, very slowly made their way across Pennsylvania in the Goliath. Each night their dinner had been a thick vegetable stew. It may have been monotonous, but to Megan it tasted like ambrosia. After a month of canned soups and tinny-tasting kippers, fresh-cooked anything tasted wonderful.

She stirred the stew and lost herself in thought. The closer she drew to Erie, the more nervous she became.

I guess I have no guarantee of what I'm going to find back home. But I've come too far to turn back.

She sprinkled the stew with a pinch of salt.

And Father William seems so certain that I need to get there, for some reason.

Is he listening to You, God? she questioned the sky. *Are You trying to get to me through him?*

Tasting the stew with a smile, she reached to add the carrots. *If You're trying to talk to me, God, why don't You just talk? I'm listening as well!*

She listened carefully. But other than the chirps of the crickets and the faint singing of Father William, the woods were silent.

If not now, God, then when? she pleaded.

Elijah's initial destination—Stonefort—only eight miles from where he stopped, had proved to be a very long journey.

Immediately following their first meeting and their breakfast with coffee and real cream, Elijah had fallen fast asleep sitting in Peter's rickety yellow lawn chair while Peter tilled his garden plot for most of the morning. It was quiet, hard work, and when he stopped to wipe the sweat from his eyes, he could hear Elijah's snoring.

Becca sat watching both men from her swing under the oak tree several yards from the trailer.

Their visitor woke slowly as the sun's rays lengthened into afternoon.

"He's awake, Daddy," she whispered. "You told me to tell you when he woke up."

"Thanks, sweets," Peter replied. "He did look awful tired, didn't he?"

Becca nodded. "And he snores funny too."

Her father smiled back.

Elijah came around the corner, rubbing his face, clearing the sleep from his eyes. "Thank you for letting me rest. I must have been tired."

Peter stopped digging, his foot on the shovel. "I'm glad to have offered it."

Elijah smoothed his beard with a practiced hand. "This your garden for the year?"

Peter nodded.

"Just this?"

Peter nodded again. "It was enough for a pantry full of canned vegetables."

Elijah shook his head. "Won't be big enough. Not this year at least. This may be all you have."

Peter stared back. *He may be right.*

"Best make it two or three times this big." Elijah looked around. "You got an extra shovel?"

"There's a couple in the barn," Peter answered.

"You got extra seeds?"

Peter nodded. "I always buy too many. The Burpee order came just before. . .just before the quakes and the Silence. And I know I could get more if I needed—farmers always order too much." He wiped at his forehead with his sleeve. "Curious thing how we've all started calling it 'the Silence,' isn't it?"

"It is," Elijah replied. "Folks back home called it that—right away."

"Maybe it's the only word that fits. The news channels used to name everything. Maybe we're conditioned to have a name so we just had to find one that works."

Elijah nodded, then rubbed his hands together as if getting ready to go to work.

"I should earn my meal," Elijah said as he turned toward the barn. "I'll give you a hand."

"Becca," Peter called to his daughter, "go and help Elijah find the shovels. . .and then go in the house and get Daddy's seed box, okay? Maybe we'll plant some cow seeds this year for your milk."

Becca ran off with a giggle.

That day Peter and Elijah had tilled a large square section of the rich, black dirt, nearly four times as large as the original plot.

"You seem to know how to handle the soil," Peter said as the shadows lengthened to dusk.

"Spent summers on my grandparents' farm near Madison. I guess I'm sort of a farmer at heart," Elijah replied. "Never thought it would come in as handy as it does now." He leaned against the shovel and wiped at his beard. A dusting of dirt filtered into the evening sun. "Peter," he said, "I been praying all the while I've been digging."

"Asking for a good harvest?"

"No. Not really. I've been trying to figure out what I should do next. After even a few weeks of being adrift like this. . .well, I don't feel settled at all." He pushed the shovel into the dirt and let it stand there. "I guess God's been saying that some folks need to keep moving and some don't. I think He's been telling me that I'm not a traveling man."

Peter stopped shoveling as well. His back hurt and his arms were sore. He had not done so much digging since. . .he couldn't remember ever having dug so much.

"I need to ask you a favor, Peter. I don't have anyplace in particular to go. I planned to head to Texas or Florida. But both seem a far stretch for me now. Missouri even seems pretty far off. And it's warm here now."

Peter waited silently.

"You got a barn over there. It isn't much, but I think I could set off a section and make it warm and cozy. You got old lumber lying about. I don't need much. I could help with the garden."

"You're asking to stay?"

Elijah looked near tears. "I know this is sort of sudden and all. But since the Silence, I don't think we have the pleasure of taking our time and considering every angle. I don't have any family to speak of anymore. I don't have anyplace to go. I can't see myself being alone for the next months. I just can't. I thought being alone was going be easy, but it's the hardest thing I've ever done. I'm not built for being alone."

"You want to stay in the barn?"

"I could help around here," Elijah pleaded. "I don't know anything about hunting, but I think I could handle the farming part."

Becca stood next to Peter and wrapped her arms about his leg. "Can he stay, Daddy? I like him."

Peter glanced down at his daughter. She stared up with expectation in her eyes. Through her childish innocence, he felt a rightness in saying yes. "Well, Elijah, I can't offer much. But if you're willing to help and settle for what we can raise or I can shoot, then I guess you can stay."

Elijah looked at Peter and his daughter for a long time, then lowered his eyes. "Praise God," he said softly.

———

After that, neither Peter nor Elijah made any hurried effort to travel into Stonefort. In fact, neither man spoke of it, despite Elijah's initial enthusiasm about Rev. Moses. Both felt that the time to prepare for the future was at hand. They plotted out their planting. Elijah discovered enough seeds for their large garden. They turned the soil, then set rows and planted. Using scraps of lumber and a few sheets of plywood, they fashioned a small, insulated room in the barn for Elijah. It was not much bigger than a closet, but it was snug and dry. Peter pulled an old, rusty Franklin stove from the back of the barn and set to cleaning it and preparing it for use. And they busied themselves with a hundred other tasks.

But a question Elijah asked one evening after Becca was in bed turned a thorn in Peter's heart.

They sat on the steps of the trailer, watching the stars. Since the Silence, there were no lights to clutter the night sky. The stars jammed the heavens with a sparkling intensity that neither man could have imagined even six weeks ago. Their brilliance was mesmerizing—as if the night glowed with a million white jewels.

"Peter," Elijah said softly, "you know I'm not a man to pry."

Peter nodded. Despite working side by side for the past nine days, Elijah had rarely asked any questions of a personal nature. It was as if both of them were just settling into friendship, a friendship not built on words but on shared loneliness.

"I always thought that a man would share his heart when his heart was ready," Elijah continued.

Peter nodded again.

"But I've been puzzling over a few things. You have a most precious daughter in there sleeping. And she talks about her mother now and again. I haven't asked about it, mind you, but children talk. I guess I've been wondering where the girl's mother is. Is she passed away, or are you two divorced or separated?"

Peter turned to the man he now considered a friend. "No, we're not divorced. Her mother is still alive."

"So she's. . .gone?"

"Well. . ." Peter struggled with how to explain this situation. *What has happened?* he wondered. *Why has she stayed there, in Stonefort, and why haven't I gone after her?* "Elijah, I don't know how to explain this, exactly."

Elijah held up his hands, bidding Peter to stop. "I'm not asking for an explanation if there isn't any. I'm just curious is all. I mean, what do I say to your daughter when she talks about her mother and all? I just felt sort of lost about it."

Peter stood up and took a couple steps into the darkness. He had ignored thinking about his marriage these past days. It hurt, and he did not like the pain. "She's with Rev. Moses. She sings on his radio show. Everybody around here would tell you that she has the sweetest voice they've ever heard. I guess those that listen are most taken by it."

Elijah sat up straight. "Is she the voice?"

"The voice?"

"I heard her that night—the night I heard Rev. Moses for the first time. It *was* the sweetest voice I've ever heard singing at the end. It was so clean and pure, it was enough to break a man's heart."

"Yeah, that would be Linda. She could do that with her singing. I think she could have done something special. . .if it wasn't for her getting pregnant and all." Peter let the silence return.

"Listen, Peter," Elijah said after a long moment, "I'm not prying. I'm really not."

"I know. . .I know you're not," he said, his voice lower than usual. "Becca was born six months after we were married. I guess that makes me a sinner, doesn't it?"

"Peter, we're all sinners. You know that."

"But this sin followed us. I mean, I know she loves Becca, but she also thinks she could have done something more with her life. I think it made her bitter—angry at me for sure. I guess that's why I've let her have free reign over most things. Or at least I did. I guess I feel guilty." He paused. "You know, I've never said anything about this to anyone ever before. I don't know if it feels good or not."

They both stared up at the stars again.

"So she's staying with the Reverend Moses?" Elijah finally asked.

"Yeah, she is. There're a few guest rooms at the parsonage that are more or less separate. I asked her to come home, but she didn't. Said the reverend needed her. Said those who are lost out there needed to hear her voice. They needed her help more than I did. And there would be no way of making that eight-mile commute every day. Used to be a piece of cake. Now—you might as well be on the moon."

From the stream across the field, a pair of raccoons squealed and yelped as they battled over a crawfish.

"Do you think that's true, Elijah? Do you think God is using her to call sinners home? I mean, if this is really the end times, like the Reverend Moses is saying, do you think God needs her more than Becca and I do? Do you think I should let her be?"

The raccoons squalled for another minute, then quiet descended again.

"Peter, I'm a simple man. Never said I was practiced at religion. But it doesn't seem right. It just doesn't."

"Sir, Ernie Hertzog and Mike Stotler are here to see you," Rolfen Devilber's adjutant said, poking his head in the doorway to the commandant's office. Mike heard nothing, then the adjutant continued. "They're the patrol that spotted the Hummer up at Lake Mojave."

Mike thought he heard Devilber say, "Show those two dunderheads in," but that couldn't have been right. Before he could figure out which word the commandant had really said, the adjutant motioned for them to enter.

Mike and Ernie shuffled into the room and offered salutes. Devilber snapped off a salute in return, then returned to his chair behind his desk. For a long time the commandant didn't say a word. Instead he eyed them with sharp-edged intensity. Both Mike and Ernie began to sweat, not knowing what was expected of them.

"Uh, sir. . .we're here about that Hummer," Mike offered weakly.

"You know. . .the one we saw up near Lake Mojave," Ernie added, trying to add a thin smile. He wasn't successful—his smile faded quickly under Devilber's baleful glare.

"I know why you're here," Devilber retorted. "I understand you requisitioned a snooper listening dish. Did you learn anything? Is he on patrol from the Nevada Militia? Did you manage to find out what he's doing on our land, in our territory, traveling without authorization? Is he armed?"

Mike and Ernie leaned uncomfortably backward a degree or two. Their faces were marked by uncomfortable grimaces.

Ernie spoke first. "Uh, sir, I think we found out where he's going. And he's not with that Nevada group."

"He's not? Where is he headed?" the commandant barked.

"He said something about Las Vegas first. Then he mentioned a town called Panora, right next to Des Moines. That's in Iowa, sir. And then he said he'll get the gold there. His exact words, 'I promised Calvin that I would get his gold there.' "

The commandant straightened. "Gold?"

"That's what we heard," Ernie said. "We didn't see anything, but he said it plain as the nose on your face."

Devilber's eyes narrowed into harsh slits.

Mike blanched, seeing the expression on Devilber's face. It was no secret that Devilber was touchy about his large nose. And Ernie had unwittingly touched on that subject. Mike hurried ahead to keep Ernie—and himself—out of trouble. "He said he would go to Las Vegas to tie up a loose end, then head to Des Moines for the gold."

"That's what he said all right. Las Vegas, Des Moines, gold," Ernie agreed.

Devilber turned away and stared at the map of the western states on the wall behind him. The UMA territory had been outlined with pink marker. Las Vegas was just north of the northernmost pink line.

Folding his hands behind his head, Devilber let the silence build to a crescendo. "Gentlemen," he said, "I have a very important mission for you."

Mike and Ernie didn't speak after their briefing until they were almost in Ernie's driveway.

"We're going on a secret mission," Ernie whispered, proud of being chosen.

A wide grin splayed across Mike's face.

"You know. . . ," Ernie began, then hesitated.

"What?" Mike asked.

"No, I better not say it. You'll get mad."

"I won't. Tell me. I won't get mad."

Ernie checked around to make sure no one had followed them. The neighborhood was quiet. "Well, I was just thinking. . . . Iowa is a long way off, isn't it?"

"Pretty far, I'd say. Especially these days."

"And we'll have the gold and the Hummer when we get there, right?"

Mike nodded.

"Well, we don't have to be in any hurry getting home afterwards, do we? I mean, we could take our time, couldn't we? We could enjoy ourselves."

At first Mike looked shocked. Then, slowly, a more secretive smile replaced his original grin. "That's what we could do. Ernie, you are one smart cookie."

The tower and spindly antenna mast were working. In the few weeks since he had begun broadcasting, scores of visitors from Chicago, Gary, Des Moines, Nashville, Little Rock, St. Louis, and Indianapolis had appeared at the steps of the Temple of God's Calling.

A tent city had sprung up near the church. The newcomers had been drawn by the power of the Reverend Moses's word and the clarity of his vision. And they were drawn to the purity of Linda Wilson's singing.

Since the Silence, Linda's voice had grown richer and more golden with every song. A man could close his eyes as she sang and feel that much closer to home and to heaven.

"Time draws nigh," Rev. Moses had thundered during the previous evening's address. "The Lord Jesus said to watch for the signs—and the signs are upon us. God has spared this poor messenger and this church to draw you unto His heart and His truth."

These days Rev. Moses had little time to prepare messages. Five times a week he had to come up with new material. Then Monday and Tuesday evenings were repeats of the Saturday and Sunday messages.

Herve had found an old wire tape recorder in the basement of the radio station. The repeated messages were full of snaps, hisses, and pops, but as the reverend said, "Beggars could not afford to be choosers."

During every sermon, the Reverend Moses shared one transcendent message again and again. "Jesus. . .yes, the Holy of Holies, Jesus. . .man and God combined. . .is set to return to this earth. He has sent the signs. He has shaken this world so all will look to the heavens for Him. You must heed my call. There is little time left. You must repent. You must accept His gift."

The first week Rev. Moses, near the end of his radio message, had asked for donations to repair and continue his ministry. But he was gently reminded that, so far, there were no signs of the postal service coming back to life. Pawlis Smidgers had made the observation after a meeting of the town's new and unofficial council.

"Rev. Moses, there's no way letters and checks can get to Stonefort. That is, unless folk start bringing them themselves. The post office was busted up pretty bad. It be awhile until we start having mail again, I imagine."

So Rev. Moses had changed the thrust of his message. Stonefort had an abundance of land, he figured. More than half of the open, arable land had been abandoned years ago. Deserted farms and grayed, tattered barns dotted the geography. Scrub grasses and brush covered the land with a tangled permanence— acre after acre of empty land.

No one is using it, he'd figured. *No one is farming it. I bet that cash money isn't much good, at least for the time being. But food. . .now there's the new currency. There's the new power. Food will be coming in right handy come winter.*

His message the following day had included a new request: "Listen to my voice. Listen to the Voice of the Lord as He speaks through His devoted and humble servant. Those who are listening, you must pray," he whispered into the microphone in the darkened chapel of the Temple of God's Calling. Every pew in the building sagged under a heavy load of people. Loudspeakers lilted his words to a crowd overflowing onto the front steps and gathered around the tower. Stranger and citizen were joined in the community of faith.

And the Reverend Moses began to call the faithful home. "You must pray. . .in this time of tribulation and sorrow. There are those who hear my voice who are hungry. You don't know if you will eat again today or this week. Your hearts are in pain. Your heart, your stomach will cry out for an answer."

His words built in volume. "And you cry out, 'Where are You, Lord? Why have You let me go hungry? Why have You abandoned me? Why have You turned Your back on my family? Can't You see that my child is crying because I can't find food to give him? Why, Lord? Why have You forgotten us?' "

He let silence pour over the crowd. Then in a whisper as soft as old velvet, he began to speak again. "He has not forgotten." Rev. Moses paused to wipe the sheen of sweat from his forehead with his red, initialed handkerchief. "He has not forgotten. I have not forgotten."

Grasping the pulpit with two hands, he leaned forward and shouted into the microphone, "He has not forgotten you!" His words echoed across the rubble that was once Stonefort as he gulped in a breath. "He knows of your pain. He knows of your sorrow. As He spared this church and this messenger, He shall spare the faithful who follow the truth of His words."

His tone now became calm and soothing. "You are scared and alone. I am here, and I am ready to receive you. In a hundred small towns and villages, there are those who are listening to me tonight who can become part of something very, very special. You cannot write to me or call me. I know that. You are lost and alone in the Silence. But we can break that Silence. We can build a new creation, a new community, a new brotherhood of faith."

Rev. Moses blinked. He craned his neck, peering into the blackness around him. "We can build a new world. We who believe have an obligation to rebuild God's world in a way that would please Him. We can build a new Eden. . .right here in Stonefort, Illinois. It can be done. God's new Eden. God's new Eden, right here, right in the shadow of the Temple of God's Calling."

The pulpit rocked forward, deeper into the harsh glare of the spotlight. The Reverend Moses closed his eyes as if he were lost in the swirl of a message from God. "If you are able, if you are well and healthy and you know how to farm or build a house or dig a well or raise animals, or if you're a nurse or a doctor. . .then I need you. I need you in Stonefort to fulfill God's plan. *I* need you. *God* needs you.

"Listen to God's plan. He wants a new Eden. He needs believers to come and build it. His church! His bride! His people! That is the message He has touched my heart with. That is the word God wants you to hear tonight. He is calling His people back home. He is using me to call His people back home. Listen to the voice of God. Come to Stonefort and be part of God's rebuilding. You must be about the business of rebuilding this nation to please the Almighty God of the universe! Listen to the voice of God!" he shouted, then slumped at the pulpit. With the barest turn, he motioned behind him with a wiggle of two fingers.

From the darkness behind the pulpit, Linda Wilson, clad in a cobalt blue robe, rose and flowed to the microphone. Her eyes focused on the ground before her. She grasped the microphone stand and closed her eyes. And then she began to sing. "Swing low, sweet chariot, coming for to carry me home. . . ."

The Reverend Moses watched, wiped at his face now soaked with sweat, and leaned against the far wall. He blinked, then let a thin smile crease the folds of his face. It was a smile that lasted until the last note carried pure and clear into the darkness of the Silence.

"May God protect you and provide a way to cross that Jordan River and come home. . .come home to His new Eden. This is the Reverend Moses saying good night from the Temple of God's Calling in Stonefort, Illinois. Good night. . .and to all of those who yearn for their homes again, welcome home."

Hours after his congrega-
tion had left and into the wee hours of the morning, Rev. Moses
sat alone in the first pew. The church was dark, save for a thin,
reedy light from the radio transformer resting on cement blocks at
the side of the platform.

I am doing the right thing, aren't I? he thought. *Somebody has to
assure these poor people that all will be back to normal someday.*

He had never felt so exhausted and exhilarated all at once. *And
I can start a new Eden here, can't I? Well, it won't be an Eden exactly,
but I can make it close. I can have a few thousand people in this valley—
maybe more—working the farmland. It can be a new community of
believers. That will be a good thing, won't it? God will bless that effort,
won't He?*

The reverend tilted his head back. *I'm sure He will. Look at how
He's blessed me so far. He won't stop now.*

By now his eyes had grown accustomed to the blackness. He
could see the pulpit and the coils of wires that snaked about the
platform. He saw the door at the far side of the platform open. A
bone-white apparition slipped into the room. He shut his eyes
until he heard the door snap shut.

"Rev. Moses? Are you in here?"

It was Linda Wilson, calling out in a mouse-quiet voice.

"Over here, child. In the front pew. Just keep walking.
Another step, one more, now one step down, and another, and
another." A smile spread across his face. "Put your hand out. Put

it out in front of you." An instant later he grabbed her hand, like
an owl snatching a mouse from the floor of a barn, and pulled her
to his side. He kept her hand in his for a long moment. Her skin
was cool and felt like silk.

"Have you had trouble sleeping?"

"No. . .I was just up and looked in your room and wondered
where you were."

"And here I am."

She lowered her head, averting her eyes from his.

Funny, Rev. Moses thought. *Watching her with her husband, I
would never have used the word* shy *to describe this woman.* He
finally let her hand go. *And now,* shy *doesn't go far enough. Or perhaps it's. . .dare I say it. . .perhaps she is in* awe *of me.* His smile broadened. His heart felt suddenly strong and full.

"Linda, why are you here? Why have you sought me out?" His
voice was low, like a rumble of a truck on a faraway interstate. *I
know why. You want the comfort of my power. That's right, isn't it?*

"I was lonely. I was lonely, and I wanted someone to talk to."

He slid toward her an inch. He took her hand in his again.
"Linda, my sweet little child with the wonderful voice in the darkness, you can always talk to me. You know that, don't you? I am
always here for you."

"I know. . .I know you are."

Peter was up before the sun rose. He walked past the garden, no
longer a simple garden, but nearly an acre of neatly tilled rows
marked with string and stakes. A cool breeze whispered in from
the north. Peter turned to face it, breathing deeply of its freshness.

I still want that cigarette, he thought, then wondered what he
would use to buy a pack with. He had perhaps a total of three hundred dollars in currency in the trailer. The First Bank of Stonefort,
if it were ever to resume operations, would show another thousand
in savings, earmarked for Becca's college fund.

Will we ever use it for that? Peter wondered. *Do banks still work? Will they be able to sort out all the accounts?*

He walked down the dirt road, past the stream. The shadows of several smallmouth bass flitted underneath him as he crossed the wood bridge.

How do you smoke and preserve fish? Peter wondered. *Maybe Elijah knows how. He seems to know a lot about those old-fashioned skills.*

The road was deserted. No more than seven vehicles had passed in the last few days. Most of those old rusted-out vehicles he recognized as belonging to farmers and neighbors who lived farther out along the road.

At the edge of the asphalt road, Peter turned back and peered east. His trailer appeared even smaller and more insignificant now that the garden plot had enlarged so. He looked over at the stand of trees and old oaks north of his home.

Plenty of firewood there for the winter. Now all I have to do is build a fireplace.

As he began slowly walking back, his heart lurched.

I should go into town. I should ask. . .or beg. . .or demand that Linda come home. Becca needs her mother. Linda needs to come home.

He stopped at the bridge and stared again at the silvery fish in the clear water below.

But Becca hasn't asked much about her mother. Should I take that as some sort of sign?

He blinked. If what he felt was a tear, he wanted it stopped.

I want her back, but maybe I never really had her all these years. After all, she left us and never looked back.

Standing on the bridge, Peter kicked a few pebbles into the water below. Then he walked sadly back toward the garden. By the time he was at the edge of the neatly tilled rows, Elijah rounded a corner of the barn, his beard and hair wet and matted to his face and scalp.

Elijah waved and smiled. " 'Morning, Peter. Sleep well?"

Peter merely nodded.

"That room isn't much to look at, but I get the most powerful and peaceful sleep," Elijah said as he stroked the water out of his beard. "Like the Lord has been wanting me to stay here all along, providing me such wondrous rest and all."

Peter smiled in return. "Good to hear, Elijah."

"I have a fire going for coffee, and I'm making some camp biscuits. I hope you don't mind that I sort of started breakfast without asking."

"Elijah, my cooking never got much past cold cereal and milk. I appreciate whatever you can do. I know Becca will love something fresh-baked."

"That's a powerful reason to do it then."

The two men walked together back to the fire crackling in a small stone ring that lay midway between the barn and the trailer. A cast-iron skillet with a cover lay to one side of the fire, resting on the wire rack of an old barbecue grill. The aroma of fresh biscuits swelled on that slight breeze. In another moment each man held a cup of coffee, splashed with a hint of powdered milk and sweetened with honey.

"It's not Starbucks, that's for sure, but it still tastes mighty good," Elijah said after taking a swallow.

Peter sat back in one of the yellow lawn chairs. It creaked with a weary yet comforting groan as he leaned back and set his feet to the outside of the fire ring.

Elijah bent over the skillet and poked at the rising biscuits with a fork.

"What do you suppose we should be doing now?" Peter asked.

Elijah glanced up and then around. "Now? You mean like before breakfast?"

"No, I didn't mean today exactly." Peter hunched forward, his hands cradled around the cup, his elbows on his knees. "I mean. . . you're a believer, right?"

"A man has to have belief to face the world these days," Elijah said.

Peter nodded. "I accepted Christ—accepted God's gift of eternal life—so many years ago that I've forgotten what it felt like beforehand. I would imagine that there aren't many lukewarm believers these days. So I guess I'm asking if we believe in the same things."

Elijah frowned. "Do you mean to be comparing theologies right now? I reckon I should be brushing up on my eschatology if you are."

"No, but a question's been nibbling away at my thoughts since you've been here. I know what I believe—and I know I should have paid more attention to the last book in the Bible than I did. Seemed too hard to figure out, I guess. And then there's that big question I think of every time you and I talk."

Elijah looked as if he was about to apologize.

"No, Elijah, it's not your fault, but your coming sure got me thinking."

"About what?"

"Well, we're both believers. And what's taken place in the past month or so has gotten me thinking that it was the end of the world. I believe that any rational person would come to the same conclusion. The world has gone crazy, and we all face a pretty troubling future."

Elijah nodded as Peter spoke.

"If we're believers, this end-of-the-world thinking is sort of a hornet's nest. If Jesus has come back, well, we're still here. It's a puzzle I'm almost afraid to think on."

A somber expression crossed Elijah's face. It was apparent he didn't relish this topic either. He nodded without reply.

"I guess we're both trusting that the Rapture hasn't happened yet," Peter said.

Elijah checked the camp biscuits. He stroked his beard again before he spoke. "I would bet everything I have—while it's not much, granted—but I would bet it all that what happened was just a string of real bad luck for America, maybe the world. It wasn't the Rapture. It wasn't."

Peter sipped his coffee. "You certain about that?"

"I can't quote you chapter and verse—never been real good at that—but if Jesus had come back, He would have come for me. I don't want to seem like I'm bragging or taking pride in myself, but I've been a faithful man. I believed with all my heart. I am a child of God. I am."

"And you know you would have been raptured if Jesus had come back?"

Elijah nodded firmly. "Yes." He stared off into the distance. "This isn't the Rapture, and it isn't the beginning of the Tribulation. I am. . .well, I am 99.9 percent sure of that. First Thessalonians 1:10 says: 'And they speak of how you are looking forward to the coming of God's Son from heaven—Jesus, whom God raised from the dead. He is the one who has rescued us from the terrors of the coming judgment.'[vii]

"I am a believer. I know it in my deepest heart," Elijah said firmly. "And I'm still here. So what I'm saying here—with as much surety as a man can have—is that this is just a whole passel of bad luck for America. Maybe it's a big warning from God—that I'm not sure of. But it isn't the Rapture, and it isn't the whole Tribulation. Not yet anyhow."

Elijah stroked his beard with a hint of nervousness. "And I would suppose that if we had only *sort of* believed and Jesus had come back and didn't make a stop for either me or you, well, then we would have known He *had* been here. We couldn't have missed it. I'd be most certain of that. If He had left us back, we would have known He'd been here."

Off to the edge of the field, a flock of crows took off in noisy flight. They wheeled and spun just overhead.

Peter set his empty cup at his feet. "That's what I had guessed too. For awhile I thought maybe He had come back and the faithful He took to heaven was a lot smaller group than anyone imagined."

Elijah managed a wry smile.

"I tried to look at our little church," Peter continued, "and while I'm not saying that I could see into men's hearts, it sure seems like a big portion of the church has always done a better job at pretending to be believers than actually doing what Jesus said—myself included."

"Amen to that, brother."

Elijah held the coffeepot, now blackened by the fire. He poured a second cup for both, the liquid now hot and thick. Peter took a sip and winced.

"So, Elijah, I'm praying, just as you're praying, that we are here and God's still in His heaven."

Elijah nodded. "That's where I put my prayers, brother."

"So if that's true," Peter said, "now what do we do? If the Scriptures—Mark, I think—say to watch for earthquakes and stars falling out of the sky, then this is one pretty big warning, don't you think?"[viii]

"I wouldn't argue with you," Elijah said slowly.

Peter leaned forward again. "If we're believers and God gave us this wake-up call, what do we do next? If the end time is near, shouldn't we be doing something about it? Shouldn't we be—I don't know—telling others or something? Doesn't the Bible say something about seventy weeks going by before He comes again?"

Elijah waited a full minute to reply. "I'm not sure when that seventy weeks is going to happen. I've read the Book of Daniel and I'm not sure if those weeks are years or decades or what. But I know what we should be doing. We should have been doing it before the Silence. Telling others about Jesus. Pretty simple stuff—Silence or not."

"Do you think God will be silent now too?"

Elijah looked angry. "Nope. That will never happen. Never. God isn't the one who is silent, Peter. Never. He'll be listening and talking to us all the time. No earthquake or dead telephone will stop Him. That's a dead-solid certainty. Dead solid. God is still here. It's us poor folks who are silent now."

"And we shouldn't be?"

"Not now. Not before, but especially not now. We should be breaking the Silence ourselves. Breaking it by telling others about God. Silence or no Silence, we know what we should be doing. And now. . .well, I guess, now we should still be doing it. I guess the Silence will be enough of a call to attention for most folks," Elijah said.

Peter nodded in response.

"People will listen if they think their time is close at hand," Elijah continued. "And maybe that's what God is doing now— telling everyone that we don't have much time left."

Quiet returned, save the hiss and crackle of the fire.

"Elijah, I know you don't know much of this Rev. Moses. But I do," Peter said in a smaller voice. "And I have to tell you that I can't imagine God choosing him to be the voice of His coming. I just can't. It may be mean-spirited and spiteful of me to say that, but I have to think God would have found somebody better. . .like Billy Graham or someone."

Elijah took a red bandanna from his pocket, wrapped it around the handle of the skillet of biscuits, and took them off the fire.

"Well, Peter, you're right in saying that I don't know much about the man. But my mother always told me that even a bucket with a hole in it manages to carry some water."

Peter smiled. "Enough for a third cup of coffee?"

Elijah rose and gently shook the coffeepot, listening for the water. He heard no sloshings from inside the pot. He smiled. "I guess the reason my mother sounded so smart to me was that she never really got down to the specifics about her sayings."

The chilled rain fell in leaden sheets as the Goliath lurched toward Titusville. Father William discovered a few seconds after the rains started that the Goliath no longer possessed working windshield wipers. He tried looking out his open window as he drove, but it was like steering a car underwater.

Wiping the rain from his face, he finally sputtered, "I don't think this is a good day to travel, Megan. I can't see a blasted thing. . .and please pardon my French."

Megan offered a weak smile in return. "Your French and my French are two entirely different dialects, Father William. Don't worry about offending me with yours."

He rolled the window up. His left shoulder was soaked through, and a puddle formed on the floor mat. "We'll kill ourselves if we try to get much farther."

"And the noise of the rain is getting on my nerves," Megan said with a sigh.

"We passed an old barn a mile or so back. I think it was big enough to get the car inside. Do you think that would work?"

"I guess so."

With a grinding of the gears, the priest turned the car around and slogged back through the rain, going no faster than ten miles per hour. Both were relieved when he drove the car into the darkened interior of the abandoned barn. Father William sighed and switched off the engine. For now they were dry and safe.

The priest stepped out of the car and ran his hands through his wet hair, trying to dry it in the humid air. "I never thought much about fresh towels before," he said, his voice echoing in the empty space, "but I most certainly miss them."

Megan got out of the car and began to walk aimlessly around the barn.

"Would you like a cup of tea?" Father William called cheerily.

When the tea was hot and strong, sweetened with a bit of honey from Henry's farm, Father William handed the mug to his traveling companion, who had slumped down against some bales of straw. "I used to love days like this," he said, gesturing to the steady rain splattering against the small overhang by the door. "I would find a chair in a quiet nook of the rectory and spend hours reading."

"The Bible?"

He turned to Megan. "Well. . .not always."

"I thought priests were supposed to read the Bible."

"They are."

"Then why didn't you?"

"I did. . .but I also read Tom Clancy sometimes," he said, ducking his head, embarrassed to confess. "Mystery novels. And I have to admit that I occasionally picked up a Stephen King novel."

"Stephen King gets pretty racy for a priest," she said with a smile.

He tried not to blush. "I skipped over those parts as best I could. But I did read the Bible as well. I really did."

Their conversation quieted, the staccato raindrops the only sounds around them.

"Megan," he said softly, "may I ask you a question?"

She shrugged. "Why not?"

"I may not be the most well-read priest, but I'm good at knowing when a person's heart is troubled. And I think your heart is troubled."

She looked away. "That's not a question."

"Are you afraid your father is dead?"

She seemed to collapse. Her head dropped to her chest and she set the cup hard on the floor, sloshing the tea about. She cradled her head in her hands and began to sob. "He's dead. I know he's dead."

Father William set his cup down and knelt at her side, draping his arm over her shoulder. He allowed her to cry without interruption for a couple minutes. Then he whispered, "Megan, I know that you hurt. Tears are natural and good."

She sniffed loudly.

"But you will see your father again. I know that you will." *Now why did I say that?* he thought, an instant later. *I don't know if he's dead or alive. I shouldn't be promising something I have no control over.*

"Are you sure?" she whispered back, her voice childlike.

I can hedge now. I should hedge my answer. I don't want to break her heart. But the words that came out of his mouth instead were, "Of course you will. You'll see him again. I know it." *What! Why did I say that?*

"Thank you, Father William," she said, "thank you for being here."

Mike worried about the blue cloud of smoke that poured out of the old truck as it wheezed along the deserted roads north of Kingman. He and Ernie were midway between Kingman and Las Vegas, no more than a half hour behind the Hummer. The two UMA members stayed on the road that led to Las Vegas and to the land controlled by the NMM.

"Will they be able to follow the smoke?" he asked.

"What smoke?" replied Ernie.

"The smoke from the truck."

Ernie sat up straight, dropped his beef jerky on his lap, and cried out, "We're on fire?"

Mike fought the urge to reach over and cuff his companion on the side of his head. "No, you nitwit," he snapped, "the smoke from the exhaust."

Ernie turned around and stared behind them. "But the truck has always done that. . .I mean, with the exhaust and all. She always burnt oil like a banshee, Mike. You know that."

Mike sighed. It was good that Ernie was such an old friend. If

"Sorry about the search," the man with the Uzi said, his voice
rming slightly. "But we can't be too careful."

"It's okay," Tom replied, trying not to let his relief show.

"You have business in Vegas? You've come to gamble, right? To
a show?"

Tom tried to speak, but he couldn't form the words fast
ough. His mind was spinning from the sudden shift. "Gambling?
show?"

The guard pulled on the shoulder strap of his weapon and it
, easy and practiced, at his hip. He rested his right arm along the
bbed barrel. "Hey, this is Las Vegas. We never close."

"But. . .but. . ."

"Yeah, that's what everybody says when they get here. It's the
n, man. Hoover Dam. All the power we could ever want. Took
than a month to bypass the computers, and we're up and run-
g again."

Tom followed the man's mouth as he spoke, struggling to
sp the import of his words. He was not keeping pace.

"Yeah," the man with the Uzi said with a broad smile. "It con-
es everybody on their first trip here since the Silence and all."

Tom watched, mute, as another guard fastened a long silver-
ored ribbon to the Hummer's antenna. He handed Tom a thick
inated pass. In the corner was a sparkling hologram of a pair
lice and beneath them bold, block letters: NMM.

"Leave this flag on your car. . .or it's ours. And that's your pass.
good for one week, and if you haven't left by then, we'll come
king for you. And we'll find you. Las Vegas isn't that big."

"But. . ."

"Listen," the guard explained, suddenly growing impatient
h Tom's befuddlement. "We're back in business. This town is
k in business. The town and everything in it is now run by the
M. . .that's the Nevada Militia Men."

"But. . ."

he wasn't, Mike would have pushed him out twenty miles ago and
left him to find his own way back home. "I know that, Ernie.
What I'm asking is if you think anybody will be able to follow us
because of the smoke—or if they'll know we're coming. That's
what I'm worried about."

Ernie arched up and rooted around below him on the seat.
The crinkle of cellophane bore testimony that he'd found the beef
jerky he'd dropped. He took a large bite and laboriously chewed
the tough meat. "Nope," he finally said.

"Nope?" Mike replied.

"Nope."

"Nope what?" Mike asked, exasperated.

"Nope, they won't know we're coming because of the smoke.
It's behind us, don't you see? They won't see it until we leave."

Mike shut his eyes tight. "What about following us then?
Won't they be able to follow the smoke pretty easy?"

Ernie thought for another long moment, finishing off the
jerky as he did. "Nope."

Mike reluctantly asked the next question. "They won't be able
to follow us?"

Ernie wiped his hand on his chest. A thin streak of grease followed his fingers. "Oh no, they'll be able to follow us all right. It's
just that we're not going to be able to do anything about it. That's
the 'nope' part. Unless we shoot them. And I don't mind doing that."

"Shooting?"

"Yeh, that and killing things. . .you know."

Mike nodded. He knew all about his partner's likes and dis-
likes. He sighed again and shifted uncomfortably in his seat. The
sun was still hot and the truck's cab was tropical. Worse, it smelled
like oil, beef jerky, unwashed clothes, and stale coffee.

"That is, unless we get ourselves that Hummer," Ernie put in.
"Bet that don't smoke. And bet it has air-conditioning."

Mike agreed. "Amen to that, Ernie. Amen to that."

The two were quiet for the next ten miles. Then Mike broke the silence. "We're a couple of hours away from Vegas. I bet the NMM start patrolling these roads pretty soon. I don't want to get mixed up with any of those guys. I hear they shoot first, then don't ask any questions at all."

Ernie nodded.

"You know what we're going to say?" Mike asked for the hundredth time.

"We're old friends of Tom Lyton," Ernie answered. "He's driving this big camouflaged Hummer with a golden-colored dog. We was supposed to meet by the lake, but we had truck trouble and he must have left before we got there. And then I'm supposed to ask, 'Have you seen him anywhere?'"

Mike knew it still sounded a little rehearsed, but with Ernie's less-than-polished natural mannerisms, it would probably work. Their weapons were tucked under the front seat. It would take an upholstery repairman to spot the hidden latch and hinge.

"And who are we?"

"You're Mike and I'm Ernie, and if we can't find Tom, we might go to the casinos if they're still open. We're sheep ranchers from south of Kingman and just sold off some of our sheep. We got nearly a thousand dollars in gold coins to spend. We're looking for a good time."

Mike smiled. *This just might work after all. Even I'm starting to believe it.* He watched as Ernie cleaned his fingernails with his hunting knife.

It was nearing dusk as Tom caught the first glimpse of Las Vegas shimmering in the distance. Tom guessed that the desert heat was creating this glowing chimera in the desert. But as he drove closer, he saw that it really was Las Vegas. The city was lit like a neon Christmas tree. Lights and street lamps and signs and searchlights beamed into the golden dusk of the desert.

At one point he stopped driving in amazement. "whispered, entranced by their multihued glow. "They

Tom was careful. He had hidden both the rifle in one of the Hummer's well-concealed storage a *really searches the car, they'll find them,* he realized, *bu one will do that thorough of a search.* The Hummer, designed for military use, and that included a heal subterfuge built into the vehicle.

As he approached the Las Vegas city limits, he snake of razor wire running across the road and stre a quarter mile to each side. Standing to either side were at least two dozen men, all clothed in black. A a stop, he saw at least half of them unsling their wea saying a word, they aimed at his head and chest. H pounding, loud and scared.

"Out of the car!" demanded the man closest to

Tom didn't hesitate. He hit the pavement with high in the air.

"If you've got guns or weapons, drop them now

He thought for only a heartbeat. "I'm unarme any guns."

"Move away from the car!" Giving the orders w a silver cording at his shoulder. He was cradling a Uzi in his arms.

Tom called for the dog, who jumped out and s a few yards from the vehicle. Three black-uniform each door and poked under the mountain of gear, the seats, opened the glove box, lifted floor mats.

God, if this is something to pray about, he though them search, *then I guess I'm asking that they not fi the gold.*

In no more than two minutes, the guards slan shut.

"You have cash? U.S. currency?"

Tom blinked and stammered, "A couple of thousand, I guess."

"Should be enough for a night or two," he winked. "The casinos will take gold or jewels or maybe even a Rolex watch, if you got one of them."

Both men glanced at Tom's wrist. His Rolex was still there.

The guard grinned. "Have a good time. Las Vegas is a great place to have a lot of fun, if you know what I mean. Just don't do anything stupid. We don't like dealing with troublemakers, but we will if we have to. Now get in your car and get out of here. Go enjoy yourself."

As if on automatic pilot, Tom climbed into the car. Revelations scrambled in after him.

"And welcome to Las Vegas," the guard cheerfully called out as he waved Tom through the checkpoint.

Tom felt like a fish—one that has just found itself yanked onto dry land, gills gaping furiously, a shocked and perplexed look in its eyes. He'd been cast onto a most foreign shore. As he drove through the roadblock and toward the glare of town, it appeared that civilization had returned to this pocket of Nevada desert—returned with a blazing vengeance. To his left was a McDonalds—open for business. There was only one car in the parking lot, but a knot of people stood by the front counter. On the other side of the street blinked a used-car lot. A portable sign carried the message ALL OUR CARS STILL RUN! The lot was filled with an assembly of old, battered cars, but a small handful of newer models faced the street, gleaming in the artificial light, their hoods open to the night air.

There were porch lights and streetlights and traffic lights. Tom encountered the first real traffic in weeks. He was the third car in line waiting for the light to change to green. He turned on Fillmore, just as the ocean of neon came into view. The Strip and its row of massive hotels and pleasure palaces twinkled like a galaxy of civilization in the dark universe. He squinted at the brightness and turned east and away from the lights. He had a mission to accomplish.

Yet amid the glitter and neon, something did not feel right. Tom knew the movie business. He knew what was real and what was simply a Potemkin village. He could tell at a glance when an elegant facade was built to mask an ugly back lot. As he drove on, the illusion of normalcy rippled and bent and curved back again. That rippling edged along his awareness like a sharp but shallow cut, drawing pain but little blood.

"It's real, but it isn't," Tom whispered into the darkness. "There's something wrong. I can feel it more than I can see it." He reached over to the dog and nudged him. "Do you feel it?" he asked. It no longer felt odd to use the dog to gauge what was normal.

Revelations looked at Tom.

"Is that a yes?"

The dog continued to stare.

"Sometimes I think we're both loony, boy."

At that the dog whimpered, then barked softly.

Tom had located Norah's last known address on the expanded map of southern Nevada. From the gridwork of streets marked on the map, the address looked to be a few miles east of the Strip. As he drove farther, the houses appeared to grow smaller and dingier. Not every storefront was lit, but most were. He passed several liquor stores, a pawnshop, and several dark-glassed locations offering a variety of massages and other intimacies. Several people walked on this section of sidewalk—all male, some in the black-and-silver outfits that Tom guessed to be the official NMM uniform. A few turned to watch him pass, though most ignored him. Must be that a vehicle in Vegas was not an oddity.

"This just doesn't seem real," Tom said aloud.

Even Revelations had pulled his head away from the open window and now cowered slightly in the seat.

Tom turned on Lovell Avenue and slowed, looking for house numbers. The houses looked tattered and tired; dusty cars littered the curb. A few porch lights glowed. He came to the number 412. He stopped and turned off the engine. Revelations stood on the seat, sniffed the air loudly, and then turned back to Tom.

"This is the address, Rev."

Revelations wagged his tail in response.

"She may be long gone. This information is, what, over a year old now?"

Revelations sat down on the seat with a furry *thud*.

"And what do I say to her? It's been so long. I don't even know if I remember the reasons why I left her."

The Hummer's engine ticked loudly in the quiet as it cooled. At the house across the street, Tom saw a drape open a crack; a second later it snapped closed. Most houses showed a slim glint of light from behind closed drapes.

"But like I said, Rev, this is going to be the only chance I get." He stepped out into the night. "You stay here and guard the car. Bark if anyone touches it, okay? You have my permission to be fierce and menacing tonight."

The dog returned a low growl.

"Good boy."

Tom adjusted his shirt and tried, ineffectively, to smooth out the wrinkles. He ran his hand through his hair to remove the tousling the wind had created. His heart began to pound. His throat tightened, and his mouth went dry. "Now, listen," Tom whispered to himself, "you've been in script meetings that were tougher than this. Remember the screaming match you got into with Spielberg? If you could do that, you can do this."

He checked the numbers again. 412. The veneer was peeling off the front door. A narrow glass panel, head-high, was yellowed and cracked. It had been patched with duct tape. He closed his eyes. He turned, took a deep breath, and knocked.

The rain didn't cease until the skies grew dark and the breeze from the north stiffened.

"We might as well spend the night here. At least it's dry and out of the wind," Father William said.

Megan nodded, her eyes still red from crying. She wiped at them again. In less than an hour, the kettle was simmering, filled with a thickening of flour and sliced vegetables. The aroma pervaded the barn's interior.

Father William put a delicate spoonful to his mouth, blew on it, and smiled again. "I must admit, I have a knack for this simple cooking."

Megan's stomach growled in response. Both laughed, the first honest laugh they had shared all day.

"God is so good," Father William added, sounding almost automatic.

Megan's face darkened and her body tensed. "How can you say—oh, never mind."

"No," he replied, "tell me what you were going to say. There isn't any reason for holding back. Not now. Not tonight. Not to spare my feelings, for certain."

She pursed her lips together, as if deep in angry thought. "It's just. . .well, how can you say that about God being good? Doesn't it seem the least bit ridiculous to you? People are probably dying by the thousands right now and killing each other over scraps of food. Maybe my father is alive, but maybe he's dead. And you sit there calmly over your little stew pot and say, 'God is good.' " She shook her head. "How can you say that? How can you even begin to think that?"

"I can say it because it is true."

She snorted in derision. "It's not. Not after all this."

"But God is still in control, Megan. He is. He has spared us and watched over us this whole journey. We have food and shelter and have not been harmed."

"But that's not the question." Megan could feel the tears coming to her eyes again. "I want to know why God let all this happen. Why didn't He step in and stop it? You say He's protecting us now. Maybe He is, and maybe He isn't. I should still be back in New York in my apartment and at my job. I shouldn't need God protecting me in some old drafty barn in Pennsylvania. I shouldn't need a priest to watch over me. I shouldn't. If God is in control, then He really screwed things up this time."

"Megan!" the priest answered sharply. "You mustn't talk like that. You mustn't."

"Why? What worse things can God do to the world? What worse things can He do to me?"

"God is always in control. You have to believe that. That's just a matter of faith."

She turned her shoulders away. "I don't have to. I don't think I really believed it before, and I sure don't now."

"But God is calling your name right now. He is, Megan. Of all the things I am sure of, this is the most sure."

"And I should listen to His call now?" she answered. "After all this?"

"Yes."

"Well, I can't. He allowed these terrible things to happen, and I can't listen."

Father William set the spoon on the rim of the pot.

"You say God's in control. Why didn't He stop all this before it happened? Why would He let all the killing and—" her voice cracked—"and all the terrible things that I've seen go on? Couldn't He just stop it?"

The priest picked up the spoon and stirred the stew one more time, thinking. "We all have free will and are free to follow our heart. God could force us all to behave—and none of us would like that. Our society became dependent on machines—God didn't force us to do that. He didn't build computers and phones and satellites. We knew that those things could break—and they did. God didn't break them."

Megan sat still and silent. She was tired of arguing.

"Megan, God is calling your name. He has called your name for as long as you have been alive. You need to answer Him, Megan. There may not be a lot of time left for any of us to answer His call."

"Father William. . .I don't think I want to. . .not now. . . I can't."

He knelt beside her and took her hand in his. "But why, child? Why can't you?"

Tears again filled her eyes. "I'm not the person you think I am, Father," she whispered. "I have done some. . .some bad things. I have done them often. Some evil things."

He squeezed her hand harder. "Megan, He will forgive you. He will."

"But I can't undo them, Father." She began to cry harder. "My father would hate me if he knew. He could never forgive me. Not his innocent little daughter."

"Megan, your father is important, but only God can forgive you. That's the only forgiveness that truly matters. Can you accept that? Megan, God's offering it to you now."

Megan collapsed in the priest's arms, weeping freely and uncontrollably.

Tom stood in the darkened doorway of 412 Lovell Avenue for more than a full minute before knocking again. He heard no noise, no sudden movement, no annoyed call for patience. His second series of knocks grew louder, bolder.

Through the yellowed glass, he saw a brightness, as if someone snapped on a light in a foyer or hallway. He heard a scuffling just on the other side of the door. He thought he heard breathing.

Perhaps someone was looking out through the peephole. In the darkness, Tom was certain that no one could see any details of any guest without turning on the porch light.

"What do you want?" a woman's voice asked.

"I'm looking for someone," Tom called back. "She lived here. . . at least it's the last address I had for her."

"Who?"

Tom leaned closer to the door. "I'm looking for a woman named Norah. Her maiden name was Westbrook. I'm not sure if she's married now or not. Do you know where she is? Did she live here?"

"Who?" The voice was edgy and muffled.

"Norah Westbrook, but that was her maiden name."

There was a long silence.

"Are you in there?" Tom called out, his face nearly pressed against the peeling veneer. "Hello?"

Silence.

"Hello?"

The voice called back, a note of panic rising in the tone. "Who are you?"

"I'm Tom Lyton. An old friend of Norah's. We used to know each other a long time ago."

"Tom?"

"Tom Lyton. L-Y-T-O-N. We were old friends."

He heard the rasp of door chains being undone and locks being unsnapped. He counted five. The door opened a mere sliver. Through the narrow opening, he could see only a woman's eye.

"Tom Lyton?"

"Yes. I'm looking for an old friend who came with me to California—"

The door slammed shut for a moment. One final chain clattered open, and the door swung wide, the pale light spilling into the night.

"Tom?" The woman before him stared at him with wide, dark

eyes. Her hair was no longer long and black but shorn tight to her face and blond.

Tom stared back, wide-mouthed in surprise. *Norah? It is her. . . older for certain and blond. Her face is a little thinner. . . .*

"Tom?"

He nodded. "Norah?"

She grabbed him in a fierce, almost desperate, hug. "I always knew you would come back," she cried, her voice muffled into Tom's chest. "I just knew it."

It took Tom nearly a full minute to extricate himself from Norah's powerful hug. To Tom, the embrace felt nearer to desperation than any embrace he'd ever felt.

He held Norah by the shoulders and pushed her back. "Will my car be safe on the street?"

Norah glanced over his shoulder into the midnight darkness. "That's your Hummer?"

Tom nodded.

"It'll be safe. No one steals anything in Vegas anymore."

She began to pull him into the house.

"Can I bring my dog in?"

"Dog? Does he bark?"

"If a stranger comes to the car, he'll set off a racket."

"Then leave him there for now. He'll be good protection if there's a knucklehead wandering by who hasn't heard of the NMM rules."

"NMM rules?"

"Come on in, let me close the door, and I'll tell you all about it."

Tom found himself seated on a tattered brown couch, hints of stuffing edging from the arms. Years of wear showed through thin spots on the dark rug. The lampshade was a light mottled brown and hung askew. The walls were bare of pictures. The room was stale with smoke and cut by a heady tracing of beer. He sat straight on one edge of the couch, with his hands resting too stiffly on his knees. Norah sat no more than an arm's length from him. She fussed at the hem of her once-pink robe as she adjusted and readjusted it, covering her bare knee and leg.

"You look great," she said.

Although she was younger than Tom, he could see her road in life had been much harder than his. Her face showed the deep lines that years of tanning, hard living, and worry caused. Her eyes, once dark pools of mystery, now seemed glazed. She had remained as thin, or thinner, than she had been when she was a teenager.

A tremendous sadness welled up in Tom's heart.

"I followed your career, you know," she said, leaning ever so slightly closer to him. "I admit that I hated you at first, but after awhile, every time I saw your name roll on the credits, I got excited."

"You did?"

"You were easy to follow. I even saved that article on you from *People* magazine." She gestured behind her with a vague sweep of her arm. "It's in here someplace. I could find it if you'd like." She turned back to him and smiled. "But then I guess you know what they wrote. I mean, you lived it."

He returned her smile. There was a rumbling richness in her voice that he had heard too often before. It was a voice mellowed and deepened by years of smoke and drink—the thick molasses-like timbre was unmistakable. A thousand Hollywood wives and some ex-wives possessed that same throaty, thick sensuality in their words.

"You kept the article?" he asked, surprised.

"And I saw you at the Emmys."

"You were there?"

She laughed, a laugh that was harder and coarser than Tom remembered. "No, you old silly. On TV. Like the rest of the peasants."

Tom smiled back, unsure of what she meant and if that was just the tip of hard feelings and bitterness edging up to the surface.

Behind her, a refrigerator must have switched on. The whir of the electric motor at first startled Tom.

"I heard you got married."

She looked up. "I did."

"To Al Calgani, wasn't it?"

"You knew about him?"

"Friends of friends, I guess. Hollywood isn't that big of a town."

She stared at her hands, resting in her lap. "Al was fun. . .while it lasted."

Tom studied the lines around her eyes. "How long were you married?"

"To Al? A couple of years."

"There was a second?" Tom knew that there was but would allow her to recall them.

"A second," she said softly, "and a third. . .and almost a fourth." Her lips tensed. "And how is Lydia?"

Tom couldn't hide his surprise.

"I actually read the *People* article, you know." Her voice had hardened and tightened.

"Did you leave her at home to make this. . .pilgrimage?"

He blinked only once. "She's dead. The quake."

Norah's face didn't change. Her voice hardly softened. "Sorry. Seems like everybody has lost so much."

Tom closed his eyes, fighting the sudden discomfort that swept over him.

Norah scooted an inch or two closer. "I missed you, Tom. After all these years, I still miss you. Did you know that? I think of you every day."

He struggled to remember why he had come. Their conversation, especially her conversation, was taking an unexpected turn.

"So are you getting by?" he asked, changing the subject. "Las Vegas seems untouched. Are you working?"

Norah laughed as she turned and fumbled for a nearly crushed pack of Old Golds. She pulled one out, only slightly bent, and used a disposable lighter to start it. The bright flame emphasized the lines around her eyes. She exhaled, coughed once, and shook her head in resignation.

Or is it sadness? Tom wondered.

"A town like Vegas isn't going to stop unless they drop a bomb on us. . .and if they do that, there'll be players who'll take odds on which street corner it's going to hit."

Tom smiled. "It's the only town with electricity that I've seen the whole trip from L.A. And I've done a lot of zigging and zagging to get here."

Norah drew in a long lungful of smoke and began to talk as she exhaled. "I figured. That's what everybody says when they get here. I work as a. . .as a hostess over at the Mirage. Worked before the solar flare and the earthquakes, and I'm still working there now."

"Solar flare? Are you sure of that? I've heard others guessing that it was the cause."

"So they tell me," Norah said. "I know a guy who said it was for sure. A huge flare. A number 5. Whatever that means. Science doesn't make any sense to me at all. . .but then you knew that about me before."

Demurely, she averted her eyes. Tom wondered if she was flirting.

"But this solar flare thing is what caused the problems," she insisted. "That and the earthquakes. Anything electronic is gone— all over the world, they say. I guess a few things here and there work, but hardly anything built in the last decade. That's why only the old classic cars work. No electronics under the hood. Casino owners went through every warehouse in town and dug out all the old slot machines—the mechanical kind—not the electronic ones."

For the first time in a long time, Tom began to feel connected, even in this slight and tenuous way, to the rest of the world. It felt reassuring and comfortable. It was as if Tom were no longer alone. There was somebody else to share the lurking fears with him.

"Were there other quakes besides L.A.'s?"

"I've heard Chicago was really messed up, as well as Japan. . .or was that China. . .someplace like that. Haven't heard much about anyplace else." She tapped off the ash of her cigarette, almost missing the ashtray, and continued. "Right after the flares stopped, the casino owners organized workers to run wires straight from Hoover Dam to town so we could start up again. In less than a month, the lights came back on."

"What about food and medicine and things like that? What about money and phones?"

Norah stubbed out her cigarette and immediately lit another. "You want a drink?"

Tom shook his head.

"Well, I think I'm a little thirsty." She rose and walked with the slightest hint of a wobble. Soon Tom saw the light from the refrigerator brighten the next room. He saw a pile of dishes in the sink and cans on the table. Norah returned and popped the tab on a can of Coors. She took a thick sip and chased it with another drag on her cigarette.

"So far there's food at Vons. Not everything like before, but there's enough. They take dollars, a few more than before, but I think the casino owners are sort of setting prices. I don't know about medicine, but they say the phones in Vegas proper will be back in a month." She settled against the back of the sofa and cupped her chin in her free hand. She stared back at Tom. "And what about you? Why are you here? No one just drops by anymore."

Tom took nearly an hour to recount the events of the last six weeks. Norah listened impassionedly, smoking cigarette after cigarette as he talked. He mentioned briefly Calvin's last request that had led him to this place. He spoke with intensity of how God seemed to be leading him on this strange journey. "I guess you might think I'm crazy, but I guess I might be searching. . .for God or something like that."

She made no comment as he spoke.

"You said something about the NMM rules," he said. "Is it the NMM who are guarding all the roads into town?"

She nodded. "I knew of a couple of those guys from before. I always thought they were on the loony edge—with all their survivalist gear and big dangerous toys. But once the power was down, they were on every street with guns and uniforms, so nobody started looting or killing like they did in other places."

"Other places?"

"I heard that San Francisco is near burnt to the ground from riots and mobs." She took another long drag from the cigarette. "And I heard the same story from a hundred other places. Everybody seems to know one more city that burnt itself up. But not here."

"So the NMM is in charge?"

"In Vegas they are. Their soldiers are everywhere, and nobody messes up. NMM rules, you know. If you steal something and they catch you, there's no trial or anything. They simply chop off your hand. You steal a car, they shoot you. You rape somebody, they shoot you. They don't fool around at all. It's serious business."

She reached for another cigarette. The pack was empty so she crumpled it into a ball and tossed it on the coffee table. "You got any smokes, Tom?"

"Sorry."

"Anyhow," she continued, "there isn't any crime because most everybody is pretty scared of the consequences. They started the executions in front of Caesar's Palace last week. A couple of out-of-towners tried to pass off counterfeit hundreds. Beheaded them in front of a big crowd at noon."

"Beheading? For counterfeiting?"

"Listen, Tom, you don't know what it's like here. You're an out-of-towner. The NMM has kept this city going; we've got food to eat, and everybody is working. You know it's not like that in too many other places—if any. Everybody does their job and stays out of trouble."

"Or they're shot, right?"

"Maybe. But everyone I know works and does what they're supposed to. You may laugh at us, but it's safe here, and everybody can still have a real good time. Real good. Englebert Humperdinck is still doing his act. There are other shows still going on, just like before. It's like nothing happened. We're still here."

Neither spoke for a few minutes.

"You know, I think I will have that drink now," Tom said quietly. "All of a sudden I'm thirsty."

Norah padded out into the kitchen and returned with a can of Coors. "Did any other town you went through have cold beer and electric lights?"

Tom shook his head.

"So then we're better off than all of those other nicer places, aren't we?" Her words were edged with sarcasm and anger.

Tom took a sip and shrugged. "Norah, I don't know anything anymore. Everything is so horribly confusing."

She stood and reached for his hand. "Including me, Tom? Including your old friend Norah? You know, it's so good to see you. I have dreamed about you coming back for a long time—and here you are. It has been a long time—but we sure had our share of good memories, didn't we? Remember that little apartment we had by the beach? Eating buttered spaghetti. Remember that, Tom? Wasn't life great back then? You and me and that beat-up old VW bug? What else did we need back then? We had each other and it was more than enough."

He willed himself to stare only into her eyes and ignore everything else.

"Well, Tom," she said in a smooth voice, "I'm not upsetting you, am I? Have you been thinking of me too? You went to a lot of trouble to find me again." She placed her hand on his chest.

He closed his eyes.

"Am I, Tom? Am I?" She took both his hands in hers. Her skin was cold and smooth.

"Of course not," he murmured.

"That's good, Tom. I wouldn't want to make you nervous. . . . Wait here. I'll be back in a moment."

Her words poured like oil over his heart, and he felt it quicken. His thoughts flew in a scattered whirl. His past had been found again. His first love could be reclaimed. Tom took a deep breath and closed his eyes, trying to still his racing thoughts. He heard the bathroom door open. She switched off the light and the room went dark, save for a bit of yellow that slipped in from the outside. Tom saw Norah pass before it, her robe loose on her shoulders but not yet open. And as she passed through that light, like the moon passing in front of the sun, he saw her silhouette.

His eyes stayed for a moment on her figure, but then a metallic glint sparkled from below.

His mind didn't consciously register the image, nor did his body consciously consider its next move. It was born out of a thousand viewings of a thousand crime and detective shows and a hundred scenes written where the hero recognizes at the last moment the true danger of his predicament.

Tom lunged to the side of the couch, turning away from Norah, spinning farther into the darkness. A roar bellowed, and a flash lit the room. A muffled thudding tore through the cushion only inches from him—the place where he had been only seconds before. As he dove from the couch, he heard the mechanical racheting of a hammer being locked into place. His ears rang from the roar. He saw her finger tighten again about the nickel-plated trigger.

Diving at her small form, he took her right hand and swung it up and away from himself and twisted her wrist back hard. He grabbed the weapon and threw her back toward the sofa. She let out a tight, high-pitched yelp of pain and anger.

Heart beating furiously, Tom uncocked the trigger. Norah remained flat on her back on the couch.

"You tried to kill me," Tom said, uncomprehending, his breath coming in spurts. "You tried to kill me."

Norah simply lay in the darkness. She made no move to escape. "So? What if I did?"

Tom shook his head. He heard Revelations barking. After all, the dog was a retriever. A gunshot meant something needed retrieving. Tom edged to the small window and shouted out. "Revelations! Hold!"

The barking stopped immediately.

He turned back to Norah. "That's all you can say to defend yourself?"

She drew the robe about herself in a defiant gesture, tightening the belt. "What do you want me to say? That I'm sorry I missed?"

Tom's eyes widened in surprise.

"That shock you, Mr. Rich and Powerful Scriptwriter?" She reached over to the coffee table.

Tom lunged toward her in response.

"Just a cigarette, ace. That's all. Don't get nervous." She lit another one, and the flame of the match upon her face made her look decades older than she was. She exhaled a cloud of smoke, then spun her feet over the side of the coach as she sat up and stared hard at Tom. "You thought you left me all those years ago scot-free, didn't you? After all, no one was hurt. We knew what we were doing back then. Free love. No commitment. We parted friends, right?" Norah's eyes were bright with anger. "You thought that, didn't you? You thought I didn't mind being dumped. . . . Well, you think I didn't mind that you got so blasted rich and I stayed poor as dirt? You think it wouldn't bother me and I should wish you well? Well, you can forget that dream, you piece of unthinking garbage. You're living in a fancy palace overlooking the ocean—I saw the pictures—and I'm living in this dump in Vegas. And you think I have no reason to be angry? You think I'm going to tell you, 'Oh, Tom, it's okay? Everything is fine?' Think again."

"But you tried to kill me."

"Were you lying about having gold?"

He was silent a moment. "No."

"Then I'm not sorry for having tried. That gold would have been a way out of here for me."

Tom stepped back and leaned against the doorjamb, gently kicking the door open. A cloud of smoke enveloped Norah's head and shoulders.

"Were you lying about all that lamebrained malarkey you said about God and all that religious stuff?"

He didn't hesitate. "No."

"Then I couldn't have asked for part of the money. You wouldn't have given it to me, would you?"

"No." His voice was small and quiet.

"I figured as much. I know all about this Christian stuff. People have been trying to cram it down my throat for years. They keep trying to reform me. I ain't buying it. They show up on my doorstep, miles away from their nice little churches and homes with picket fences. They spend an afternoon on the wrong side of the tracks and feel good about it. They think I need saving because I'm not like them. They think I'm going to hell because of what I do."

"You are. I probably am as well. A lot of us are, I guess."

"It's all bull," she replied, stubbing out her cigarette and lighting another. "A load of bull."

"It's not, Norah. It can't be. I may not know the answers—but it's not make-believe."

She wiped his words away with the sweep of a hand. "Yeah, right, whatever you say." She puffed again, then glared at him, a determined, hard edge in her eyes. "I said I was a hostess at the Mirage. Well, Tommy, my knight in shining armor who happens into my life a few decades late, it may not please you to know that I'm not a pleasant little hostess with an apron like the little old ladies at the all-night Waffle House by the freeway."

Tom wanted to run away. He knew what she was about to say. Somehow he'd known it the moment he saw her again.

"I'm a whore, Tom. A whore. Does that shock you? Your old flame has become a cheap hooker?" She took another drag on her cigarette. "Well, not so cheap, actually."

Tom shut his eyes.

Norah coughed. "I'm blaming this all on you. I was so mad when you left that it was a great way to get back at you. And it worked. It made me feel a whole lot better. And you know what? Some of my best customers are from the good side of the tracks. Those johns are the same solid family men that show up in some lily-white church every Sunday."

Dragging hard on the cigarette, she continued. "I was doing fine on my own until the stupid earthquake and the Silence. Now the NMM sets the rules and prices and shifts. It's like working a factory job now." She inhaled again. The room was blue with a thick fog of acrid smoke. "Your gold would have gotten me out of this. Tom, it's your fault I'm stuck here."

She reached for a fourth cigarette in less than ten minutes. "What's that do to your search for forgiveness, Tommy-boy? I saw that 'please forgive me' look on your face as soon as I opened the door. Well, sorry to say, that blasted Bible isn't always right. You're not getting any forgiveness here. Not from this girl. Not now. Not from me. Not from anyone. I have made a living of reading men's faces. You're guilty, Tom. I saw it the minute the light hit your eyes. You're guilty. You know it. I know it. You left your wife and baby back in Malibu just like you left me. You get off scot-free and the rest of us suffer."

Her face narrowed and hardened. "And I saved the absolute best till last, Tommy-boy. Remember all those years ago in California? Remember when you just walked out on me without a word? Remember when you never even returned my calls? Remember that, Tommy-boy?"

He averted his eyes and nodded.

"Well, the reason I was calling you then, Tommy—proud and rich Tommy—is that I was pregnant with your baby."

He turned and stared at her in disbelief. He felt his heart stop beating.

"Don't look so surprised. You know it was possible. . .after all, it was before safe sex."

"But. . .but. . .I never. . ."

"Of course you never knew. After your silent treatment, I wasn't going to give you the satisfaction."

"A child?"

"You bet, Tommy-boy. No abortions for this natural girl. I gave up your son. I gave him away—just like you gave me away. Without a second thought or ever looking back. Gone, Tommy. Gone." Her words dripped with angry venom. "Your son is gone."

"But where? How?" Tom's thoughts raced.

"You'll never find him, you loser. Some podunk farm town in Illinois." She cackled. "Like you could drive to Illinois now. Even in your blasted Hummer. Not likely."

An angry smile coarsened her features. "Hurts, doesn't it? Hurts right down to your imported socks, doesn't it? Kind of twists your heart into a little ball, then feels like some fat person stomps on it, doesn't it?"

She glared at him, smug and satisfied. "I can't tell you how good I feel right now, Tommy. Even better than if I'd shot you. Much better. Now you can have the same pain I've had every day of my life since you tossed me aside like a piece of garbage. Feels real good, doesn't it?"

His face was a blank mask. "What small town?" he whispered.

"I don't know. I don't especially care. Starts with Rock or Stone or something." Her laugh was brittle. "Boy, does revenge taste good. Good luck on your trip, Tommy. You'll be dead before you leave this town. I have friends in high places. . .and low places as well. You'll be dead before dawn," she screamed. "Dead! You'll be dead!"

may 28

The first delicate tracings of dawn etched the sky as Tom prepared to leave Norah's house. He had slept fitfully on the couch and felt no better about what he had done the night before.

After Norah had told him about their son, Tom had tied her to the bed with a bandanna across her mouth. He had written this scene a hundred times in a hundred detective episodes, and he had followed his own blueprint.

Now, as he prepared to leave, he decided it best to keep her bound. "Forgive me, Norah," he said softly. "I know you'll call the NMM as soon as I leave if I don't do this. I know you'll get loose in a few hours—or they'll come looking for you."

He peered out to the street. Nothing looked out of the ordinary, whatever ordinary now looked like. Revelations yipped twice when he saw Tom in the doorway.

"Steady, boy," he called. "Hold."

Back in the house, he tested the security on the knots once again. *They'll hold long enough for me to get out of town and into the open desert. I hope.*

Turning back to Norah again, whose eyes were blazing with malice and anger, Tom withdrew his wallet. He pulled out two thousand dollars in one-hundred-dollar bills. He laid them on the nightstand where she could see them.

"I know it isn't much, but it is all I can do."

Norah thrashed against her constraints. She screamed a series of invectives and threats, muted to mumbling by the thick cloth.

"I know you can't forgive me, Norah. But I had to ask." At the doorway, he turned back one more time. "I. . .I forgive you for trying to kill me. I do."

She thrashed about, more frenzied and wild than before. The ropes held.

"And I'm going to find my son."

Tom slipped into the faint light of first dawn. Without looking back, he quickly drove north, past the casinos and the neon lights and the swarms of people that washed across the streets at five in the morning with desperate, scared looks in their eyes.

Tom squealed to a stop at the checkpoint on the northern edge of the city and returned his flag and pass to the thicket of guards, plus a handful of fifties—just for insurance. Bribery never went out of style.

From that moment on, the wind whistled hard through his open window with a reedy whine. The speedometer only slowed when Tom could no longer see the tracings of Las Vegas in his rearview mirror. He continued another ten miles and then pulled off to the side of the road. Slipping from the Hummer, he promptly threw up. To clear the images dancing in front of his eyes, he poured a thermos of water over his head.

After a couple minutes, he scrutinized the map, growing tattered with use. "A clear shot, boy. A clear shot. And after Des Moines. . ." His voice trailed to silence.

Scanning the road southward, behind him, he saw no movement, no squad of NMM nipping at his heels. At the far edge of the southern horizon, he saw a thin blue wisp of smoke. It may have been a fire or a simple gathering of dust by the dawn breeze. Dismissing it as harmless, he climbed back into the driver's seat.

"Let's head north, boy. We have some miles to cover."

A thick white fog flowed around the barn, carried by the faint winds. Father William awoke early and stood, stretching and yawning, at the wide barn door. The first rays of sun tinted the hills to the east a pale, hazy rose.

Father William lost himself in a fog of memories. So many souls he had known. He had touched them, had been part of their lives. But now, after the Silence, they were lost to his world forever.

Why didn't I touch them with God's grace when I could see them? Why didn't I take things more seriously then?

He pumped gas into the campstove and struck a match. He would make a strong pot of tea and toast the remaining few slices of bread they had. He would wake Megan with the scents.

At least she is here. I can still touch her and show her the way. If I have no other chances, then I will make my last chance count for God.

He nodded solemnly.

I know we must hurry. The blackness is still there behind us. . .or maybe it's in front of us now.

Obeying a tug at his heart, the priest slipped to his knees. *Lord, protect Megan. Help me help her. Allow her to see her father once more, Lord. Help her know where You want her to journey.*

He kept his head bowed until he heard the bubbling of the water. He rose, stared hard at the whiteness outside, then turned to prepare breakfast for Megan and himself.

Confronting evil is always easier with a cup of tea and a good piece of toast.

As he held the bread with a fork near to the flame, another thought struck him: *What if this blackness has always been here— what if it's always been clouding around me, and I didn't see it? What if this blackness I'm sensing is just the evil that pervades the world? What if now—and only now—I'm noticing it?*

He turned the bread over. It was slightly burnt at the edges. *Maybe this is just your run-of-the-mill evil. Maybe it has always pursued the righteous.* He looked over his shoulder. All he could see through the barn door was white. *And if this is just a garden-variety blackness,* he wondered, shuddering, *what if Satan himself gets involved? I think I'll need more than tea if that happens.*

<hr />

The birds had never sounded as sweet as they did this morning, Rev. Moses thought. He stood at the open window in his bedroom and surveyed the green and rubble that was now Stonefort. From behind the parsonage, the faint chug and clatter of the two generators formed a comforting rhythm. Herve and his sons had built a tall fence around them to block out some of the noise. Yet Rev. Moses had grown to like the sound. To him, the noise and the faint, sickly sweet smell of the diesel fumes gave evidence to the power of God.

"My, my, my. This day is something to rejoice over."

He scanned the wide field that lay to the west of the church. New tents had sprung up like mushrooms after a spring rain. Blue and red and orange canvas and nylon squares dotted the acreage like so many flowers.

"They have responded to God's calling," he whispered. "They have listened and been obedient. They are here to start the new Eden."

The Reverend Moses dressed carefully, selecting a deep blue shirt with a deep blue tie. *Blue is my color,* he said to himself as he buttoned his collar.

The kitchen was empty. Rev. Moses toasted four slices of bread and prepared a full pot of coffee. By eight-thirty he had finished eating and left the dishes on the table, slipped on his blue sport coat, and set off to find Mayor Smidgers.

<hr />

Linda stood by the window of her bedroom and watched the Reverend Moses stride off. Before he had gone a single block, a group of people gathered around him, and his pace slowed. She watched him as he shook hands, clasping one hand over the other. With some, he placed an arm over their shoulder and bent close to their ears to speak briefly. She watched for five minutes until he turned west and headed into what remained of Stonefort's downtown.

Drawing her robe about her throat, she knotted the belt tighter. She turned back to her room and looked at her bed. The coverlet was pulled tight to the pillows, which had remained fluffed overnight. *I need a shower,* she told herself, *a long, hot shower.*

Megan woke to the smell of burning toast. It was a skill that Father William never quite got accustomed to.

"It's a matter of seconds from golden brown to burnt black," he complained as he explained one more piece of blackened toast.

"No matter," she said as she slathered a thickness of jelly on the hard bread. "It's not eggs and kippers at the Ritz—but I'll take it."

As she chewed, Father William stirred the tea. He had a tendency to chatter on and on in the morning. It was a trait Megan found both charming and disturbing.

"So you liked Manhattan? Living in New York City, I mean?"

Megan nodded. "I did. I loved the energy of it, the pulse. It was so different than Erie."

"Did you have a lot of friends? Anything like that *Friends* show on television?"

"No, life in New York was nothing like that. Well, maybe the hooking up part was the same."

"Hooking up?"

"That was what they called sex, Father William. A lot of people were pretty casual about it. Sex with no expectations."

"Really? I mean, I guess I knew that—I must have read about it somewhere."

"I wasn't into that at all," Megan said, perhaps too quick to defend herself. "But some of the girls at the office would wind up going home with half the men on the trading floor in a month."

"Seems sort of desperate," Father William replied.

"Maybe it was," Megan said. "Nobody wanted to be alone. And in such a big city with so many people, so many people were so alone. Sex was better than facing an empty room, I guess."

"Not for you?"

They had discussed many things, but nothing so personal.

"No. I mean. . .I'm no angel. I'm not going to lie to you. It would serve no purpose now. But hooking up seemed to make everyone even lonelier than they were before. Cheap and fast doesn't make for happy feelings."

"I'm glad you weren't like that, Megan," Father William said. "It's funny. I have an image of you back then, and I just can't imagine you doing anything wrong."

Megan offered a weak smile, perhaps in gratitude to Father William for his kind assessment.

"Mayor Smidgers," Rev. Moses said, smoothing at the large map showing the land plots within a ten-mile radius of Stonefort, "how current is this map?"

"Survey was done. . .let's see here. . .about six years ago."

"Nothing more current? We need to know who still lives where and which farms have been abandoned. We need to know where the fallow fields lie so God's servants can till them and bring forth crops."

Pawlis Smidgers stepped behind Rev. Moses and peered over his shoulder. The two men stood in a large field tent requisitioned from the badly damaged National Guard armory. Pawlis had rescued his desk from the town hall. The building's collapse had left deep gouges across the top, but no other damage. Both men stared at the large map that covered the entire surface of the desk.

"Well, Rev. Moses, I don't think it will be that much of a problem. Stonefort lost population over the last few years. If I don't know who still lives where, well then, I bet Cal would. If anybody knows, he's your man."

The Reverend Moses nodded. He knew as well as the mayor that Sheriff Killeen was one of the town's most prolific gossips. Arrests, parking tickets, and domestic squabbles made up Cal's job and were a staple in his diet of restricted information.

"And between the two of you," Rev. Moses continued, "you would know which farms are vacant and which houses might still be inhabitable."

The mayor stroked his chin. "Now a fair amount of them might have been done in by the quake, but we could soon enough find out. Seems like barns weathered the quake better. Fewer walls to fall down, I guess."

"Good, good, good." Rev. Moses straightened up and stepped toward the open tent flap. The small crowd that had followed him to the mayor's tent rose when he appeared at the tent's opening. He turned back to the mayor. "I suggest that you get Sheriff Killeen to scout all the houses and farms within a half-day's walk from right here. Tell him to find out which are still standing and if they're empty or not."

"We'll get right on it," Smidgers agreed. "I bet we'll have it all scouted out in a couple of days."

The reverend then turned his attention to the waiting people. "Faithful friends," he began, his deep voice rumbling across the quiet, "I know many of you have come a long way. And I want to thank you. In a few days we will be marking out farmland for each one of you. We will be assigning people to different tasks. We will soon be about God's business of creating a new Eden."

A few in the crowd applauded and a smattering of "amens" rang out.

"But for today," Rev. Moses continued, "you can lend a hand to those residents of Stonefort. Help clear the rubble or plow their gardens. Help a stranger. That kindness will bring a smile to the Almighty's face. Will you do that for Him?"

A chorus of affirmatives sounded from the group.

"Then God will bless this day," Rev. Moses pronounced. "And God will bless you."

He pivoted back to the tent. "Mr. Mayor, I need you and the sheriff to come to the church this evening. We need to discuss land allotments."

Smidgers focused briefly on his feet. "But Rev. Moses," he stammered, "I was planning on giving my brother-in-law a hand with clearing the brush from his—"

The reverend's smile quickly faded.

"Well, I guess. . .I guess I can do that tomorrow. We'll be there. . .about five?"

The Reverend Moses nodded and stepped into the brilliant sunshine, a thin smile set lightly on his face.

———

Steam billowed out of the bathroom. Linda reached out from behind the shower curtain and groped for the towel. She had only stopped as the hot water began to slowly grow cooler and cooler.

Her skin, reddened from the harsh washing, grew even redder as Linda used the scratchy towel to dry herself.

As she prepared for the day, no whistle, no song, no humming crossed her throat or lips. The only sound was the repeated rough rubbing of the towel on her skin.

———

"It's a good day for a walk," Elijah said as he wiped dry the last breakfast dish.

Becca looked up, her face wide with a smile. "Yes, yes, yes," she cried, "let's take a walk, Daddy. Let's take a walk."

Peter closed the cabinet door. Dishes were done, and a small part of him felt most settled and at ease.

"Yes, Daddy, Elijah said it's a good day for a walk. Elijah wants to take a walk too. Can we, Daddy? Can we? Please? Please?"

"Well. . ."

Their smiles met.

"Please, Daddy, please?"

"I guess it would be okay. Maybe we can pack a picnic."

Becca jumped up and down, clapping her hands joyfully. "Yahoo! A picnic."

Peter gathered up a loaf of homemade bread, some farmer's cheese, a jar of last year's peach preserves, and some three-bean salad. He filled a thermos with springwater. He loaded it all, plus three plates and a blanket, into his worn backpack.

The trio set off, heading away from town, into the promise of a beautiful morning. No more than two miles away lay a secluded shore of the river, with shallow shoal for wading and a wonderful willow tree for climbing. Becca loved that spot. They walked along the main road, in the middle of the lane, unafraid that any car would interrupt their quiet stroll. Becca kept thirty or so yards ahead, her hair dancing as she skipped along.

When Becca cleared the top of a small rise, she stopped dead in her steps and stood, motionless as a statue, with only the breeze lifting her hair from her shoulders.

"Becca?" Peter called, unaccustomed to her being still, "what is it, Becca?"

She neither turned nor answered.

"Becca!"

She remained stock-still. Peter, a sudden clamminess pervading his being, took off at a sprint to his child.

With Elijah panting right behind him, Peter reached the hill in a matter of seconds.

Spread out on both sides of a level stretch of the roadway, twenty or so tents flapped in the slight breeze. Some bore flags and streamers at their open ends. Some were painted with a rainbow of tie-dyed colors. In the middle of the roadway, people gathered, milling around a fire set in a stone ring.

The three walkers gaped at the crowd.

Where did they come from? Where are they going?

A tall man in his early twenties looked up from the circle, smiled broadly, and waved, swinging his arm in a wide semicircle over his head. "Hey! Fellow travelers! Pilgrims! Welcome. Join us! We're harmless. Join us if you'd like, man."

Peter, a hand on Becca's shoulder, exchanged a puzzled glance with Elijah.

"We're on our way to Eden, man. We're on our way to the Garden," the young man called out, offering an explanation for their being there on the road to Stonefort.

Peter sniffed the air. There was a thick tracing of something sweet, pungent, and burnt. He saw Elijah sniff at the same time and nod at him in silent agreement.

"Come on, man. We won't hurt you. We're heading to Stonefort to wait for Jesus."

A chorus of agreements and affirmations drifted out from the rest of the crowd still milling about the fire.

The young man took a few steps toward Peter, grinning and wiping his hand on his tunic. His brown hair was done in tight dreadlocks that hung down along his back, each tied with a bead. As he walked, a chorus of soft clanks marked his every step. "We're from Ann Arbor, man. We've been hiking south ever since that Moses dude started being on the radio. Since he started talking 'bout the Garden and all, we've been moving faster. You should join us. He says he can use people like us who know. . .who know how to farm and grow things."

Peter accepted the young man's vigorous handshake.

"My name's Leo—like the lion, you know?"

"Glad to meet you, Leo. I'm Peter Wilson," Peter replied and introduced Elijah and Becca in turn.

"That's so cool, man," Leo said. "Since you ain't carrying much, you folks must be some of the locals. Or else you're traveling mighty light."

Peter nodded. "We live only a mile from here."

"Then, man," Leo confided, standing closer, "can you tell us where this Stonefort is? We're not too sure. None of us brought a map, but a dude two days ago said to stay on this road, and we did. Is Stonefort near here?"

"Uh. . .yes, Stonefort is only another eight miles or so down this road. You'll come to a river and a bridge—be careful on the bridge—it's pretty rickety since the quake. Stonefort is right across the river."

Leo beamed.

"What's left of it, anyhow," Peter added. *But that's not where they should go!* The thought plagued him. Then an idea grew. *They could stay with Elijah and me. I should offer them sanctuary. . . .*

Peter smiled. It was the first thing he'd felt certain about in a long time: *I'm to offer them a place to stay.*

"Listen, you can stay at my farm. We're just over a ways. Lots of space and land for planting. Stonefort is getting crowded, I heard. And I won't force a lot of rules and regulations on you, like they would in Stonefort."

Leo looked surprised. He turned to the group. One or two shrugged. Most smiled. The rest smiled broadly, nodding in agreement.

"Really? We could stay with you?"

Peter thought for just another moment. This felt so very, very right. "Really."

"Well, that's cool, man. We're coming here to rebuild. Jesus needs us to help. Jesus said that this was the start of the end of the world, and He wants us to build the Garden so He'll take all of us to Paradise. Your farm would be as primo for that as Stonefort, I bet. And I'm hip to the hassles of too many rules, man. I got a good vibe about this—a really good vibe."

Peter could tell that this group had known rejection. Any small acceptance would be music to their ears. He assumed that was why they so quickly accepted his invitation.

"That's what happened?" Peter asked. "You think that's what happened? The end of the world?"

Leo leaned close and whispered, "I don't know what the blazes happened, man. The world went kaflooey and nothing works and people are killing each other over bread and booze. That preacher on the radio—Rev. Moses—he says he's building a Garden 'cuz Jesus told him to or something like that. And we're coming to help. At least that man knows what he's doing. I mean he's on the radio and all. That man knows the truth. They wouldn't let him on the radio if he wasn't legit, would they?"

Peter couldn't think of a truthful response.

"You want to show us the way, man. . .to your farm, that is? We're pretty tired of walking."

Becca ran through the tents and ribbons as Elijah and Peter waited until the small band packed up.

"When you said come stay with us," Elijah confided to Peter, "I thought you had gone plumb crazy."

Peter nodded. "Not your typical houseguests, are they?"

"But as soon as the words left your mouth, I found my heart growing happy. . .like it was pleasing to God that you made the invitation."

"I felt the same thing. I know it doesn't make sense, but I had such a nudge to my soul."

Laughter pealed out of the tents as Becca held a tambourine over her head and danced around.

"Do you think they really believe in God, Peter," Elijah asked as he watched, "or are they a bunch of tired hippies who are too stoned to make sense out of what happened?"

Peter shrugged. "We said we were going to try to tell others about God, didn't we? They think the world is ending. They think Jesus is coming back in a few months or something. Don't we have an obligation to tell them the truth?"

"Peter, they need to hear about God. That's what you and I

can give them. That's our obligation."

"That's what I thought, Elijah. That's what I thought."

———————

Before the Silence, it would have been easy to set the cruise control and head off on an interstate at ninety miles per hour. The roads had been straight and open.

But no longer. Now too many vehicles littered the roadway. Debris from abandoned trucks littered the asphalt, and burnt hulks of cars sat like mute charred skeletons along the roadway. Tom consulted the map again and charted his course for Iowa.

But his thoughts kept going back to his short time in Vegas. *Isn't that what I'm supposed to do—ask others for forgiveness? And look what happened!* He would not think of Norah herself—at least not yet. *I almost got killed for begging for forgiveness. Is this how this religion stuff works? Maybe believing was only for the times before the Silence. Maybe none of it works anymore. Maybe. . .maybe some people are just—I don't know—destined to be religious. Like Calvin was. And maybe some people like me are just destined to be on the outside looking in.*

He breathed in deeply. The dryness of the desert was slowly giving way to a greener scent of pine and moss as he drove north.

"Didn't Calvin tell me that once?" Tom asked Revelations, trying to remember his conversations with Calvin. "Didn't he say that God selected—no, he said God chose—the people who were going to believe in Him and get to heaven. That He chose them before they were even born. And if God chose only some people, then maybe He didn't choose others. . .like myself. Maybe God simply left me off His list of those who were going to understand all this. Does that sound right, Rev?"

The dog glanced up with sleepy eyes.

"I mean, that God may have picked Calvin and not me? Does that sound right?"

The dog stared a moment, then laid his head in his paws and

returned to his slumber.

"That's not much of an answer, boy. Not much at all."

And if I'm not one of God's chosen, then why should I even bother being good and doing the right thing? Why don't I just keep the gold and find a small place and buy myself a whole bunch of privacy? Doesn't that sound like a good idea?

"Revelations?" he called out, wanting to test his new idea on the dog. "Rev?" But the dog would not stir from his slumber. So Tom drove on in silence.

———

By midmorning the fog had lifted, and the Goliath was chugging toward Erie, Megan's childhood home. Father William prayed as he drove that Megan's father would still be alive and that God would honor his most foolish promise to Megan.

As they drew closer to Erie, signs of destruction mixed with the ordinary and untouched. Charred rubble was all that remained of what looked to be several large discount stores. The skeletons of several supermarkets also dotted the roadway. Grocery carts, shelving, and piles of paper and trash swirled about the parking lots, filled with abandoned cars.

Megan leaned forward in her seat and called out directions. The priest slalomed about the increasing maze of inert vehicles clogging the roadway. Twice in three miles he had driven onto sidewalks, steering around snaked barricades of dead cars and trucks.

"Turn left at that gas station," Megan directed.

As they headed into the older part of the city, he felt more and more conspicuous and more vulnerable. He could feel eyes dart from behind closed drapes in the houses they passed, as occupants peered hard at a strange car violating the absolute quiet of the neighborhood. He prayed that the Lord's angels would be increased around them and that they would not be set upon by a roving band of neighborhood vigilantes.

On each block, empty lots held piles of burnt and charred wood and brick that had recently been houses.

"Over there by that. . .well, it used to be a minimart. Turn right there," Megan instructed.

They were now in a residential neighborhood, guarded by towering, stately oaks and elms. Fewer homes had been torched in this area. If Father William squinted his eyes and ignored the abandoned cars littering the roadway, he could still imagine what it felt like before the Silence.

Through a gap in the trees, he could see the blue shimmer of Lake Erie and the white roughness of the waves as they struck the shore.

"Turn right here. . .down this street. . .the fourth house. . .the stone one with the white fence."

Megan had her hand on the door latch. Her face was drawn tight. The priest saw both relief and panic. The door latch clicked open even before he turned into the wide drive. By the time he switched off the engine and its last clattering gasp sounded, Megan had already bounded across the lawn to the front door of the house. She tried the door, but it was locked. Thick sheets of plywood covered most of the windows that faced the front, preventing her from peeking inside.

Her knocks rumbled in the stillness of the neighborhood. As Father William walked up behind Megan, a female voice, older and frightened, sounded from inside. "Who is it? What do you want?"

Looking as if she would soon begin to claw her way inside, Megan shouted back, "Aunt Sophia? Is that you? This is Megan. I just got here from New York. I'm looking for my father."

Her words came in a torrent and were followed by the mechanical clinks and turns of dead bolts and locks being undone.

Seconds later an old woman in her seventies blinked in the sunshine. "Megan, my little muffin," she cried as she pulled the younger woman to her in a tight embrace. Both women were sobbing with equal passion. "Come in! Hurry—you must not stay outside."

The old woman reached out and grabbed the priest by the forearm. Her grip was steely despite her age. "You drove in that car?" she demanded of the priest, eyeing his upturned collar. "Are you a holy father?"

"Yes to both questions."

"Then get back out there," she hissed.

"What?"

"Get back out there and drive the car to the back of the house. Drive it over the lawn and park it on the patio. You leave it there, and those hooligans will steal it from under your nose. Move it now. Maybe no one saw you come in here."

Aunt Sophia roughly pushed Father William back toward the driveway. As he parked the car on the middle of the brick patio, a sliding door in the back of the house opened, and the old woman beckoned him. He stepped out of the car, grabbed both of their packs and remaining food, and stepped into the house.

A thick wafting of lavender, Old Spice, and Vicks Vapo Rub nearly swept him back toward the lake. It was Aunt Sophia's bony death grip on his forearm that pulled him farther into the maelstrom of scents.

"You are a real priest? With orders from the Vatican?" she whispered urgently into his right ear. The smell of lavender came from her, he gauged, a thick application of some discount perfume. Her hair was bundled in a tight coil at the back of her head. Despite the warmth in the house, her dress looked to be black wool and was buttoned to her neck. The thick fabric flowed about her like a dark wave, almost dancing with the ground.

"Yes," he obediently replied. "I am Father William, and indeed I am a real priest. My order is authorized by the Vatican and the pope."

She craned her neck up. Father William never considered himself a tall man, yet he towered over this wizened old woman.

She narrowed her eyes. "You have your kit?"

"My kit?"

"You know, the beads and the oil and books for the ceremonies."

He nodded, thinking that no priest worth his salt is ever without them.

"That's good then," she firmly replied. "You'll need them."

"Need them?" His thoughts spun in a hundred directions.

"For Megan's father. He's dying."

Mike slowed the truck and leaned out the window, almost turning completely around in his seat.

"What? Whaddaya looking at?" Ernie mumbled, a half-chewed mass of beef jerky in his mouth.

"Just checking to see if we're being followed. Didn't like the looks of those guards." Mike tossed in his seat, getting comfortable again. "We're lucky that we saw the old boy and his Hummer this morning."

"And you're lucky I was sick or we would have zoomed right past him."

"We just need to stay behind him a few miles. He'll never know we're here," Mike said firmly. "And then. . .boom, we'll have him where we want him."

"Yeah, and this is a lot more fun than being on KP or guard duty back home," Ernie added with a grin. "When we get there, there may be more gold and more stuff in Des Moines. And when we get it, we'll be heroes when we get back."

"Panora, not Des Moines."

"Yeah. Whatever. Heroes," Ernie repeated, almost dreamily. "Being a hero would sure be nice."

Mike smiled. "It sure would, Ernie. It sure would."

Ernie smiled too. "*If* we go back, that is."

Mike reached over and twisted the dial of the radio. "See if you can find that Rev. Moses again. I really like that guy."

Ernie began to fiddle with the radio knob. "How far do you think he is from Des Moines?"

Mike shrugged.

"Be cool if we could see him," Ernie said as the wind whistled in the open window. "Real cool."

———

"The Garden will be remade right here in Stonefort."

Loudspeakers trebled the Reverend Moses's voice into a metallic and tinny chatter. Old speakers, some thirty feet in the air and clamped tight to the radio tower, vibrated with each word. His voice reached across the greening fields.

"In Stonefort! Indeed in the very midst of our humble town of Stonefort. The very place where God spared His faithful and His church and the very place where God has given us the vision of what He requires of His children. This church—yes, His church—remains standing. That is a miracle of God's holy and awesome power. He has enabled us to carry out His plans. He has given us the vision and will give you the strength to fulfill it. Just as each of you is required to fulfill the Great Commission, you now will likewise be given the power to herald His second coming. Let us prepare His church by rebuilding the Garden. The Garden of Eden will bloom again. There is land here, and people with wonderful, godly skills are coming, even as I speak, to help me and to help God rebuild the world that was destroyed."

Goodboy Slatters stood guard on the church steps, one of several guards in black uniforms that had once belonged to the Stonefort Police Department. A dark spot of virgin material lay across Goodboy's shoulder—the position of the official embroidered police patch up until now. In its place was a thick cross done in gold thread, tilted at a slight angle. Ringing that cross like a halo was a tangled vining of ivy done in greens and browns. Stitched in red letters above and below the new emblem were the words THE NEW GARDEN—STONEFORT SECURITY FORCES.

The crowd outside the church numbered three hundred. Half of them were locals; the rest were newcomers to Stonefort. All sat in rapt silence. In the field beyond the crowd, a sea of tents and cobbled-together shelters had risen.

People were not just curiously listening, they were responding. They were doing what the Reverend Moses was telling them to do.

"So, dear friends, I know that for many of you your world has gone cold and dark and evil. Satan is alive and well. It is up to the believers to fight back. And it is up to this radio station in America's true heartland. It is up to you and me. . .and to God. You know the Silence. You know the Silence is everywhere. The air is silent, save this one small voice in the wilderness."

He paused dramatically.

"And yet. . .and yet this one small voice," the reverend said, his voice growing louder and louder, building in strength and timbre until the loudspeakers and tower hummed in response, "this one small voice is crying out—speaking for the truth of God!" He paused, then declared at full volume, "You know the truth! You are hearing the truth! This *is* the truth!" His voice rang across the fields.

"And you who can hear me," he continued, his voice no more than a whispery counterpoint, "you must respond to the call of God. He wants His church rebuilt. He wants the Garden restored."

Silence reigned with a deafening intensity for a long time.

Then Rev. Moses said, "God has called, and you must follow. You must obey His commands. You must—no, we must—we must repopulate the Garden."

Silence again roared out, the loudspeakers' hum the only sound. But soon a chorus of mumbled "amens" rippled across the crowd. Then, in what could only be described as all the angels of heaven descending to earth and proclaiming the truth and beauty of God in song, Linda's voice slowly filled the air about the church and Stonefort. People closed their eyes and saw the flickering image of a radiant angel of God, with bright drapings of purples and gold and silvers.

Following her song, there was a moment when the entire world seemed suddenly right and normal again. An incredibly sweet, soothing balm of righteous silence floated over the multitude.

Then the loudspeakers crackled one last time that afternoon. "This is Rev. Moses in the Temple of God's Calling. Hear the voice of the Lord and His angels. Come and join us. Rebuild His church. Rebuild His Garden."

After the broadcast, Linda sat in her room, looking out over the chasm in the parking lot. She picked up a pen and began to write:

> *Dear Peter and Becca,*
>
> *I trust that you are both well. Things at the church are certainly exciting. More and more pilgrims and visitors are arriving every day. A lot of them mention my singing. I know it's a sin to be proud of a gift, but I am—a little. But I promise I won't let it go to my head.*
>
> *Rev. Moses wanted to know if you needed any food. The Garden will produce more than we need, he said, and if you wanted some extra, he would be willing to bend the rules a bit for me. Let me know.*
>
> *Peter, I need to ask you a favor. I miss Becca so much. Could she come and stay with me at the parsonage for a week? Maybe we could share the time with her? I wish I could be in both places, but my work is important right now. You know that Rev. Moses was sincere in offering you both a place to stay here. I know how much you like open spaces—so I have not pushed you to move to town. I know you don't like towns. But you could. I hope that you will let Becca come and stay with her mommy for awhile. She will have her own big bedroom and everything.*

Rev. Moses has big ideas for Stonefort. Farms and dor-
mitories and new buildings and food halls and kitchens. I
don't understand what happened with the earthquake and
all, but I can attest that God is blessing this work. People are
coming to the Lord, Peter, hundreds of them. I am so blessed
to be a small part of this ministry.

Please, Peter, don't be angry with me. Don't be angry
with Rev. Moses either. He is trying to do his best.

I will send this letter with a messenger. You can tell him
to wait and give me your answer about Becca. If you say yes,
maybe I could meet you halfway to town next week sometime.

. Thanks so much for your patience and understanding. I
love you both very, very much.

Always,
Linda

She signed her name with a flourish, hoping her words would
convince her husband and daughter.

Picking up a china teacup with unaccustomed delicacy, Father William sipped at the strong brew sweetened with real sugar. He smiled, closed his eyes, and enjoyed every warming sensation as the liquid rolled down into his stomach.

Megan's aunt Sophia shuffled about the kitchen. Her tattered thick wool robe covered her to the floor, making her appear much like a wind-up doll on wheels, Father William thought.

"Toast will be ready in a minute," she called out, louder than necessary. "Can't get used to toasting over a flame again." She was maneuvering an antique toaster that sat directly on top of a gas burner like a pyramid. She poked at the bread resting against its sides with a long fork. "Thought these toasters went out with the ages. Good thing my brother was a pack rat; otherwise we'd really be in a tight pickle—I mean, no toast and all."

The door to Megan's room had been closed when the priest made his way to the kitchen that morning. It had been hours past midnight when she had left her father's room. Megan had looked on the verge of collapse. Father William possessed no medical skills, but from the father's chiseled and drawn face, his flesh pearly and nearly translucent, his time had to be drawing near. His breath rattled like gravel down a pipe all through the night.

Father William thought it best to let Megan sleep. He took another sip and prayed that she would have time enough to say all that needed to finally pass between father and daughter.

She needs his forgiveness, he thought, *as well as God's.* Father William turned and listened for the surf through the open patio door that faced the lake. Blustery winds buffeted the shore and waves crashed, small and angry, against the rocks and sand.

He stood up and crossed to the counter that separated the kitchen and dining room. "Sophia, we didn't get to talk much yesterday. What was it like here. . .I mean, after the Silence?"

She slapped the toast onto a plate and slathered it with butter and jam. Father William's stomach rumbled in delighted anticipation.

"It was hell," she said. "Pardon my language, Father, but it was hell."

She gave the plate to Father William, poured herself another cup of tea, and then immediately bent down and shuffled about in a lower cabinet. She stood back up, holding a bottle of clear liquid. "Kimmel," she said with authority as she unscrewed the cap with a practiced twist. "Good for what ails you. Want a few fingers in your tea?" She winked at the priest.

The cloying scent of the alcohol made the priest's eyes water. "No, thank you, Sophia," he said kindly.

"My father used this every day of his life. Lived to be ninety-two. Never sick a day. . .well, until he keeled over at the bar. Said it was the Kimmel that kept him going so long." She poured three fingers of the liquid into her tea and took a long swallow. She blinked hard and long, then snapped her eyes open. "You asked a question?" Her voice edged to a thin wheeze.

"So how was it here? Was it as bad as everywhere else?"

She stared back at him. "Don't know. Haven't been anywhere else. But here was bad enough, Father. Bad enough for a lifetime." She pulled up a stool to the counter, took another swallow, a bit smaller this time, then hoisted herself onto the stool's seat. "For sure, no one knew what hit. We heard a week or so later what happened. The neighbor a few doors down has a radio station in his

233

basement—a whole boatload of tubes and wires—and he heard from somebody who heard it from somebody else in Washington."

He watched her take another sip of her tea.

"Solar flares." She snorted. "How could something so far away screw so much up so fast? Can you answer me that, Father? Just how in blue blazes did something that happened a million miles away ruin everything? I can't even watch *Guiding Light*."

Father William shrugged. *If I say it was God's will, people laugh with scorn. If I say it was just an accident, they ask where God was in all this. If I say it was all part of God's plan and that good things will happen because of it, they stare at me as if I've just told them the biggest lie in the universe. . . . She doesn't want an answer, and I don't want to try to give one.*

"Solar flares," she repeated and ran her fingers over her fine white hair, patting at the bun at the back of her head. "Then the animals came out. Burnt all those stores on Route 8. I don't know what they wanted to prove. Maybe they were hungry. Or had kids at home who were hungry."

"What about the burnt homes we passed coming here?"

"I don't know for certain. Some might have just been fires, some could have been those hoodlums looking for something." She drained the rest of her tea in one gulp. "Want another cup, Father?"

He had drunk three already. He did not need to be more jittery, so he shook his head.

She wobbled up and poured another for herself, this one nearly equal parts alcohol and tea. "They say it will all be back to normal soon. The fellow down the street says he gets radio now and again from Washington—or was it Harrisburg? Doesn't matter. None of them are telling the truth, as if they ever did in the first place.

"Normal they say! Be patient! Bunch of addle-headed, pig-brained nonsense, if you ask me!" she exclaimed. "But the truth is,

I still hear gunfire every night. They can't tell me that any of this is normal." She grabbed a single sheet of newspaper from the pocket of her robe and waved it in the air. "Someone said the police are welcome to come back, but Megan's father, Luther, wasn't called. I bet it's not the police at all. I bet the police turned and ran."

Father William reached out and took the paper. It was dense, with black type on both sides. A headline at the top read CITIZENS URGED TO STAY CALM. POLICE RESTORING ORDER. The paper carried a tiny tag line at the bottom of the page: PRINTED UNDER THE AUTHORITY OF THE MILITIA OF ERIE.

Sophia cocked her head toward the priest. "Bunch of loonies. Luther thought they were crackpots. But. . ."

"But what?"

"They're the loonies with the most guns. Been preparing for this for years, and now I bet the loonies are like kids in a candy store with a fistful of twenties. They have the guns and the guts, and they just took over."

Scanning the paper further, Father William read that the Militia of Erie had set up food distribution points and that their security forces enforced a dusk-to-dawn curfew. Another article urged citizens to plant gardens. A small paragraph read that the militia commander assumed temporary control over city hall. The commander warned that unauthorized activity would not be tolerated and that disobeying a member of the Militia of Erie would result in extreme punishment—up to imprisonment and even death.

The priest shivered, despite the warmth of the tea.

"Luther has been stocking up on his own for years. He's not a survivalist, mind you—just your run-of-the-mill pack rat. I guess shopping was a hobby for him after Megan left. Had no woman in the house, and I lived too far away then to keep tabs. Good thing I was here on a visit when it all happened, or I'd be gone for sure. All I have in my pantry are crackers and ketchup. Luther has enough food for a long, long time."

Father William chewed on his second piece of toast.

"Maybe two years' worth. Thirty cans of coffee! I mean to say, Father, what would any normal person do with thirty cans of coffee? And him a widower all by himself."

Father William shrugged. "I don't know, Sophia. I don't drink coffee."

Sophia polished off her second cup of Kimmel-tainted tea and readied a third. She poured the Kimmel in, looked at the near-empty bottle, shrugged, and emptied the rest in with a grin.

She propped her elbows on the counter and balanced her chin on her upturned palms. Father William thought it was an effort to keep her head from weaving.

"So, Father William, let me ask you something," she slurred slightly, "before my sweet little muffin wakes up."

"Go ahead, Sophia. Now that I've had my toast and tea, I'm ready for anything."

She looked around, as if making sure the two of them were alone. "So why the blue blazes did all this happen? Wasn't God supposed to be in control of all this?"

"He is."

She stared at him with a growing anger. "Fat chance, Father, pardon me being mean to you and all." She gestured toward the street with her hand, and her head wobbled a bit. "But those animals were burning churches as well as Wal-Marts. You mean to tell me that God had all this figured? That He wanted the churches burnt? I bet a lot of people who fancied themselves as religious folks and had been going to church all their lives wound up dead. You mean to tell me that God wanted *that* to happen to them?"

The priest focused on his teacup. *How do I answer her? I know what to say. . . . I know the right words. But I'm not sure if I even believe them. I suppose it doesn't make sense. It just doesn't.*

"Well, Sophia, God does have a plan for everything that happens," he replied. But he was really thinking, *Do these words sound as hollow as they feel when I say them?* "And His plan is perfect. . .but we don't always understand it—"

Father William stopped in midsentence. It was as if he felt a draft curling in around his ankles and grasping at his legs and body with cold, wet fingers. He shuddered, a chill slowly crawling up his back, in spite of the warmth of the house.

It is the darkness! It saw my unbelief! He closed his eyes and tried to focus.

"Sophia, I don't know for certain what's going on. But I know with all my heart that God still controls the universe. He loves me. He loves you. And He will give all of us the strength and wisdom we need if we ask Him for it."

As he spoke, his words became forceful and heartfelt, and Sophia's features relaxed and softened. The priest was never sure if it was his doing, the Lord's prompting, or the alcohol. Sophia sat still for a long moment, then nodded.

"It's not up to us to know. We need only to serve God. He'll take care of us. He will," Father William concluded.

"He will what?"

Both Sophia and the priest spun around. Megan stood in the doorway, her auburn hair tousled, her clothing of the day before rumpled, and a thick veil of sleep still clouding her eyes.

"Megan," Sophia called out, a bit wobbly. "Just in time for breakfast. Is your father up?"

Megan shook her head. "He's still sleeping, Aunt Sophia. He looks more peaceful than he did last night."

"Mornings are usually good times for him, Muffin. The nights seem to do him in."

Megan slumped into a kitchen chair, lifeless and sad. "He looks so weak, Aunt Sophia."

Sophia busied herself in the kitchen, clattering the toaster to the front burner. "He is, Muffin. It's the cancer. It came back. Found out just before the Silence. Dr. Roberts opened him up, then sewed him right back up. There wasn't anything they could do. Said the tumor was the size of a grapefruit. . .or was that a cantaloupe? Anyhow, it was some big fruit. You know, I warned your father not to do the surgery in the first place. You let the air get at these things, and they just explode. I bet that's what really happened. The air got at it."

Megan recoiled at the words. Aunt Sophia was always direct—too direct at times.

"Muffin, I know I'm talking harsh," Sophia said, sawing thick and uneven slices of bread, "but now isn't the time to be polite. There may not be much time left. Your priest here even agrees with me. It might be the end of the world."

Megan shot a jangling stare at her traveling companion.

"If it is, you need to know the truth and be able to talk with your father. If it isn't, then you still need to hear the truth."

"I know, Aunt Sophia," Megan said. "And it's okay. At least I'm glad we made it here when we did." She accepted the plate of toast and cup of tea Aunt Sophia set before her.

"Dr. Roberts said that at least this cancer doesn't cause too much pain—except right at the very end. Then it's *boom*, and you're gone."

"Could they have done anything else?" Megan asked. "I mean, I know they can't now. But could they have, you know, made him well. . .before the Silence?"

The old woman shook her head. "That's why they sewed him up. They said they could have taken the tumor out with a shovel, but that winds up killing the patient most of the time."

Megan stared at the food in front of her. The tears began. "It's not fair. I've come all this way, and now I'm going to lose him. Why didn't he tell me earlier?"

"Muffin, he didn't want to worry you. He knew you'd leave your job, and he didn't want you to do that."

Megan stared first at the priest and then at her aunt. A cold look of resolve filled her eyes. She lowered her head for a minute, then looked up at her aunt again. She squared her shoulders and sat up straight. "Aunt Sophia, I was stealing at work. I was using the company's money to make illegal trades. I was doing it in my mother's name. The only thing that saved me from getting caught was the. . .was the Silence. I'd be in jail now if it hadn't happened. If my father knew, it would break his heart."

Megan's aunt moved a chair close and sat, shoulder to shoulder, with her niece. With her bony fingers, she smoothed Megan's hair behind her ear. "He knows, Megan. He knows."

Megan blanched.

"In the mail. There was something about contracts or. . .option orders sent to your mother. He opened them and he knew."

Megan could only manage a whisper. "How long has he known? How long, Aunt Sophia?"

The old woman shrugged. "Don't know for certain, Muffin. He spoke to me about it last time I was here. What's that? About five—no, six—months ago."

Megan winced. "He knew from the very beginning." Her voice rattled off into a soft sob.

Sophia wrapped Megan in her arms and pulled her close. "My sweet muffin," she cooed, "I'm going to have to tell you something now that you need to hear. While he's still alive."

Megan refused to look up. She didn't think she wanted to hear what her aunt had to say.

"You broke his heart, Muffin. You did. Since your mother died, you were his pride and joy. He was so proud of you all the years you were growing up. When you started to make all that money, he was downright amazed. Never did he think such money was out there for a woman to make.

"He thought you were a good Christian girl, Megan. He always said that. Then that incident with Jerry and that other boyfriend of yours—the one you said stayed in the other room of your apartment at school. I never believed you. I figured you were shacking up. I don't know why, but he said he believed you, though I don't think he did really. And now this with using your mother's name. That hurt him, Muffin. That hurt him most of all."

A thin wail was the only sound Megan could make. She scrambled out of her aunt's arms. Tears blurring her vision, she stumbled from the house, across the patio, and toward the lake.

Megan knelt in the sand, her face cradled in her hands, waves lapping only inches from where she fell.

Father William stood at the top of the dune and watched her. Then he walked to her. A gull landed a few feet from him and bobbed around, watching him warily, hopefully. The barrenness of the beach was evidence that it been many days since anyone had walked by the waves and many more since any human had fed the cawing gulls scraps of picnic leftovers.

"I broke his heart," she wailed, her face tight and pained. "It's not fair, Father. It's not fair. I came all this way to see my father, only to find that he's dying. . .and that he hates me too."

Father William knelt beside Megan. "He doesn't hate you."

"He does too. Aunt Sophia said it."

He placed a hand on her shoulder and turned her toward him. "You hurt him, Megan. But hurt does not mean hate."

She turned her shoulder away and stared out across the lake. The graying sky married the graying water at the horizon, and the world seemed to disappear at their joining, fading to an infinite gray softness.

"You wronged your father here on earth, and you wronged your heavenly Father. You hurt them both."

"I hurt God?" Her voice wavered with a teary anger. "I hurt

God? And for that He takes my father from me?" She stood and stalked away, her purposeful steps the only marks on the smooth sand.

Father William rose. He said a short prayer, then followed her. He was mere feet behind her when he asked, "Megan, what was your father like when you were a child?"

She turned, clearly puzzled. "Why?"

"What was he like?" he repeated.

"He was a wonderful man. Everything he did he made seem special. He made me laugh every day."

"When did he change?"

"Change?"

"Yes, change. From what you say, he's not like that anymore."

"No, he's still a wonderful man. He tried to make me laugh last night. . .sick as he was."

"Did you ever break anything big when you were a child?"

"Break anything?"

"I mean, did you ever break something big or really valuable?"

She lowered her head and stared at her feet. "I once let off the emergency brake on the car. It rolled into a tree and smashed the bumper. I was eight."

"And then your father hated you?"

"No." The lines by her eyes and forehead began to soften. "No. . .he was angry, but he hugged me and forgave me."

"And then he changed as he got older?"

"No, he's the same man now as he was then."

Father William took a step closer. "So, if what you're saying is the truth, if you ask your father to forgive you now, he will?"

A tear tumbled from her eye, then another and another. "But I hurt him. I hurt him so much. I'm not the sweet little girl he remembers."

"If you don't ask him to forgive you, he can't."

She looked at him, her eyes liquid, her chin trembling.

"He wants to, Megan. I know that." He waited a moment. "It's just like with God, Megan. God's waiting to forgive you too. You have to ask, and He will. It will lift the burden and shame and hurt from your heart." He waited for her eyes to harden and her smile to vanish, as it had often in the past when they'd talked about God.

But this time she asked, "He will?"

"He will," the priest replied. And the confidence of that statement rang in his own heart too.

Megan sat in her father's darkened bedroom listening to his reedy breathing. She took his hand in hers and squeezed it lovingly. His eyes, now a thin watery blue, were fixed upon his daughter.

"How could I not forgive you, my little girl," he whispered, catching his breath. "You're my precious daughter. Of course I forgive you."

"Really, Daddy? For everything?"

"Megan, all you had to do was ask."

He coughed hard, and his entire body rattled in response. She helped him with a sip of water. After a minute of labored breathing, he continued. "I knew you were doing wrong, Megan. But it was your life. I raised you as well as I could. If you went wrong, it was your choice. I couldn't protect you anymore."

"And you can forgive me, just like that?"

"Megan—" He coughed repeatedly. His face reddened from the effort. "I tried to do the best I could, taking you to church and Sunday school. It wasn't easy with your mother gone. But I thought you understood. I thought the camps and retreats talked about forgiveness and faith."

Megan shut her eyes and tried to remember. She had vivid memories of the tents and the counselors and the cute boys, but nothing spiritual.

"You told me once that you came to God back then. You were seven or eight. I thought it was enough."

She squeezed his hand again and bent to kiss his forehead. Such intimate gestures were not easy for either father or daughter. "I don't remember that, Daddy."

Soul-breaking pain slipped across her father's face. "Megan, I forgive you. There is no time for grudges or unresolved issues."

Megan began to weep. She bent down and tried to lose herself in her father's frail arms. They were father and little girl again, and she felt his heart thumping against hers. She felt at peace.

"Megan, open the nightstand drawer."

She did and pulled out an ancient transistor radio.

"I gave this to you when you were in the second grade. Found it after the Silence in an old strongbox in the basement. Works like a charm."

Megan turned the device over in her hands. The black imitation leather case had cracked and peeled, but the pearl-white plastic brought a rush of memories.

"Switch it on, sweetheart. The station is set."

At first there was only static, then a chorus sounded, as if on a hill far away. A woman's voice pierced through the static with a sound that chilled Megan's heart with its beauty.

"It's time for Rev. Moses. He's building a new Garden of Eden someplace in Illinois. Gives me hope that all isn't lost. I know it sounds crazy, but it's true," said her father.

Through the radio, Megan first heard the sounds of a man's voice, deep and calm.

"I would love to go there, Megan," her father said. "I would love to see the Garden. Any garden."

A hush fell across the fields and forests.

"Be dark soon," Elijah said flatly.

"Peter," Elijah said, soft and quiet, "does your heart feel settled tonight?"

Peter was slow to answer. "You mean about Becca visiting her mother? No, not at all. I'm mostly troubled." Since that morning, when the messenger had delivered Linda's letter, it had been all he could think about.

"Didn't mean that, Peter, but I can see why you're upset about it." Elijah stroked his beard as he always did when he pondered matters. "I meant with the reverend and the Garden and all them pilgrims in town. I mean, does all of it seem like God has His hand in it? Does it seem like the Lord wants it to happen just as it's happening? Is there something there that makes a soul twinge—or is it only my soul that notices it?"

Peter was silent.

"I mean, it *looks* like a good work and all, but there's something that seems just a bit off. Just enough to get me all cattywampus."

"Cattywampus?"

Elijah laughed. "It's not exactly a biblical term, but that's the way I feel."

Peter's smile soon disappeared. "I wouldn't have known that was the right word until you used it Elijah. . .but there's something cattywampus about it in my soul too."

Smoke curled out of the Hummer's window. Riley, smoking his fifth cigar of the day, remained in the driver's seat while the other three agents stood about the vehicle, stretching their muscles, twisting out cramps in the chilled darkness.

It had been a trip of odd proportions, Riley thought. Hours and hours of tedium followed by more boredom. Then, in response to a call or a fax, they would slip into a hamlet and do the government's bidding.

These jobs, often extreme in nature, were a heart-thumping mix of adrenaline and terror and agency professionalism at its cold and calculating zenith.

Riley had been right. The government had made long strides toward taking back control. New York appeared contained.

Washington, D.C., after mobs had stormed up and down Pennsylvania Avenue, returned to quiet as federal troops spent weeks collecting the city's dead. An uneasy stillness returned to what was left of Chicago. The West Coast, ravaged by the quakes, faced a question of survival, not control. Other areas—the Midwest, the South—carried on as best they could.

"It's time, gentlemen," said Riley.

His team quietly opened doors and got in.

"Our next stop, Fort Knox."

From the rear, Mark Macaluso spoke. "Do we get to take samples?"

Riley laughed. Though almost hidden, his head bobbed in a gentle nod.

june 30

Tom and the dog sat quietly, yet very awake. It was now past midnight. The thick of the night had slipped over central Iowa. The Hummer lay hidden from view behind an abandoned roadside diner. Tom was tired—tired of driving, tired of being confused and scared, tired of feeling lost in the gray circling fog of his thoughts. He was only a few miles from his goal—and feeling a mixture of relief and regret. He was relieved that he had made it, that Calvin's wife's house lay no more than a fifteen-minute drive away.

But after this, then where? Where will I find home?

Tom switched on the Hummer's map light, reached into the pocket on the door, and silently slipped out his journal. He thumbed through the pages to review his last month of traveling.

May 29–June 25, Parachute, Colorado
Left Las Vegas with my thoughts in a hurricane. I spent one night sleeping in the Hummer someplace in Utah. Kept driving without really seeing until I began to climb through the Rockies. Overwhelming cloud of grief and depression and anxiety swept over me like an avalanche. I could not go on. Found secluded spot by a stream in a deep valley by Parachute, CO. When I first set camp, my thought was to stay forever and let the world go crazy without me. Days slipped past, and I paid scant attention to anything. Revelations looked worried—as worried as a dog can look—and kept

nosing me, as if encouraging me to move. Finally he resigned himself to lying in front of the tent and watching me. I felt more paralyzed than a man in a wheelchair. Even feeding myself took supreme effort.

Feel crushing weight of guilt and remorse over Norah and what happened to her and how evil her heart has become. But what could I do? If I'd stayed, I would be in jail or dead.

I try not to wonder too much about the son I never knew existed, but it colors every moment of every day and night. Is he still alive? Would he want to see me?

Dislocation and isolation are difficult. I begin to agonize over the small details of life and what I have lost: stopping in a donut shop for coffee, reading the newspaper while eating buttermilk donuts, doing the crossword. Small things, but those tiny stitches held the fabric of life together. I'm not even thinking of bigger losses—still too painful to put into words.

Occasionally think that someone is watching us. Used my binoculars and scanned the distant tree lines and would swear that we are alone. Yet Revelations growls at night sometimes. Maybe it's a deer. . .or a bear.

After a few weeks of nothingness, I began to pick through Calvin's books for some hint of how to deal with what has gripped my heart like the jaws of a shark. What will happen next? To both me and the world, that is. The subject scares me—I don't like to think about it. I don't even like reading about it.

If this is the end of the world, part of me cries out to remain blissfully ignorant. For if this truly and positively is the end, then I would give up hope and end it all here and now. To have no hope is a fate much worse than death. That is why I have hesitated. If God has come and gone, then I have no reason to live. That's my deepest, darkest, soul-shaking fear.

Thinking that a glimmer of hope is there, that the earth remains, gives me the barest of reasons to rise in the morning. Without that hope, there would be no reason to go on.

And yet there is a small voice inside me, saying that we will survive, we will rebuild. There is that faint illumination of hope. . .and I have to feed the dog as well. Funny how such mundane tasks provide an ongoing will to live.

I've been reading a lot lately. As near as I can figure, the Tribulation is going to be one bad time. I found this in my Bible the other night: " 'Scream in terror, for the LORD's time has arrived—the time for the Almighty to destroy. Every arm is paralyzed with fear. Even the strongest hearts melt and are afraid. . . . They look helplessly at one another as the flames of the burning city reflect on their faces. . . . The heavens will be black above them. No light will shine from stars or sun or moon. I, the LORD, will punish the world for its evil and the wicked for their sin.' "[ix]

Maybe some language is poetic and not literal. But what has scared me most is what happens before the really horrible stuff. I read this list in one of Calvin's books:

*Drunkenness (happened in L.A. all the time)
*Illicit sex (so did this)
*Gross materialism (and this)
*Rise of false messiahs and prophets
*Terrible worldwide famines (I know they're coming, if not here already)
*Disastrous earthquakes (I certainly know about that. . .more in other locations?)
*Fearful heavenly signs and disturbances (check)
*Stars of the heavens to fall upon the earth (satellites? could be)
*Events to steadily go from bad to worse (check)

*Time of thick darkness and utter depressions (firsthand
    experience with that)
*Worldwide drug usage (at least that's what CNN reported)
*Universal idolatry and devil worship
*Unchecked citywide fires (L.A. burned to the ground. How
    many others?)
*Total destruction of earth's religious, political, and economic
    systems (Since nothing works, I would say this has come
    to pass.)
*Most frightful plague in all of history (With water and
    purification systems down, who knows what horrible
    disease will spring up?)
*Famine for the very Word of God itself (It's true—I feel like
    a man at a banquet who cannot eat. I have the words in
    front of me, but they swim before my eyes. I struggle to
    understand, but it is so hard. It is as if I'm hungry, but
    even with food in my hand, I go unsatisfied.)

I have checked my supplies; without rationing, I have
more than three months' worth of food. That could stretch to
five if I am careful. With streams full of fish and gold to
trade, I don't worry about hunger.

Yet it is my soul's hunger that I find harder to satisfy. I
think I understand a little of what the Bible is saying and
what Calvin told me, but it seems so simple and too easy.
There must be more to the journey to God than this. I am
journeying to find myself, the center of myself, again. I keep
getting closer.

With each passing day, a sliver of who I was before the
Silence returns to me. It has been like going to a therapist—
without the therapist being here. After weeks of paralysis,
movement—any movement—is a joyous thing.

I can continue my journey now. I feel I must move or

*wither and perish. I need to honor my promise to Calvin.
Perhaps that is why I have the gold—to keep me moving so
I don't lie here and slip away in the wilderness.*

*Packing up the Hummer. Revelations is most joyous—as
joyous as a dog can be, that is.*

June 27, Heartwell, Nebraska

*Beautiful spring morning. Clouds like sheep in the heav-
ens. Birds chirping. Air fresh and clean and pure.*

*Then the world became dark and evil. I jammed on
brakes in disbelief. From telephone poles, for probably a mile,
hung bodies—over a hundred dead bodies, bloated and
swollen in the summer heat. Each hung from a thick rope,
gently swaying in the breeze like a macabre decoration.
Underneath one body—a young man with long hair—was a
hand-painted sign that read THIEF. Another body bore the
sign ADULTERER. The next, DISOBEYED POLICE. The next,
LOOTER. Each one hung there on a lonely, desolate stretch of
asphalt road outside Elwood, Nebraska. After the last one, a
huge billboard greeted all travelers. It was hand-painted in
black and white and done with a shaky, unprofessional hand:
"This is what happens to criminals and lawbreakers in
Elwood. If you want to break the law, don't stop here." A
small line at the bottom read SPONSORED BY THE ELWOOD
HOME MILITIA & SECURITY FORCES.*

*A hundred yards beyond was an arrow pointing north
that indicated BEAUTIFUL DOWNTOWN ELWOOD—2 MILES.
The sign had been placed well before the Silence.*

*I hit the gas hard—did not slow until I had put miles
between that horror and myself. Revelations remained curled
in a ball in the passenger-side foot well, his head tucked
beneath his paws. Heartwell isn't a paradise, but it feels especially welcoming after the ghoulish sights of this morning.*

June 28, Ulysses, Nebraska

Did not fall asleep until well past midnight, then awoke to the sun high in the sky.

Nebraska has been a horrifying juxtaposition of images.

Passed through small town of Friend, Nebraska. Pleasant little village with a welcome sign on Main Street. Had a real lunch at a restaurant: real coffee, fresh meat, good vegetables. Bartered an eighth of a gold coin for it. It was worth it. They tossed in two cans of Alpo for the dog. Rev loved every scrap.

Pleasant waitress. Asked me where I was spending the night. Said I planned on camping outside of town. She looked puzzled. "Nobody camps out in Friend. They stay at one of the houses."

"Houses?"

She winked. "You know, the houses. Didn't you see the signs?"

I said I had not.

She almost blushed, but explained. I must be dense, but it took another five minutes to understand that Friend has prospered during the Silence because of three large brothels set up in two old hotels and an abandoned elementary school. She said I could have my pick of race, sex, or age. "And you've got gold," she said. "That could buy you any pleasure you want." She winked again. "I mean, any pleasure at all."

Cold shuddered in my bones. Hard to believe a quaint Midwestern town would rely on prostitution to survive— especially in a school. What has happened to us?

Later that day I passed two other towns that left their criminals either hanging from telephone poles or tied to them, slumped and distended in death.

Yet there are small rays of hope. I see the green lushness of corn and wheat overflowing fields and farms. Can that be enough to support America?

At dusk I finally heard that preacher again—Rev. Moses, from Stonefort. His voice came in loud and clear. First time I have been able to get his radio show since those few minutes in Death Valley. Only heard last several minutes of his message. Told listeners to come to the Garden that he is rebuilding.

Odd, but I felt so much better after his calming words, like things would come back to normal. And at the end the singer—Linda, I think he called her—her voice was (I know this is cliché, but it's true) that of an angel. I did not know the song, but midway through it, tears filled my eyes and I stopped the car and wept. I wept for what I had lost—and for what that voice promised I might find again.

I'm reading Matthew in the New Testament. Near the end of the book, Jesus says of the future, the Tribulation, I guess, "'How terrible it will be for pregnant women and for mothers nursing their babies in those days. . . . For that will be a time of greater horror than anything the world has ever seen or will ever see again. In fact, unless that time of calamity is shortened, the entire human race will be destroyed. But it will be shortened for the sake of God's chosen ones.'"[x]

Why would pregnant women be so singled out? Have they done something wrong?

June 29, Tekamah, Nebraska

Driving east toward Missouri River and Iowa. Traveled north—out of my way almost a full day—because I kept encountering blockaded roads and armed guards. My usual approach is to stop as soon as I spot the barricades, then back up and drive away. I do not ask if they are charging a toll for passage or who they are looking for. I just drive away as quickly as I can. No sense in a confrontation with these militia nuts or with a few nervous farmers with shotguns.

Today I headed over a sharp rise and slammed on brakes.

Wheels screeching, smoking, and sliding. Came within six inches—literally six inches—of crushing a woman walking alone in the dead center of the road. She turned her head, her face a clenched mask of fright. Then she turned all the way around and I saw her belly. She's pregnant. After the fear left her face, an angelic smile radiated from within her. Revelations sniffed at her hand and grinned, wagged his tail.

I opened the door, and the dog climbed into the back without being told. The woman sat, folded hands in her lap, then fell asleep.

Our new traveling companion is Mary Keller, 23. She is eight months' pregnant. From Trenton, New Jersey. Moved to Albion, Nebraska, in March. Husband on business trip to England when Silence hit.

"He's gone," she said flatly when I asked after she woke up. "He'll never be back."

Mary knew no one in town, ate most of her food in two weeks. She had heard radio broadcasts of Rev. Moses and his promise of a new Garden of Eden. So she headed to Stonefort by herself. "I'd rather starve to death on my way to something better than hide and die alone and scared, huddled in a cold house."

She carried a box of saltines with her, her only food for a week. She had two blankets and one change of clothes. "It's all I could carry." She had no idea how far Stonefort was, only that she needed to travel east. It appears that this Garden in Stonefort is becoming a beacon of hope. I pray it is what the Reverend Moses has promised.

Tom closed the journal, switched off the light, and leaned back in his seat. He turned his head slightly and listened to the calming sounds of Mary's rhythmic breathing. Tom narrowed his eyes but would not sleep. He would merely watch—and wait through the night for the first gold glint of dawn.

In the battered, littered truck cab full of beef-jerky wrappers, stains, sweat, and other unpleasant odors, Mike and Ernie sat three thousand yards from where Tom, Mary, and the dog rested in the safety of the Hummer.

"We're getting closer," Mike whispered. "It looks like only a thumb-width on the map."

Ernie, his mouth full of jerky and warm soda, nodded vigorously. He peered into the darkness and swallowed audibly. "You know," he whispered, "I've been thinking."

"About what?"

"About our plans."

"What about them?"

"Well, we been following this guy for what? Over a month? Camping out all that time in, where was it again, Colorado?"

Mike nodded and kept his stare fixed on the distant horizon.

"Well, we knew all the while where this gold is. In Iowa. Why didn't we just drive there and take it ourselves?"

Ernie turned, and even in the faint light of the rising sun, Mike could tell he had a proud, smug look on his face for having thought of this. Mike didn't want to ask Ernie why it had taken him over a month for the thought to surface.

"Because there may be more than one person there, you doofus," Mike answered. "If this guy gets the gold, then leaves with it, we can take him easy. It isn't the same trying to take the gold off a dozen people."

Ernie looked confused at first, then finally began to nod, as sagely as he could appear.

"Megan," Father William began, breaking the stony silence of the last twenty miles, "we do not have to make this trip. Your father said as much to me. He didn't want this to be a dying man's last request."

"I know that. I really do," she said as she gathered her long auburn hair into a ponytail. "But there is nothing to hold me to Erie. Aunt Sophia has enough food and water for a hundred years. The neighbors will look in on her every day. The only thing she'll run out of is Kimmel, but not for at least a year or two. We'll be back by then."

Father William smiled. "Had the times been normal, I would have counseled her to battle that appetite for drink. It's not healthy."

Megan smiled too. "You know, Father, she'll outlive us both."

The priest nodded in agreement.

"Father, I know we don't have to go to Stonefort. But you heard my father. You heard him talk of how he wished he could see green fields and a golden harvest. You saw him almost weep when he heard that true Christians were gathering to rebuild this nation, with God as their foundation. How could I ignore something that meant so much to him? How could I not honor something that brought him so much joy in his last days? How could I not make this pilgrimage? He wanted so much to taste the fruits of that Garden. . .even if it had to be through me. I can't ignore his last wish. I just can't."

Megan paused. "It's not like we have anything else to do," she said, grinning. "So I guess if we're living on guesses, then I guess we should keep going."

She's right, Father William thought. *There's nothing holding us anywhere. It truly feels like God wants me there, in Stonefort, too.*

"Your father was a nice man," the priest said softly. "If only I could have known him better."

Megan's smile was thin, hinting at the pain of her loss mixed with the pleasure of her memories. "He *was* a wonderful man." She blinked away a tear. "It wasn't long enough—just two weeks. Yet I am so grateful that at least I had those."

Father William glanced over at his traveling companion. Her

sleeves were rolled up to her shoulders, and her skin was now toasted the color of caramel. It suited her green eyes, he thought. She leaned one arm out the open window of the Goliath. The early morning breeze lifted her hair, and the golden-red tendrils fluttered in the sunlight. For the first time since they met, Megan appeared to be at peace. There was a softness about her mouth. The tension had drained from her eyes. She finally seemed comfortable within herself.

The priest recalled Megan's last few days with her father. She had crawled into his pale, sticklike arms and wept like a lost child. The priest had seen the grace of God flow through the man, a man ravaged by disease and pain. Her father had struggled to stroke her hair with a weakened, shaky hand and had whispered that everything would be all right and that he still loved Daddy's little girl. He had once again told Megan that he forgave her for everything. And as he forgave her, the heavy, invisible burden slipped from his daughter's shoulders. All she could do from that point on was to stay in the comfort and safety of her father's arms.

Two days later, as the morning sun poured like honey into his room, Megan's father had fallen asleep. He never woke again.

It had taken the priest six hours to dig a grave on the bluff overlooking the lake. Only three mourners gathered at the site. Had one or two of his friends from the police force been alerted, a hundred friends and fellow officers would have been there to say farewell. But Megan insisted that to do so would jeopardize her aunt's long-term safety in the house. A hundred people knowing she was alone would spread to two hundred, then three hundred, and soon one person who should not know of her solitary existence would know. In a time of Silence, silence was often the best protector.

Now, two weeks after his death, Father William and Megan had set out to find the Garden—the Garden that had provided a thick ray of sunshine and hope to her father in his final hours on earth.

The little Goliath, jam-packed with food, gas cans, sleeping bags, tents, and camping gear, strained over the rolling countryside of western Pennsylvania. It gasped up the hillocks and roared down the valleys as the warmth of spring gave way to the heat of summer. The priest sighed. His gut, his heart, perhaps his soul, relaxed. Troubles lay behind them, he thought, and what lay ahead was a new and wonderful adventure—a time of discovery, a spiritual pilgrimage.

And perhaps, even a glimpse into God's working in the world, he ruminated. *How else could anyone explain the Reverend Moses?*

But as he finished that thought, the inner blackness that seemed to haunt him these days reappeared, nipping at the edges of his awareness and filling his sidelong vision with the flickering, ghostly image of evil. He blinked rapidly, trying to clear the sight from his eyes. A cold rivulet of sweat trickled down his back, and he felt the blood drain from his face.

And as they drove toward Stonefort, the panic rose further.

⬥

Megan sat quietly in the passenger seat. She closed her eyes, and the dream came back.

I'm walking along a quiet stream in the woods. This man appears. He's older than me, but he's blond and very handsome. But why is he here with me? Why am I giggling and blushing?

She held her eyes firmly shut, enjoying the wave of emotions.

He takes my hand, and we walk along the stream. And then we kiss. It is so pure and sweet and innocent, and I enjoy it very much.

The car swerved, but she kept her eyes tightly closed.

Then I see this little girl. Is it his daughter? She is crying, and I don't know why. It looks like there's blood on her hands. She cries, but I take her in my arms and she stops. She looks at the man and smiles, then hugs me back. . .like we all have known each other for years.

Megan's eyes flickered open and she smiled.

I don't understand any of this, but I am willing to wait until it happens.

Leaning back in his chair, the Reverend Moses offered his beatific smile to all who gathered around the table. In the space of only a few months, Stonefort had become the unofficial nexus of all Christianity in North America. Just outside the doors of the parsonage, in the fields and farms around Stonefort, nearly ten thousand people had gathered, all in response to the power of his voice and the truth of his message.

He leaned back farther and interlocked his hands behind his head. *Others are on the air now,* he thought, gazing at his loyal assistants who waited for his words during the daily staff briefing, *but I was the first. And so far, according to Herve, we're still the most powerful station. He says that because of where the tower is located, on a clear day we can reach all of America!*

He drummed his fingers on the arm of the chair. *No sense in starting before the coffee gets here. I hope Marliss will have some of those chocolate donuts. I really love those donuts.* He sniffed the air, trying to detect a hint of the sweet frosting.

Marliss Soderburg shuffled in from the parsonage kitchen. One hand drooped close to her waist, carrying a full pot of freshly brewed hazelnut coffee, and the other hand bore a full tray of three dozen small chocolate donuts, dripping with a thick layer of homemade chocolate frosting.

The Reverend Moses's eyes sparkled. "Marliss, my sweet lady," he called out, motioning her close to his side, "I swear to the heavens above that you are planning to spoil me right into a larger vestment."

Reaching over, Moses took three warm donuts in his hand and popped one into his mouth. A thin chocolate halo had formed about his lips. He mumbled, "Marliss, is that true?"

She blushed, set the coffee down, and shuffled back out of the room.

After the coffee and donuts had made their way around the

table, the reverend was most glad to see that two donuts remained on the tray for the second loop around the table. The two did not make it past his plate.

"Gentlemen and ladies," he said after a mouthful of coffee washed down the last donut, "it would be best if we begin."

All fell silent.

"Shall I pray?"

There were no objections, so he began, "Dear Lord, please bless us, Your servants, in our efforts to follow You and to rebuild the Garden. We know that You are watching over us. Let us show Your love to all those who have traveled so far to serve You."

He looked up. Every head was still bowed. "Amen," he said softly and watched as every head bobbed back to upright. Then he asked, "First order of business?"

Sheriff Cal Killeen produced a series of maps and colored overlays. The first map indicated abandoned farms and farmland. The second overlay indicated which farms had been parceled out to the first pilgrims to Stonefort and the Temple of God's Calling. Sheriff Killeen had made sure that every two dozen pilgrim planters had one experienced farmer in their midst. These men—and a few women—were promoted to captains of the Garden and were instructed to teach those less knowledgeable about proper planting techniques and tending-to-the-garden skills. The third and fourth and fifth overlays indicated which lands were still empty and the order in which they would be filled. All land in a twenty-mile radius of Stonefort was labeled, indexed, and categorized.

"You need to consult me, Sheriff, about who will be stationed in which fields," Rev. Moses warned in a quiet voice, "for Jesus needs to be part of this decision. I need to give guidance in such important matters."

The sheriff nodded quickly. He also indicated that the new and expanded security forces ensured a peaceful transition from isolated rural farmland to the pilgrim-saturated Garden. Nearly five hundred men, most with police, military, or security backgrounds, were deputized into the New Garden–Stonefort Security Forces. These men, some who worked on the farms as well as carrying out policing duties, were fanned out in a wide circle, preventing any unauthorized movement through the Garden and ensuring that those workers assigned to specific tasks actually accomplished those tasks.

Other than the couple hooligans who attempted to steal a tractor and another few stragglers who attempted to make off with some very green corn, there had been no executions in Stonefort.

Mayor Smidgers outlined the procedure for designating which pilgrims were placed in which locations. Those with absolutely no experience in farming—the white-collar workers who had a plethora of office and computer skills—were assigned to farms and farmers who needed simple, brute labor to till and cultivate and water what used to be done by machines. The only requirement for these jobs, Mayor Smidgers said laughingly, "was a strong back and a weak mind—no, a willing spirit." Everyone, including the Reverend Moses, laughed.

Mayor Smidgers assigned to his former town councilmen the task of collecting seeds and supplies and ensuring their equitable distribution. A smaller task force was in charge of collecting necessary medical supplies. Mayor Smidgers gave these men the authority to "use whatever means necessary to keep the workers in the gardens healthy." Three tractor-trailers, locked and guarded in the church parking lot, housed the supplies that the medical committee had previously secured from the surrounding communities.

Herve Slatters stood and presented a rambling, disjointed report on news he gathered with the town's ham radio. From parts scrounged and taken from several sources, Herve had built a formidable listening post to the rest of the world.

From what Rev. Moses could gather, there was no one or no area that had been spared the disastrous impact of the Silence. It sounded as if Japan had been nearly leveled by tidal waves and earthquakes. England suffered from riots and the first signs of the return of what Herve called "the Black Death plague." South America was in chaos, but the more closely the economy was to a subsistence level, the better off the peasants were. Other reports, Herve said, came from countries he'd never heard of. "But they're all in bad shape," Herve said, "so I guess it doesn't really matter—since I can't do anything about it, that is."

There were splinters of the United States that continued to function as best they could. The president and much of the government had managed to return to Washington. Next to Rev. Moses, the president was most often heard on the radio. He had promised every week that the situation was returning to normal and that soon solutions would be found that would have society back on track. His messages, Herve remarked with a caustic laugh, were "full of lies, smoke, mirrors, and more lies."

"But we in Stonefort are doing well," Smidgers interrupted. "Wouldn't you all agree? That we're making progress? That God is blessing our work? That He will grant us a harvest sufficient for our numbers? That no one is going to bed hungry in Stonefort? That Jesus is being honored here? That we will have enough stores and provisions to truly rebuild the Garden in the coming year?"

There were nods all around.

A farmer by trade and the president of the Grange, Bob Kruel spoke for the first time. "From the acreage we have planted and from the labor we have at hand, there'll be enough food for twenty thousand over the winter. It may get monotonous—corn and oatmeal and bread and the like—but we'll have food. We'll have meat too—not every day maybe. We still have a couple of big dairy operations, some hogs and chickens too. It should be more than enough."

Rev. Moses gave a contented sigh.

"Of course," Kruel explained, "we know we have God with us.

That is a tremendous benefit. The rest of those heathen countries—well, God only knows what temple they bow down in, if any at all."

Again a chorus of nods followed his statement.

Ternell Slatters, recently appointed head of construction, reported that much of the rubble in town had been cleared away, most of it by a laborious passing, hand-to-hand, of every stick of debris from the center of town to the town dump. The human conveyor belt had stretched for more than four miles and had been in place for nearly a week. But now Stonefort looked clean and ready for the rebirth of the Garden. New barracks and shelters were being constructed.

"And the addition to the parsonage?" Rev. Moses asked, tapping his pencil on a clean yellow legal tablet that lay before him.

"Uh, um. . .that was started last week," Ternell mumbled.

"Well, nothing has been accomplished in nearly four days—other than tossing lumber around and digging a big muddy hole at the side of the building," the reverend countered, his tone darkening. "I need the extra sleeping quarters for important visitors. We will need our privacy for our private deliberations."

All of a sudden the atmosphere became chilly. Ternell's eyes darted about the room, looking for support. He didn't find any. "Should I set a bigger crew of workmen on that?" he asked timidly.

"Yes, Ternell," the reverend responded. "That would be a *most* appropriate response."

Silence settled over the group.

Rev. Moses reached for his cup and sipped at the lukewarm drink. "Any other reports?"

No one raised a hand. Mayor Smidgers coughed, squirmed in his seat, and tentatively said, "Uh, we said last week—I think it was last week—that we were going to discuss the matter of what happens to lawbreakers and the like. I mean, those two incidents that Sheriff Killeen mentioned. . .well, none of us wants those repeated. Bad for morale, I say. We need to be following some written-down rules."

The reverend offered a loud sigh that could have been a sigh of boredom.

"Sorry to make the meeting go long," the mayor apologized, "but we need to figure out what sort of. . .well, what sort of legal system we're going to use. Is it the state and federal system we had? Or because that all flew out the window with the Silence, do we do something different? Judge Larimar is dead, and the county isn't going to be having elections anytime soon. I mean, who is going to decide things? Do we need to elect somebody?"

Mayor Smidgers appeared as uncomfortable as a man can get. His face reddened, and beads of sweat formed on the crown of his head. "I mean. . .like take for instance, Peter Wilson."

"What does he have to do with any of this?" Rev. Moses squawked.

Mayor Smidgers looked down at his hands. Two drops of sweat fell to the table, reflecting in the morning sunshine. "Well. . . I mean, don't all of you know? He asked me over ten times now. I mean, his daughter is here with her mother. We all know that, don't we? I mean, we all know Peter brought her into town like her momma asked nearly a month ago now. The little one wanted to see her momma, and that was fine. But Peter's been asking to see her as well.

"I sure don't want to pry into other families' business and all, but the little girl hasn't been allowed to even come back to visit him, he says to me. And he says that isn't right. Peter's asked me what I'm going to do about it. I mean, I am the mayor of this town. That should count for something, he said." The mayor pawed at the sweat above his eyes with the sleeve of his shirt. No one spoke.

Rev. Moses stared hard at the mayor. "A child should be with its mother. That's obvious."

Gulping, Mayor Smidgers continued. "But who's making it legal? That's what's confusing Peter. . .and me as well. Who's setting the laws on this?"

The Reverend Moses turned and faced the mayor front on. The mayor seemed to shrink in response.

"Why, Mayor Smidgers," the reverend replied, his voice tight and in control, "that law comes from God. If anybody around here needs God's laws interpreted, I suggest you send him to me. I will tell him that God's laws supersede any of man's laws."

The mayor blanched a shade whiter. "And so you're saying that you'll do the deciding in such cases."

A full minute passed as Rev. Moses glared at the hapless mayor. "Yes," he finally said, a dark iciness in his words, "that is indeed what I am stating." He stood and pushed back his chair. "Any other questions?" He did not wait for a response, but turned and walked from the room.

<hr />

From the barn behind them came rhythmic tapping. The group of travelers from Ann Arbor had settled down on Peter's land. They shored up the barn's supports, built walls, added insulation, cut windows, and soon the rickety structure was transformed into a dormitory of sorts. Today Leo and a team of five others were nearly done shingling the barn's leaky roof, using shingles that had lain in the barn for nearly a decade.

Peter formulated no plan in regard to these people, no organized agenda, save that he knew he had a chance to share the Word of God with them. Something in his heart had called him to make the offer to these few dozen stragglers. They were lost and had no true idea of just how lost they were. Peter knew it was time to put his faith into action. If they lived on his land, he could easily share Christ with them. If they moved on to Stonefort, they would only have Rev. Moses's voice in their ears.

Scarcity of land was not a problem. Peter had land enough for all. Most of the farm he inherited had lain nearly dormant for years. More than fifty-five acres covered with thick, black loam were available for pasture and planting. Another thirty acres stood dense and green with hardwood and pine. A stream full of fish ran through the center of his parcel. It could provide food for twice their number. And Peter, not the Garden, still laid claim to this plot of earth.

In the midst of weeding a bed of lettuce, Peter folded his arms, rested his hands on the end of his hoe, and stared off at the western horizon. His back was wet, and beads of sweat clung to his brow. He stood motionless.

When a tap came on his shoulder, Peter was so startled that he dropped his hoe.

"Looking for Becca?" Elijah asked.

Peter nodded. "It isn't right what's happening. I should be able to do something about it. I can't stop Linda from staying in Stonefort—she's an adult. But aren't we bound by law to share in raising our child? Don't I have rights to see my flesh and blood?"

Elijah rested his hand on Peter's shoulder. "Isn't the mayor going to talk to the council or whoever's running the town? He should be able to do something about it."

Bending, Peter retrieved the hoe and began attacking the weeds between the rows of lettuce. Each time the blade fell, a hissing chop of green leaf and black dirt sounded.

"Mayor Smidgers?" Peter snorted. "Nice man, but he won't stand up to Moses. And if he says no, then that's where the discussion stops."

"You can't be so sure, Peter," Elijah replied. "God's still in this, isn't He? You've been praying about this, haven't you?"

Peter whacked at the ground, harder than usual. He turned over a thick clump of dirt, alive with worms wriggling to flee from the sun's bright heat. "God? I hope you're not saying that God is only favoring Rev. Moses." Peter laughed. "If being on the radio and running that town and having a couple thousand new people move into Stonefort means that God is on his side—well, I guess that's true."

Elijah stepped back to his row and began weeding again.

Peter recognized this discussion. It was a repeat of the discussion of the day before, and the day before that, and the day before that.

"And I *am* praying, Elijah. I tell you that. For the first time in my life, I'm in prayer nearly all the time." Peter stopped and wiped his face with a stained bandanna. "Some of my prayers—like knowing what to say to our friends from Ann Arbor and praying for a good harvest—well, they're prayers that I think God would want to answer. Those are easy prayers. But what I struggle with are my angry prayers, prayers about Linda and Rev. Moses. I'm not sure if God likes those as much. I know I don't like them. They don't provide much comfort when I'm done.

"She's living there with a man who calls himself a man of God. Doesn't anyone else see that? Why else would she abandon her husband? Isn't it troubling for the rest of them? And that isn't right—not in front of my daughter. All I have to say about that is that he'll pay if I find out for certain that they're sinning right in front of my child."

"But Linda told you, didn't she, Peter, that she's not doing a thing that God would frown on? She said that to you, Peter. Her word counts for something, right?"

Peter only snorted in response.

The suppertime fire crackled and popped, sending sparks dancing into the sky.

Becca used to call them angels, Peter remembered. *Fire angels that were heading back to heaven.*

Sadness threatened to overwhelm him—he wondered if he would ever see his daughter again. He fought the feeling and stuffed it away, along with his anger and bitterness. *These people from Ann Arbor need to hear about the love of God, not my anger,* he told himself, *and that's what I'm going to give them.*

Leo sat on an overturned plastic pail next to the fire, warming his hands. Others from his group made a circle around the flames. Scraggly, prison-thin with long, braided hair, Leo looked nothing like a leader. Yet the group had followed him from Ann Arbor to Peter's farm without complaint. And when Peter insisted that the group give up all drug use, Leo stood in support of the decision, though at first he'd been shocked, then angry, then heartbroken. But he'd agreed.

"If we need to hear about this Jesus guy," Leo had finally said, "then I think we need to hear it with straight heads."

Peter had no doubt that a few of the group wandered off now and then and indulged, but at least such behavior was no longer condoned or practiced openly.

Tonight Leo appeared deep in thought, almost meditative, a departure from his normally bubbly self and his assortment of weird mannerisms.

"Leo," Peter asked, "what's on your mind?"

Leo stared at the fire. "Been thinking a long time about this. We heard that reverend guy on the radio, and then we met you, and then we're supposed to be reading this Bible and all." Leo stopped and tilted his head, as if hearing a high-pitched whistle from across the fields.

"And the question is?" Peter asked, trying to get him started again.

"Oh, yeah," Leo answered, his eyes focused on the flames. "What I want to know. . .is this the end of the world or what?"

Peter smiled. It was a question oft asked. In fact, he'd asked it himself. "Well, Leo, that's a big question. And even though we've talked about it before, I don't mind talking about it again."

"Cool, man."

Peter scanned the faces in the group. Some were older—in their fifties—the lines in their faces hinting at a generation of peace marches, joints, drugs, and rock and roll. Others were no more than teenagers, their faces wide and open with promise. Yet each face glimmered with a determination to find a place in a world gone topsy-turvy. Some of their friends had given up, lost that spark of hope, and were still in Ann Arbor, lost behind the haze of drugs and self-indulgence.

"This isn't the end of the world," Peter insisted. "It isn't. I know there are others—some you've heard on the radio—who are saying it is. But Jesus will spare the believers from the Tribulation."

"And this isn't that?" Leo asked. "It feels like a pretty big tribulation to me."

"Nope," Peter replied. "It'll be a lot worse. A whole lot worse." Peter paused and looked at each face again. "I don't think God would end the world with a slow crumble into anarchy and chaos. If He decided to end it, you would know for certain that He was behind it. You know, in the Book of Romans it says: 'Since we have been made right in God's sight by the blood of Christ, he will certainly save us from God's judgment.' "[xi]

Paddy Brian, a hulking bear of a man with the fringe on his mostly bald head tied into a ponytail, called out, "So this Silence and the earthquake wasn't powerful enough for God? Man, what more does He have in store for us if that wasn't enough?"

The group laughed, but the laughter was tinted with nervousness and fear.

"Paddy, God is in control now," Peter said calmly. "And He was in control then. I don't understand everything He does. Maybe He wants all believers to realize that the end is near—the end of the world and all. Maybe He wants us to get busy telling others."

"Like you're doing with us? You know, man, like telling us about Jesus and stuff?"

"Yes. Well, at least what I'm trying to do."

Peter stood up. His thoughts ran clearer when he stood and walked. It must have been because of his years of pondering the mysteries of the universe while walking the woods with a rifle in his arms.

"I know that I'm seeing this. . .well, it's like the Bible says, through a mirror.[xii] There are some folks, like Rev. Moses, and I'm not picking on him exactly, but you know what he's been saying. They claim to have what the Bible says about the future all figured out. You've heard him talk about the seventh seal and what the white horse means and what the seven riders mean. If he's right, then he has the future down cold. And maybe he does. But my question is, Who are we to think that God has to follow our interpretation? I mean, no matter how well reasoned and researched our interpretation is, does God have to make His actions fit into our scenarios?" Peter stopped and looked down at his feet. He cleared his throat and continued.

"You must remember one thing. Whatever happens, God will be in control. Maybe a year from now, or ten years from now, we'll stop and look at our past and see how all of it fit together today. Don't think for a minute that those who say that what's happening right now is exactly as they said the Scriptures said it would happen. Maybe, just maybe, some of what they claimed would happen matches the Bible, word for word. But some of it may have been coincidence. Maybe some things that the smart people said would happen have turned out to be just one big lucky guess."

Peter let several heartbeats pass, then spoke again. "God is in control now."

Leo's brow furrowed in concentration. "So then, what do we do?"

"You know the answer to that, Leo," Peter replied.

"You mean all we have to do is follow Jesus?"

Peter nodded.

"And do what He said to do?"

Peter nodded again.

"Man, it seems too simple. There's gotta be more to it than that. I mean, if what you say is true, then it was harder for me to join the Cub Scouts than it is to get into heaven."

"That's right, Leo. It is simple," Peter replied. "Follow Jesus. Take up His cross and do what He would do. It's real simple. Love one another. Serve one another. Honor God. Simple stuff. But it means giving your life away. You didn't have to do that to become a Cub Scout. But with Jesus you do. You give your life to Him, and He gives it back tenfold."

"What about all this seventh seal and white horse and pale rider stuff?"

"I can't explain all of that to you. I don't get half of it myself. But even if you knew exactly what it all meant, would it mean that you shouldn't fix the barn roof? Should you put that off since it's not raining now?" Peter replied.

"Well, I guess not."

"Does it mean you shouldn't plant and put up for the winter?"

"No."

"Does it mean we might not have much time to share Jesus with others?"

"Well, man. . . .I guess it does mean that."

Peter smiled. "Then I guess we know what to do."

As the fire died down, Leo's face faded into the darkness. But his answer rang clearly: "A simple answer. So alrighty then. Let's do it."

—⚙—

"My fellow Americans, this is President Garrett. I wish you well this evening and trust that you are safe and secure during these turbulent times. Thank you for tuning in to my weekly address. For those of you who have just acquired a radio, I will recap much of the information from previous broadcasts, as I've been doing these updates for some weeks now. Please note that while many of my words are known to you already, there is much information that is new and of the utmost importance to your survival and our survival as a nation.

"Though these times look dark, I urge you to take heart. Take heart, for though we have been battered and bloodied by nature and the cosmos, we have not been beaten. Take heart, for we as a nation are persevering—persevering through a time of extraordinary calamity and chaos. Take heart, for no matter what the obstacle, it will never be big enough to defeat the indomitable spirit that resides in the heart of America. We will never be beaten. We will never give up.

"As I speak, order has been restored in many areas that have suffered greatly by civil unrest. Units of the armed forces of our nation have regained control of New York, Philadelphia, Boston, Newark, and Washington, D.C. As I speak, peace and calm are being restored to other cities across this great nation.

"The military has been given powers by my executive fiat to set up *pro forma* governments in the newly peaceful cities. I urge all citizens to heed their instructions. Until civil law and civil security forces can be reformed, the military will be in charge.

"Perhaps you have heard rumors of tragedies overseas. As you well know, since the Silence, the truth is hard to ascertain and verify. There have been unverified reports of unrest throughout the Middle East. Some have said that the area is reported to be in flames. According to those sources, units of the Russian republic's army have pressed southward in order to gain control of the Middle East's vast oil reserves. Yet I am not convinced, nor are our sources convinced, that these reports are genuine. In much the same fashion, there have been scattered and unreliable reports that a plague is sweeping across Africa and parts of Europe and threatening Asia. I report these to you so that you may know that these are unverified and speculative. Pray that these are exaggerations and that our sister nations will be able to recover, even as we are doing.

"By no means has America remained unaffected, as you well know. California suffered a series of massive earthquakes, unparalleled in recent history. Chicago and much of the Midwest have also been struck by quakes.

"Whether the solar flare was in some way responsible for such events is unknown. Our scientists claim that no one could have predicted such an event, and given such information, there was no means to defend against it.

"But despite loss of life, destruction of property, and dislocation of great numbers of our citizens, we are pulling together as a country. We know that many of us are gone—some without notice or explanation. But those who remain must carry on. And that is what I urge every one of you to do. Carry on in the great spirit of great Americans. Look to George Washington and Abraham Lincoln, men who carried on in the face of danger and disappointment. They carried on because they had a vision and because they were assured that God had a plan for this country.

"And God still has a plan for America. Whether your god is Mohammad, Buddha, the Great Spirit, the god within us all, or the God of the *Holy Bible*, we must look to that higher power to give us strength to carry on and wisdom to know what to do next.

"I urge each of you to stay where you are. Avoid travel. It is dangerous and unnecessary. Stay where you are, plant a garden, and prepare for the winter.

"I want every citizen to take heed to what I am about to say: You must obey anyone in a U.S. Army uniform. They represent the new law of the land, at least until order is completely restored. If they have not set up a command post in your town yet, they soon will. When they arrive, you must obey them.

"Until they come, stay where you are and plant your gardens. We can turn America into a garden—a true Garden of Eden. Remember, no one man has an exclusive franchise for building such a garden. It is the right of every American to share in the bounty of this good earth.

"So I urge you all to remain calm. Remain where you are, for our country will soon be restored to its former grandeur.

"Thank you, my fellow Americans. Take heart, and may God bless you all."

Riley smiled and clapped his hands in a slow, theatrical gesture. "Very inspiring, Mr. President. If you keep giving these speeches, eventually someone out here will believe you."

Riley's team chuckled as the Hummer continued down the interstate, alone, slaloming between the carcasses of dead and abandoned cars and trucks.

"Surely, Mr. Lyton, you must be mistaken. I haven't seen Calvin for nearly twenty years."

Tom could see only an eye and a slice of Deborah McClure's mouth as she spoke from behind the still-chained door. From what he could determine, she was a most attractive white woman in her early fifties, with short, sandy-blond hair. Her voice was strong, with barely a hint of fear. Tom thought he saw the glint of a pistol in her right hand.

"I don't blame you for thinking I'm some sort of lunatic. But I assure you, Ms. McClure, that I am indeed on the level. I have a bag of Calvin's gold that he wanted you to have, and I'm delivering it as my last favor to him."

"It's *Mrs.* McClure," she said, leaning several inches back into the darkened and well-boarded house, "not Ms. I never liked that title. It's *Mrs.* McClure. I was married and proud of it."

Mrs. McClure's home lay just off a country road covered with a green shading of trees. It had taken Tom all night, all morning, and part of the afternoon to get up the courage to approach Deborah. In the fading light of a warm summer afternoon, Tom had missed the entrance twice. The Hummer barely fit between the towering oaks that lined the narrow drive. The windows and doors of the rambling farmhouse were covered with sheets of plywood and corrugated metal. A few second-story windows were covered with only slats of wood, and those alternated with open space, providing some ventilation. From what Tom had seen as he drove up and parked, the front door was the only unbarricaded opening into the house. With a whisper, he had told Mary and the dog to stay in the car while he finished his cross-country errand.

"It's not that I don't want to believe you, Mr. Lyton, but your story is just. . .well, a little crazy."

Tom shrugged. He had expected this reaction, yet he hadn't been able to fashion a response that would make it all sound normal.

The woman behind the door angled about, staring beyond Tom to the large, mud-caked vehicle in her driveway. "And who is that with you?" she asked. Tom knew she was carefully masking any fear in her voice.

Tom couldn't help but grin. "Mrs. McClure, it gets even crazier. That's your ex-husband's dog, Revelations, and the woman is Mary Keller, who is very pregnant. I picked her up on the west side of the border between Iowa and Nebraska."

"Revelations?"

"Yes, that's what Calvin called him. I've been calling him Rev."

"I want you to answer me honestly, Mr. Lyton. Promise?"

Tom nodded.

"Was Calvin a Christian? Had he come to the Lord? I'm asking because I don't know why else any man would call a poor dog Revelations."

Tom peered over his shoulder at the Hummer. The dog had his head out the window and a doglike grin on his face. Tom was sure by now that the dog had extrasensory powers and knew when others were talking about him.

"Mrs. McClure, I'm not a man who can judge. But if any man should be called Christian, Calvin was that man. He was kind and decent and knew a lot about the Bible."

The door shut with a harsh click. Tom's eyes widened. *What did I say?*

Then, just as abruptly, the door swung open, and there stood Mrs. McClure, dressed in an Iowa State sweatshirt and jeans, with work boots and thick white socks. On a table just inside the door lay a very large handgun, at least six inches larger than the pistol Tom carried.

"Mr. Lyton, you pull that vehicle of yours around to the side and into the garage. It should fit—the doors are big enough for a tractor. Then you bring that poor girl and that dog inside. Plain enough to see you've been traveling a long way without a decent meal or a bed."

―――――

Only a few minutes after Tom pulled off the deserted road, a rattling and smoking clatter followed in his tracks. A rusted pickup, now wheezing badly and listing heavily to the left, sailed past the nearly hidden drive.

"That's it!" Ernie screamed, pointing out the window as the truck rumbled along.

Mike jammed on the brakes. There was no squeal or swerving, just a long mushy groan as the truck sighed to a tired stop a quarter mile down the road.

"That's what?" Mike shouted back, worn and frazzled. He was only a word or two from throwing Ernie out of the vehicle.

"The Hummer! The Hummer! I saw it back there at the end of the drive. I saw the brake lights."

Mike eyed him suspiciously. "Are you sure? You saw a lot of Hummers in the last month. Most of them wound up being piles of old beer cans."

"Nope. I'm sure this time. It's even the right address. This is the real McCoy. He must have been going to hide the Hummer on the far side of the house. I saw the red through a gap in the trees there. I'd know the back side of that Hummer car anywhere."

Ernie rubbed his hands together in eagerness. "That's going to be the house where he gets the gold. We're going to be rich!"

Mike stared at his traveling companion. They had been together for too many long weeks. They hadn't washed in days. Their hair had grown long and greasy. Both were tired beyond belief of eating beef jerky and saltines. Both were exhausted from scanning the horizon before them. They had waited and planned and plotted for this day and this location—the junction of two lonely country roads in Iowa. If nothing else, Mike and Ernie were doggedly loyal and committed to their mission. They would succeed or perish in the attempt.

A chilling, gut-tightening anxiousness washed over Mike. Now they would have to act. Now they would have to use force. He turned the truck around and pulled it off the road, nosing it into a thicket of weeds near the house and switching off the engine. The motor snorted and coughed for another thirty seconds before limply falling into silence.

"Well, then," Mike said, "I guess we best be reconnoitering the area. Establish our perimeter. Set up fire lines. Stuff like that."

Ernie jumped from the truck and squished into calf-high mud, swearing and hooting. His feet made oozing, sucking sounds as he slogged toward the road. "Be a bear to get out of the mud," he said, shaking each foot, clumps of mud and grime loosening with each shake.

Mike eyed his partner. "Won't need to."

Ernie appeared puzzled.

"After this," Mike said, reaching into the bed of the truck and shuffling boxes and tarps aside, "we're going to be driving a Hummer." He pulled out a long orange sleeve and unzipped it. He extracted a nicked and dusty M-15. He wiped off the dust, licked his thumb, and cleaned off the rifle's sight. "Well, Ernie, it's time."

Ernie glanced at his wrist, a blank expression on his face. "Time?"

"Time to lock and load." Mike shouldered his weapon.

"But what if there're a bunch of them there? Didn't you say that we would wait until he gets the gold to take him down?"

Mike grimaced. "Yeah. . .maybe—aw, the blazes with this." He spit on the ground. "You know, I'm sick of waiting. I'm sick of beef jerky. I'm sick of following this fool around the country. I don't care if there's a hundred of them in there. We're going to get what we have coming. We are." His eyes narrowed to a slit. "Time to lock and load, and rock and roll."

Ernie giggled and repeated in a childlike, singsong voice, "Lock and load, lock and load, now we're going to get that big fat toad."

Mike rolled his eyes, then hissed, "And the big fat toad's stash of gold too." He slipped a clip into his rifle. "Now let's find out how many people are in that house."

After parking the Hummer in the garage, Tom stepped onto the back porch. He peered into the darkened house. Windows were boarded shut. Electric lights remained mute and dark. Thin wisps of candles broke the darkness, and their pools of weak light camouflaged the dimensions and colors of the room. Only yellows and grays were visible.

Tom sniffed. The house was alive with smells. A rich, heady scent of fresh bread permeated the space. Below that richness ran a sweeter scent. . .sugary and laden with cinnamon and apple. Tom closed his eyes and inhaled deeply. It had been so long since such richness had enveloped him.

A second later Deborah pulled Tom into the house with a firm grip. The dog clattered in behind Tom, his tail swishing. His nose was up, pulsing, drawing in the unfamiliar smells. Deborah nearly pushed Tom aside as she went to Mary's side, linking arms with the very pregnant woman and escorting her into the house.

"I've got bread just out of the oven," Deborah spoke, primarily for Mary's benefit, "and I traded a dozen eggs for a gallon of milk from the neighbors down the road. You'll need to drink most of it, you poor thing."

Mary seemed to be on the edge of swooning. Even in the candlelight she looked pale. So Deborah encouraged Mary to sit down on a couch just inside the door.

"Here's a footstool for your legs. And there's a comforter at your shoulder. Take it and cover yourself. Don't need you catching cold—especially in your condition."

Mary remained silent, her speech lost in the torrent of scents and sounds.

"How long yet?" Deborah asked. "A month?"

Mary remained mute, but smiled and nodded, her bottom lip quivering slightly.

Deborah turned to Tom. "Mr. Lyton?"

Tom nodded. "But please, call me Tom."

"Tom, then. You come into the kitchen with me. You can help with dinner."

Deborah stopped after only a few steps. She turned and eyed the dog, who was following them both. "He housebroken?"

Tom cocked his head at the dog, who looked up at them, grinning. "You know, I'm not sure. I've never been in an actual house with him."

Deborah lifted an eyebrow.

"But he has never gone in the car. He whimpers a bit and then I stop," Tom added hopefully.

The woman stared at the dog and bent toward him, wagging a finger at him. "You need to do your business, you bark. I'll let you out. Nothing in the house, you hear?"

The dog appeared to nod and wag his tail, smacking the side of the doorjamb with a furred thump.

Deborah fussed with an oil lantern, and soon a husky, oily glow pushed the darkness out of the large farm kitchen. Three loaves of bread lay on a cooling rack by a smoky, wood-fired stove. Next to the bread were a fat square of butter and an opened Mason jar of apple preserves.

"Down through there," she said, pointing to a narrow door by the sink. "Take a candle and fetch me some cheese, milk, and a few zucchini. We need to fix up a proper dinner for that poor child."

Nearly kneeling in the tiny, cool cellar, Tom gathered the foodstuffs. In the chilled darkness, there were barrels, drums, and crocks—all filled with cabbages, pickles, and potatoes, strips of dried beef, eggs, and gallons of oil.

These country people can survive for years I bet, thought Tom. *And I wouldn't even know how to start.*

Within ten minutes Deborah had silently fixed up a full meal: scrambled eggs, cheese, fried zucchini, bread, apple preserves, milk, and cold springwater. The wooden tray groaned under the weight as Tom carried the repast into the dining room.

Deborah bent to Mary and gently touched her shoulder, awakening her. "Time for dinner. You have to get up and eat."

———

Within an hour nearly all the food was consumed. Even the dog ate an entire loaf of bread, dipped in cooking fat, and was now busy gnawing a large beef shoulder bone that Deborah had used for soup. The grinding and crunching crackled in the darkness.

Immediately after the meal, Mary rose to help clear the dishes.

"Nonsense," Deborah said, escorting the pregnant woman to a bedroom. "You let the dishes be, child. Tom will be a gentleman and take care of them while I get you settled."

His arms wet to his elbows, Tom methodically washed each plate and set it on the drain board. There was plenty of fresh water, pouring under pressure from the large cistern on the roof. As he reached for the last platter, Deborah came to the door, leaned against the jamb, and smiled.

"You're doing very well, Mr. Lyton."

Tom smiled. "I guess I'm out of practice being civil—and being in a house."

"Your friend is settled in the guest bedroom. The poor thing fell asleep in less than a minute." Deborah reached up to a shelf over the stove. "Coffee?"

"You have coffee? I used the last of my instant weeks ago. I would love some."

Five minutes later the two sat in fat upholstered easy chairs on either side of the fireplace, sipping on the dark brew.

"Feels almost normal here," Tom said softly. "Like the Silence never happened."

Deborah nodded. "We're not too bad off around here. Mostly farmers, and we have a way of making do. Except for not having a car or electricity, I bet most of us are living as well as we did before. . .in terms of food and shelter, that is. I know I am."

"Where is Mr. McClure?" As soon as the question was in the air, Tom tried to grab it back and apologized for asking.

"No, that's fine. These are odd times, and I think that formal rules of etiquette have changed."

She smiled, then said, "Mr. McClure is dead. He died five years ago—a heart attack. A farmer's life is not stress free. Since then I've sold off part of the farm, but I still handle what's left myself. It's hard work, but what else would I do with my time?"

The burnished glow on her arms and face and the healthy thickness of her shoulders and upper arms offered silent testimony to her farming activities.

"No problems with militia or looters around here?"

"Some," she replied. "There's a big militia group in Des Moines. Some of them came around here and asked if I needed protection. I don't. And I bet every farmer said the same thing— we've all got gun cases full of rifles. Looters aren't keen on attacking when they know the farmer's bound to be home and is well armed to boot."

"What about farming? Without tractors, how is it getting done?"

Deborah offered Tom a cookie, then took one herself, dipping it into her coffee. "Most farmers have an old John Deere somewhere on the farm that doesn't have a lick of electronic gizmos on it. They all seem to work just fine. Mine does. Built in 1954, it runs as smooth as the day it came off the assembly line. And my neighbor down the way is a whiz with engines. Took him a few weeks, but he figured out how to rig his new tractor so it runs. Has to fuss with it more—the thing's more temperamental now, but he's got it running. If he has his new tractor working, then I'm sure others do the same."

Nodding, Tom sipped his coffee. It was such a rich pleasure that he couldn't help but smile and simply enjoy it.

"But anybody who doesn't have land or an old tractor, them I don't know about," she concluded. "Maybe they have other ways to survive."

"So it will be awhile till things are back to normal? Has anyone said anything about that?"

Deborah shook her head sadly. "With all my heart, I believe that the world will never be back to normal, Tom. Never."

Scratching their way to the far side of the house, Mike and Ernie sweated in the darkness. A thicket surrounded the house and barn and outbuildings—several acres of bramble, brush, and trees. Corn and beans and wheat lay in neat rows across the road.

Ernie stopped and wiped his greasy brow. Mike was red-faced and gasping; he could feel the veins in his neck pulsing. Each man was scratched and torn from the brambles.

"To blazes with all of this," Ernie swore loudly.

Mike hushed his partner, hoping that no one heard.

"Why didn't we bring a machete?" Ernie complained.

"Just shut up and get ready," Mike insisted. We don't got time to complain."

⟞⟞⟋⟍⟞⟞

"Does this spot feel okay to you, Megan?"

Megan shrugged. "It's as good a place as the last dozen you've suggested. Seems more than fine to me. We've got a stream over there for water and more than enough wood for a fire. Haven't seen anybody for miles. Looks as safe as we're going to get for the night."

After a late dinner, Father William walked twenty paces from the camp. Then he stopped and placed a hand over his heart. From that point, he turned and began to walk in a wide circle about the car and tent and campfire and young woman. As he took each slow step, he prayed that God would send His angels of light and power to guard them during the night.

It wasn't the first time in their journeys that he had secretly invoked God's name for such protection—especially for protection by heavenly and spiritual guardians. But it was the first time that something in his soul demanded it. He felt the blackness again, strong and malevolent, and warded it off the only way he knew how. With each measured step, he prayed. His slow walk took ten minutes.

"What were you doing?" Megan asked. She sat by the fire with her arms folded over her knees. Her knees were tucked under a large University of Pennsylvania sweatshirt.

"Just taking a walk, doing a little praying in the darkness."

Megan nodded. The priest knew she had not fully reconnected with God yet. He knew she stood at a distance from faith, acknowledging its power and beauty but never truly setting foot on the landscape of God. But he also had a strong desire—and an unshakeable belief—that she would someday.

He stood and searched the black limbs of the surrounding trees silhouetted against the firelight. It was as if their small fire was the only light in the world, standing as a flickering sentinel against the cold dark.

At the side of the fire, a pot full of water bubbled. Megan

carefully poured the steaming liquid over two new tea bags. As the pair sipped the strong sweet brew, they agreed the taste was a luxury of decadent proportions.

"We have six full boxes of tea bags," Megan said. "Good thing Aunt Sophia considers tea a bad way to drink Kimmel."

They both laughed. The priest got up to add a couple of arm-sized branches to the fire. Megan leaned back against a tree trunk. She sipped again and appeared deep in thought.

"Can I ask you a question?" she said.

The priest sat up straight and nodded.

"Is there still time to believe in God? Or should I have believed my friend Angela, who said that the Rapture has taken place and the rest of us are fooling ourselves to think that God is still watching over us?"

The priest focused on his teacup for a long moment.

Megan spoke again before he had managed to formulate a reply. "What are we supposed to be doing? Are we two big fools?"

Father William stood up and gazed across the sparking fire into the darkness again, trying to decide on the best answer.

"Well?" Megan said a bit impatiently. "I thought a priest would know the answers to these things."

Father William turned to her and smiled. "Maybe some priests do, but most of us didn't specialize in Revelation or prophecy. That was never taught as I studied for the priesthood. But I continued to read on my own. And I was friends with several preachers in our small town. They were fascinated by all of this theological speculation. They said that the Bible speaks of a global leader who will rise up and rule the world—that will be the Antichrist."

Megan gestured to the black sky above. "But how could anyone rule the world now? How would we know anyone would be in charge? How could anyone lead a world so badly changed?"

The priest listened carefully to her questions. "This is where I'm most confused. My preacher friends would say that this

Antichrist person shows up after the Rapture of the church—you know, after the believers are taken to heaven."

Megan continued to sip her tea. "But if every true believer was taken up, then you'd have gone with them, right?"

"God sees the heart of every person. Only He knows whether someone is truly a believer or not, because He sees their hearts. And, yes, I'm confident that I would have gone with Him." He rubbed his hand over his chin.

Megan focused her eyes on the ground. "But the Rapture could have happened, right? I'm pretty sure I wouldn't be one of the faithful who gets a free pass to heaven, not with all I did. And I don't want to be mean, but maybe you weren't good enough either, Father William." She winced as she saw the pained look on his face. "I'm sorry, Father, but I mean, maybe you were overlooked. Could that have happened? Could you have been left here on purpose?"

"I don't want to consider that," the priest said, obviously upset by the thought. "Since the Silence started, I don't know who is and who isn't truly gone. Even back home there were a lot of people who disappeared when the Silence hit, but I attributed that to the fact that they just couldn't get back home or simply stayed where they were."

"But they *could* have been raptured is what you're saying," Megan replied, leaning closer to him. "It could have been the Rapture, and we wouldn't be 100 percent positive."

The priest stood up and dusted the dried leaves from his knees and shins. "No. I don't believe it was the Rapture. I think we'll pull through it. I think that in a few years, things will be more normal and then we'll see things more clearly. I'm willing to stake my soul on that."

He breathed deeply in the chilled night air.

"I hope you're right, Father. I don't want this to be the end of the world. Not yet anyhow. I still have too many unanswered questions."

Smiling, the priest poured more hot water over the tea bag in his cup. He sipped, feeling a moment of peace.

Then, suddenly, the darkness that had been following him for a long time swept toward him and the girl like a tidal wave, closer and closer, chilling the air with a sense of dread and death. In the blink of an eye, that dark force, that black energy, shrilled and shrieked in silence just at arm's length.

It is real! The priest clenched his fists in an involuntary response. *It is real! And we have to fight it.*

That solid darkness pulsed only feet from the priest. But a shimmering—a gilded, clean shimmering—held firm between the priest and the blackness! It was then that Father William realized: God's angels were holding that evil blackness at bay! And, within a minute, the darkness began to retreat, slowly, grudgingly, giving ground an inch at a time, until it hovered, almost out of sight, in the stand of trees.

Father William stood and stared, the muscles in his jaw tight, his heart pounding, his hands trembling. Pieces of this new puzzling reality began to fall into place. *If the Rapture had occurred, then this evil, this darkness, would have devoured us by now. And since we are still here, that means that God is still in His heaven and is still protecting those who love and trust Him. Now I am sure of it. Why didn't I see this sooner?*

"So tell me again how you knew Calvin, Tom," Deborah McClure said. She had swept back some errant hair behind her ear. Even in the dim light, the woman's healthy skin seemed to glow, and her smile, though slow to arrive on her face, was now bright. Tom's heart warmed in her presence.

The room was filled with overstuffed furniture, the kind that had fallen from fashion in trendy homes. Tom liked the fullness, the softness that surrounded him. From the corner of the room, Revelations softly snored, the partially eaten bone nestled like a treasure between his front paws.

"I worked with him on a couple of projects in Hollywood. We cowrote a script that won an Emmy. He lived a few miles from me. I went there right after the quakes hit. And I promised him just before he died that I would find you."

Her smile dimmed.

"I'm sorry, Mrs. McClure. I guess I've lived with the knowledge and the memory long enough that I'm sort of calloused to the sound of it. I didn't think how you might react."

She waved off his apology with a gentle sweep of her hand. "It's fine, Tom. Like I said, it has been twenty years. I knew he had done well for himself out in California. But the death of a person who used to be close—very close—well, it hurts." Deborah reached up and touched her cheek. She may have brushed away a tear.

She is still a most attractive woman, Tom thought. *I can understand why Calvin would have loved her. But. . .*

"I can see you're puzzled, Tom," Deborah said evenly. "I can tell, even in this terrible light, that you're trying to work out the details of twenty years ago and reconcile that to the woman you see in front of you."

"Mrs. Mc–McClure," he stammered, "I have no right to ask any questions—Silence or not."

Rising from her chair, she went into the kitchen and returned with the coffeepot. She refilled his cup and ladled cream and sugar into the hot brew.

"Tom, please call me Deborah. The past can't hurt me anymore. Mr. McClure is gone, and my daughter. . .well, she lives in New York, and since the Silence I have not heard from her."

Tom bowed his head slightly. "I'm sorry."

"I know God is in control, Tom. And He does not want any of His children to worry about things they cannot change. Her safety is one of those things that I have left to the Lord. He'll be able to take care of her better than I will right now."

Tom nodded, though he did not truly understand her acceptance.

"And you're wondering about my history with Calvin?"

Tom blinked. It was exactly what he was thinking.

"It was twenty years ago and a whole world away. I'm from here, Tom. I was born here. I went to New York City to seek my fortune as an actress, of all things. I was good enough to be a star in Panora. I wasn't good enough for New York." She stared at the floor. "During all that rejection, I met Calvin at an actor's workshop. He was a visiting student playwright—a dashing, angry young man, full of life and energy."

Her eyes turned soft and moist. "We fell in love. A starry-eyed white girl from the farm with a streetwise, brilliant black man from the ghetto. And we scandalized everyone—here and in New York—by getting married. Back then it was very, very shocking. Within ten months my precious little Kallita was born. And a month after she arrived, Calvin got a call from a Hollywood producer. It was a writing job, a writing job in the Promised Land. It didn't pay much, and the three of us couldn't afford to live there at first, so he dropped us here—my parents were still alive then and their farm was pretty successful. He promised that he would come get us as soon as he was settled."

She spoke the next words slowly, as if each word caused pain by uttering it aloud. "He never came back. He called, he wrote, but his words began to grow more distant. Then one day divorce papers arrived." Pulling out a red bandanna, she wiped at her eyes. "I let him go. I had no other choice. So I stayed here with my daughter."

Tom let her words fade into silence before speaking. "And Mr. McClure?"

"Kallita was nearly seven when he came to our church. You can't realize how painful just being out in public was. Me and my daughter, who was more black than white, we were a sight. Eyes would turn; jaws would drop. It was agony for my parents." She wiped her tears again. "That dear man fell in love with me and never once treated my little girl as anything else than his own flesh and blood. I could not understand how he did that, but he did."

Words failed Tom.

"He was a wonderful man," Deborah continued, "and he showed me what believing in God is all about. He lived a truthful life. He led me back to faith."

On the verge of tears, Tom swallowed a mouthful of hot coffee. He did not want to cry in front of this woman.

"That's the short version of Calvin and me. I haven't heard from him since the divorce papers came," Deborah sniffed. "Other than what I read in the entertainment section of the Des Moines newspaper. I saw his name every few years or so."

She sat up straight, smoothed her hair, and forced a smile back onto her face. "So, Tom, you said you brought gold. Was that the truth or just a way to get a free meal?"

"It's the truth," Tom said, intensity in his voice. "It's a bag of Krugerrands. Before the Silence, that many coins were worth at least a hundred thousand dollars. I'm certain that now they're worth a lot more than that."

If Deborah was surprised, she showed no sign of it in her demeanor. "Calvin felt that guilty all these years?" she asked quietly.

"He must have. But he never said anything to me about you until the very end."

"That would be like him. He liked the surprise ending, didn't he?"

In the quiet of the room, Tom nodded and smiled. It *was* just like his old friend.

Crash! Tom and Deborah jumped. The front door splintered in with what sounded like a sledgehammer blow. A shoulder was forced against wood, and the door smashed back against the wall. The glass panel cracked into jagged pieces and fell on the floor.

Two men, dressed head to foot in camouflage and brandishing rifles, burst into the room screaming, cursing, and shouting, "Give us the gold! Give us the gold!"

⸺⸺

"Well," Rev. Moses puffed as he collapsed deep into a leather chair, "this has been the most trying of days."

His evening message finished, he had retired to his dressing room, filled with mirrors, closets, chairs, a sofa, and a dressing table. He loosened his tie and tossed it toward the valet stand. It missed and snaked on the floor. Without undoing the laces, he pried off his shoes and kicked both toward the valet. Within minutes he stood in front of the full-length mirror, tying the belt on his plush velour robe. The suit and shirt he wore for this evening's message were strewn at the valet stand. His vestments remained in a thick plastic wrap in the closet—those were for Sundays only.

He heard a tap at the door, tapping so faint that he stopped and strained, trying to locate the sound. "Yes?" he finally called out. "Is someone there?"

The door opened the width of a finger, no more. He heard a soft rustling, then a mumble of words from the other side of the door.

"Yes?" he called again, his tone edging up in a petulant manner.

The door opened a few inches wider. Seeing the black glint of coal-colored hair, he smiled and tightened the belt of his robe even more. "Linda," he said, forcing his voice deeper, "please come in."

She never truly opened the door but slid into the room sideways, keeping close to the wall.

"You wanted to see me, Rev. Moses?"

His smile broadened as he extended his hand to her. Her hand hesitated at her side, then fluttered up toward his. His beefy palm enveloped her petite hand and he tugged, escorting her to the sofa. She sat and pulled at the hem of her dress, stretching it to cover her knees. Her eyes darted about the dimly lit room, failing to find an object that felt safe to stare at. She settled on gazing at her hands, one of which was still in the reverend's grasp.

"Is the little one settled in, snug and warm?" he cooed.

For a moment, a frantic look clouded Linda's eyes, as if she were unsure which "little one" he was talking about—her or her child. Quickly she responded, "Um, yes, she's in bed. She seemed tired today."

"Such a sweet child," the reverend said soothingly. "I look at the children and I see the promise of tomorrow. Tomorrow. . . yes. . .yes. . .but I know that today is only the beginning. Stonefort will be the new Jerusalem. Perhaps God will bless us and allow us to usher in the new millennium. Imagine, poor little Stonefort as part of God's master plan. Awe inspiring, that God would use me in such a fashion."

He swung his arms as he spoke. The arm closest to Linda found a perch behind her on the top edge of the sofa. Rev. Moses thought he saw the skin on the back of her neck twitch as the fabric of his sleeve brushed against it. "Awe inspiring, that God has selected us to be his servants."

Linda nodded, eyes downcast.

"A tremendous responsibility. A tremendous challenge. So much pressure and strain and worry."

Linda kept still. His fingers enveloping her left hand uncoiled. She slipped her hand away and settled them both on her knees.

He smiled at her. "Sweet Linda," he hushed, "you will never know how important you are to spreading the word to the nation. They yearn and hunger for your sweet voice and your pure soul. They can hear it when you sing. They are blessed. You have the gift of calming men's souls."

"I do?" she asked in a timid voice.

"Everyone is seeking out a peaceful place to rest, Linda. Everyone's soul needs to find rest and peace."

She backed away an inch as he leaned toward her.

"Everyone needs to be at peace, Linda," he said, his voice an oily whisper. "Everyone. . .including me." And with that, his hand coiled back about her left hand, still resting tightly against her knees. His fingers squeezed her small fingers. She did not move, save to flutter her eyes closed.

He leaned forward, his mouth only inches from her ear. "Everyone needs peace, Linda. Everyone."

Peter wrestled with the sheet for more than an hour after going to bed. No position gave him peace. Finally tossing the sheet into a corner, he grabbed his jeans, a sweatshirt, and sneakers and slipped out into the moonless night. A throaty chorus of bullfrogs sounded from the stream, mournful and sad. Crickets and owls filled in the gaps.

He listened for a moment, then headed back inside the trailer. Standing on tiptoe, he felt around the top of a kitchen cabinet until his hands tapped against a small package. He retrieved the package, tilted the opening back, and drew out a single cigarette. He had found a full carton in an abandoned car along the main road to town and had hidden them in the kitchen.

No one would tell me I couldn't, he thought as he slipped the cigarette behind his ear, *but no one would tell me that I should either.*

He reached for matches and returned outside, walking slowly away from the barn and toward the open field. *I don't want to wake anyone else,* he thought.

A second guilty thought arose. *And I don't want anyone to catch me.*

In thirty or so steps, Peter sat beneath the tall oak tree that stood at the curve in the dirt road near the stream. He could hear the faint bubbling and gurgling of water and the splashes of fish and frogs. Wild onions scented the night. He slipped the cigarette to his lips and struck a match, illuminating his face in a golden ball of flame and light.

"Couldn't sleep?"

As Peter jumped to his feet, he nearly tumbled forward, clutching at his heart and flailing out in fright. His feet stumbled frantically for solid purchase of ground. "Good heavens!" he exclaimed as he regained his balance and a sliver of his composure. "Don't ever do that again!"

Elijah merely shuffled toward him in the dark.

"Sorry," Peter said, "I thought I was going to be alone."

Peter's heartbeats still sounded almost as loud as the bullfrogs.

"You've taken up with the wicked weed?" Elijah asked.

"Not the first time, but again." Peter scowled. "Since Becca left, I can't sleep. Thought they might help."

"Do they?"

"No, but it gives me something to do in the dark. . .other than being scared to death by friends hiding."

Elijah laughed softly. "Sorry! And I don't have any right telling you what you can and can't do. A few cigarettes won't make too much of a difference, I imagine."

The glow from Peter's cigarette lit the night air, and he exhaled a fat cloud of smoke. "Since when can't you sleep, Elijah? I thought yours was the sleep of an innocent."

"Wish it were so, friend, wish it were so," Elijah replied. As he began to pace slowly back and forth on the dirt road, the gravel crunched under his feet. "But it isn't. A couple of weeks now sleep's been hard to find."

Another puff and another exhale. "And the reason?" Peter queried. "Is it the company in the barn? Are they too noisy?"

"No, not that in the least. After dark the whole crew goes quiet as a church mouse in winter."

Even in the faint light of the stars, Peter could see Elijah stroking his beard. That's when he knew his friend was worried or frustrated. "Then what?" Peter asked.

Elijah stopped pacing. "It's the dreams. They're like a nail in the shoe of sleep—keep pricking me, canceling my rest."

"Dreams?"

Elijah nodded. "Dreams," he repeated. "Dreams of gloom and obscure things and a black sort of. . .a black sort of evil. Wakes me up in a sweat. I don't want to go back to sleep most nights."

Peter was midway through a drag on the cigarette, now all but consumed, when he gasped and coughed and hacked. It was a full minute until he regained his voice.

"Told you those things are bad for you, Peter. Told you."

Peter crossed over to his friend and clamped a hand on Elijah's shoulder. "You said a blackness. . .a darkness."

Elijah nodded. "It's not that I can truly see a blackness. It's just like the air, all around me. Like it's waiting for me—or somebody—to fulfill some grand destiny."

Peter spun around and stared behind him. "Elijah, I don't know if this means anything, but that's the same dream I'm having."

"A black sort of evil?"

"The same, Elijah, the very same. And it's out there waiting for me."

———

"Where's the gold?" one of the intruders shouted through the wool ski mask that covered all of his face, save his eyes. "Where is it?"

The other man jumped about, spinning and turning, as if he expected guards to leap from the shadows, bayonets drawn. He thrust his rifle toward Deborah first and leered as she flinched. His finger tightened around the trigger. It was a slight but horrifying gesture.

The first intruder walked over to Tom with a deliberate swagger and placed the tip of his barrel at Tom's throat. The warm metal dug into his flesh. "Where's the gold? We've followed you since Arizona, and now we want that gold! You got that?"

The other man, the shorter and squatter of the two, lifted his weapon to his shoulder and aimed it at Tom's chest. "We want the gold, you big fat toad," he shrieked in a high-pitched squeal.

Deborah had slumped backward into the thick sofa cushion, as if trying to hide herself. From the corner of his eye, Tom saw her lips move. He was certain she was praying.

"You! Woman! Stop talking!" the taller man shouted.

Deborah stopped moving her lips and closed her eyes. Tom knew she had not stopped praying.

The taller man removed the tip of the rifle from Tom's neck and then, in a casual move, swung the gun butt around in a wide sweep, with Tom's head at the end of its arc. The thick wooden stock thumped against Tom's head, and he tumbled from his chair to the floor. His attacker stood over him and pointed the gun square at his face. "So, big man in the Hummer, think you're better than we are, do you? Now you'll see who the professionals are and who's just a dumb-jerk amateur."

He bent at his knees and rested the gun barrel on Tom's left cheek. "Tell us where the gold is, or we'll show you what a professional does to. . .does to. . ." He looked over at his accomplice.

"Squeal pigeons?" responded the shorter man.

"No, that's not it."

"To double-crossers?"

"No, you moron," the taller intruder responded.

"To slackers?"

"Ernie, don't you know anything? That isn't the word I'm looking for."

"If I'm a moron, Mike, then how's come you don't know the word?"

The man identified as Mike stood back up, clearly frustrated. He pointed the rifle again at the middle of Tom's chest. "So, big man, you aren't so big now, are you? Where's the gold?"

"Yeah, you toad. We want the gold," said the man called Ernie as he stepped forward and pointed his rifle at Tom as well. Tom, the back of his head throbbing and bloody, wasn't about to move. And until this moment, there had been no time to speak.

From where he lay, Tom could see Deborah's eyes grow wide with fear. She began to sit up and lean forward, her right arm rising, her palm held out. Ernie must have seen it too—the sudden movement from the woman at his back—for as he turned, his finger tightened on the trigger. Deborah attempted to stand and call out to someone in the distant shadows across the room. . .and Ernie pulled the trigger.

The gun erupted in a deafening flash and roar that pulsed, howling, through the room. The shell tore low into Deborah's shoulder, splaying her backward against the sofa. Crimson splattered across the far wall like a rainbow.

The eyes of the two intruders met in that instant. It was as if neither man separately would have had the courage or foolishness to pull a trigger, to cleave flesh and spill blood. But together, the combination of their egos and personalities tending to the dark produced a more evil, more malevolent, entity. And it was that entity that pulled the trigger. But first it had needed the darkness that dwelt in both men to combine. Then the black evil could grow, strengthened and nourished, until it filled the room with malevolent power.

Tom saw for that instant, amid the grinning, leering evil, a look of terror and confusion and shock on both the men's faces. They froze for a brief heartbeat.

There was but a heartbeat to react.

Tom swiveled to his right and brought his foot upward as hard and swiftly as he possibly could into the groin of the man hulking above him. Mike huffed once, his eyes dulled, and he doubled over, collapsing like a rag doll, his rifle clattering to the floor.

Tom rolled from under him just as he fell. Ernie swung his rifle toward Tom, but as he did, from behind came a fierce barking as a golden, furry animal launched itself at his back. At the same moment, another woman entered the room from a darkened hallway carrying a candle.

Ernie fired wildly. The wall above erupted in plaster and dust. Tom stepped toward him and cracked an elbow across the man's nose. He dropped like a stone in a well.

Tom grabbed both men's weapons and shouted, "Mary, get me some rope! I saw some in the garage—and towels or sheets for bandages. Hurry!"

⸺⸺

Within twenty minutes, Tom had both men tied painfully tight in a pair of ladder-back chairs as Mary tended to Deborah. He had bound their legs, waists, arms, hands, and necks with baling twine and slapped a section of duct tape across their mouths.

He turned then to the two women. Mary sat by Deborah's side, a large handful of towels pressed against the gaping tear in her shoulder. The bandages grew heavy with blood. Her breathing was coarse and labored. Her face was ashen, and her eyes were barely open.

"Deborah," Tom whispered, "is there a doctor nearby?"

She struggled to shake her head. "Nearest one," she whispered back, "some twenty miles south. Never find him. . .or get back in time."

He leaned over her. "Nonsense, Deborah, you'll be fine. We've got the bleeding under control."

She licked her lips and tried to smile. "You're a nice man. . .but a terrible liar." She opened her eyes and told Mary, "Fetch me my Bible from my room. I want to have it when I go."

"Go?" Tom said loudly. "You're not dying. You're not." *Not again*, he thought, *not like Calvin.*

With the smile of an angel, she looked at Tom. "I am. Maybe I'll get to see Calvin and thank him for the gold."

The blazes with the gold! Tom raged. *If it hadn't been for the gold, none of this would have happened.*

"And don't blame yourself for this, Tom. God is still in control. It isn't your fault."

He wiped a thin bead of sweat from her forehead. "But it is my fault. If I hadn't come, then those two wouldn't have shown up."

He glared over at the pair. They were both staring at Revelations, who sat growling, teeth bared, no more than a foot from their unprotected legs and stomachs. Tom made no attempt to call the dog back. Every moment or two, the dog would lunge at them, snapping his jaws closed only inches from their flesh.

"I know why you're here, Tom. It has nothing to do with gold."

Surprised, Tom turned to face her. Her color had improved, but her shoulder still pulsed with blood. Tom knew that if he took the bandages away, a gaping hole would remain.

"You do?"

"You don't really know Jesus, do you? You don't really know the truth."

He gazed into her eyes. They were clear and sharp, at least at this moment. Mary returned with a well-worn black Bible.

"That's a good girl, Mary. Put it in my right hand, would you?" She turned back to Tom. "You don't know, do you?"

He bowed his head.

"It's simple," Deborah gasped. "It truly is." She struggled to raise her head and her skin paled. "Obey, Tom, that's all you have to do. Obey."

Her voice grew reedy and faint. Both Tom and Mary leaned close. "Tell those men that I forgive them."

Tom rocked back as if he'd been struck. "What?"

"I forgive them. . .please. . .you must tell them." With those words, Deborah slumped over, her eyes fluttering once before closing, her chest slowly collapsing, her last words trailing off into a faint whisper of forgiveness.

⸻

Two hours later, Tom reentered the house. His hands were coated black with dirt, and there were streaks of mud on his cheeks and in his hair. His boots were muddy, and his jeans were stained and wet up to the knees.

He had just finished digging another grave. It had not gotten any easier.

Revelations still sat, growling, by the two men. They hadn't moved since they'd first attempted to struggle free from their restraints. Each man now bore a set of teeth marks on his calf for his effort. Tom now reached over and tried every knot and rope. They were all tight and fast.

The Hummer sat in the drive, fully loaded with fresh food and gasoline, candles, and a set of garden tools. Mary waited for him there, her hands in her lap, her eyes moist with fresh tears. Tom had removed the spark plugs from the tractor and thrown them as far as he could into the brush behind the barn.

Now he glared at both men. He stood in front of the shorter one called Ernie. "You heard, didn't you? You heard that she forgave you for what you did to her. She forgave you for killing her, you lowlife, thieving scum. *She forgave you.*"

He stared into Ernie's eyes, wide and frightened. "Maybe even God forgives you," he continued. "But I don't." Tom swung his right arm hard and fast, smashing it against the captive's nose. It streamed blood and mucus. Tom ripped off the duct tape from the captive's mouth with a hard yank. "So you won't suffocate." Before he stepped out the door, he turned back. "But I don't forgive you at all."

As he stepped through the doorway, he shook his hand, hurting from the punch. He took all of Deborah's weapons, plus all the guns and weapons the intruders had left in a duffel bag by the garage door. Their restraints would hold them for awhile—at least long enough for Tom, Mary, and the dog to escape and continue their journey eastward.

Maybe the two of them will make it home, Tom thought, his mind ragged and tired. *Or maybe they'll starve to death in those chairs. I'm glad that's up to God.*

Taking a deep breath, he climbed into the Hummer. "Everything will be all right once we get you to Stonefort and the Garden," he told Mary. "You'll see."

Tom maneuvered the Hummer down the narrow lane again. He didn't know what to do with the two men. Maybe there were police in Des Moines, but he had no time or energy to search. And how would he be able to explain it all? No doubt he would place the gold and Mary at risk. Tom did not want to see Calvin's gold used to fund further violence. Even though he hated these men for what they had done, he couldn't bring himself to execute them. Then he'd be no better than the militia extremists he'd been dodging all along. He had to leave them.

As Tom started down the road, he spotted a pickup truck mostly hidden in a thicket near the house. Guessing it was the attackers', he stopped. When he investigated, the Arizona license plate confirmed his suspicion. He emptied two cans of gasoline over the cab and bed of the truck. As he pulled away, he tossed a lit flare back at the vehicle. The flames brightened his rearview mirror for miles down the straight-running country road.

july 15

You're saying that Rev. Moses is leading people astray?" Elijah stood with a canvas bag over his shoulder. Rising early, he was set to travel downstream to gather cattails. Cooked, the white roots tasted like a cross between an onion and a potato. Elijah had caught Peter by the big oak near the stream. Six crushed cigarette butts littered the ground by his feet. "And you been staying up all night thinking about these weighty ideas?"

"Sleep isn't part of my life right now, I guess," Peter replied sarcastically. "The night gives me time to put a lot of thoughts together."

Peter became more and more agitated every time he listened to the reverend's sermons on their small radio. Anyone who lived too far to attend the evening services received a free radio, a crude crystal set, from the reverend. That meant just by using a few batteries and a tiny speaker, everyone who fell under the umbrella of the New Garden could partake in the messages. The wooden base of the radio bore a hand-lettered warning in red ink: "This device is to be used only during Reverend Moses's and the Temple of God's Calling broadcasts. Any other usage is prohibited."

Peter often railed at the message. Elijah knew that Peter saw the reverend veering further and further from the truth, using the broadcasts to recruit new pilgrims, to solicit specific gifts of supplies, and to draw more and more attention to himself rather than to God. Peter's obvious agitation grew to the point where he couldn't even be within hearing distance of a radio when the sun drew near the horizon and the Reverend Moses drew near to his microphone.

Elijah looked worried. "I can't say you're wrong about this, Peter. Except I'm not the one that needs talking to. It's Rev. Moses. He claims to be open to all. Why not sit across a table with him and talk it out?" He hesitated, then added carefully, "Be good to talk about Becca as well. I miss her too."

"Maybe I'll do that," Peter replied. "Are you busy today? Do you want to walk into town?"

Elijah toyed with the idea. It would be good to see other people. It was exciting to see the changes that took place in Stonefort almost on a daily basis. It was good to see God at work, even though Peter dismissed it as one man's venal folly.

"Well, Peter, maybe we might travel tomorrow? I was set to get a sackful of cattails today. I wait much longer, and they'll be old and mushy."

Smiling, Peter waved to him as he set off down the stream, splashing in the cool water.

—————

The sun stood overhead, and Elijah dipped his hand in the stream, splashing it over his face and neck. His canvas bag was half full, and the wet cattails grew heavy. He bent down, reached into the water, and with a small blade cut near the bank of the stream. Pulling up the sweet white tubes, he sliced off the tops and slipped them into his bag.

From behind him, on the west side of the stream, he heard a rustling, then the snap of broken twigs. When he turned, he saw two men, silhouetted by the sun looming above him. Their faces were hidden by the noon glare.

"What's that you've got there?" the first man called out. His words were sharp and hostile.

"Cattails," Elijah said. "They're right tasty when fried."

"Who are you?" the other demanded.

"I'm Elijah Woods. I live over at Peter Wilson's place."

"Woods. . .Woods. . .Woods. . . ," said the first, running his finger down a long sheet. He flipped the pages, mumbling to himself. "You're not registered."

Elijah took one step forward. "No one said I had to register."

"You don't listen to the radio? You're not listening to Rev. Moses?"

"I have, but I haven't heard anything about registering."

"You said Peter Wilson's farm?"

Elijah nodded, shielding his eyes from the sun. The men's features were still hidden. They were dressed in olive, and each wore a baseball cap with a cross stitched on the forehead. The shadows erased their eyes and mouth.

"I don't even have a record of a Peter Wilson, let alone a farm."

Elijah's neck tensed. A drop of sweat rolled down his spine. It felt cold.

"You're not registered. You don't live on one of the Garden farms," the first man said. He placed his hand on the black wooden baton that hung from his belt and took a step toward Elijah.

"Listen," Elijah explained. "I've been living with Peter Wilson for almost two months. It's his wife that sings on the reverend's show. You can ask him."

The second man stepped forward toward the stream. Elijah heard the grass hush as the man stepped through it.

"I don't think you're in any position to be telling us whom to ask about what," the man said sternly. "We're the security around here—not you."

"I'm just saying—"

"You're saying nothing. Now give me that bag. You're taking food that don't belong to you. That's a crime in the Garden."

Elijah held his palms open. "Look, nobody's been along this

creek for weeks. Nobody else is taking these cattails. They'll go rotten in a few days."

"Do you have a hearing problem? Is that it?" one of the men asked. "I said you're in violation of the law. I don't think you have any say in the matter. You do what I say, and that's that."

"But I didn't know. . .no one said. . . ," Elijah protested.

Both men stepped to the edge of the bank. Both had their hands on their batons.

"Listen good now," the taller one said, "because I'm not saying it again. You're breaking the law. Give me the bag. Otherwise. . ."

I can't believe this, Elijah thought. *Over cattails?* "Otherwise what?"

Without a second's hesitation, the shorter one snapped the baton from his belt and swung it in a wild roundhouse. The club landed with a hollow thump against Elijah's right temple. He had no time to block the blow, and he tumbled backward into the knee-high water.

The taller man jumped down, grabbed the bag that had fallen in the shallow waters on the bank, and scrambled back up. Elijah's arms were slowly flailing in the air; he was gurgling, struggling to hold his head out of water. His eyes were dazed and unfocused. The current, slow in this part of the stream, nudged and edged him downstream. Elijah could not determine the passage of time. It might have been a minute; it might have been five.

"Is he hurt bad?" the tall man asked.

"Nah. That little tap just shook him up a bit. You know, addled his brain for a minute. He'll be fine. I bet it's no worse than a bad hangover."

"Should we. . .I dunno. . .get help or drag him up on the bank?"

"Are you nuts? He's disobeyed a direct order. And there's no record of him. He's just some worthless drifter who's trying to take advantage of the Garden. I say leave him there. He'll perk up soon enough."

"But you hit him pretty hard. I thought you just wanted to scare him a little."

"Listen—he'll be fine. Now let's go."

"But—"

"He's a no-account bum. If he dies, no one's going to miss him. Now let's go."

july 16

A bird singing. . .I hear a bird. . .or is that a door swinging. . .and why do I feel so wet. . .why am I so cold. . .where are my hands. . .why can't I stand up?

Elijah sputtered and coughed as the waters carried him downstream another twenty-five yards until he came to rest on his back on a shallow bar of rocks and mud. He lay there, staring up into the sun, blinking hard from the pain.

He thought he saw the moon against the glorious darkness and heard the shriek of an owl, flapping its wings in the pearl moonlight. He thought he heard the bullfrogs trumpet and bellow inches from him, calling for mates in their sad and lonely voices.

He thought he was awake as the dawn broke and the mists filled the meadow and stream. He thought he heard his name being called through that mist and fog. The sound grew closer. He thought he raised his hand into the first rays of the sun; he thought he called back to the sound, yet the words stayed garbled in his mouth.

He thought he felt hands upon him, calling his name, washing his eyes, lifting his body. He thought he drifted on a cloud until he landed warm and dry on the bed in his little room in Peter Wilson's barn.

Peter stood in that small room and listened to Elijah's labored breathing. A bruise, angry and purple, snaked its way across his temple and head. Elijah had opened his eyes, taken a few mouthfuls of

305

warm soup, raised his hand, and whispered, "Thanks for looking. . . for me."

A few minutes later, Elijah tried to sit up. Peter bent close to hear Elijah speak. "Peter. Warn them. You're right. . .the Garden. . . wrong. Warn them." Elijah's voice sounded like velvet tearing. He then slipped back into a deep sleep.

Peter shuddered. *I'm right about the Garden? What does he mean?*

He knelt beside the bed and prayed. *Heal him, Lord. Heal his body. And if You are calling me to speak out, then show me the way, Lord. I am only one man against thousands. Show me the way, Lord. Show me the way.*

Sweat beaded on the preacher's forehead. In the sanctuary, the humid air ebbed and flowed like languid water. Six overhead fans labored ineffectually to cool the sweating congregation. A beam of white light engulfed Rev. Moses's head, adding another layer of heat to an already steamy night. The reverend wiped at his forehead with a handkerchief.

"Is this the end of the world?" he shouted. "Have we been overlooked by God?" He let the words echo and fade until the only sound was the hum of the fans and the ruffled murmur of several hundred people breathing.

"No!" he exclaimed, answering his own question. "God is not done with this nation just yet." He wiped his head with his left sleeve, his right grown soggy and damp. "Let me list again what will happen to the church at large in the last days."

He opened a compact leather notebook and laid it flat on the pulpit, then picked up the Bible in his left hand. "Churches will turn liberal"—he spit out the word *liberal* as if it were a bitter seed in his mouth—"and they will reject the Bible and its true doctrines. Before the Silence, everywhere I looked I saw the sickening crawl of liberalism spreading its evil stain on the pure white garments of the Lord. You saw it too. Churches ordaining gays. Gays marrying in the church. Praying to God the Mother. It was sickening."

Rocking back and forth on his heels, he continued. "Communists, atheists will rise up, take arms, and oppose the church. Has that not happened in Russia, in China, and among the heathen Arabs?

"Then—I hesitate to call it a conspiracy, but that's what it appeared to be—many well-known preachers actually endorsed and worked for a world gathering of churches so that no church would stand for truth, but all would stand for 'godless inclusion' and 'fairness above righteousness.'

"And who here has not seen the moral chaos that resulted from so-called Christians fleeing from biblical doctrines, getting into spiritism, the occult, and even the worship of Satan, who masks his presence under the guise of a mother god?

"But you may ask, and I hope you do, what of those Scriptures in Matthew?[xiii] Don't they apply to now? Aren't they coming to fruition, even as we live and breathe? Matthew, who records the words of Jesus, says that there will be wars and rumors of wars. . . and do we now know for certain which nation rises up against which? Or which nation is in conflict with which? It is all rumors now. We know little of the rest of the world since the Silence. The Word states that there will be pestilence and famine. Again, that is coming to pass. . .everywhere perhaps, save for God's chosen in His chosen town of Stonefort.

"There will be earthquakes—you all know that to be true. It has occurred. The Word says there will be martyrs. New arrivals to Stonefort have told me stories of the godless rising up against the righteous—killing, maiming, destroying. Jesus says love will grow cold. I have heard stories of mothers abandoning their living babies along the roadside for scavenging beasts to feast upon—for their love was gone. Their hearts grew cold as stone.

"Matthew records that Jesus said that the entire world would hear the gospel."[xiv] Rev. Moses paused and looked heavenward, then tapped his right hand at his heart. "Do you not see our role in completing that prophecy?"

He bent to the pulpit and flipped through his well-worn Bible. "Yet there are several Scriptures that have not yet come to pass. There are Scriptures that remain unfulfilled. Take, for example, Jesus' warning of false messiahs and false prophets."[xv]

Stepping from behind the pulpit, he strode across the dark stage, the spotlight trailing him in a circle of brilliant whiteness. "You may think it odd that I would mention these Scriptures, but I have heard distant rumblings and midnight whispers. Some say that if the Scriptures caution against a false prophet, then I should look no farther than the mirror in which I shave every morning—for there is the image of a false prophet.

"Does that frighten me?" Rev. Moses paused. "It does not," he answered in a whisper. "That is why we still wait. That is why I am not afraid that the end times draw nigh. For a preacher who is ashamed of his words or who is preaching falsehoods and heretical doctrines would never mention these Scriptures. And yet, here I am, bringing them to their full disclosure before you."

He swung his arm over his head, the Bible pages riffling like leaves in autumn. "If I was a false prophet, if I had designs on being a false Christ, I would tear this page from my Bible and never speak on it again. But I have not done that. I am not afraid. I am not a false prophet nor a false Christ. Because I say these words and you know them to be truth, the predictions Christ made in the Book of Matthew have not yet come to pass—at least not all of them.[xvi] The times close in around us, dear friends, but the predictions are not yet fulfilled. There is no false prophet speaking this night. There is no beast of an Antichrist. There is not."

His hand gripped the pulpit. He lowered his head. Drops of sweat fell as he slowly shook his head. *They'll never get the sweat stains out of this suit. Land sakes, is it hot up here. We have to get the air-conditioning repaired. I need to remember to set a fire under Ternell—or Herve—to get the AC pumping again.*

"I am not afraid. God is in control. He will not take us until the Garden is restored, until Israel is rebuilt on the dark, rich soil of Stonefort. God is waiting for us to rebuild Israel and Jerusalem and the Temple right here in Stonefort. He wants us to join together in that great undertaking. He has provided land and seed and laborers. He has provided food and clothing and shelter for every pilgrim who has made the long, hard journey to the Temple of God's Calling."

Rev. Moses gazed out at the crowd with an embracing smile— the smile that might pass between a man and his lover. "You came to Stonefort to obey God's Word and to rebuild the Garden and the temple. That is a sacred, holy undertaking. You will be blessed."

He mopped at his sweaty face with his handkerchief. "But," he bellowed out, his voice rising in warning, "there are those among us who do not follow Jesus and who do not seek to be part of this Garden. Who do not seek to rebuild the Temple but to destroy it."

He felt, rather than heard, a shocked murmur ripple in the darkness. "Yes, it is true. There are those who have stolen the fruits of other men's labors and did not labor themselves. There are those who will not register and sign their names in God's Book of the Garden. And God is not pleased."

Gripping both sides of the pulpit, he added one last warning. "Dear friends, fellow laborers, all of us must work together. We must sacrifice together. We must not tolerate those among us who seek to pursue their own ideas and their own plans. For if they do that, we will all suffer and God will be grieved. You must be ever vigilant to guard yourself. You must warn the church of the voices that rise up to speak against this work. You must steel yourself against those who would destroy us, who would attempt to destroy the work of the Temple of God's Calling and God's appointed preacher. You must!"

It does look like a garden here, doesn't it, Megan?" Father William asked as the little Goliath puttered along the roadway no more than ten miles from Stonefort. "And the cars—there are so few abandoned cars in the roadway that I can actually enjoy driving."

Megan nodded. Illinois, at least this part of southern Illinois, was green and gold with crops. There were scores of workers tilling the land. As the car puttered past, those closest to the road would stop their labors and wave. Usually Megan waved back.

Her dreams had intensified, though she had not told the priest of their power and clarity. She kept seeing a little blond girl, a man with hazy features, whose name she heard in her dreams but could never remember.

Megan and Father William had puttered and wheezed across Pennsylvania, Ohio, Indiana, and then had headed west toward Illinois. Once, west of Columbus, the Goliath's engine clattered, wheezed, and shuddered to a stop. Father William said it was God's provision that had stopped them a quarter mile from a church and a pastor who had worked part-time as a mechanic. However, it took days to make the needed repairs. After that, the Goliath progressed even slower than before, sometimes groaning to reach a top speed of ten miles an hour. They broke down twice in Indiana. Father William searched for days until they found someone who was willing and able to help with repairs. Each time they found refuge with small groups of church people who opened their homes and hearts to the priest and Megan as the pair of them made their pilgrimage.

After a month of stop-and-go traveling, they were finally nearing their goal. Megan smiled at the warm sunshine. She looked over at the priest, his last collar and dark coat tattered and soiled. *Maybe we can find him a new one in Stonefort.*

Suddenly she winced, as if a pain sliced her side. *What was that? Just thinking about Stonefort and—* Another pain stabbed at her. She shook her head, trying to clear her thoughts. *I'm not supposed to go to Stonefort?*

She narrowed her eyes in concentration and tried to think about the hymn Father William was whistling.

And the Goliath puttered on, heading down a sharp incline, and turned into a blind curve of a hill by a stand of oak trees.

"Just breathe in and out, Mary. I know that sounds stupid, but you need to breathe real regular and smooth. Regular and smooth. Focus in on something that you love—a favorite vacation spot or a tropical beach somewhere."

Tom was frantic as he drove. His only map of Illinois was a gas station variety, and the road he was on didn't appear to be drawn with any great precision by the cartographer. He would have sworn that Stonefort lay to the east—the direction he was now heading—perhaps five miles ahead.

It had taken Tom, Mary, and Revelations a full month to travel no more than four hundred miles. After the horror of the shooting and the death of Deborah McClure, Tom had attempted to put as many miles between him and Panora as possible. But just past Pella, Mary had begun to cry out in pain. She had looked up at Tom with pleading eyes, her lap stained red with blood.

It had not taken him long to find a safe campsite hidden by pine and oaks on the shore of Red Rock Lake. With a painful jolt, Tom had recalled Lydia's pregnancy. Lydia had had bleeding also, and the doctor had prescribed absolute bed rest for several weeks. So Tom insisted that Mary do likewise. They had stayed at the campsite for nearly a month, until Mary had insisted that she was well enough to travel again—no matter that the child was close at hand. Both of them hoped that Stonefort and the New Garden that Rev. Moses promised would offer them safety and refuge.

"Cape May," Mary gasped through clenched teeth. "Cape May."

"What?"

"You asked what my favorite vacation spot was." She clenched her teeth and grunted. "It was Cape May."

If I don't find a town soon, I'm going to have to deliver this baby myself. Tom had neither the training nor the desire to do that.

Revelations, relegated to the backseat, whimpered and whined. He nudged at Mary with his cold nose, causing her to shriek and Tom to skid off the road, narrowly missing a faded billboard for Salem cigarettes.

Good heavens, he thought. *Where is Stonefort?* He grabbed the map, wrestling with it in the wind of the open windows. He held it against his thigh and tried to trace his position as the paper flapped and fluttered.

He glanced up. A small hill lay ahead. *If I don't see anything from the top of this hill, I'm turning around and heading back.*

⸻

The tiny Goliath was no match for the massive Hummer. Tom's lumbering military vehicle came roaring over the crest of the hill, squarely in the middle of the road, the safest place to be. The Goliath was headed for that same piece of roadway.

Tom looked up once again from the map and saw the little car and a beautiful woman, screaming, in the front seat. He slammed hard against the pedal, setting off the antilock braking system. The Hummer went into a controlled, screeching, straight-ahead slide, smoke from burning rubber billowing from all four wheels.

The Goliath did not brake as well. It swerved and spun to

Tom's right. The Hummer's nose smashed the driver-side fender of the Goliath, crumpling it back almost to the windshield. The Goliath then bounced and spun to a stop several yards from the point of impact. Tom was amazed at the damage to the old car. The engine had broken from its mounts, the left front wheel was in shreds, and the front axle had snapped in two. He prayed that the occupants of the vehicle had survived.

———

A blond man jumped out of his military vehicle and ran to the Goliath.

Megan was shaken up, but there were no obvious broken bones or wounds. Father William was rubbing his head. Megan was relieved to see that there was only a smudge of blood there.

She stepped cautiously out of the passenger side, the wind catching her hair and lifting it from her shoulders. She turned her green eyes toward the man who had hit them. "Are you hurt?" she asked.

"No, I'm fine. How are you two?"

Father William climbed out, felt his ribs and arms, and said, "I'm scared and surprised. But nothing hurts—too much."

A wail came from the Hummer, followed by a furious barking.

"She's having a baby," the man said. "Do either of you know anything about childbirth?"

Megan's eyes widened. *Is this the child? There was no baby in my dreams,* Megan thought. She stared hard at Tom. *Is this the man?* The image in her mind was strong and insistent.

"Do you?" the man asked again.

"What?" she stammered.

"Know anything about childbirth?"

"I do," Father William said, smoothing at his hair and tugging at his coat. "I know enough, I think."

Megan stared at the man, blinked several times, then licked her dry lips. "Is that your wife?"

The man looked surprised for an instant before he turned back to the Hummer, with Father William in tow. "Uh. . .no, actually. Her name is Mary Keller. I picked her up in Nebraska."

"Where are you from?" she asked.

The man was helping the priest climb into the Hummer. Megan couldn't help but notice that his vehicle had only a scratch on the bumper and a small dent. The man turned and called over his shoulder, "California. My name's Tom."

And with that, a sudden awareness swept over Megan's heart. *His name is Tom. Yes. . .yes. . .his name is Tom. And he's blond and so very handsome. I think this is the man from my dreams.*

For the first time in a long time, Megan felt a warmth begin to grow in her heart—a heart that had once despaired of ever knowing a temperature other than cold again. And she smiled.

august 1

And the child's name?"

Mary smiled, her face shining with sweat and relief, then shut her eyes. Father William, draped in a clean sheet, sat beside her, holding her hand. Two women, Anna and Lindsey, from the Ann Arbor group, worked quietly nearby, cleaning the baby, tying off the umbilical cord, and wrapping the infant in a blanket.

Opening her eyes, almost as if from a dream, Mary turned her head to the priest. "I don't know, Father. What does he look like?"

The priest's smile broadened. "Mary, he looks like a wonderfully healthy baby boy."

She laughed, then winced, the pain from the birth slowly washing from her body.

After the accident between the Hummer and the Goliath, Mary's labor had seemed to stop, as if the baby had been jarred into reluctance. Within several minutes after the accident, a swarm of people poured across the field from a nearby farm and swept Mary, as well as the other three, back to their dwellings to attend to the birth of her child. The priest was told it was Peter Wilson's farm, and the visitors were made to feel most welcome. Mary was put in Peter's trailer for her comfort. Her contractions had begun at nightfall that same day and were sporadic for the next six hours. Her cries of pain echoed through the walls of the trailer and into the moonless night.

Many years ago, Father William had taken a yearlong emergency medical training course so he might offer himself as a chaplain for a volunteer ambulance service. Occasionally he had ridden with the paramedics, offering what prayer and comfort he could. Yet he had never dreamed that he would be in charge of an emergency delivery.

But as the analytical, logical side of the priest took over, he smoothly called out orders, issued instructions for Mary, and guided her through childbirth. Despite the duration of the labor and Mary's obvious pain, the delivery went smoothly.

The child arrived with squalls and cries just before dawn on the first day of August. He blinked his eyes, looked at his mother, cried loudly one more time, and then slipped into the sleep of an innocent.

Mary gazed at the priest who had helped deliver her child. She appeared very tired, and with good reason. "No, Father William. I meant, when you look at him, what name is there? What name does he look like?"

The priest glanced at the sleeping baby cradled in Lindsey's comforting arms. He was wary about naming another's child. Besides, all he saw was a face, red and wrinkled, a pug nose, and a head rounded to a soft point.

Mary spoke again. "Father, what is your middle name?"

He pivoted quickly toward her. "No, Mary, you will not saddle him with that. I struggled hard enough with it—almost enough to steer me away from the priesthood."

She laughed. "But what was it? It can't be that bad."

He grinned. "It was indeed. Anyone who names a child Crispus, in my opinion, is not doing the child a service."

"Crispus? Sounds like a breakfast cereal."

"He was Paul's first recorded convert in Corinth. I guess my mother thought it would be a guiding inspiration." He squeezed Mary's hand. "It wasn't."

Mary furrowed her brow in thought. "Does Nathaniel work?"

"Nathaniel? That's very nice. The name means 'gift of God.'"

"It does?"

He nodded. Lindsey beamed as the baby stirred and twisted in his blanket.

"Then Nathaniel it will be," Mary said firmly and happily. "For that is what he is, a true gift of God." Then her smile wavered. "Father, this child does not have a father. . .at least not now. Will you. . .will you watch over him? Will you help teach him?"

He leaned down toward her. "Mary, I promise that with all my heart, I would give my life to keep this child from harm."

She smiled one last time, closed her eyes, and drifted off to sleep, exhausted from her labors.

Father William held her hand until her breathing slowed, then gently placed it on the bed. The baby was wrapped tightly in his blanket and placed in the middle drawer of the dresser.

Lindsey sat next to Father William, watching mother and son. "Go ahead, Father, you can go. Someone will be cooking breakfast in the fire pit between here and the barn. You're tired. Go. I'll watch them."

He nodded gratefully. His thoughts were swimming, swirling in the miracle that he had just participated in. Nothing short of a rebirth in Christ could match the miracle of the birth of a child. From the smallest portion of a man and woman grew a perfect reproduction of themselves, nestled beneath a woman's heart, nurtured by her, and sustained by God above.

To enter a world so alien would be a shock, the priest thought, but how perfectly prepared they are. Tiny toes and fingers, tiny nails perfectly matched to each. Eyes and heart and lungs and ears that function within seconds of birth.

Dear Lord, he prayed just before standing, *thank You for this opportunity to help birth this child. Thank You for the reminder that You are still in control and that You still care about us. Bless this baby and his mother. Allow him to grow healthy and strong and be of great service to You. For he is made in Your image—allow him to follow Your perfect path. Amen and amen.*

Father William got up and stepped outside, into the fresh air and the light of early dawn. After the accident, events had been such a tangled mess that he'd scarcely had time to collect his thoughts. So now he viewed his surroundings clearly for the first time since his most abrupt arrival the day before. He approached three men who were gathered at a large fire ring set midway between the trailer and a large gray barn. The men fussed at the fire, moving wood and logs about, lifting pans and lids on a blackened rack, tasting, comparing, speaking in low turns to each other.

A patchwork of new windows pocked the face of the weathered barn. The roof looked new. Three doors, freshly painted by the looks of them, divided the barn's long exposure. *Looks more like a dormitory than a barn,* he thought.

" 'Morning, Padre." The rail-thin man who spoke wore a tangle of braids and beads; his dark beard looked like a swarm of honeybees resting on his chin and cheeks.

"Good morning, gentlemen. I apologize for not having an opportunity to meet you before this. I'm Father William."

"I'm Leo, this is Clive, and that's Sid." They gave short waves in greeting.

Leo bobbed his head up and down as if it were attached by a rubber band. "Breakfast is nearly done, Father William. Would you like some?"

"Breakfast?" The priest's stomach growled in response. He had not eaten since yesterday noon. Since the Silence, mealtimes lacked regularity and consistency. "I would love some."

Soon a plate full of steaming oatmeal and wild blueberries and honey was warming his hands. A thick, grainy slice of bread slathered with peach jam rested on the rim of the plate.

"We have coffee—real coffee, Father. Would you like some? We found two hundred one-pound bags in an abandoned truck north of here."

sound. Peter held his hand tight, longer than necessary, longer than custom.

"I suppose it was fortunate that we had our accident where we did. A most fortuitous event," Father William said.

"God's planning," Peter replied. "His timing is always right." Soon he added, "We'll let the mother and child stay in the trailer. It's the most comfortable place we have."

The priest smiled, the dark fog lifting from his thoughts.

"And the young woman with you. I put her things in the trailer as well."

"That's good."

"I'm putting both of us in the new rooms in the barn. I hope that's acceptable to you. I have a lot of theological questions to ask, and you're our new resident scholar."

The priest smiled. "I'm not much of a scholar, I hate to tell you. Seminary was a long time ago. And I have placed too high a reliance on printed matter from the diocese rather than on my own exploration of the Scriptures."

Peter clasped an arm around the priest's shoulders. "Well, that may be, but nonetheless, you have just been elevated to supreme rabbi here. That might give you an idea of where the rest of us are in our biblical understanding. We need you, Father. That's why I said it's God's perfect planning."

No, this man is not the darkness, Father William realized. *But it's something else, something close.* He shivered, then tried to set his concerns aside as Peter walked him to the barn and showed him through the warren of small rooms stitched into one side of the barn and hayloft. One side of the barn's interior remained clear for storage of corn and crops soon to be harvested. In the hayloft twelve closet-sized rooms nestled against each other. None had doors, but each was equipped with a few shelves, a bed platform, and a small porthole cut just below the eaves. Two Franklin stoves stood at the ready for winter in the large open balcony of the hayloft.

"You can have this one," Peter indicated. "It's not much, but it's warm and out of the rain."

"It will do nicely, Peter."

The priest looked around. There must have been room for nearly four dozen people in the barn, between the lower level and the hayloft. "Peter. . . ," he began, not sure of why he hesitated, "may I ask you a question? I mean, after all, I've only been here for a day. Hardly gives me the right to ask anything."

"Nonsense," Peter replied.

Father William looked down at his feet for a moment, confused. "We're near Stonefort, aren't we?"

"Eight miles that way," Peter said, pointing to the west.

"Then you know Rev. Moses and all about the Garden?"

"I do." Peter's voice grew a shade colder.

"Then are you part of that? Is this farm part of God's Garden. . . or the New Garden?"

Peter stared at the priest. Voices carried from below, laughter mixed with talk. "No," he replied. "If you want to be part of Rev. Moses's Garden, then I'm sorry, but you won't be able to stay here."

Revelations bounded up from the stream, dripping water and river weed. The dog spun about, splashing water over the tent. Then he dove into the grass, rolling and nosing on his side, rubbing furiously against the green, plush earth.

In the short span of hours since arriving, Revelations, in a most miraculous transformation, became more of a dog and less of a confidant to Tom. Tom could have sworn that when the dog first saw Megan yesterday after the accident, he smiled, then padded off toward the stream. It was as if he was grateful that another might take the place at Tom's side.

Yawning and stretching, Tom stuck his head outside the tent. He had pitched it the night before near the stream, several hundred yards from the barn. After so many weeks of living a solitary

life, sleeping in close quarters with others sent a shiver through his bones. He had seen to it that Mary was in good hands; the priest and the women looked more than competent. And then he had fallen into a nervous, exhausted sleep sometime after midnight.

Now, as dawn seeped through the nylon walls of his tent, he noticed the smoke curling from near the barn and trailer. He sniffed the air. It smelled of harvest and burning oak and. . .perhaps coffee. "I think I may need to greet our neighbors—especially if they have fresh coffee."

Tom rummaged through the clothes and socks and shoes on the tent floor and pulled on a pair of jeans and a T-shirt. In the months since the Silence, his body had become lean and hard. Food had been sufficient but not to excess. He had worked hard at setting up camps and cutting wood for fires. And during the last few months, the extra pounds that he had struggled with in California had melted off. He felt a tautness in his frame that had been missing for a decade. He yanked hard at his belt to tighten the jeans. He pulled on a sweatshirt that read NBC WRITER'S GUILD. It had hung in his garage for years and was one of the few items he had rescued from his old life.

He roughed his hand through his hair, not really knowing why. Most days his appearance mattered little to him. He would see no one who would care how he looked.

I could use a haircut—a real haircut. When you cut it yourself, it looks like it.

The dog barked and whined in a friendly manner.

It's not a rabbit—that deserves a much angrier bark. I guess it could only mean. . .could only mean a visitor. He had better check. There was no telling as to a stranger's intent these days.

In the distance the stranger was bathed from behind with a soft halo of morning light. Revelations bounded and jumped by the stranger's side, his tongue lolling out, cheerful barks sounding loud in the quiet of the field.

Startled at Tom's sudden appearance, the intruder took a step back and nearly stumbled. He saw two cups in her hands. As she stepped back, the steaming liquid sloshed and a few drops fell to the ground. "I. . .I. . .I didn't mean to startle you," she called out. Her voice was throaty and rich in the early morning stillness.

Tom stood up straight, loosening his arms and fists. "No, I'm sorry. I hadn't expected to see anyone."

The dog stopped barking and sat at her side, his head resting against her thigh.

"Um. . . ," he stammered, "I see you made a friend with my dog."

She laughed. The sound was crisp, and something pleasant twisted in the hollow of his chest.

"I don't know if you drink coffee, but I thought it smelled so good. . .and I haven't had a real cup in months and months myself." Her voice trailed off.

Tom wished that she would have kept talking. "No, no, I love coffee," he replied. "I'm Tom. Tom Lyton. . .from California."

She smiled. "Megan Smith. . .from New York City. We sort of met. . .by accident. . .yesterday." She extended the mug of coffee to him.

Tom glanced about sheepishly. A fallen tree lay six yards from his tent. "Uh, would you like to sit down?"

She laughed again.

He smiled as if he were hearing a symphony.

"She had her baby."

Tom blinked. His eyes were blank, as if he could not register the thought.

"The baby," Megan repeated. "The woman in your car—she had her baby."

Tom snapped back to the present. "Oh yes. That's wonderful. Did everything go well? I would have stayed, except I figured that the priest—what was his name again?"

"Father William."

"Yes, that's it. I could see that Father William and the others had things well in hand. To be honest, it was a miracle that we all found each other yesterday. I know nothing about birthing babies."

Megan laughed at the comment and then took a sip from her mug. Without the artifice of makeup, her lips were full and pleasant. Her eyes sparkled in the early light. Her long auburn hair tumbled past her shoulders.

She relayed the story of the birth to him. She kept talking and began to tell him of her journey—her struggling to get out of New York, meeting the priest, traveling to Erie, and burying her father. She spoke for nearly an hour. As she talked, Tom sipped at his coffee, nodded, added a few appropriate words at appropriate times, and relished her monologue.

He watched the flow of her hands as they helped illustrate her story. He watched her eyes, growing greener and darker as she spoke of her father, lighter as she described the travails of the tiny Goliath in the mountains. He watched her lips move and her tongue and her teeth. He stared at her arms, bare to the shoulder, tanned a deep caramel color.

"And that's how we got here to Stonefort—or at least close to Stonefort," she said, her voice thicker now, deeper.

Tom simply stared, silent and unmoving.

She stared back into his eyes.

The dog, sitting next to her legs, stretched and groaned, then lay on the ground and let his head fall on her feet. Still Tom offered no comment.

"Tom, are you all right?" Her words tightened with concern.

He glanced down at his hands and the empty coffee cup. Then, lifting his head, smiling, he replied, "Megan, I'm fine. I really am. It's just that since the Silence, I haven't had many normal conversations. I couldn't even imagine ever having such a pleasant conversation again. It's like. . .it's like nothing has happened, and the world feels normal again."

His hands gripped the coffee cup. His words came out short and choppy. "I'm sorry. It's just so hard—because I know it's not normal. It's not. . ."

Megan reached over and took one of his hands. Tom almost shrunk back in shock from the gesture, but he found himself enjoying human contact too much to do so.

"I know," she whispered. "Everyone's story is hard. Yours, mine, everyone's." She gave his hand a squeeze. "But we have to continue. We have to go on."

Tom looked into her eyes. "I know. I know we do."

<hr />

Sheriff Killeen shifted uncomfortably, sweat starting to pool under his arms. The rest of the council had just left, and Rev. Moses had asked him to stay for a private dialogue.

The Reverend Moses sat in his leather chair, tilted backward, and thumped his feet onto the conference table, his black leather boots shining in the morning light. He was running his hand through his hair, which curled at the long ends hanging well over his collar. The more he waited to begin, the more nervous the sheriff would become. That suited Rev. Moses just fine.

After a minute or two of silence, Rev. Moses finally spoke. "Sheriff Killeen, how large is the Garden? How many people?"

"Nearly ten thousand total as of our last census. About five thousand in town and within a mile or so, which is just about what the population was before the quake. The new farms and workers make up the rest." He scratched his head, staring hard at the yellow pad in front of him on the table. He turned to the reverend and tried to smile. "New people keep coming every day, so that number may be a bit on the low side. We're growing." He blinked, then added, "And it's all because of you, Rev. Moses, and your radio program."

The Reverend Moses enjoyed flattery, but he also recognized it for what it was. He dismissed it with a flippant wave. "And,

Sheriff Killeen, the food stores, the harvest? Do we have enough food set aside to feed all these mouths?"

"I'm told we have twice as much as we need to feed everyone. If we wanted, we could use the surplus to trade for things we don't have. . .like, I don't know. . .tools maybe, or parts."

The reverend stood and paced to the window. He stared at the diesel generator chugging away in the parking lot. In a few weeks it would be disconnected. Herve Slatters had located a bigger unit midway between Stonefort and Cape Giradeau. He claimed it would power most of Stonefort and produce an even more powerful radio signal.

"Such is music to my ears, Sheriff." Rev. Moses also knew how to dish out flattery.

The sheriff broke into a wide, loopy grin.

The reverend returned to the table and bent down, palms flat against the polished wood. Both left slight smears of sweat. "You know why I'm pleased?"

The sheriff shook his head.

"Have you read Mark 13:5–8 recently?"

The sheriff shook his head no again.

"Jesus replied, 'Don't let anyone mislead you, because many will come in my name, claiming to be the Messiah. They will lead many astray. And wars will break out near and far, but don't panic. Yes, these things must come, but the end won't follow immediately. Nations and kingdoms will proclaim war against each other, and there will be earthquakes in many parts of the world, and famines. But all this will be only the beginning of the horrors to come.' "[xvii]

The reverend, pleased that he made it through the verses from memory, walked back to the window. "You see, Jesus said there would be famines and then the end would be near." He spun back to the sheriff. "Don't you see? No famine, no end of the world. Makes so much sense. What we are doing in the Garden is preventing the end of the world. We are given the great gift of having more time to reach others with the Good News."

The sheriff smiled again, though it was a confused smile.

"You see, Sheriff, people are power. Food is power. With the people of the Garden and the food we create, we can stem the tide. We can hold back the apocalypse with our hands in the soil." He turned to the window and spread out his arms. "God is pleased and is blessing this ministry and our harvest—our harvest of souls and our harvest of the soil."

"Sheriff Killeen," Rev. Moses whispered, changing to a more serious voice, "what of our security? Have you undertaken all that we have discussed? We want no evil men thwarting God's plans and blessings. For as Mark says"—he closed his eyes and spoke, stumbling over the verses only once—" 'So keep a sharp lookout! For you do not know when the homeowner will return—at evening, midnight, early dawn, or late daybreak. Don't let him find you sleeping when he arrives without warning. What I say to you I say to everyone: Watch for his return!' "[xviii] He opened his eyes. "You see, God wants us to be vigilant. Are we vigilant, Sheriff Killeen? Are we awake?"

Again the sheriff nodded.

"Have you, as I instructed, visited our neighbors?"

"We have, Rev. Moses. We are prepared." The sheriff outlined the expedition of a couple days prior, when he and a handpicked team of security personnel had traveled to over twenty small towns within a hundred-mile radius of Stonefort. Each town had an armory or a National Guard facility. Three old, wheezing farm trucks had left Stonefort on Monday empty and had returned home on Thursday filled beyond capacity—laden with weapons and ammunition and military supplies. A few of the armories had already been emptied, but there were enough weapons left over to equip an army of perhaps a thousand soldiers.

The reverend paced from the window to the large map of

southern Illinois framed and hung on the wall. "That news sets my soul to peace." Then he spun around so fast that the sheriff nearly tumbled from the edge of his chair. "Listen to 2 Thessalonians!"

Rev. Moses closed his eyes again and recited. " 'And now, brothers and sisters, let us tell you about the coming again of our Lord Jesus Christ and how we will be gathered together to meet him. Please don't be so easily shaken and troubled by those who say that the day of the Lord has already begun. Even if they claim to have had a vision, a revelation, or a letter supposedly from us, don't believe them. Don't be fooled by what they say. For that day will not come until there is a great rebellion against God and the man of lawlessness is revealed—the one who brings destruction.' "[xix]

The reverend leaned over the table. His breath was coming faster. His eyes were wide and animated. "Don't you understand? If we prevent the rebellion, which the Scriptures say must happen first, then the lawless one will not be revealed. Think of it. Using our security forces, our people, our food—we can prevent the coming of the Antichrist. If we stop him. . .or even slow his entrance by a month or a year or a decade. . .think of how many souls we can win for Christ in that time. Think of it! Souls saved for the kingdom simply because we are obedient in the Garden!"

He again paced to the window, hands behind his back, clasped so tight as if to prevent them from flailing about in excitement of their own accord.

"It is amazing, Sheriff Killeen, spiritually amazing. God has blessed us. He has spared this church. He has given me a radio program. He has given this new Garden laborers in the fields. He has given the church a vision. We are blessed. God wants us—wants you and me—to succeed in leading this Garden to be the center of all things good and Christian in the world. He wants that."

The sheriff, riding along on the reverend's wave of excitement, smiled widely.

The room grew quiet. A sour and sweet aroma slipped into the room, a thick smell of donuts. Suddenly the reverend slapped both palms on the table again. The pencil in front of the sheriff trembled and rolled to the floor.

The reverend glared at the sheriff. "You must remain vigilant, Sheriff. Do you understand? Do you truly understand?" His voice rose from a low rumble to a shout in the span of a dozen words. "Beware! Keep alert; for you do not know when the time will come!"

Leaning forward and glaring at the sheriff, the reverend continued, his words hard and dark. "Mark warned us. Beware! Keep alert!"[xx] Now his words fell to a raspy whisper. "Jesus was crucified before He was truly finished. That will not happen in Stonefort, Sheriff Killeen. That will not happen in this town, will it? You won't let that happen to me, will you, Sheriff Killeen?"

The sheriff merely shook his head.

The reverend stood straight up and screamed, *"Will you?"*

"I thought we would be in Illinois by now," Dave Ox said as the three operatives and Riley sat at the curb munching fried chicken in the shadow of their dusty Hummer. "I thought you had family there, Riley."

Wiping his chin on his sleeve, Riley swallowed and nodded. "I do."

"Then why are we stuck in Nashville?"

Riley pointed his drumstick at Dave. "You unhappy with the work here? You not busy enough?"

Dave shrugged. "Busy enough, I guess. But don't we keep hearing about this Moses guy? I thought he would be higher on our list of imperatives."

They had been in Nashville for nearly all of June and July. Federal law had been well established in the city and much of the state for weeks. Riley had been back and forth to Washington twice, picked up and delivered in a Cobra helicopter. Each time he had come back with local operations that delayed their westward march.

"We'll get there in due time. And my relatives out there are doing fine. That much I know."

"So Illinois is next?" Macaluso asked in between bites of chicken.

Riley did not answer but smiled in reply.

The four men, after so long in the field together, knew exactly what he meant.

august 15

The after-midnight air glistened with a fine mist, raindrops all but invisible, the only sound a faint breathing hiss. Peter stood in the doorway of the barn and looked about. He saw no one. He reached up and felt behind a loose board above the doorjamb. Finding his hidden cigarettes, he jumped down and stared out into the mist.

Can't hide 'em in the trailer since I don't really live there anymore. He adjusted the baseball cap on his head and zipped up his coat. *It's not raining that hard, and I don't want to smoke in the barn—too much stuff to catch fire.*

Tucking his head against the rain, he began to walk toward the oak tree and the creek. Halfway there he stopped and peered into the darkness. He unconsciously looked for Elijah, though he knew his friend wouldn't be there.

It had been four weeks since Elijah had been found, nearly dead, floating in the stream. He had not yet regained consciousness, though they were managing to get food into him, sturdy broth mixed with oatmeal. On some days, his body grew restless, looking as if he were a blink away from waking; other days his body stayed still, the only movement the rise and fall of his chest.

Peter narrowed his eyes, trying to gain definition in the dark mist. He peered downstream, toward Tom's campsite. Tom had moved his tent to a less visible place, fifty yards downstream, on a small rise under a branching of fir trees. Peter had expected that he might see the shadowy form of Megan there, for their friendship had blossomed quickly. But the campsite and tent remained dark and quiet.

Peter turned back to the barn. All was dark and still. He peered hard toward the oak tree. There was movement—a slight figure standing under the canopy of leaves and branches.

Peter smiled. Immediately he knew who it was from the figure's definition against the darker sky—it was the priest, Father William. His back was to Peter, and Peter was certain that if he did not speak, and simply walked up, he would scare the living soul from the priest's body by tapping him silently on the shoulder.

So Peter coughed loudly instead. The priest spun about, and Peter waved, calling out in a tight whisper, "Father William, over here."

The priest waved back.

"This must be the spot for insomniacs," Peter said, laughing. "Elijah and I used to meet here before he was hurt."

"A pity, such a pity," the priest replied. "Has he been able to say what happened? He doesn't respond to me at all. An unfamiliar voice, I guess."

"No," Peter replied. "He was lucid only for seconds when he first came back. Said a few words to me, then drifted off. Never thought it would be this long."

The priest nodded in sympathy. "Head injuries are hard to figure. Doesn't look like any swelling is there, but you can't know without X-rays and a CAT scan. I imagine those are out of the question."

Peter nodded. "You heard the president last night, didn't you?" In spite of the warning on the crystal radio set, all those on Peter's farm had tuned in.

"Nothing new," the priest replied. "The same message he has been giving for months: Give us a few weeks, and everything will be back to normal."

With a bitter laugh, Peter added, "And obey everyone in an

army uniform. Well, I don't think normal is coming back for a long time, no matter how many speeches Garrett gives."

An owl hooted from near the barn. A slight breeze whispered in from the west and shushed among the rows of corn, lush and full in the field by the road. The crop was nearing harvest and smelled rich, green, and sweet.

"Father, I don't know if this is good manners or not," Peter said as he withdrew a cigarette pack from his jacket, "but I was raised to always offer a guest whatever it was I was having."

Through the darkness, the priest peered closer, as if expecting candy.

Peter extended the pack. "Are priests allowed to smoke? These may be a bit stale."

"Cigarettes?"

Peter nodded. "Only at night, only when I can't find sleep, only outdoors."

The priest extended his arm partway, pulled it back, then shrugged. "No. . .I think not. Back in seminary, decades ago now, a few of us would sneak out and have a puff or two. We were rebels back then."

"And now?"

"What's left to rebel against?"

Peter laughed softly. "By being here and not in Stonefort, you've already established yourself as a rebel—at least as far as Rev. Moses matters."

"Is that true?"

Peter nodded glumly. He wanted to open up to the priest but was unsure of how much to tell him. Then he decided to hold nothing back. "You've heard enough of Rev. Moses to realize that all is not perfect in the Garden."

The priest nodded. "To me it seems his vision as to what is happening continues to shift. Once he intimates that the Rapture has occurred. Then later he says it hasn't." The priest glanced down quickly, as if ashamed of speaking ill of another man of God. "But then, I haven't known him from the beginning."

"No, Father, you're right—and you're a diplomat. But I think he's just plain wrong. He's telling people falsehoods." Peter thought for a moment. "Let me ask you a question. The true church will be spared from the Tribulation, won't it?"

Father William answered, "Depends on whom you ask. The Catholic Church is nearly mute on the subject. The more evangelical and fundamental a church's theology, the more likely they are to believe that."

Fumbling for his lighter, Peter looked into the sky. "I hate to admit this, but many results of the reverend's work are good. People are coming to Christ. People are being given work and food and a place to stay. But they work so hard. There seems to be so little joy."

"Times are hard, Peter. Everyone has to work hard to stay alive."

"But believers should have attitudes of grace and joy and love regardless of their circumstances, regardless if this is the end of the world or not. I keep hearing that verse in Matthew: 'But those who endure to the end will be saved. And the Good News about the Kingdom will be preached throughout the whole world, so that all nations will hear it. . . .'[xxi] Aren't we supposed to endure and spread the Word? And how can you be dark and angry if you have the Good News in your heart?"

"You can't, Peter, you can't. That's what I noticed the first day we arrived here at your farm. All these people were smiling and inviting and happy to share."

Peter lowered his voice to a whisper. "You've seen the darkness? I saw the fear in your eyes—for a second—the first time we met."

The priest closed his eyes and nodded. "It's been there since Megan and I crossed the bridge between New Jersey and Pennsylvania. I thought it was after her, and I tried to protect her. But now I am not so sure. I think it might be after someone else."

"I feel it," Peter said urgently. "It's there in my dreams. It's there at the edge of my thoughts. Before the Silence, I'd never have considered this possible, but now the darkness is alive."

Peter lifted his hand, struck the lighter, and lit his cigarette. After the brief flicker of light, shadows returned and their faces were lost in the mist.

———

Mike and Ernie had walked across much of Iowa in the full glow of a summer sun. Ernie had sniffled and snorted the entire trip, his broken nose healing slowly and the pollen of the corn and wheat reeking havoc on his allergies. His sneezing and gasping slowed them to a snail-like crawl.

One full duffel bag of food was salvaged from the burnt truck outside Mrs. McClure's farm. The bag had been left to the side and was only charred at the edges. Mike had carried it most of the way, in deference to Ernie's obvious pain.

The shedding of blood had changed them. It had made them hard and angry. It had made them more dangerous. In the middle of a moonlit night, they had broken into a small frame house in Monroe, Iowa. Only one person lived there—an old woman who wore a jumble of colored scarves. She had offered little resistance as Ernie strangled her with her long, paisley scarf. They left a couple of days later with her gold jewelry and two rusty revolvers.

East of Brighton, an old farmer never lived to leave his barn again. Mike and Ernie remained hidden in the barn for a week, until his small cache of food was gone. Now they carried his shotgun.

Neither man spoke much as the days passed. When their duffel bag was light, with only a few days' worth of food remaining, they'd come upon a farm, nestled in a cutback of the Mississippi, just outside Nauvoo, Illinois. A thicket of corn grew higher than a man holding his hand above his head. From the road, they saw a small house a hundred yards distant. In the growing dusk, a man and a woman tended to a tiny garden plot.

Mike and Ernie had waited in the cornfield for the couple to go inside and retire for the night. As they waited, Mike had pulled the last of the beef jerky from the duffel. He'd offered half to Ernie and took the other half himself. Their chewing had sounded loud in the green rows of corn and the softness of the thick black loam. Slowly the croaking of frogs and the hum and buzz of mosquitoes sounded around them. An owl hooted. The calls of river ducks filled the air.

When the house was dark and not even a candle flickered, they had drawn their guns, entered, and slowly made their way up the stairs to the bedrooms. A trio of booms echoed in the dark, then another four, then two last shots, then silence.

As the sun climbed to morning, they had searched the house for food and guns. Then they dragged the elderly couple out and buried them in shallow graves behind the barn.

They had stayed in Nauvoo for weeks. But this morning, as Mike stoked the fire to cook breakfast, Ernie said, "We have to get to Stonefort. I'm plumb tired of wasting time. I'm going to kill that toad that busted my nose. I can't breathe, and my head hurts all the time. You said it would go away when it healed, but it ain't going away. Everything still hurts. I can't take it no more."

Mike's smile dimmed.

"I'm going to enjoy blowing off his nose before I shoot his heart out," Ernie added. "He'll learn he can't go busting people's faces without somebody busting back."

Mike's smile dimmed further. "You want to leave today?" Mike asked, hoping that his friend's anger would pass.

Ernie glared at him. "I want to leave now." He sniffed loudly, his nose whistling. He touched it gingerly, as if the merest pressure would rebreak it. "I'm going to kill him for what he did to me."

⸺⸺

If it was possible for a frog to appear desperate, this particular frog did.

Revelations saw the small splash from the bank of the stream and dove in after it, paddling and splashing furiously in the shallow water. The frog darted down, then left with a fast kick. The dog stood in water up to his chest, snuffling and searching for his prey, ducking his head in the water, and snapping at the ripples.

"Rev, come back! It was only a frog. You don't eat frogs."

Tom stood a few feet from the edge of the grassy bank and called to the retriever. The dog turned, water streaming from its jaws and snout. He turned once more to the water, barked twice, then sloshed to the shore, shaking himself vigorously.

Megan, several feet behind Tom, laughed. "First time I've seen a frog retriever in action."

Tom smiled and nodded. "He'll go after anything in water. On cloudy days, when you can see into still pools and below the surface of the water, he'll dive in after fish."

Megan laughed again. It was music to Tom—pure, wonderful music—and he couldn't help but grin wider.

The afternoon sun glowed orange and warm. Tom took off his sweatshirt and tied it around his waist. It was cool for an August day, but their walk had been long and ambitious.

Back on the farm, an informal rotation of duties ensured that all shared equally in the work. Tom and Megan had added their names to the list and were kept busy weeding or cooking or harvesting or fishing. There was much work to be done, yet each week every person on the farm had several afternoons free from work or duties.

During the past two weeks, perhaps out of coincidence at first but then out of choice, Megan and Tom selected the same afternoons off. And they spent much of that free time together. Tom had even shared with her the story of his son and the possibility that he might be in Stonefort.

"You have to go to town and ask about him. There must be some records still there."

"I've thought of it, Megan," he said seriously, "and even

talked to Peter about it. But he said that it would be unlikely that Rev. Moses or anyone on the town council would help anyone from this farm."

"Why?"

"I'm not sure of all the reasons—some bad blood and something about Peter's wife."

"But you still need to look for him, don't you?"

Tom nodded. "After so many years of not knowing, I guess I'm pretty scared to find out anything more. And it's not like I have any rights or claim to the boy. I know it would be hard on the boy, finding out that his biological father never even knew he existed. I'll look for him, but I'll know when the time is right. It's not right now."

Megan took his hand and squeezed it.

⸻

On this day, Tom and Megan and the dog were exploring the stream as it meandered south of Peter's farm. It ran through fields that had never been farmed. Some acreage had been cut for pasture. Brambles and brush spotted the open land, and tangled trees and vines grew by most of the stream bank.

Birdcalls broke the quiet stillness. They could hear the gentle lapping of water as it tumbled over rock and gravel. Revelations bounded ahead, water spraying in all directions. He stopped on a rise overlooking a small bend in the stream where the water ran deeper and silent. A shaft of afternoon sun cut through the trees and bathed the spot in delicate warmth. The dog turned back to wait for his companions, then barked once. He circled around a half-dozen times, then lay on his side with the sun warming his golden fur. By the time Tom and Megan arrived, the dog was snoring.

A fallen oak tree, a perfect bench, lay in the dappled shade and sun. Megan sat and stretched her legs. She wore a pair of baggy khaki shorts and a man's plain cotton shirt. Clothing had been gathered from the hundreds of abandoned cars and homes that lay east of Peter's farm. They never traveled west—it was understood that that land was claimed by the New Garden of Stonefort.

She leaned her head back, exposing her neck to the sun, and closed her eyes. "I could stay here forever," she said, her voice a whisper. "This is such a magical place."

Tom sat cross-legged on the ground just in front of her. She had hoped he would sit next to her on the tree. She had picked her seat knowing that the branches would have made it difficult for him to sit anywhere but close to her side. She looked down at him, then at the space on the tree beside her, then back at him. She thought she held an invitation in her eyes, but he either hadn't noticed or chose not to accept.

During their free time over the last two weeks, as well as the delicious time after dinner and before dark, their discussions had lasted for hours and hours. Megan knew all of Tom's past—his wife, his work, his journey to Stonefort, and the horrible experiences in Nevada and Iowa.

Megan listened intently and shared as much of her life with him as he did with her. She began to feel a certain intimacy with him, deeper than she had ever felt with any man.

She looked down at him. He was lying flat on his back, one hand locked behind his head as a pillow. His eyes were closed, and the sun poured over his features. His bronzed skin and long blond hair made her think of a surfer who had aged very well.

Megan blinked her eyes several times and stared off into the woods. *We're friends. Maybe that's all he can offer now. Maybe he still needs time to grieve his family.*

Tom stirred, and a thin strip of his stomach became exposed to the sun.

But the luxury of time is something none of us has. She put her hands on the rough bark and pushed herself up. She brushed the bark off the seat of her shorts. Tom did not stir, but the dog wearily lifted its head.

It is now or never, she thought, setting her jaw firm. She knelt down next to him, perhaps a foot from his frame, then lay down on her side facing him, her elbow on the ground, her head cradled in her upturned palm. This time Tom stirred.

"You looked so comfortable here," she whispered. "And I was tired of sitting."

He smiled at her, rubbing his eyes with his hand. "I must have dozed off for a moment."

"Just a moment." Megan smiled and extended her free hand to touch his arm. "Tom," she whispered, "I know all about you. I know all that you've lost. I know you better than I have ever known a man before."

His expression was not one of surprise, nor fear, nor revulsion. She saw a flicker of something pass his eyes, like resignation or surrender.

"Megan, I. . .I. . ."

"Am I too forward?"

"No, it's not that," he said with a smile. "I'm flattered beyond belief."

Her expression grew puzzled. "Then you don't find me. . . attractive?"

"No, not that in the least," he whispered. "You are very beautiful."

"Then what? I know it's been only a few weeks, but there's something between us. I can feel it. I know you can too. I'm not imagining this. Tell me that I'm not imagining this." Megan's words tumbled out.

He sat up and pulled his sweatshirt back over his T-shirt. "You're not imagining it at all. From the first day I knew. I knew from the moment I met you, when we hit on the highway."

"Then what? Why?"

"Because if I reach out to you. . .it means that. . .I mean. . .then my wife and child are truly gone. If you and I, you know, become. . .

you know. . .then a huge part of my life has to end, officially and totally, for good."

Megan propped herself up on both elbows and stared at him. "I know that, Tom. But aren't all our lives—I mean the lives we used to have—aren't they all over? None of us can go back. None of us. You know that our only hope is to hold together and move forward. We will always have memories, but there is so little time. Shouldn't we take advantage of the time we have left?"

Tom nodded, then added in a low whisper, "I know. . .I know."

Megan was aware of his breathing, his warmth.

"There is one other thing," he said, his voice flat.

"There is?" She braced herself for a monumental revelation.

"I'm still searching for God, Megan. I don't know if I have faith or not."

She smiled. "That's all right, Tom. I'm. . .I'm not sure either."

Surprise colored his eyes. "I thought. . .you know, traveling with the priest and all, that if anyone believed, it would be you."

"No, Tom, I. . ." Instead of trying to explain something that she could not, she reached for his shoulder. She pulled at him, drawing him close. He resisted for a heartbeat, then engulfed her in his arms. Without speaking for a long time, Megan held tight, feeling totally safe and protected for the first time since the Silence.

"It's okay for people to be together," she whispered in his ear. "It's okay to feel again. It is."

He kept her tight in his arms.

"This is okay, isn't it, Tom? Just to hold each other? Just to feel each other's heartbeat?" Her words flowed slow as honey. She felt him nod.

He pushed back a little, and their eyes locked. She was captured by his brown eyes, the color of an oak tree. She could not resist. She leaned over and let her lips touch his. It was the gentlest of first kisses, like a butterfly tasting the sweetness of a rose. She let him draw back a few inches.

"This is okay, isn't it, Tom? This is only a kiss between friends."

It was clear he was finding it hard to breathe, let alone speak. "I–I guess it is." His words were chopped and throaty.

She bent forward and kissed him again, this time more insistent. "I hope so," she whispered in his ear, breaking apart from him. "I hope so."

She kissed him again. Passion would only be dammed so long; then the restraints would crumble, loosening the torrent.

It was at that moment that Revelations snapped alert and spun to a crouching position. He growled threateningly.

Tom broke the embrace and sat up with a start. Megan knew Revelations to be a good guard dog from Tom's stories and knew that he only growled when danger was near. The dog's eyes were locked on the far bank to the west. Tom lay back on the ground and placed a finger to Megan's lips, bidding her to remain still. She had no intention of moving.

A rustle and a man's voice carried across the quiet stream. "Over here, Max, over here. We can mark this tree."

Two men scrambled through the brush, the first one whacking at twigs and vines with a machete. They wore the black uniform of the Garden security forces.

"Isn't this near where we found that vagrant with the bag of moldy plants?" the one with the machete asked.

The other man, shorter, with dark sweat circles under his arms and on his back, looked about. "Nah, farther downstream I think."

"Well, get the sign. Put it on that tree there by the water."

Tom held his palm at the dog, who kept up a low growl. He stopped and glared through the tall grass at the two strangers on the opposite bank. Tom could make out the bold words, printed red on black: NO TRESPASSING. BY ORDER OF THE NEW GARDEN SECURITY FORCES. VIOLATORS FACE SEVERE PUNISHMENT.

The short man pulled out a hammer and tapped three nails

into the tree. He tugged at the sign. It held tight. "That should be enough warning."

The tall man gave an evil snort. "I can't wait until we catch our first trespasser. I can't wait."

"You and me both," the shorter guard replied. "Give us a chance to put our training to work."

The tall man snapped a pistol from a jacketed holster, aimed toward the far bank, and pulled the trigger. The explosion sounded huge and violent. Clumps of mud and dirt flapped into the air and settled like a dirty, wet cloud over Tom, Megan, and the dog, still hidden in the grass.

"Hey, don't be wasting ammo like that," the other said.

"Like there isn't a hundred thousand more back at head-quarters. Nobody's going to miss one bullet."

More than five silent minutes passed before Tom raised his head to see if all was clear. It took many more minutes after that for Megan's heartbeat to return to normal.

The sun had just dipped to the western horizon as Tom, Megan, and the dog finally made it back to Peter's farm. They had walked and jogged much of the way, and sweat streaked their faces.

They turned the corner by the fire pit, where virtually every-one had gathered, all talking excitedly, gesturing, pointing. Leo spotted them as they turned the corner. He called, "Did you hear? Did you?"

"Hear what?" Tom gasped.

"Elijah woke up a few minutes ago. He's talking and every-thing. He's back among the living."

⚊⚊⚊

Dinner that evening was a thanksgiving celebration. Most of the band had not ceased praying for Elijah's recovery, and this day proved to many that God was active in their lives. While the mer-riment continued after the dishes had been cleared, Peter, Tom, and Father William offered prayers of praise in Elijah's tiny room.

Elijah looked thin and pale, but he had managed to eat a full bowl of noodle soup and two slices of honey-sweetened bread. He was now sitting up, propped up by pillows.

Peter knelt by the head of the bed. "How do you feel, Elijah?"

"A mite tired," Elijah said. "But well. Arms and legs are working as expected."

"You had us frightened."

Elijah smiled. "Is a month too long for a nap?"

"Friend, it was. It surely was," Peter said as he squeezed Elijah's forearm. Peter scanned the faces of the men gathered about the bedside, then asked, "Elijah, do you remember what happened? Did you fall?"

Blinking his eyes, as if the memory pained him, Elijah shook his head. "It was nothing like that," he said softly. "It was one of the Stonefort militia that did it. Came on me gathering cattails. Told me I wasn't registered and neither were you." The words spilled out as if they had been stored for a long time and were anxious to be spoken. "Said we weren't registered—and they had no record of your farm. Said I was gathering illegal food since I was on the New Garden grounds."

Peter looked up at Tom, who nodded. Tom had shared the details that he and Megan had overheard that afternoon.

"That isn't right now, is it, Peter?" Elijah asked. "I mean, who gave them the right? It isn't their land, is it?"

Peter squeezed his friend's arm again and tried to hide his anger.

———※———

As news of Elijah's story spread, the rest of the people on the farm became outraged.

Leo stormed back and forth in front of the fire, his arms gesturing wildly, his head bobbing and weaving in the dark. "We have to stop this, man," he cried, his words harsh and angry. "What they did isn't righteous, man. It isn't their place to go caving heads in. That stuff went out in the seventies, man."

All heads nodded in agreement.

"You have to do something, man," Leo said, looking straight at Peter. "You have to do something."

———

Just before midnight, Peter rummaged above the door one more time. He was down to his last two packs of cigarettes and wondered what he'd feel like when they were gone.

Maybe I'll have to search for more, he thought. Then he realized that Rev. Moses and his security forces would already have scoured the county looking for valuables. *I bet that cigarettes are one valuable commodity these days.*

He walked into the darkness to the oak tree. *Perhaps east of us? Maybe no one really looked that way. There might be cigarettes there.*

As he shuffled along, he heard a cough. It was Father William's way of alerting him that company was expected.

"Father William," Peter called.

"Shh," was the priest's response. Peter quieted until he reached the cleric's side. The priest pointed downstream. "Megan and Tom are visiting by his tent. I don't want them to think I'm spying on them."

Peter smiled. "Are you?"

Father William suppressed a laugh. "Well, yes. And if she goes in his tent, I'm making as much noise as possible."

"Well. . ." Peter grinned. "Let's hope we don't need to resort to that tactic. They seem like a pretty levelheaded couple."

"And she needs to be reassured and loved. It's a good thing, but I don't want anyone to get hurt," the priest said.

———

Five minutes later, his cigarette gone, both men sat on the fallen tree. Megan and Tom's soft conversation and laughter drifted upstream on the warm breeze scented by the ripening cornfield beyond.

Father William broke the silence. "What are you going to do

about what happened to Elijah? Everyone is pretty upset."

Peter shrugged. "What can I do, Father? We're a couple of dozen people against thousands. It will be their word against ours."

The priest stood up and paced back and forth. "You have to confront evil, Peter. I learned that for the first time a few months ago. I never did until then. If you don't battle the devil, the devil will think you're on his side—and so will everyone else."

"Do you mean that?"

"You remember a movie awhile back? The main character said, 'Stupid is as stupid does.'"

"Forrest Gump."

"Yes, that's it," the priest replied. "Well, I can paraphrase that line and truthfully say that evil is as evil does."

Peter remained silent.

"I've talked to the people on your farm, Peter. What you've been teaching them is solid, proper Christian faith. And now you've run into a real-life application of being a Christian. And they're watching you. Do you fight? Or do you simply walk away and say nothing? They're watching you, Peter. They want to know what you'll do."

Peter reached in his pocket and withdrew another cigarette. "It's a two-smoke night, Father."

In the distance an owl called, and a raccoon screeched.

"Peter, I think you have to confront evil. . .if that's what this is. You have to do battle."

In a small voice Peter asked, "Is that what Jesus would do?"

"They were only thirteen against an entire world, Peter. They may have been afraid, but they stood for truth."

Peter took a long drag and watched the smoke curl into the night.

"Father, will you come with me when I go to town?"

The priest stepped toward Peter and placed his hand on his shoulder. "Of course I will, my son. Of course I will."

august 16

A heavy rain pelted the rich black loam of southern Illinois. A low scud of clouds hung low over the horizon, promising a full day of the same. Only halfway to town, Peter said ruefully, "I'd say we picked the wrong day to take a walk, Father."

"Nonsense, Peter," Father William responded. "One of your friends lent me this wonderful raincoat and these very dry and comfortable rubber shoes. I feel like a duck out for a Sunday stroll. Dry as a bone and happy as a clam."

Peter did have to admit that the priest looked very comfortable. And in civilian clothes and raincoat he looked more like a fisherman than a cleric.

Peter figured that with the couple-hour walk to town, the hour in town to meet with Rev. Moses, and the couple-hour walk back, they could be home by supper. Last night they had spoken of confronting evil. A realist, Peter had limited expectations. He didn't expect the reverend to admit that his security forces had attacked and nearly killed Elijah. Since Elijah had been left for dead, Peter knew no one would own up to the attack. And though Peter's heart hurt every day in Becca's absence, he didn't believe that Rev. Moses would allow her to come back to the farm this day. However, he might be able to share some time with her and Linda.

All Peter felt he might accomplish was to set the scene for other discussions, another round of negotiations.

The rain had intensified by the time Peter and Father William ascended the steps of the Temple of God's Calling. Under the eaves in front of the church doors stood five men Peter had never seen before. Each man wore the same black uniform, and each displayed a pistol hung from his belt. None smiled, and only one spoke.

"You have business here?"

"I do," Peter said. "My wife, Linda Wilson, sings on Rev. Moses's radio show. My daughter is with her. I've come to see Becca and to talk with my wife."

No one moved.

"Who's he?" the guard asked, angling his head toward the priest.

"William." For some reason Peter hesitated to identify the man as a priest. "He's a friend."

"You have an appointment?"

Peter glared at the guard. "Are you saying that a man needs an appointment to see his wife and child? Is that what you're saying?"

The guard slumped an inch. "No, I guess not. You can go in. See the receptionist. He'll let them know you're here."

The receptionist, a young man with a pocked, swarthy complexion, picked up a two-way radio and whispered into it. In response, there came a burst of heavy static, then a garbled voice that apparently only the young man could decipher. The radio was held together with duct tape.

I guess someone figured out how to rework such things, Peter thought. *And if that technology exists in Stonefort, then what else might be coming back?*

Five minutes later Becca charged through the doors of the sanctuary and leapt, giggling, into her father's arms. "Daddy, Daddy, I have missed you so much. Mom said that you couldn't come because of all the work on the farm."

Peter stiffened at the lie, but smothered his daughter with kisses. He held her, asking questions, being questioned, embracing his daughter tightly. "And how's Mommy?"

Becca's eyes darted to the ground first, then to the priest who sat a few yards away in a folding chair, then back to the center of Peter's chest. "She's. . .she's. . .Mommy's fine, Daddy. She's fine."

"She is? You sound like you're not certain." Now he was worried.

Becca avoided his eyes. "She's happy here. She likes singing." The little girl looked up with a forced smile on her lips.

"Where's Mommy?" Peter asked again.

Becca's eyes darted to the ground again. "She's upstairs. I think. . .maybe she doesn't feel well. I'm never supposed to disturb her in the afternoon ever again."

Peter hugged her hard. "Maybe we can get you back to the farm, sweets. Maybe you could stay with Daddy sometimes."

"Could I, Daddy?" Becca squealed. "Could I? They said you didn't want me there because of all the work. Could I go back?"

As Peter held his daughter, the sanctuary doors banged opened. Everyone in the narthex jumped, most of all Becca, who buried herself in her father's arms.

"Peter Wilson," Rev. Moses boomed, "nice to see you again. Who's your friend?"

Peter stood up and stared. The face he saw was fleshier than he remembered, the skin whiter, and the hair blacker and more contoured. The extra weight gave the reverend's presence a more threatening bulkiness.

"This is William," Peter said. "He's been staying with me for. . .for a time now."

"Has he registered, Peter?"

"Registered? For what?"

"Don't tell me you're not listening to my radio show. You have been given a radio, haven't you?"

The receptionist flipped several pages in a book and nodded vigorously.

"Then you've heard. Everyone in Stonefort must register with us," Rev. Moses insisted. "Peter, you must register your farm as well. How else are we to keep track of everyone?"

Peter squared his shoulders. "I don't have to register with anyone. The farm is mine, and I can have anyone on it that I choose."

"Peter, the farm is half yours. Linda has rights too, you know."

The reverend's words were spoken slowly. They were deliberately ominous, Peter thought.

"Rev. Moses," Peter said, holding his voice cold, "I want to see my daughter. I want her to spend time with me on the farm. It's only right. I have a father's right to see her, you know. I've been patient. I've talked to the mayor. I thought going through channels was the wise, Christian thing to do."

He shut his eyes for a long heartbeat and shuddered inside. *The darkness is here,* his thoughts screamed. *That bone-cold darkness is in this room.* His arms closed in protection around Becca.

The reverend rocked back on his heels, listening with eyes half closed and lips pursed. After Peter spoke, the reverend waited for nearly a minute before responding. "Peter, do you have a school on the farm?"

"No," Peter replied softly.

"Do you have a hospital and medicines?"

Peter simply shook his head.

"And other children? And playgrounds?"

Silence filled the room.

"There, you see, Peter, she's better off here. After all, a child belongs with her mother. That fact every Christian should understand. You may see her"—the reverend scrutinized his fingernails—"you may see her twice a month on Sunday afternoons, after church, of course."

Peter straightened and clenched his fist. He was very tempted to strike Moses.

"Peter," Rev. Moses said, his words dark and chilled, "do not even think of taking one step closer. Do not. I am the law in

Stonefort now. You will abide by what I have said." He turned and began to walk back to the sanctuary. "Becca," he called out as he walked, "go back inside. Your mother would like to see you now."

"I want to see my wife!" Peter shouted. "I have a right!"

Moses spun around, his eyes flashing. "Rights! Rights! Who are you? Who are you to stand in the way of the Garden being rebuilt?"

"I'm a father and husband—those are my rights!"

Taking two steps toward Peter, Moses shouted, "They will both stay with me! I have need of Linda. She is important to the Garden. She is important to me!" He turned and looked at Becca, still in her father's arms. "I told you to get to your room. *Now!*" he shouted.

Becca gazed once more at her father, a distant, lonely look in her eyes, and then slid down from his arms. She ran off quickly in the direction Rev. Moses pointed.

When the shouting had started, the doors of the church had opened and the five guards had rushed in, hands at weapons or batons.

"Wait a minute!" Peter shouted back. "You cannot dismiss me like this—nor my child! We need to talk about your security forces as well. They almost killed a man—Elijah—who lives on my land. He was doing nothing wrong, and he was attacked by your security guards—for gathering cattails!"

Rev. Moses came closer, and the guards edged closer as well. He stabbed his finger against Peter's chest. "Listen, and listen good. I have nothing further to discuss with you. Nothing at all! If an unregistered person has a problem, let him register and maybe we'll talk about it. But until then, Peter, you and your Catholic priest friend are dismissed!"

Father William's face blanched.

"You think I don't know, Peter?" the reverend said in a sinister voice. "You think I am ignorant of the comings and goings around here? I am not. I have to be aware. Christ calls us to be aware. I am following Christ's orders. Are you with me, Peter, or are you against me?"

"Talk to me about my child! Talk to me about your goons nearly killing an innocent man!"

The reverend sniffed at the air as if an unpleasant odor had crept into the room. "We have talked of your rights, Peter. And hardly ever is an innocent man harmed." He glanced toward the guards and stated flatly, "Our discussions are through. See that these. . .gentlemen. . .are escorted out of town."

Father William and Peter didn't say another word as the phalanx of stern-faced, mute guards surrounded them and walked them to the far side of the bridge. The formation parted, then stood in a line, shoulder to shoulder, preventing any thought of Peter's returning to the church.

Peter glared at the guards, none of whom he knew, none of whom spoke; then he turned and began walking home.

Perhaps a mile later, Peter stopped and faced the priest. "What would Jesus have done, Father? Would He have gotten angry? What did I do that was wrong?"

Father William placed a hand on his shoulder. "You did nothing wrong, Peter. And I don't know what Jesus would have done. I know when it came to the end of His time, He did not fight with the guards. But He did spend a long time in prayer. Perhaps. . . perhaps on the walk back we might give this all to God as we pray and ask for direction."

Peter sighed. "I am so angry, Father. I want my little girl back."

"If God wants that, then it can be accomplished, Peter. It can. No power, no security force, no Rev. Moses will stop God."

"But doesn't anyone see what a charlatan that man is? Doesn't anyone realize that he is preaching heresy? How can anyone live in this town under his authority? Isn't God at work in people's hearts anymore?"

"People have always been misled," the priest said thoughtfully. "People want to believe the easy answer. But God is still at work here, Peter."

"How?" he angrily shot back. "Tell me how God is here and at work. Tell me how it is that God hasn't packed up His bags and left Stonefort to fend for itself."

In a whisper the priest said, "Because He left *you* here, Peter. He left you here to tell the truth. He left you here to stand up to evil and darkness."

Peter dropped his head and let the tension flow from his body. "I'm not the man for this. I feel so unprepared and unready."

"Welcome to the club," the priest said with a knowing smile. "I have felt unworthy my whole life as a priest. Only now do I feel like I am making a difference in people's lives."

"Why now?"

"Because the need is so great, Peter. When there is silence, people suffer. They search for something to fill that silence. An honest man, an honest voice, breaks that silence."

"But, Father, how can I really make a difference? I am just one man."

"One man can't make a difference," the priest said, "but one man in prayer can. You need to pray, Peter—more now than you have ever prayed before."

Peter stopped walking and let the rain pelt his head and shoulders. The rain was warmer now, and the water felt cleansing and purifying. "You're right. I know you're right," Peter whispered. "Prayer is the wise response."

"Very wise indeed, Peter."

august 18

The reverend bent low over the back of Sheriff Killeen's chair and angrily hissed into his ear. "If I ever hear of another unauthorized abuse like this, I will have your hide."

Beads of sweat rolled down the sheriff's face. "It won't happen again," the sheriff said, cowering.

Moses arched an eyebrow in disbelief.

"It's true. I found out who was responsible, sir. It took awhile. We have a lot of guards. But we found them. They were on duty by Wilson's farm that day. They confessed."

The reverend did not smile, nor move, nor speak.

"And I have made certain that they will never do it again."

The reverend stiffened but offered no response other than to arch his eyebrows again.

"Dead certain, sir," the sheriff whispered, his face reddening.

"*Dead* certain?" the reverend replied, his voice cold and stony.

"Yes, sir. I know that such brutality is never to be tolerated."

Rev. Moses scanned each face gathered around the highly polished table. Each face stared back in a sidelong fashion, not willing to make full eye contact, not willing to be singled out.

"I'll hear your reports now." Rev. Moses sighed and relaxed back into his leather chair.

One by one, each member stood and presented a three-minute summary of his department's activities. Each knew not to speak longer than three minutes, five on a pleasant day, for Rev. Moses would simply interrupt by calling out loudly, "Next!"

The flow of pilgrims had stabilized; housing continued to be constructed to meet the demand; land under cultivation increased; crops were being harvested with record yields noted; and the future looked bright. The newly formed Livestock Control Department reported that the size of the Garden's herd increased from a few hundred at the time of the Silence to the current several thousand. The growth was due to good management, the director said. What he did not mention was that his officers aggressively searched all of southern Illinois, Indiana, and parts of Kentucky and Missouri to "liberate" many cattle, claiming that those farmers did not have the ability to feed and board them over the coming winter.

After all had stood and reported, Sheriff Killeen gulped, then raised his hand.

"What?" barked Rev. Moses.

"Uh. . .sir, we have several cases of a judicial nature that await disposition."

"Such as?"

"There was a rape a week ago at Castine's farm. A reported robbery of hen stock and eggs at Soderburgs' two nights ago, and two men stole a Garden vehicle, damaged it, and tried to flee."

"Are they guilty?"

"Uh, I'm not sure, sir; that's why I have brought them up."

The reverend gestured with an open hand, and their official folders were quickly passed to him. He flipped them open and scanned through. "The rapist is guilty," he said evenly, without looking up. "The chicken case is a joke, and the two men who took a joy ride are guilty as well. No one saw the chicken thief. Let the one in custody go free. The rapist and the two who stole the car are to be dealt with in the most severe manner possible. Understand? The most severe. They are guilty, and the law must be observed."

"The most severe?"

"Yes," Rev. Moses said with finality. In the last several weeks, more and more judicial power had migrated to the reverend alone. He claimed that any efficient operation had but one leader, one head. No one challenged his claim of authority nor spoke in opposition. "The most severe. Do you understand?"

"Yes, sir."

Rev. Moses pushed back his chair, stood, glared at everyone, and walked from the room without saying another word.

The lights went dim, and Linda stood up into the spotlight, her dark hair shining like a black diamond. She reached for the microphone, closed her eyes, and began to sing. When she finished, Rev. Moses hustled to take the microphone from her. He pointed at the piano player, who continued to play, striking soft chords as the reverend spoke.

"Dear friends," he soothed, his words flowing like oil, "you have heard the message tonight. You have heard the sounds of God Himself in this song. God is at work in your life. I know it. You know it. God is not silent. The world may have become silent and mute, but God has not."

He walked to the edge of the platform and stared at the crowd crammed into the sanctuary. "Even here, even now, I know there are those among you who do not know the Lord. I want you to come forward now. I want to pray with you. I want to see that God has filled your heart."

He scanned the people, then raised his face to the ceiling. "Please come, please come."

More than fifty people made their way down the narrow aisles and crowded about the platform. Tears streaked their faces. Some were mumbling prayers and praises. Some could do no more than weep. With slow, methodical movements, Rev. Moses bent to each person, praying, offering words of forgiveness and encouragement. They would mumble words of thanks and grasp his hand, their faces beaming with newfound or rediscovered faith. An usher would slip up behind and offer them a Bible and escort them out for others to pray with. Every night scores and scores of new faces would make the journey to faith at the edge of Rev. Moses's pulpit.

Perhaps it was only Linda who saw the subtle culling that the reverend did each night. He would kneel with the old first, then the very young, then the men, then the women. He would start with the plain women first. The last person on the platform invariably was a young woman—a young attractive woman. Linda had listened before as he whispered, kneeling head-to-head with these women, placing a firm hand of comfort on their shoulders.

If they did not shrink back when he squeezed, he would pray longer, often insisting that they remain in prayer with him after he dismissed the congregation. Linda saw them nod, smiles and tears mixed on their upturned faces. They remained there as everyone filed out and Rev. Moses returned to them.

After that, Linda could do no more than surmise what "prayers" they engaged in. But like the members of the Garden council, she saw but remained mute. Like others, a blanket of silence fell upon her outrage and indignation, smothering it, keeping it from flaming, keeping it small and dark and hidden. And tonight she once again saw another innocent face, gazing so hopefully into the leering face of the Reverend Moses. Linda watched, held back a tear, and closed her eyes. For it had happened to her too.

september 10

Mike and Ernie inched their way south, their route mirroring the flow of the Mississippi. The river was quiet, with only a few fishermen marking the water with the wake of their boat.

Ernie, now bothered by severe headaches, stared forward as they walked and kept repeating, "Lock and load, lock and load, we're going to squash that big fat toad." He mumbled the words like a mystic's mantra, just at the edge of hearing. After days of the singsong repetition, Mike no longer heard it, but he saw Ernie's jaw move. He knew what he was saying.

As they walked into White Hall, they slipped into a dark and rambling house at the edge of a state park. To Ernie's absolute glee, the owner—wherever he was now—was a serious gun collector. Now they had all the firepower they needed.

They stole an ancient battered Dodge pickup in Medora, and for the last hundred miles of their journey, they once again traveled in style. The truck had rolled down a small dimple in the road and crested a short, low hill. Mike looked up and began to pump the brakes on the pickup. After a long squeal, they rolled and tilted to a stop. A quarter mile ahead stood a large wooden arch, hulking over the road. From where he sat, Mike could see at least twelve men scrambling to various positions. Most of them carried weapons. "Ernie," he said, "looks like we've found the Garden."

Ernie snapped awake from his nap. "Hot dog. We found him."

Mike and Ernie declined to enter the Garden. If they had given up their weapons and willingly submitted to relocation on one of the Garden farms, they would have been granted entrance. Neither man was willing to go that far.

As they spoke to the commander of the guards, a fat, sweating man with a southern accent, Mike noticed that every guard was outfitted with the same rifle—an ancient, grease-soaked M-1 from World War II. Mike lowered his voice to a dark, conspiratorial tone. "You like that M-1?"

"This piece of worthless junk? I don't like it one bit, but that's all they gave us to guard this place with."

"You want an Uzi? I have an Uzi to trade."

Mike and Ernie had five Uzis, taken during their stop in White Hall.

The fat man's eyes widened. He actually licked his lips in anticipation. "Who do you want me to kill?"

Mike and Ernie waited a few seconds too long to laugh at his remark. There was that serious, literal side to his offer. . . .

"You hear of a man driving into Stonefort in a Hummer. . . with a golden retriever dog?" Ernie asked.

The fat guard consulted the sky for a second, then his face brightened. "I heard of him, by gum. Came in along the southern road. Staying at a place called. . .called. . ." He scratched his head, then barked to another guard standing nearby. "What's the name of that place that we were watching a few weeks past? That farm where none of the people are registered?"

"The Wilson place?"

"That's it," the guard said, turning back to Ernie. "I know it now. You want to meet him?"

Ernie's lips parted in a huge grin.

The guard kept talking. "Well now, you could drive around south and get there all right, but you'd have to head through that moron Jamison's checkpoint, and he's a real stickler. You would never get through that way. You see, we got that Wilson farm surrounded by the Garden lands now."

The fat guard thought for a moment. "I could get word to that fellow with the Hummer that you're here. Would that be worth something to you?"

"We were sort of hoping to surprise him. We're old friends." Mike leaned close and whispered, "Would you know if the Hummer came to town?"

The fat guard's head bobbed up and down enthusiastically. "Holy cow, a Hummer in town would be all over the radio in a gnat's eyelash. I would know for sure."

Mike smiled again, long and satisfied. "Listen friend, we don't want to join the Garden. That isn't who we are—you know— farmers. We're soldiers, just like you. But tell you what. You tell me when that Hummer comes into town and close your eyes for a minute, and I got not one Uzi for you, but three of them. Brand- new, never been shot."

"Three?" The guard's eyes widened farther. It was apparent that Uzis were part of the new platinum currency. The guard focused on his feet. "I think I can—I know I can let you know when he shows up. We can talk back and forth. I can let you know."

"That'd be great, friend."

"But where are you going to be? How will I find you?"

Mike pointed back to the top of the hill and a grove of oaks. "We'll camp there. You let me know when that Hummer shows up in town, and you'll get the Uzis."

The guard jiggled back and forth on his feet. "I suppose that it's a deal then. Should we shake on it?"

Mike extended his hand and the two men grinned as their sweaty palms met in midair.

They unloaded their tent and supplies in silence. From the edge of the trees, Mike could see the guard outpost and arch over the road.

"Mike?" Ernie asked. "How do you know he's still there? He could have stopped at that farm and kept on going. And why do we need to wait for when he's in town? Why not just plow through to the farm and get him?"

Mike squinted hard. "Not on his own turf. Too hard to find and get. Once he's in town, he'll be a sitting duck. And besides, this guard gate will swing wide open."

september 15

The baby gasped and cried and tossed its head back and forth as if every breath brought pain, rather than life. Mary held him close to her breast and looked up at the priest with panicked, pleading eyes. "Do you know what's wrong, Father William? Can you do anything about it?"

The priest knelt by her and stroked the baby's head. He knew that Nathaniel's tiny lungs were filling with fluid. It had begun as a simple cold. The illness was a common enough condition—and treatable—before the Silence. But now that simple, innocent cold metastasized into a much more serious condition and became life threatening.

While Father William wasn't a medical doctor, every indication pointed to infant pneumonia. A healthy dose of antibiotics would clear things up in a few days, but considering the current situation, antibiotics would be as scarce as hen's teeth.

"Will he die, Father?" Mary asked, her voice cracking, tears beginning to flow. "You won't let him die, will you? You won't, please, Father? Please? You promised you'd watch after him."

The priest placed his hand on her shoulder. He lowered his head and began to pray.

―――

"There's nothing you can do, Father?"

"I know some about medicine, but that won't do us much good with Nathaniel. We need antibiotics. Some simple penicillin would do, I think, but we don't have any."

Father William, Leo, Peter, Tom, and the women who had helped with the birth gathered in a somber huddle on the far side of the barn.

"Can we make some?"

The priest shook his head. "It's controlled mold—like on cheese—but I'm no expert. It's not something that we can produce."

Peter stood at the side of the group, staring off toward town. "Would they have it in Stonefort?"

The priest shrugged. "They might. I heard someone say that they raided every hospital within a hundred miles of here. If anyone would have it, the Garden would."

"Who will go with me?" Tom asked. "If they have it in town, we need to get there now. We can take the baby in the Hummer. They would not refuse a sick child medicine."

Peter scowled. "But don't you see? The man is preaching heresy. He's evil. To go there on your knees just plays to his ego and his power. Don't you see?"

Tom's face reddened. "You're making an ethical and moral stand and holding a baby's life in the balance. You would sacrifice that child for your principles?"

It was Peter's turn to redden—this time in shame, not anger. "I. . .I guess not."

A tense quiet settled. And then baby Nathaniel began to cry.

"Forgive me," Peter said, addressing the whole group. "I let my feelings stand in the way of reason. Take the baby into Stonefort. Barter what you need to so you can get the medicine."

⸺⸱⸺

Tom and Leo unloaded everything in the Hummer. Tom did not touch the gold or the hidden weapons. The fewer who knew about them, the safer it was.

Mary and the baby climbed in the back with Megan, who offered what help she could. The priest and Tom climbed in the front. Revelations circled the Hummer, whining, barking nervously, pacing back and forth. It was the first occasion when he wasn't in the vehicle when the engine started.

Tom pulled away. But by the time he reached the stream, he noticed Revelations bounding after him, barking and tossing his head back and forth. Sliding to a stop, Tom jumped down from the car. The dog actually took his sleeve in his teeth and pulled, trying to return Tom to the barn.

"Revelations," he said, patting the dog's head, "we'll be back. We're just going to town."

Leo had run to the vehicle, panting. "I'll take him and tie him so he doesn't follow you."

Tom nodded and got back in the Hummer. The dog continued to lunge and bark and whine. "First time I've seen him so agitated," Tom said. "Like he is trying to warn me or something."

As they reached the main road, Tom turned and watched Leo pulling and dragging the dog back toward the barn.

<hr />

Upon arriving in the Garden, the small contingent found themselves shuffled and directed to a large canvas tent, just in the shadows of the church building itself. There sat six clerks in dark uniforms behind folding tables, backed by a long row of black file cabinets. Each clerk wore a similar expression of disinterest and implacability.

Tom's face was growing angry as he waved his arms in the air. "What do you mean the child can't have the medicine? You do have it, don't you?"

A slight blond woman with hair cropped close to her scalp sat unperturbed, staring back at Tom as he ranted. "Whether we have it or not is not the issue here."

"Then what's the blasted issue?" Tom shouted.

"The issue is," she began with an icy, callous tone, "that none of you, including the child, is registered with the Garden. That means you are not members of the new Garden and, as such, are not entitled to any of the Garden's benefits. It's a simple matter. I believe even Rev. Moses discussed this very issue with Mr. Wilson some weeks ago."

Tom bent over the table, hulking over the woman as best he could. "You mean to tell me that no registration—no medicine? You'd let this child die?"

"That is not my decision, sir," she replied, ready to dismiss him. "It was yours in the first place."

Tom slapped the table with his palm. The rest of the people in the tent stopped what they were doing and began to stare. "Then, blast it, we'll register. If it means saving this child, then we'll sign whatever stupid paper you have."

The woman sighed, turned behind her, clattered open a file cabinet, and withdrew a thick file folder. She presented Tom with a handful of papers. "Fill these out."

Tom scanned the multipage document. "We don't have time for all this. I'll sign my name, we'll get the medicine, and we'll come back to finish up."

"Well, sir," she said coldly, "that is not how it works. You have to fill this out, all of you, then present yourselves to the Office of Relocation for your housing assignments, then to the Labor Office for your work assignment. You'll also need to go to the Reclamation Office and turn in what materials and possessions you brought with you. Then to the Outfitting Office for uniforms or clothing, depending on your labor assignment."

Tom was furious. "We just want the blasted medicine! Now! Don't you understand? The baby is sick! We don't have time for this!"

The clerk weathered Tom's storm with no change in expression. "Well then, you should have thought of that earlier. This process takes at least a week until you're properly registered. There would be no chance of receiving any benefits, other than food, for at least a week. You could stay in the temporary shelters until you're all processed."

At the end of his patience, Tom slammed the papers down on the table. "Don't you understand? Does anyone understand? We need the medicine now. Not in a week. *Now!*"

"Well, sir, there is nothing I can do. My hands are tied. I suppose you could take it up with the mayor. He might have an open moment this afternoon or perhaps tomorrow."

Tom glared at the woman, the veins in his neck and forehead pulsing. He turned and stomped out of the tent with Megan, Mary and the baby, and the priest in tow. "I'll get in to see the mayor," Tom said, seething. "I'll get to see the holy Rev. Moses himself if that's what it takes. I'll get this medicine if I have to tear people apart."

Tom walked quickly toward the church. Father William watched for a moment, then saw the sun glint off a pistol that hung from a guard's belt. Then another glint and another. The guards shuffled toward the edge of the steps, watching Tom's slow-burning charge. Tom's words and shouts could not have gone unheard.

"Tom!" the priest shouted. "Tom! Wait. You must wait!"

Five minutes later the four of them and the baby settled down on a shady spot of grass under a stand of elm trees at the far side of the church property. To their left was the sea of tents, to their right the church and town.

Tom paced back and forth. "I'll get the medicine. I'll get it if I have to break some heads to do it."

Father William nodded. "I know you want to do that, Tom, but face the facts. You are one man against hundreds of armed guards. How far will you get if they say no?"

Tom glared at the priest. "Then what do you suggest, Father?" His words dripped with sarcasm. "Perhaps we should say 'pretty please'? Perhaps we should just turn and slink home and hope Nathaniel gets better?"

Father William didn't respond immediately. The only sound was the gurgling rasp of the child's breath as it rattled in his chest.

"Father," Mary whispered, "can you do anything? His breathing is getting worse."

Tom stopped and stared. Nathaniel's arms grew limp, his color paled to ash. His eyes closed, and his lips tried to produce a weak cry.

"Father, we cannot wait," Tom declared. "That child will die. You know that as well as I do." Tom began to march toward the Hummer that they had left on the east side of the bridge. "I have a rifle hidden under the floorboards. So help me, if I have to shoot my way into the hospital, I will. This baby will get that medicine."

The priest stood up. "Stop where you are, Tom! Stop this instant!" The priest's voice was shrill and commanding. "Get back here. I will have no one take up a weapon. You'll be killed, and the baby will be no better off. Get back here now!"

Tom rattled back to them. "Then what do we do, Father? Wait for awhile so you can perform last rites?"

Mary began to cry.

"No, Tom, we shall not wait, nor will one lone, crazed man march out and start shooting people!" Father William glared back at Tom. "We have more power than that!"

"Power? What power?" Tom sneered back.

The priest waited to answer. He waited until the anger dissipated from the air. "We have God's power."

Father William knelt beside Mary and Nathaniel. He placed one hand on her shoulder, one hand on the infant's head. He looked up at Tom. "I suggest you join us."

Tom's demeanor shifted suddenly. "But I am. . .I mean, I don't know if I believe. . . ."

"Obey, Tom. Simply obey for once," the priest ordered. "Kneel with us in prayer. We're all sinners, Tom. We have all failed. But God calls us to obey, not to be perfect."

Tom hesitated.

Megan slipped over to Mary's other side and knelt.

"Tom?" the priest called out.

"But. . .I'm not sure."

"Who among us *is* sure all the time?" the priest answered back sharply. "You think a priest has all the answers? You think I know for a fact what will happen and what will not? You think I know who will live and who will die?"

Tom was mute.

"Even I'm not sure, Tom," the priest said more softly. "But I *am* sure that God listens. He has promised to always listen."

Tom bowed his head.

"Tom, obey your heart. Kneel with us and pray with us. God has room for your doubt."

Tom hesitated, took one step, and stopped.

"Obey, Tom. Do not think. Simply obey."

Tom finally knelt beside the priest and bowed his head.

Summer still held a humid warmth in the air as the fat guard came wheezing up the hill. He bent over, palms on his knees, gasping for breath. Mike and Ernie knew what this meant.

"He's. . .he's. . .he's. . . ," came the gasping words. "The Hummer. . .it's on the east side. . .side of the bridge. . .and he's headed. . .for the church. . .with a priest. . .and two women. . .and a baby."

Ernie smiled, walked to the truck, and hefted out a canvas bag. "Here's your three Uzis, my friend."

The guard stood up, still gasping, and grasped the bag to his chest. He managed a smile.

"Now you'll have your men take a little nap?" Mike said as he walked to the truck.

The fat guard nodded. Between gasps, he managed to croak, "But only. . .if you. . .give me. . .a lift. . .down the. . .hill."

Ernie nodded, held the door open, slid to the center, and said, his voice oozing happiness, "Come on in, friend; you've earned it."

———————

Father William waited until each bowed his or her head. Then he waited a minute longer until all was quiet around them.

Today is the first step in the battle against this evil, Father William prayed silently. *I think that is what You have told me, Lord. And I am trusting You now. I would never have done this before the Silence. But now I have no alternative. I have no other place to go save to You, Lord.*

The priest gulped once. *Lord, I beg You to hear this prayer.*

"Dear God," Father William began, his voice reedy and scared, "we are sinners, humbly coming before a holy God." His words warbled with nervousness, for he knew what he must ask. He knew that lives depended on God's response to this prayer. He had no fear of what God could and could not do, but he had absolutely no inkling as to the unfolding of God's plan.

"We are sinners," he continued. "We have no right to be here, other than the right You have given us through the gift of Your Son and His death, in order that we may live with You forever. Without Jesus, we know we would be lost forever. We have taken that gift to our hearts. Lord, there are those in our midst who struggle with doubt and uncertainty. Please use this day to show them the truth. You are the Truth and the Light and the Way. You know our hearts, Lord. You know what must be done."

The priest gulped again. He knew the next part of his prayer was for, as he had said before, all the marbles. He had seldom, if ever, prayed with such bold supplication. God's will—yes, he had prayed for that, but he had never presumed to offer his own plan to the Lord. "God, there is a tiny baby here nestled in his mother's arms. He is Nathaniel, God's gift. His mother is Your servant, Lord. We are scared and frightened. The child is sick, Lord; his breathing comes hard. We have no medicine, save the medicine of the Great Physician. We are hopeless without Your hope, God. We are helpless without Your help."

The priest opened his eyes. Tears had begun to streak down Mary's and Megan's cheeks.

"Lord, I come before You today a broken man. I cannot save this child under my power. Only You can. And I come before You with a bold request—a most bold supplication. I come before You humbly, and I earnestly ask You to heal Nathaniel's body. I am asking that You lay Your hand upon him and heal him."

Father William opened his eyes again. Tom was staring at him with anxious, incredulous uncertainty in his eyes.

The priest continued to pray, eyes open. "Lord, it is in Your hands. We place this child in Your hands. Heal him, Lord, heal him." He closed his eyes again and bowed.

Mary repeated in a low whisper, "Heal him, Lord, heal him."

For nearly five minutes, the four remained nearly motionless in that silent tableau. Mary and the priest repeated over and over, "Heal him, Lord, heal him."

And the miracle began to happen. The change was imperceptible at first. But Nathaniel's breathing gradually strengthened—without rattle, without wheeze, without gurgle. The child's skin, a pale, ashen white no more than ten minutes prior, began to change to a robust and healthy pink. The tiny infant opened his eyes and blinked, gazing up at his mother's tear-streaked face. Then his tiny mouth quivered and he let out a lusty cry.

Megan's tears tumbled out in a torrent.

Mary looked to her child, then to the priest, then to heaven, and whispered, "Thank You, sweet Jesus, thank You." She turned away, taking the child to her breast. His cries muffled and stopped as he began to feed in earnest for the first time in days.

Tom's face, expressionless and mute, gradually dissolved into tears also. "Is he healed?" he whispered, hoarse with emotion. "Are his lungs clear?"

Father William hesitated only a heartbeat before he nodded at Tom. "The child has been healed."

"How did you do that?" Tom asked the priest, placing his hand on his shoulder.

"I didn't. God did."

"And you believe that?"

"Tom, you were here," Father William said, amazed at Tom's stubbornness. "You listened. You saw. And still you do not believe?"

Megan's tears continued to roll down her face. "You saw what we saw, Tom. How could it be anything other than a miracle from God?" she asked between sobs of joy.

"That was God? God healed him?" Tom said, appearing shocked.

The priest and Megan shared looks of incredulity.

"Yes, Tom, that was God's power at work," the priest said. And it was something he believed with all his heart.

Tom, Father William, Megan, and Mary and the baby slowly walked through the grove of elms, the first leaves of autumn crunching underfoot. The sun streaked down through the branches, dappling the ground with golden light. The hum of insects and birds surrounded them.

Father William couldn't recall a time when he felt more energized and awestruck in his life. He knew he was not a healer, nor did he possess any special conduit to heaven. Yet God had smiled on them that day and had poured out His blessing on them. Nathaniel's life had been spared, and for that the priest rejoiced. He also prayed that such a dramatic demonstration of power would make an impact on Tom and Megan, would soften their hearts, would prepare a way for their rebirth.

But the priest was a patient man. Even after the Silence, such matters could not be hurried. When God's time was right, it would happen.

They made it to the end of the line of trees and walked in front of the church. As they crossed the deserted street to get to the Hummer, the priest saw, out of the corner of his eye, a battered pickup truck swerving along the main street.

Lord, do not let this day end badly, the priest prayed as soon as he saw the truck. *Do not let this be the darkness that I have seen in my dreams. Do not let evil win.*

Any vehicle was now an unusual occurrence and cause for a longer look. Two men rode in the truck, one driving and one standing in the bed of the vehicle. It lumbered at the small group, roaring closer, now only a block away. The priest hurried the two women ahead of him, ushering them toward the church, wanting them to escape danger, placing himself between the oncoming truck and the women.

Then a flash of light glinted across the priest's face. The glass door of the church swung open and caught the sun's reflection. He looked up, and there on the top steps of the church stood Rev. Moses, a trio of somber-faced men in casual clothes whom he did not recognize, and an attractive black-haired woman. They watched as the priest and the women reached the curb below them.

The pickup truck barreled down the street, its muffler loose and its engine braying loudly. From where the priest stood, he saw the sun flash off the dark metal barrel of a weapon. Without thinking, he pushed Megan and Mary and the baby to the ground. Mary landed hard on her side, protecting the baby with her body. Megan fell flat on the sidewalk. The priest dove on top of them, trying to straddle both of them with his body, keeping his head turned toward the truck.

Tom still stood, apparently not seeing the danger. He faced the pickup.

The truck slowed as the man standing in the bed raised the weapon and, cackling with laughter, pulled the trigger. The sound of gunfire fractured the air with a furious clatter. Puffs of exploding concrete stitched along the curb and across the sidewalk. The shooter tried to hold the gun steady as the bullets clamored about Tom's feet like lethal wasps in an angry storm. Tom could find no shelter as the shells hissed about him, yet none found purchase in his flesh. A full clip was expended, and the shooter slapped in a fresh clip and kept firing.

The driver accelerated, and the truck lurched forward. The shooter spun, off-balance, and screamed, his finger still holding the trigger. Shells exploded and climbed the stairs, two at a time. The glass doors of the church exploded into a thousand deadly shards.

Father William turned to face the front of the church. Rev. Moses stood, slack-jawed with shock, at the scene unfolding below him. One of the men with the reverend took several shots to the chest and pitched forward, eyes gone dead and glassy. Another shell struck the woman in the shoulder just above her heart. She screamed once as she was thrown backward against the shattered doors. Guards and the others dove for cover as the bullets continued to whine and whistle in the air. The last shell fired from the Uzi found Rev. Moses's left arm. It spun him around like a child's top. He screamed as he fell.

A few of the guards regained their footing and began returning fire. A storm of bullets splattered into the truck and its tires. The truck slowed and began to smoke as its two occupants leapt from it.

"Take them alive!" Rev. Moses yelled. "Take them alive!"

A storm of guards and nurses and doctors had been posed at that very moment, readied for just such an attack. They streamed out into the sunlight, carrying black satchels and bottles and stretchers, running from several tents on the far side of the church's old parking lot.

A mob of guards corralled Mike and Ernie, clubbing and spitting and manhandling them on the way to the newly constructed jail. Both men had escaped injury during the return hail of bullets, but by the end of the two-block journey to the jail, they were bruised and bleeding.

Rev. Moses, braced by two young nurses, sat on the top step as three doctors tore off his sleeve and bandaged the wound, stanching the blood flow. He turned and saw Linda carried off, a dark crimson flood staining her dress below her left shoulder. Her face was chalk pale.

A stretcher arrived, and four men carefully positioned the reverend onto it. They hefted it back into their hands. Before they turned, Rev. Moses sat upright with a howl and pointed down to the priest and his group. "You! The Catholic charlatan and the rest of you! You caused this! They were after you and your hippie scum! Don't think I don't know what goes on at that farm. I know! I know everything!"

One of the doctors attempted to push the reverend back down on the stretcher. He batted him away, indignant that somebody would try to manhandle a man of his stature. "Get out of Stonefort! You are no better than a noxious weed in God's Garden. You are malcontents and evil! Leave and never return!"

He watched with distaste as the priest and Tom gathered up the women and child and led the band of heretics back to their commune.

Rev. Moses, held upright by two nurses, shuffled toward the jail as the light of day began to fade.

Three doctors had spent nearly an hour on the reverend's arm, cleaning away metal shell fragments and bone chips. A liberal dose of morphine flowed through the reverend's bloodstream, so the pain from the wound remained masked. The wound was large, but not serious.

Mike and Ernie—their names per the official report—sat in twin cells, shackled at their ankles and wrists and chained with a very short tether to a huge iron ring in the wall. They could sit, barely, but not recline. Both men looked miserable. Their eyes swelled nearly closed. Bruises colored their faces and necks. Their clothes were torn and bloodied.

The nurses navigated the reverend to a chair and helped him sit. "Now leave me alone with these men," he said, his words slightly slurred.

The three men stared at each other through the bars.

Rev. Moses spoke first. "You weren't trying to kill me, were you?"

"No," Mike replied, "we were after the blond guy with the Hummer."

"Where are you from?"

"Arizona," Mike replied. He gulped and then started to cry.

"Shut up," Ernie hissed. "We're not crying. We're not crying."

But Mike wasn't to be quieted. Rev. Moses let the sobs echo around the room for several minutes. Then he asked, "Why did you follow him from Arizona? That's a long journey for just any reason—short of. . .revenge." The reverend was a superb judge of men's motives and logic.

"We're not saying," Ernie snarled. "We're not, and Mike, you aren't saying either."

Rev. Moses nodded. The morphine made him feel like he was floating, and he was beginning to enjoy himself.

"I mean, we're sorry for killing that other fellow," Ernie said, "but that's all we're saying."

The reverend narrowed his eyes. "You dunderheads shot me too, and my lov—I mean, my singer, Linda. The man you killed was the sheriff. You have very bad aim."

"Sorry," Ernie grunted.

Mike continued to sob.

"You know we have to hang you for this."

Mike sobbed louder, tears puffing his eyes up even further.

"You sure?" Ernie asked with a waver in his voice.

"Oh yes, most sure," Rev. Moses replied. "An eye for an eye.[xxii] It's in the Bible."

Ernie grunted.

"That is, unless—" the reverend added.

"Unless what?" Ernie asked quickly.

"Unless there is something else you're hiding from me."

"Hiding?"

"Something you know and I don't. It might save your filthy necks."

Ernie gave the reverend an intense stare. "You mean you'd let us go if we told?"

"If it's important."

Ernie snorted. "It's important all right."

The room was silent, except for Mike's crying.

"You promise that if it's big enough, we get to walk?" Ernie asked.

The reverend smiled slowly, then nodded. "Of course. You give me a big secret, and you get a get-out-of-jail-free card. Sounds fair to me."

Ernie checked around, then whispered, "It's the Hummer. That guy has a million bucks worth of gold coins in it. He got it from some lady in Iowa. It's in his Hummer. I know it. It wasn't in the lady's house. He's got it in that Hummer."

The reverend arched his eyebrows in surprise. "Well now, a million in gold?" He stood, wobbly, and called toward the door, "Nurse!"

Ernie's face twisted into a mounting painful awareness. "Hey, when do we get to leave?"

"Nurse!" Rev. Moses called again.

"Hey! You promised!"

The reverend turned back and laughed. "I said if the secret was important enough. Needed to be two million dollars to get you out. Sorry. You'll still hang by nightfall."

The two nurses rushed in and wrapped their arms around Rev. Moses's waist and began to help him walk away.

"Hey!" Ernie shouted. "You promised! You promised!"

The reverend draped his good arm over one of the nurse's shoulders and said just loud enough for Ernie to hear, "I must inform the guards. These men are to be hanged tonight before the service. I do not want anyone—no one at all—talking to them before then."

The nurse nodded and closed the door. The light switched off, plunging the room into total darkness. Mike and Ernie remained in their chains, Mike's sobs punctuating the darkness.

—⁂—

At the western horizon, the faint tickling of dusk etched a pale crimson on low-hung clouds. Six guards in black uniforms surrounded both prisoners in a tight circle as they walked toward their final appointment. A handful of people stood in attendance—the new sheriff, a few high-ranking security people, and half of the town council. Riding in a wheelchair pushed by a nurse sat Rev. Moses.

Gags prevented either prisoner from speaking—orders from Rev. Moses. He said he wanted no last-minute incendiary speeches being made that might corrupt the innocent. The gallows hulked in the shadows behind the jail. This was the third time they'd been used in the month since their construction.

Both prisoners kicked and struggled in mute agony as the guards dragged them up the rickety steps onto the platform. The scent of fresh-cut pine followed their struggles. A red-faced guard slipped knotted ropes over the men's heads and pulled the noose snug to their necks.

Mike halted his struggles, lowered his head, and let the tears flow. Ernie twisted and stomped and tossed his head back and forth, trying to break free, trying to slip from his gag. With the noose in place, he pushed the gag against it, harder and harder, scraping his cheek raw. Before anyone could make any official pronouncements, the gag fell past his chin.

"This ain't fair!" Ernie screamed.

Mike snapped his head up, his swollen eyes wide with surprise.

"That man over there," Ernie shouted, angling his head toward the reverend, "the one in the wheelchair—he promised that we wouldn't hang if we told him about the gold! Well, I told him, and I'm up here with a noose around my neck about to be hung!"

Rev. Moses, still woozy from the morphine, struggled to keep his head from wobbling.

"This ain't fair! This ain't right!" Ernie continued to scream. "We're sorry for that other fellow, but we told him 'bout the gold! He said we would go free! He promised!"

A number of heads turned and stared at the reverend. His hands, tucked under a blanket spread across his lap, suddenly burst forth and waved in the air. "That man is a lunatic," Rev. Moses slurred. "He never spoke of gold to anyone."

The small crowd turned back to the prisoner, who was still shouting and cursing. "That's a lie and the two-timer knows it! He promised! This ain't fair!"

With a petulant wave, the reverend swung his hand as if batting at flies. "Silence him!"

On the gallows, the guard pulled up hard on the gag, muffling Ernie's curses.

The reverend's eyes swept over the assembly, taking each face in, then locking on the guard. He stared hard for a moment; then his head tilted back, as if he were appealing to the heavens for guidance or perhaps a sign. His arm flailed in the air, a wobbly command. "Hang them!" he called out, his words pitched high and thin.

Without a second's hesitation, the guard yanked at the lever. The trapdoors clanged open. Silence followed, broken only by the wheezing gasps of the dying men.

As Rev. Moses was being wheeled back to the parsonage, his blanket slipped from his lap, tangled in the wheels, and nearly tossed him from the chair. He lay there, half in and half out, as several men leapt to right the chair and its rider.

I can't tell them of the gold, Moses thought as they pushed him back into the leather seat. *I can't tell them now, and I can't go after the gold just yet. But the Hummer isn't going anywhere. I can make sure of that. And when the time comes, we'll have that treasure.*

An odd, deliberate smile creased his lips. *And then God can have the gold to use as He sees fit. You continue to bless this Garden, don't You, Lord? The gold will be Yours. And the evil has been eliminated. Thank You for protecting your faithful messenger.*

The reverend's head lolled back. He closed his eyes and began to snore, happy that such an evil had been eradicated from the Garden.

That evening doctors had gathered in the reverend's room. One had pulled out a hypodermic and tapped it with his finger, clearing the air bubbles. In the milky fluid was a powerful stimulant that would quickly counteract the effects of the morphine. The reverend had insisted that he preach an important message tonight and demanded something to keep him awake and alert.

Now, fixed in the glare of the spotlight, gripping the podium with hands that would not stop trembling, stood a sweating and angry Rev. Moses.

Linda would not sing tonight. She lay in a hospital tent, clinging to life. Doctors had done what they could. It was now up to the Lord and to her will to live.

He stared out at the crowd, sweat glistening off his forehead. He would not bother to wipe it away this night. *Let them see how much pain I am in. Let them see how I have suffered for God's Garden. Let them see how courageous I am to stay in the pulpit. Let them see*

how God has protected me yet once again in a most miraculous manner.
He could not help but smile as those thoughts raced in his mind.
I am blessed by God. I am chosen.

He bowed his head, trying to collect himself as odd visions
and strange images floated past his consciousness. The pages of his
notes, and the words on them, swam before his eyes. He blinked
to clear his head.

"Brothers and sisters of the Garden," he began, "by now you
have heard that the forces of evil have tried to silence God. They
tried to silence God's messenger in the Garden." He lifted his arm
and the sleeve of his robe fell open. A massive bandage encased his
upper arm. A thin dot of crimson marked the bandage.

"Two or three inches more and this bullet would have struck
my heart." He heard a gasp in the sanctuary. "But God has blessed
me and spared me once again. You may have heard that the men
who are responsible for this heinous attack have met biblical justice. They have met the Old Testament code of an eye for an eye.
Sheriff Killeen is dead. Linda Wilson lies near death. I have been
wounded."

He leaned back and nearly stumbled. "And those men who did
this are dead. God is now judging their souls."

He stepped forward, swaying slightly. "There are those among
us who seek to do evil and sin. Charlatans, women without hus-
bands bearing children in barns, men who horde treasure,
landowners who exploit others and cross legal boundaries. There
are those who are not members of the Garden and who sin and
preach heresy and evil."

He motioned and a doctor scurried toward him. Whispers
were exchanged and the doctor ran, returning with a glass of water.
The reverend gulped it down.

"The assassins were after those in our midst who seek to
destroy the Garden. Evil force against evil force. They have brought
death and bullets into our peaceful Garden."

The reverend struggled to focus his thoughts. His head was swimming in a dense fog. "That's what I must tell you. Be alert. Be aware. Be on guard that you are not polluted by the evil of others."

He turned and motioned for Linda to sing, then remembered that Linda was not there. He pivoted back to the congregation with panic on his face. Just then two doctors slipped out and placed their arms around him, ushering him back into the shadows as the pianist began softly picking out an old hymn.

A trio of women gathered by the microphone began to sing as the light diminished. Darkness crept in, bringing with it an autumn chill, a foreboding of the winter to follow. A volley of gunshots sounded, faint and distant to the west. But only for a heartbeat did the singing waver.

september 25

Peter's mood had grown dark and sour. When Tom and the rest had returned and told their story, Peter had flown into a desperate rage. He had pulled his old motorcycle from the barn and torn off to Stonefort. The others had tried to stop him, warning him of the reverend's anger, but he would not be dissuaded.

Well after moonrise, he had returned home. Guards had met him at the bridge and, without provocation, had fired warning shots over his head to stop him. A second volley, fired only inches from his feet, followed. Passage into Stonefort was denied.

One guard, an old friend, Ted Krienbrook, did share news of his wife's condition. "Don't be stupid, Peter," he said softly. "They have their orders. I've seen Linda. She seemed fine—more scared and shook up than hurt. But don't try to cross the river now, Peter. You'll wind up in jail. . .or worse." He then whispered in Peter's ear to wait until the furor of the shooting died down. If Peter returned with a letter, Ted would be sure that his wife received it. "And Becca is fine, Peter. Marliss dotes on her. She'll be fine."

Peter—angry, desperate, frustrated, and growing bitter—had no choice but to comply with the galling conditions. He had returned the following morning with three letters—one for Linda, one for Becca, and one more for Mayor Smidgers, requesting a more formal hearing on his rights to visit his daughter.

Ted smiled, took the letters, and promised that he would deliver them. Peter left, his heart heavy, but somewhat comforted by knowing that his letters would be delivered.

The days had dragged on. Peter spent most of his time standing by the stream, watching the water flow.

Everyone had heard of the hangings, and Peter's bleak mood spread. There was no doubt as to the guilt of the two, but such swift and harsh justice took the group's collective breath away.

This evening, after the meal was finished, most of the members of the farm sat in a semicircle around the fire. The breeze from the west carried the fire's warmth. The nights had begun to chill.

Peter sat to one side, his feet propped near the fire pit. The priest sat beside him. Elijah busied himself with serving and cleaning. Peter listened to the murmur of conversation around him. The group talked around him and not to him, each knowing that Peter's words had grown short and cold over the past ten days.

Peter fidgeted, as if struggling with a decision. Then he scanned the group and stood. He coughed loudly to get everyone's attention. "I need to ask your forgiveness. I haven't been a very good role model these last days."

"Hey, man, we understand," Leo called out. "You've been through some heavy stuff."

"Thank you, Leo, I appreciate that. But then, haven't we all been through a lot?"

A chorus of amens followed.

"But I don't think the Bible ever talks about a Christian having it easy." Peter's face tensed. "And the Bible never guarantees that everyone who calls himself a believer is a believer. Just because a man says it, doesn't mean he is."

"You talking about the man?" Leo asked.

"The man?"

"You know, Rev. Moses," Leo said.

Peter studied his hands. He had rehearsed this answer many times in his mind, but now, when the time came, the answer was no clearer. "Leo, I can't see into his heart. But some of what he's said is wrong. There is no need for God's people to live inside an armed camp and be registered in some master file. Justice has been too swift and too severe. And there is no reason for God's people to give up everything they have to follow one man. If they were following Jesus—but they're not. They're following Rev. Moses."

"But, like," Leo interrupted, "didn't Jesus say toss everything away and follow Him? Isn't that giving everything up?"

"Leo, you're not alone in being confused. Some of what the Garden has brought about is good. Rev. Moses and the Garden. . . well, they have taken in a whole lot of pilgrims and stragglers who may have died without his help. That's good."

"So what's the problem? I mean, I understand about your little girl and your wife, but does that make the guy evil? Maybe there's a side we don't see," Leo said. "I'm confused. It looks to me like this Garden is a good thing, most of the time. I mean I know I'm honked about what they done to Elijah, but I've been busted enough times by the cops before. Sometimes I was guilty, and sometimes I wasn't."

Peter sighed. "I want to tell you that you shouldn't confuse doing good with being holy. They're not the same. Do not confuse progress with God's will. Not all successful things please God."

"I can dig that, Peter," Leo continued. "But what do we do now? Do we battle with the bad guys because you say they're bad? Do we pack our bags and move? Do we wait it out?"

Peter became more and more mired in his anger as he spoke. "Listen, I don't have the answers to everything. All I can tell you is what I know. We have to do what Jesus would do. He witnessed to others. He helped. He cared. He shared. He loved. We can do that, can't we?"

Peter took a cleansing breath. He wanted to end his anger. "We need to be ready. We need to witness to others now. We need to be aware that Christians are not going to be magically spared from suffering. Christians may die of starvation like anyone else.

We have to remember that God's will gives us grace and peace and strength throughout whatever bad things we have to endure. You must lean only on God's strength, for our human preparations will be fruitless. We need to be prepared to be martyrs, if necessary. That's what Jesus meant when He said, 'Give up everything and follow Me.' We might die in the process."

"So what should we do?" Leo asked, scratching his dreadlocks. As he did so, his beads jangled.

"Leo, I have to repeat one thing. What you should have done before the Silence—if you were a believer—was to witness. What you should do now after the Silence—if you are a believer—is witness."

Leo smiled. "Is that really all there is to it?"

"It is. If the Silence goes on forever, do you think the survivalists will have enough food for all eternity? No. Will the militias be able to survive forever? No. But a believer will."

"But what about food, man?"

"Have you ever read Mark? I think it's in the eighth chapter. 'If you try to keep your life for yourself, you will lose it. But if you give up your life for my sake and for the sake of the Good News, you will find true life.'[xxiii] That means that if you work so hard at saving your life and neglect God, then your life is lost. Only those who live for Jesus will truly know what living is."

Peter gazed at every face before him. "We may not survive the winter. We may all die at the hands of a crazed militia or the Garden security forces. But if we die following the words of Christ, then our lives will have meaning.

"Don't you see, none of us knows when Jesus is coming back. We have to do two things while we wait—and have to do them with equal enthusiasm. We have to work as if we have ten or twenty or thirty years to live; we have to live as if we have a week left."

Leo looked confused.

"We have to be smart and lay up food and take care of ourselves and anyone else we can help as best as we can—and we have to share the Good News with others every chance we get. That's what Jesus wants us to do."

A long silence followed.

"Cool, man," Leo replied.

The moon rose, heavy and full over the soon-to-be-harvested fields. A thick, rich scent lay over the darkened landscape like a blanket. Tom sniffed the air. While not a farmer, his nose could tell that the crops were ripe. Megan walked beside him, a golden oak leaf in her hand. She twirled it, and it caught the moonlight.

"Fall is here," she murmured.

"I love this crispness. It's been a very long time since I felt that early nip of coolness. California was wonderful, but it insulated me from what life was really like."

"I guess New York City was no better. Occasionally I'd take a cab through Central Park. That's as close as I got to nature for a long time."

"But since the Silence. . . ," Tom began.

Megan laughed. "Seems like a lot of conversations start that way."

They came to the stream. Revelations had not tired of diving in, but at night he was content to walk beside them. He waded in a few feet and lapped at the water instead. Tom brushed some leaves off a fallen log and sat down. He held his hand out to Megan, who took it and sat beside him.

"Megan," he whispered, "I. . .I don't know how to say this. . . but I want to ask you a question."

She turned to him and smiled. "Ask me anything."

"Am I too old for you?"

She stared hard at him for a long minute, then began to laugh.

"What's so funny?" he asked, puzzled.

"How much older are you anyhow?" she asked, her voice lilting.

"Well, I'm forty-one. That used to be pretty old. It feels pretty old."

She squeezed his hand. "I'm thirty-one. You just wait, and I'll catch up pretty soon."

He stared back, and they both laughed.

Revelations clambered out of the stream and nosed at Tom, a curious look of concern in his eyes. Tom reached over and patted the dog's head. "I know it sounds odd, boy. You haven't heard much laughter these past months."

Megan sat up and straightened her sweatshirt. "We risked death a hundred times getting here. The world may be coming to an end. And here you are, worried about a few years' difference in our ages. Tom, you are a man of odd sensibilities."

He grinned. "I think it's just that I'm so aware of how hard life has become. . .how terrible it is and will be for so many millions. It almost seems like we shouldn't be happy. It seems like we don't deserve this relationship."

"I know, Tom. I know what you're saying. But regardless of what is happening, we don't have the luxury of wasting time."

He nodded. Then she reached up, put a hand around his neck, and pulled him close, meeting his lips with hers.

A hundred yards away, Father William and Peter sat under their customary tree. Father William hushed their conversation so as not to disturb Tom and Megan, and Peter swept at the cigarette smoke with his hands.

"Father, this is a big farm. And it's mine. Those two could go someplace else for privacy."

The priest glared at him with mock seriousness. He knew Peter was still in pain and hoped that Peter's words of this evening had helped vent that crippling emotion.

"The darkness hates love, Peter. You know that. I can feel it recoiling at their laughter. I can sense it being driven farther and farther from this farm by the power of the love that emanates from this small plot. If Tom and Megan are falling in love, then I do not want to stand in the way of that love."

"I guess you're right, Father," Peter said with a cheerful resignation. "So why don't we move to the other side of the barn? There's a bench over there, and it would be more comfortable."

Father William snorted. "And leave them unchaperoned? Not yet, Peter, not yet. I will not have them move too fast."

"Good Lord above," Chuck Martin said as the government-issue Hummer crested a slight rise, "I never thought I would see this day."

Before them lay the Ohio River and just north of the river lay Metropolis, Illinois.

Riley turned to face the riders in the back and grinned. "Didn't I tell you we would get here?"

"Yeah, but you didn't say it was going to take so blasted long," Chuck said.

Riley flipped his lighter open and set flame to the end of a well-chewed cigar. "Don't see why it would make any difference anyhow. None of you has family here."

Dave Ox laughed. "But we have heard so much about yours that this has become the search for the Grail. None of us thought we would ever get here. We thought you'd made up this family just to keep us going."

Riley settled back against the seat and let the smoke cloud cover his face.

The last months had been hard. Terminations, replacements, and adjustments were part of every week. Each of these men left family back in Washington. Safe in the Pentagon, to be sure, but apart. He had promised that after Illinois, they would all return home for some leave.

"Why are we so worried about this Moses guy, anyhow? I know he sounds a little off sometimes, but he's got southern

Illinois under control, doesn't he?" said Chuck. "That should be a good thing. A lot of people farming and living simple-like. Shouldn't we be happy with that?"

"And I sure like that singer he has," Dave added. "Makes me pretty glad we have a million dollars of electronic gear with us."

Riley puffed, then shifted the cigar to the side of his mouth. "He isn't that dangerous—yet. That army chaplain back at base says he's drifting. Says he's getting closer to thinking he's not only called by God but a member of God's ruling order. That sort of man gets mighty dangerous."

The men in the vehicle grew quiet.

"Does this mean assault with extreme prejudice as well? I mean, he is a man of the cloth," Dave pointed out.

Riley shut his eyes. "That's a call I'm not making. The brass upstairs will. And we'll know when we get there."

No one spoke as they crossed the muddy Ohio River into Illinois.

september 26

The new day was only an hour old. Tom tossed and turned for a long hour before rising, slipping on a sweatshirt and jeans, and walking to the stream. The moon, a giant circle of gold, reflected in a still pool. The air carried an innocent nip of autumn's chill.

Behind him, Tom heard a scrabble of paws against the nylon tent. He smiled. A second later a very wet nose pressed against his back. Tom reached around and tousled the dog's hair. Revelations sat down with a yawn.

"I know it's late. . .or early, boy, but I can't sleep."

The dog inched his way to the ground and rested his head on his paws.

"I think Megan has interrupted my sleep."

The dog kept staring up at Tom.

"Well, I know she has."

Tom picked up a dry branch that lay next to him and stripped it of the leaves and twigs. The stream burbled only feet away. Without thinking, Tom tossed the branch into the water. And also without thinking, Revelations leapt up and tossed himself with abandon into the cold water, splashing after the stick.

The dog returned, wet and happy, and laid the stick at Tom's feet. Revelations stepped back, grinning in that loopy dog fashion, and silently urged Tom to repeat the process. Cold water ran off him in rivulets, and his coat steamed in the chilly night air. Tom reached for the stick and tossed it again. He knew the dog would never be satisfied with one retrieval. Two stood as the bare mini-mum; three was preferred.

The third time the stick was retrieved, Tom said, "Good boy! Now hold," and tousled the wet hair on the dog's head. The dog seemed to nod and began shaking the water off. Tom had learned that trying to shield himself from the water was a losing proposi-tion so he simply smiled, shut his eyes, and waited until the dog finished his gyrations.

In that mist of cold water and darkness, a jolt of insight surged through Tom's body. *Revelations obeyed. He didn't think. He just obeyed. And that obedience made him happy. He didn't fight it. He didn't wonder why the stick was thrown. He didn't debate if the stick was intended for him or not. And he didn't resist when the game ended. He simply obeyed. He simply obeyed his master.*

Is that what this dog is teaching me? Tom wondered. *Just abandon my resistance? Just give up and obey? Just accept it? Just accept the gift?*

Tom stared into the dark vastness of the sky that stretched into the infinite heavens. Like a sparkling streak from a falling star, Tom suddenly felt so absolutely right about this new revelation. Nothing moved or shook or trembled, but Tom knew that what he was about to decide and embrace was totally and certainly correct.

God, thank You for leading me to this decision through a dog. Every time I wanted to obey, something in my heart told me that I couldn't. That I was too much of a sinner. That I had caused too much pain in my past. That I had done too many bad things to even approach You. Something made me think that I just couldn't let the past go. Something made me stop, wait, then say no. I was convinced that You wouldn't want to be bothered with me since I'd done too many bad things or had too much money to need You.

But now the pieces seem to fit. I was waiting for something, but all I really had to do was stop being analytical for a moment and obey. I can do that. I can do that. I can give You my past and ask Your for-giveness. I can do that, Lord.

Tom lowered his head and closed his eyes. Quietly he began to pray aloud: "Lord, You have brought so many people into my life that explained all of this to me. I don't know why I couldn't listen. But this dog. . .Revelations. . .he opened my eyes. I can obey. I can accept what Jesus did. I can open my heart to that. I can obey."

He opened his eyes, not knowing for certain if the prayer was enough, or if the words were correct, or if he had covered enough theological ground. But the dog's eyes were set on him, and his wide canine mouth turned to a grin again.

"Is it enough, boy?"

The dog whimpered once, excited, then barked. He barked once more, then laid down his head and closed his eyes.

"I guess it was, Lord. I guess it was."

september 27

Peter carefully held the crumpled letter in his hand. Inside were two short pages, both typed. One page was signed by his wife, but the signature was shaky and light. The other bore the childish scrawl of his daughter. Ted Krienbrook brought the letter to the farm and placed it into Peter's hand as night fell.

"I hope it's good news, Peter," he said as he quickly departed, as if unwilling to stay on the unregistered farm any longer than necessary.

Linda's letter read:

Dear Peter,

I am getting stronger every day. I am grateful that there are doctors, as well as medicine, available. I know it is unpleasant, but I am glad that my attackers met with God's swift, ultimate punishment. God will punish those who break His laws. I am looking forward to returning to my singing. I hope you will see that registering with the Garden makes so much sense. I am sure that the differences between you and me and sweet Becca would be easily straightened out if that were to occur.

Your loving wife,
Linda

The letter from his daughter read:

Dear Daddy,
    I miss you. I am fine. Everyone here at the church is very
nice. I have my own room. I hope you can come and visit me
soon. Rev. Moses is a nice man.

Love,
Your daughter, Becca

Peter reached into his breast pocket, looking for a cigarette.
Then he remembered that he'd smoked the last of his stock some
days earlier. He sighed, knowing that it didn't matter anymore.

They didn't write these letters, Peter realized, near tears. He
brushed away the wetness from his eyes. *I miss them so much.*

A rustle of dry grass alerted Peter that Father William was
making his not-so-quiet way across the field. At first Peter thought
the priest was simply calling attention to himself as he walked, so
as not to surprise anyone. But by now he knew the truth. Father
William was simply not a man comfortable in the woods. He
stumbled over roots, he chopped down healthy plants trying to
weed, he slipped on wet rocks by the stream, and he made amazing amounts of noise in the woods for being such a slight man.

Peter smiled and turned to greet his guest. The two of them
sat companionably in the still of the evening.

"Why doesn't the moon set at the same time every day like the
sun?" the priest asked. "Sometimes I see it early, sometimes late,
sometimes not at all. Why is that?"

"I'm not sure, Father, but I thought a man of God like yourself would simply take such things on faith."

"I can be faithful, Peter, and still have questions. Are the letters happy?" Father William asked.

Peter shook his head. "Not happy or sad, but they weren't written by Becca or Linda. Someone else wrote them."

"Are they signed? Are their signatures real?"

"Maybe. I think so. But I'm not a handwriting expert."

"Why would anyone want to do that?" the priest asked. "I know Rev. Moses may not be the most honorable man in Illinois, but why would he forge a letter from your wife and child?"

"Maybe to keep me quiet," Peter surmised. "Or to get me to come to town. I don't know for sure." He looked down at the letters in his hands, fighting the urge to say the real truth. Then, finally, he realized he had to come clean with the priest. "Father, I take that back. I know. I know why he sent the letters."

Looking surprised, the priest asked, "You do? Why?"

"You know, Father."

"I do? Peter, I'm sure I don't."

Extending the letters to the priest, Peter added, "I'm sure you do."

With a puzzled look, Father William took them. Peter watched as the priest stiffened, as if a cold surge of energy tore at his arm. The priest clutched at his chest, as if he'd been squeezed hard—and suddenly. The letters fell from Father William's hands and tumbled end over end, coming to rest in the high grass.

"I felt the same thing when I opened the envelope," Peter said, his words dipped heavy in resignation. "It's the darkness. We both knew it was there—waiting. We both knew it was waiting—for us."

The priest shut his eyes, as if fighting off the power of the evil that filled his mind.

"It won't do any good, Father William. Evil is as evil does. Didn't you say that awhile back? Or was that me?"

The priest could only shrug.

september 28

Linda Wilson blinked as she slowly sat up and waited for her room in the parsonage to stop its agonizing spin. Her hand reached out for the water glass by her bed and then jerked, sending the glass crashing to the floor. Two intravenous lines dripped into her left arm. Massive bandages and packing formed a disfiguring lump over her left breast.

That terrifying moment when bullet shattered bone flooded back over her like a tidal wave. In her mind's eye she relived the flames from the gun, the bark of the shells crackling into concrete, the shriek of exploding glass, the pain imploding into her left shoulder, the horrifying spin as her body twisted under the bullet's impact.

Heavy beads of sweat coursed down her face. The sheet draped over her grew wet and clung like a skin to every inch of her body. Under the bandages and packing, she felt a pulsing wetness. She knew it had to be blood.

Dear God, I don't want to die, she thought as she brought her right hand to her face. She touched her eyes and then her dry and cracked lips to make certain she still existed, that she still had life and animation.

Her hand fell, lifeless and drained, at her side.

I must hold on, she commanded herself. *I must hold on.*

From beyond the window, she heard the faint chug of generators and people shouting. The voices were too faint and far away to make out individual words. A bird's song—bright and brash and joyous—broke through the clatter. The feathered singer's trills and chirps were so beautifully audacious that Linda found a smile trembling at her lips.

There are still wonders in the world, she thought. *It hasn't been ruined yet. We haven't ruined it all.*

She let the songbird's calls resound in her ears and mind. She licked her lips and began to speak in a mouse-quiet voice. "Dear Lord, I know that I am near death. I know it. My body knows it." She closed her eyes. "In my dreams I have seen such visions, such tormenting visions. Are they from hell, Lord? Have You let me see through the doors of hell?" She spread her fingers on her right hand and fiercely grasped a handful of sheet and mattress as a buffer to the pain. "If I have seen the evil, Lord, I have to make it right with You. I cannot bear that pain. I cannot. If I still have a chance, would You hear my prayer for forgiveness?"

After a minute her fist relaxed and her hand opened.

"Thank You, Lord," she whispered. "I have sinned so badly, Lord, that I am worried that even You cannot forgive me. I have sinned against my husband and child. And, worst of all, I have sinned against You and Your holy church."

A rattling breath filled her lungs. "I am asking that You forgive me for all the horrible evil that I have done, evil done deliberately and under the very cross of Christ." Tears pooled in her eyes and slowly streaked down her face. "Please forgive me, Lord, and take me into Your arms again. I am so sorry. I am so, so very sorry."

She cried, unabated, for nearly an hour as she recounted her past sins and cast them to the Lord.

Then the bird called out again from beyond her window. She sniffed and coughed once. Her body recoiled in pain. But she smiled as a new peace washed the pain from her.

"I will make amends, Lord," she promised. "I will lead the others to seek Your forgiveness in the time I have left." She sniffed again. "Thank You, Lord," she whispered. "Thank You, Lord."

I'm told that you have asked to see me." Rev. Moses slid a chair a few feet from Linda's bedside, as if not wanting to catch her pain.

Linda narrowed her eyes in the cool light of the evening.

Rev. Moses turned to the nurse with a smile. "You may leave us now. I shall need this time to remain as private between pastor and parishioner."

The nurse scuttled out of the room.

"Jerry," Linda whispered, then saw his eyes harden. "I mean, Rev. Moses—sorry."

With a wave, he dismissed her slip. Use of his first name was too revealing, he insisted, and from the time of their first meeting on, he could only be addressed as "Reverend."

"I understand, child, you are in pain. The doctors tell me that you are making a remarkable recovery."

She tried to smile through her cracked lips. "I *will* recover, but it will be in heaven."

"Nonsense," he said quickly. "The doctors have promised me that you will get well. I have prayed for you and their efforts."

"Then I must thank you, but I know what I know."

Rev. Moses stared at her, then glanced toward the door, to his watch, then to the window as he waited for her to speak.

"Rev. Moses, I have asked Jesus to forgive me," she finally said, weak and tired. "And He has. He has forgiven me for everything."

Rev. Moses nodded. "That is wonderful, Linda. Confession is

good for the soul."

Her face tightened, and she managed to push upright a little on trembling arms. "And *you* need to ask forgiveness too."

His face twisted into a mask of shock, bordering on outrage. "Me? Ask forgiveness? For what? The pastor of the largest church in America? I don't know what you're talking about."

Linda continued to stare at him. "You know. I know. For what we did. What we continued to do under the very shadow of the cross. It was sin, Rev. Moses. Every time you came to my room. Every time I slipped along the dark hallway to your room. We need to make it right. You need to ask forgiveness. You have to."

He slid back on his chair as if a snake had slithered under it with venomous fangs spread wide. "You're in pain, Linda," he called out. "Obviously a great deal of pain. You do not know what you're saying." A thin trickle of sweat ran down his left sideburn and darkened his starched shirt collar.

"You have to confess, Rev. Moses. There isn't much time left. I have confessed. I'm confessing to you. It's what you must do. You must tell the church and ask for forgiveness. I must tell Peter and Becca and beg for their understanding and forgiveness. You must do the same and tell the church."

"Tell the church?" he cried out, incredulous. "Linda, the pain has made you delirious. There is nothing to tell the church about."

She fell back to the bed, her face ashen, her breath rapid, her words hoarse. "You have to come clean," she whispered. "I have. If I'm going home to Jesus soon, then I want to enter the gates of heaven with all sin confessed. Don't you see, Rev. Moses? You may not have much time."

He snorted in response. "Time? I have all the time in the world," he said, but his eyes seemed frantic to her. He consulted his watch again. "And now I must be going, Linda. I will see to it that the doctors come in with a heavier dose of morphine for you—for the pain. We can't have you hallucinating. That just won't do." With no further words, he slipped from the room and latched the door.

⌐⌐⌐⌐⌐

My lands, Rev. Moses thought. *I can't let her speak to anyone. What if someone overheard her rantings? That would be horrendous.*

The nurse just outside the door looked at him with a warm, inviting smile. He smiled back, took his time to stare at her features, and then he remembered. *Did she hear what Linda was saying? She's still smiling, inviting me to stare back, so she probably hasn't.*

The nurse leaned forward suggestively. He was certain her move was intentional. *Good. She didn't hear. But now what? Did Linda tell anyone else?*

"Uh, nurse. . . ?"

"I'm Cindy Fox," she purred. "We met a couple weeks ago at the hospital."

He scrambled for that memory, but no image came to mind. "Yes, of course," he said, hoping she would not ask for details. "Tell me, has Linda had any visitors today other than myself?"

The nurse smiled longer and harder than needed. "Well, her daughter came in after breakfast. And then the doctors came in after that. They stayed for at least forty-five minutes."

"And that was all?"

"Well. . .no," she said, her face brightening as she remembered. "Just before lunch a Mr. Ted. . .Ted Krienbrook stopped by."

"Who?"

"I never met him before. He was in a security uniform though. Seemed like a nice man."

The reverend began to breathe a sigh of relief. He had, for a moment, entertained the idea that Peter had slipped through security and had managed to hear his wife's impertinent confession.

"And I'm sure her husband was happy that Linda was well enough to write him another letter," the nurse added.

The words exploded in the reverend's ears. "Another letter?"

he gasped, the color draining from his face.

"Yes, I remember you saying she wrote him a letter a few days ago, and today she wrote to him again."

"A second letter?" Rev. Moses gasped again as his voice nearly disappeared in shock.

"Mr. Krienbrook picked it up and said he would deliver it to her husband. That seemed to cheer her up a great deal."

Rev. Moses wobbled and held his hand out to the wall to steady himself. "At noon?" he wheezed.

She smiled wide and nodded.

It was now nearing seven. There would be no way to intercept that letter.

"Rev. Moses," Cindy said, clearly nervous, "are you all right? You don't look so good. Can I do anything to help? Anything at all?"

He filled his lungs with a huge gulp of air, then shook his head. "It's nothing. Just a little dizziness. I'm fine now." He lurched down the hall, still holding one arm out to steady himself, grazing his fingers along the wall.

I've got to stop this, he thought frantically. *I've got to get to a doctor for a healthy increase in Linda's pain medicine to keep her quiet. That will take care of the problem one way or another. If the dose is too much for her frail body to handle, then her life will. . .then her life will be in the hands of a just God.*

He nearly stumbled down the steps. *And then I need to get to Goodboy Slatters. Peter has to be stopped. He'll come here for sure. Maybe if Goodboy thinks that Peter's out to do some damage to the church? Maybe if he thinks he's armed and dangerous? But it has to be only Goodboy. I can't spread this more than it's already been spread. Just Goodboy. I can trust Goodboy.*

⸺⸺⸺

The doctors had kept Becca outside for a long time while they changed Linda's bandages. As they left, Becca slipped past them and tumbled back into the room. Linda could tell Becca was trying not to cry as she stood next to her mother's bed.

Linda's breath came in scratching wheezes as she reached for her daughter's hand.

"Does it hurt, Mommy?"

Linda turned and smiled at her daughter. "A little. But Mommy won't suffer much longer." Her words were tinged by the hint of finality.

"You look sad, Mommy," Becca said as she carefully climbed onto the bed and nestled into the comfort of her mother's good arm.

"No, my little one," Linda replied, "I'm not sad or scared. Not now."

"Why?"

Linda smoothed at the wisps of her child's blond hair. "Well, Becca, it's because I told Jesus about a lot of wrong things that I did, and He forgave me."

Becca wriggled around. She sat up and looked into her mother's eyes.

"Sometimes mommies do things that are wrong, Becca."

"I know," Becca answered softly. "I still love you more than anything, Mommy."

"Do you mean that? Do you really? After everything that has happened?"

Becca nodded and embraced her mother.

Linda pulled her daughter tight, willing to suffer any pain the gesture might cause. "I love you too, sweet one, more than anything. I just sort of forgot it for a little while."

"I know," Becca answered, matter-of-factly, "and that's okay. I know you love me."

Linda tried to smile. "And your father loves you too. You know that, don't you?"

Becca nodded. "I know he does, Mommy."

Linda held her daughter close again for a long, long time.

"And if Mommy has to go away, you'll always know that she loves you so very, very much?"

"I'll know, Mommy," Becca whispered. "I'll always know that. Always and forever."

Linda pulled her daughter fiercely to herself, ignoring the pain, ignoring the fact that her time was running out. Their salty tears began to flow. . .and mixed with one another's until they both fell asleep, nestled in the love and comfort of each other's arms.

september 30

A thick scud of clouds hovered overhead as the day broke gray and ominous. Peter awoke early and stood a few rows deep into the cornfield, testing the kernels with his thumbnail. He estimated another week until harvest.

From the road, a voice called out softly, "Peter, is that you in the corn?"

Peter recognized Ted's voice and stepped out of the field, brushing at wisps of stalk and corn silk clinging to his jacket.

Ted smiled for a moment; then his face returned to a somber visage. He held out his hand. "Letter from your wife. I left last night but didn't make it. Got too dark and I slept in an old car. Anybody asks, I didn't deliver a thing, okay? I was never here."

Peter nodded and took the letter. Ted turned without saying another word and disappeared.

As Peter read, his face, his lips, his eyes trembled, then tightened, then trembled again. With great care, he folded the one-page letter and slipped it into his breast pocket. He looked up at the sky for several minutes, his lips slowly moving in silent prayer. Then he turned and ran toward the barn, hoping and praying that he would not be too late.

He yanked off the canvas sheet that was covering his old, battered motorcycle. He quickly unscrewed the gas cap and jerked the bike to one side. A slight sloshing indicated that there would be enough gas for the trip but not much more. Pushing it from the barn, he wheeled it far enough from the structure so as not to wake anyone. From out of the early shadows appeared Father William, hair tousled into a point, eyes bleary.

"I have to go to town, Father," Peter said calmly.

"But what about the reverend's warning? It's too dangerous, Peter. Let me go. Whatever it is you have to do, I could do for you."

"Grateful for your offer, Father. But it's Linda, and she wants to be forgiven. It's something only I can do." Peter climbed on the bike and rested his foot on the kick-starter. "I'll be careful, and I won't cross at the bridge." He kicked once, and the engine sputtered to life, smoke pouring out of the exhaust. "Father?"

"Yes?"

"Pray for me, would you?" Peter shifted into first and charged off toward town.

He knew that crossing into town over the highway bridge would be foolish. Even if Ted Krienbrook was a friend, Peter would be a marked man for every other Garden security guard. With a lurch, he turned off the main road about a mile east of town and followed an old footpath that led to a narrowing of the river.

By this time in the fall, the river ran shallow. Peter parked the bike, took off his shoes and socks, rolled up his jeans, and waded across thirty yards of cool water.

The church and parsonage lay no more than a mile to the west. Circling north, Peter kept hidden by stretches of shrub and woods. By the time the church was in sight, Peter figured the time to be no later than 6:30 in the morning. He had to sprint across on open field, the parking lot, and slip in the back door without being seen.

He closed his eyes, prayed again, harder and more earnestly than ever before. Then, with his head lowered and his shoulders hunched, he took off over the open space, praying that no guard would sound an alarm at his presence.

In less than a minute, he was at the side door of the parsonage.

The door, a flimsy storm-and-screen combination, remained locked. Peter wedged a penknife behind the lock and yanked, and the door popped open easily.

He prayed that no one would be standing guard in the upstairs hall this early in the day. His prayers were answered. He found Linda's room and slipped inside.

"Linda," he whispered, "it's me, Peter." He stroked her hand as he knelt beside her bed. *She looks so pale,* he thought. *Lord, she looks close to death. They said she was recovering. They lied to me. They lied, and I believed them!*

"Linda, can you hear me? It's Peter. I got your letter."

Her eyelids fluttered open, and she stared at the ceiling, unwilling or unable to turn her head and actually look at her husband. "Peter?"

Gently he squeezed her hand. "I'm here."

"Ted brought you my letter?"

"He did."

"And. . ." Her voice sounded as if it were rising from an inner part of her soul, struggling to find the energy to be heard.

"Linda," he said, his voice low and caring, "I am tired of being angry at you. I am tired of holding on to that pain."

She turned and looked into his eyes. Peter could see that only a sliver of her passion and power remained. He could see the heavy burden of pain she carried—physical, emotional, and spiritual.

"I am too, Peter," she whispered. "I am too."

As he gazed down at her slight body, wrapped white in a sheet and disfigured by bulky bandages and IVs, he no longer saw merely a woman but the wonderful girl he had fallen so desperately in love with almost a decade ago. As he stared at her and his tears came, he saw that beautiful woman with the flashing dark eyes and the sleek, dark hair that he had loved to caress. His heart began to swell and pound.

"Do you. . . ," she began, then sniffed. "Do you forgive me,

Peter? I have been so. . .so terrible. *Can* you forgive me?"

He bent down and kissed her lips with the light touch of a butterfly. "Linda, all you had to do was ask. I thought you would never return. I was wrong. God touched your heart. I knew that from your letter."

With a great effort, she pushed up on her left elbow, lifting her shoulders from the bed. "Do you forgive me, Peter? I need your forgiveness. I. . .I don't have much time."

Peter leaned over and, with great deliberation, enfolded her in his arms. "Linda, I forgive you. I forgive you. If God can forgive you, I can forgive you."

He felt sobs rise in her chest, and then they broke into the stillness of her room like waves on a rocky coast. "I love you more today than I have ever loved you," he said. "You have filled my heart. Remember the first day we met? From that day on I have never loved any woman but you. I will always love you. Always, Linda. Always and forever."

Her tears flowed as Peter gently lay her back on the bed.

"Peter, I love you too. I wish I could make these last months just disappear. I have been so foolish, so sinful. I've hurt you so much."

He held a finger gently to her lips. "You need not speak of this again. We have said all we need to say."

She reached up and caressed his cheek with her hand, then pulled him close and kissed his lips with a trembling passion. "Peter," she whispered, "can I come home? Can Becca and I come home?"

Through his tears, Peter nodded. "Yes, sweet Linda. You can come home." He bent and kissed her forehead. "But I have to go back to the farm to get a proper vehicle. I rode my old motorcycle here, and I don't think it would get you home in one piece."

She attempted to smile. "Peter, I would do anything to ride behind you once again. Maybe—"

"In the spring, Linda."

"I'll be here waiting for you. I'll be here, Peter, I will."

As he reached the door, she called out in a voice that was as soft as a cloud, "I love you, Peter."

"I love you, Linda," he whispered back.

Peter stood by the broken screen door for a heartbeat. He brushed the last tears from his eyes. *I don't think she has much time left*, he thought and winced as that truth twisted into his gut like a knife. *But if she wants to come home, then she's coming home.*

A sharp crackle lit the sky, and a rolling boom of thunder pounded the heavens over Stonefort. Peter zipped up his jacket and pulled up the collar. The first few heavy drops of rain splattered the sidewalk as he opened the door with a screech. He stepped out and began to run as hard and as fast as his legs would go.

Rev. Moses sat bolt upright in his bed, sweat dripping from his face. Still as a stone he sat, his eyes darting around the room.

Was that gunfire? his mind demanded. A bolt of lightning lit the sky outside his window, and another boom followed, and he began to relax. *No, it's not gunfire. . .yet.*

He slipped from the bed as quietly as he could, not wanting to wake Nurse Cindy and be forced to actually talk to her again. *Last night's few minutes of conversation were more than enough*, he thought with a crooked leer on his face. He grabbed his clothes and slipped out into his study, dressing as he walked. *She knows the way out*, he assured himself.

He sat at his desk, peered out at the rain and lightning, then pressed the small red button fastened to the desk's edge. He heard the buzzer sound loudly and insistently in the kitchen. Smiling, he knew that in minutes donuts and coffee would be placed before him.

And now I have to attend to important matters, he said to himself, *like preparing for tonight's message.*

He thumbed through a dozen pages of a book of sermons on Revelations. The opening of one caught his eye and he folded the book back, breaking its spine further. He pulled out a yellow high-lighter from his desk drawer. Only two pages into it, he heard the tap at the study door. He sniffed the air. *Mmm. . .donuts.*

Only crumbs remained on the plate when Rev. Moses finally pushed it away. The last notes, freely copied from the book, were scrawled on a pile of four-by-six cards.

A man who must preach so many times a week surely deserves some help, Rev. Moses told himself as he neatly stacked the cards and bound them with a thick rubber band. Slipping them into his pocket, he walked to the window and watched the rain.

If he craned his neck just so and stood on tiptoe, he could make out the shadowy figures of Goodboy and several guards jammed in the lee of the front entrance of the church, huddled there out of the rain.

He picked a few crumbs from his lapel. He was tempted to pop a large crumb into his mouth, then thought better of it and brushed it to the floor.

He walked to the thick door that separated his study from his bedroom. His bath was on the other side; he would have to cross the open hall or walk through his bedroom. Placing his ear flat against the painted wood of his bedroom door, he listened and shut his eyes, hoping to hear better.

There were no sounds. He opened the door and peeked in. The room was empty, the bed linens strewn about, and pillows tossed on the floor. *Good, she's gone. . .and perhaps back on duty with Linda.*

Standing between the study and the bedroom, he looked back to his study lined with books and souvenirs. On the wall was a large map of southern Illinois, the lands of the Garden outlined in blue and shaded a deep yellow. The tinted areas expanded and expanded. Rev. Moses couldn't help taking great pride in that growth. He walked to the map and lovingly traced the entire yellowed area with his finger. Then he placed his palm against it, and the yellow radiated out, bigger than his hand, bigger than two hands, bigger than four, than eight.

This is God's blessing, he thought. *It must be, or else why would such abundance fall to this small, backwater town? God has a plan, and I am part of that plan.*

He peered out to the front of the church. Even in the mist and rain, the metallic glint of weapons was unmistakable. Goodboy leaned back, and Rev. Moses watched his soundless laugh explode.

I have to protect what God has blessed. I must prevent people like Peter Wilson from spreading false teachings and malicious gossip. He seeks to undo God's work. All he wants is revenge for imagined slights and injuries. It was not my doing. It never was my doing.

Rev. Moses walked to the window and placed his hands flat against the chilled hard glass, his forehead resting against the pane. *A man in my position has awesome responsibilities. To provide solace and succor to a man in God's work is not a sin but a blessing.*

A guard came running toward the church. Rev. Moses's heart lurched, yet he couldn't stop from staring. From under his black raincoat, the guard extracted a large thermos and proceeded to pass it from one guard to another. The reverend's heartbeat settled.

I will not have Peter or his delusional wife bringing shame upon the Garden. There is too much at risk. I cannot allow such mean-spirited and small people to destroy what I have worked so hard to build.

He turned away. The window bore an outline of his palm prints and an oily smudge from where his forehead rested. *I must protect God's work. God's people must have their leader. I will not let anyone tear down the walls that I have built.*

Riley spread the map out over his knees and peered closely at the small grid of Stonefort. He traced the contour lines with his finger, back along a creek bed to where the Hummer now sat.

"How much farther?" Macaluso whispered.

"No more than three miles," Riley replied.

They had easily slipped past the inexperienced security forces manning the roadblocks and checkpoints. Riley peered behind the Hummer. No one had followed.

"We'll drive to this stand of trees here," he said, stabbing at the map with his finger. "Then we'll gear up and walk the rest of the way."

"Gear up for extreme prejudice?"

"That is our order," Riley stated flatly. "The brass has spoken."

Each man slowly drew his hand to the holster on his belt, checking his personal weapon.

"I don't care if they have a thousand guards," Peter shouted, his face flushed, his arms waving wildly. He, Tom, and Father William stood in the open area of the barn while the rain pelted the walls. "I am going back to get my wife and daughter. If she wants to spend her last days on earth on this farm, then I am not going to deny her that."

Father William grabbed him by the shoulders. "Peter, don't be a fool. If you go there again—especially in the Hummer—you won't get through. Hasn't Rev. Moses said so?"

Peter brushed off the priest's hands and stomped several feet away. "Listen, I don't care what that fool has said. My wife wants to come home. And I'm going to get her and my daughter. I don't want to debate it any longer."

"And you're going to just drive up to the church and ask politely? And Rev. Moses and all those guards are simply going to open the doors for you?"

Peter spun around, as angry as he had ever been. "Listen, Priest! You're not married! You don't have a child! You can't understand. This is what I have to do," he shouted. "Linda's in pain and asked that I forgive her. I did. I forgave her for everything. And now I am bringing her home with me—where she belongs. Isn't that part of God's plan? That a husband and wife be together? Or are you suggesting that I simply let the *good reverend* do what he chooses? Doesn't somebody have to say no to evil?"

Peter glared at both Tom and the priest. He took a step toward Father William, with every indication that he might actually strike him. "Or are you afraid, Priest? Are you scared of the dark?"

The priest stepped forward, almost head-to-head with Peter, although it was more like head-to-chest. "I'm not afraid, Peter! I'm not afraid of the darkness! I'm just trying to do the smartest thing and not get killed in the process!" The veins in the priest's neck bulged and throbbed as he shouted. Most of the people in the barn had come out of their rooms, yet milled about at a respectful distance. From the trailer, as silence slipped between the two men and the raindrops, a baby's cry poured out, innocent and sweet.

Tom stepped between the two men. "Come on, now, come on. This is not the time for fighting among ourselves."

Neither man answered.

"Is it?" Tom repeated.

Father William and Peter slowly shook their heads.

"Good," Tom said, rubbing his hands together. "Now if you want to get into town, I think we should discuss a plan."

Both men turned to Tom, their anger slowly dissipating.

"Peter, can I take the Hummer over the river anyplace other than the bridge? A shallow ford somewhere?"

Peter thought for a moment. His crossing this morning would not work. The bank on the west side slanted up thirty feet of steep, root-gnarled, sandy soil. No jeep or Hummer would be able to climb it, especially in a driving rain. "Well, downriver about three miles there is a narrow stretch, and I think the west bank isn't too bad. I bet the Hummer could make it."

"What about access into town then? The less noise and attention the better."

Peter shrugged. "I guess we could stick to the brush by the river. Maybe get the whole way to town without being seen."

"Good," Tom said enthusiastically. "Sounds like a good plan."

"What happens after you get there?" the priest asked.

Peter turned toward Father William. In an instant he had shifted from anger to acceptance, from pain to transcendence. "Father, this is my destiny. . .our destiny."

The priest nodded. He knew.

"Where will your daughter be?" Tom asked. "We get your wife first, right? Then where would Becca be?"

"Becca will be at school on the south side of town," Peter explained. "It's being held in a big striped tent maybe ten blocks south of the church. And you're right—we should get Linda first, then Becca."

Tom grinned and clapped both men on the back. "Sounds like an even better plan now. Besides, if Linda *wants* to come home, who is going to stop her? Not even the reverend is foolish enough to hold somebody against her will. And her daughter? There may be some arguing, but that's all. I say we go."

"Wait a minute," Peter interrupted. "I'm the one who's going. There is no need for anybody else to go."

Tom slipped an arm around Peter's shoulder. "Peter, driving a Hummer is not as easy as it looks. You'd wind up stuck in the middle of the river. This just makes sense—I go as the driver. You go as navigator."

"What about me?" the priest demanded.

Tom smiled. "You have to come along—you're going to pray."

As the Hummer faded into the distance, a cloud of mist churning behind it, Elijah stood watching. He felt a painful twist in his heart.

"Everyone!" he shouted. "Everyone! Gather here with me and pray. We need to pray. We need to pray right now!"

Elijah knew that a husband simply getting his wife and daughter from a church should be neither dangerous nor life threatening. But this trip would be anything but normal and safe. Just as certain as he knew that his three friends faced danger, he also knew that to try to stop them would have been wrong.

In the past Elijah would have dismissed that heart nudge as a simple working of his own subconscious, fulfilling desires that he himself held. But recently those nudges came from the left field of his mind, thoughts often so odd and curious that he knew he had not simply dreamed them up himself. So now he listened, stayed connected, and obeyed when the nudges became strong and insistent. "Outside, people," he commanded. "I believe we need to be outside to pray."

"But, Elijah, it's raining!" Leo cried.

"God lets it rain on the righteous as well as the unrighteous. Let this rain fall more heavily on the righteous."

Leo obeyed. Two dozen men and women gathered around Elijah in the chilled mist. The rain quickly puddled at their feet.

"I'll handle the out-loud praying. If you want to add to it, feel free," Elijah explained. "If all you do is bow your head and keep saying amen, then that's okay too." He bowed his head and began. "Dear Lord, our three friends are on their way to Stonefort to fetch back Linda and Becca. You know that weeks upon weeks have passed, and they aren't back here with their husband and their daddy. We know, Lord, that isn't the way You planned families. So we are asking that protection be granted upon them and that You hold them tight in Your arms."

At that moment Elijah felt an actual, hard touch against his heart—so hard that he stopped praying. A gentle wash of amens kept the silence from filling the air. "And, Lord, we need You to protect this small group. . .no, this family. We'll be holding true to Your Word as best we can. We ask that You be true to us too. Amen."

Everyone in the circle looked up in surprise. Elijah was not known for short prayers.

"I need to be there in town at that church with the three of them," Elijah claimed. "I don't know why for sure, but I know it to be truth."

Leo appeared about ready to cry. "But what do we do now, man?"

"You pray. You pray until I get back. . .or until. . .until whatever happens."

Leo reached out and grabbed Elijah's arm, as if he might try to prevent Elijah from leaving. "But you can't go. We need you here, man."

Elijah gently placed his hand over Leo's. "I know. You're scared. Right now, I have never been so scared. But I am obeying what I think God's telling me to do. You keep praying now, and I'll be back."

"But what happens if. . .you know. . .you don't come back?"

Smiling, Elijah lifted Leo's hand from his arm. "You've listened to Peter now long enough. What he tells about Jesus is simple. You act like Jesus acted. You do what He would do. You understand that? It's just that simple."

Leo, now with tears in his eyes, nodded.

Elijah continued, "You do that always, and you'll do fine. If you do that, then you'll have all the teaching you need. Just do what God tells you to do." He turned to the barn. "Now one of you will have to show me how to ride that motorcycle of Peter's."

Father William had never ridden in such a massive vehicle. As it bounced and twisted, he felt tossed like a cork in an ocean. His knuckles grew white and stiff from his death grip on the seat belt.

Tom had slipped off the main road nearly three miles before the bridge. "If anyone is waiting, they won't suspect us here," he said, laughing as they crashed down one drainage ditch and roared up another.

Tom finally stopped at the edge of a cornfield. Even as tall as they were in the Hummer, the corn grew taller yet. "Peter," he called out, "watch the compass. I guess I need to head due west to catch the river at the shallows you talked about. Yell if I go too far north or south, okay?"

Peter nodded.

"And you, Father, you need to pray that we don't drive into a stump or something and break an axle. Okay?"

Father William nodded but was unsure of his abilities to call on the Lord to rearrange topography on demand.

"Then let's go." Tom mashed the gas pedal to the floor, and the Hummer took off with a rush. The field corn rustled and hissed as the vehicle tore straight through it, the greens and golds of the corn stalks slapping at them. Father William felt claustrophobic in the ocean of corn and began to sweat, redoubling his prayer efforts.

In no more than five minutes, the Hummer burst through to a dirt road that ran parallel to the river, no more than two hundred yards away.

"North or south, Peter?"

Peter squinted both directions. The rain poured down in fits, then stopped, then poured again. "North."

Tom spun the wheel, and the vehicle leapt from the edge of the field, jumping and bouncing along the potholed road.

In less than a half mile, Peter shouted, "Stop!"

The Hummer slid in the loose muck, winding up sideways on the road.

"Turn here and head straight through this field," Peter directed. "Up by those willows, that's the shallows. We can cross there."

Five minutes later the Hummer stood idling at the far southern edge of Stonefort.

"How far are we from the church?" Tom asked.

"No more than four minutes," Peter replied. "Just down this hill, and we're on the main road."

"Well, are we ready?" Tom asked.

"Wait," Father William called out from the backseat. "We need to pray first. We must do that."

Tom switched off the engine. Silence surrounded them.

"Dear Lord," the priest began, "we are scared. The darkness that we have felt is near, and we know that we must stand up to it. We know that during this Silence, men must not remain silent about their faith. We must be bold. We must have courage. We must be willing to stand up to evil—despite any consequences. You are our Savior, Lord. You will protect us. You will open the doors of heaven for us if we should die.

"Lord, we lay our lives in Your hands and allow You to take them as Your kingdom requires. For Yours is the greatest good, Lord. Yours is the highest calling. Your will be done, today, Lord. Your will be done. Amen."

Megan paced back and forth in front of Tom's tent. Revelations continued to bark and whine and pull at his chain as if his life depended on gaining his freedom.

Leo was pacing about in the rain, his hair drenched. This day he appeared very worried. "What's wrong with the dog, man? Is he getting spooky on us? Is he trying to tell us something's going wrong?"

Megan spun about. "He just wants to be with Tom. He's. . .he's worried, that's all. Nothing bad is going to happen. It isn't. When he left, Tom promised that nothing bad would happen."

Leo backed up, cowed by her outburst. "Okay, man, I was just asking."

Megan stared to the west. "How far is it to town? I only went there once, and that was in the Hummer."

Scratching through his dreadlocks, Leo thought before he answered. "A couple of miles? Eight miles? Peter said once, but I forgot."

Megan peered once more to the west. She bent down and untied the stout rope that held Revelations in check. "Are you up for a run, boy? I bet we can make it there in less than an hour."

Tom turned the key in the Hummer, and the engine roared to life. "We ready?" he asked.

Peter smiled and nodded.

The priest called out, "Ready, with God's help."

I know God wants us here this day, doing just what we're doing, Peter thought as the Hummer charged out of the brush and onto the road. *And just as certain I know that I will not see the sun set tonight. I know that, Lord. Maybe I see it clearer than the priest. But I am not afraid. Watch over my sweet Becca—but God, You have assured me that she will be fine. I understand, Lord, and I am not afraid. Truly I am not. Allow me to serve You well. You have my life, Lord. You have always had it. And please be with Father William. Give him courage as well.*

Father William held on to the handrails as the vehicle lurched and bounced over the rough and twisting road. *Dear God, let Peter be brave. I know that You have called me here as a sacrifice. I am in awe that You would choose me, an old man who has never truly tested his faith before all this happened. I trust that others will see the truth, Lord. To die for You is gain, Lord. Let me do honor to the kingdom and all the martyrs that have come before me. Let me stand for Your truth and Your love. Let my life have meaning, Lord.*

The Hummer roared through town as fast as the engine would allow, shattering the silence of the day with its powerful, metallic roar. Spinning the wheel when Peter called out "left" and "right," Tom swerved through the narrow streets. He slammed on the brakes, and the vehicle fishtailed, spinning in a semicircle, leaving wide, black smears across the pavement next to the church. The left wheels banged against the curb, and the Hummer tilted for a long dizzying second, then lurched back to level, tossing the occupants about like dolls.

"Sorry for the landing," Tom shouted, "but we're here."

Three guards stood outside the church doors. Two of the doors still contained sheets of plywood where the glass had been shattered by bullets. Crossing their arms, each guard took a step closer, almost out from under the eaves and into the rain. No one made a move for a weapon.

Peter stared for a moment. "Not the church doors. The parsonage door is around the side." He jumped out of the Hummer and took long, silent strides across the wet grass. Father William gulped once, then followed. Tom was no more than a few steps behind them.

"Hey!" one of the guards shouted. No one answered.

"Hey!" Tom saw the guard's hand slip from his belt to the hilt of his pistol.

"Listen," Tom called out to the guards as Peter and the priest continued walking. "I'm Tom Lyton, from across the river. We have to make one stop at the parsonage. There are two passengers waiting for us. It's all been approved. Some sort of medical emergency. We have the papers in the Hummer. I'll get them when we get back. Don't want to get you more wet than necessary. We won't be more than two minutes."

Tom had written this scene in one of his movie scripts. *If someone asks you to stop doing something, simply tell them it's been approved. Offer to get the official papers, then do what you have to do. Guards just don't want to be held responsible, that's all.*

The stern-faced guard visibly relaxed, and his hand came away from his pistol. "All right, then. But I need to see them papers."

"You got it," Tom shouted cheerfully. "We'll be right out."

Peter was at the door. The screen door was still broken. He took the steps two at a time to Linda's upstairs room.

The four agents silently and carefully made their way past the tent city and the new dormitories. Dressed in black, everyone assumed that they were part of the security forces. Not that the regular security forces carried such elaborate firepower, but most observers paid little attention.

"How come the police always dress in black?" Dave asked quietly as they walked toward the church. "We've done this what—fifty times now?—and the new cops on the beat always wear black."

Riley turned his head. His cigar poked out like a brown tongue. "It's a fashion statement for the times," he snarled past the unlit cigar. "Now shut up. We got work to do."

Rev. Moses paced across the platform, wiping his face with a lavender handkerchief in front of a jammed church. Sweat glistened off his brow, and the bright light seemed to explode off each drop in reflection.

His thoughts were difficult to draw together because he was distracted. Linda's threat troubled him. He knew that if she survived, it would bring trouble upon the Garden. That he could not tolerate.

By this afternoon, he thought as he paced, *all of my worries will be over. The doctor said he would visit during the service so fewer people would notice.* He found himself smiling.

A portly gentleman in the first row gestured to the closed window, then pantomimed wiping the sweat from his brow. Then he mouthed broadly, "Do you want me to open the window?"

The reverend smiled and nodded.

The man pushed himself up from the pew and lumbered to the window, straining to get it open. With a series of low grunts that Rev. Moses was sure were picked up by the sensitive microphone, the man managed to slide the window open. Swollen wood scraped against swollen wood.

Rev. Moses nodded in appreciation, then walked toward the window, feeling the cool, humid breeze slip into the room. He stopped midstep, his eyes widening, his jaw dropping, his sweat becoming more intense.

An enormous Hummer sat by the curb, glistening in the rain, windows fogging with condensation. Rev. Moses could not swallow. *There's that Hummer, parked right beside the church! The one with the gold in it! If he's in town, then Peter is here as well. He got the letter from his crazy wife, and he's here to expose me! Where in blazes is that oaf Goodboy? Where are the gunshots? I told him to shoot Wilson on sight! Why haven't the guards fired? They let them park at the door?*

A quiet, nervous rustle swept through the packed church. The Reverend Moses had not said a word for nearly three minutes. Instead he continued staring hard out the window. He heard a few whispers, then a few more, each asking, "Is there something wrong with the reverend?" "Why isn't he talking?" "What has he seen? Is it another vision?"

He looked around frantically, his eyes wide like those of a frightened, wounded animal caught in the jaws of a steel trap. Turning to the darkness behind him, he sought out the faces of the three women who sang in Linda's absence. Grabbing at the mike and covering it with a great, sweaty palm, he hissed, "Get up here and sing!"

Turning to the congregation, he shouted out, "And now we'll spend some time praising God in song!" And then he ran toward the rear door—the door that led to the back staircase of the parsonage and the guest rooms beyond.

———

"My wife is in this room," Peter said to the sputtering Nurse Fox as he elbowed her out of his way. "And I've come to take her home."

"But she's not well. She needs a doctor's care," the nurse shouted. "Doctor! Doctor!"

Peter banged open the door and found a doctor, empty syringe in his hand, standing over Linda's bed. "You can't come in here!" the doctor shouted. "This is restricted. The reverend ordered it. No one is supposed to be here."

Linda's skin had grown even paler, and her breathing had become shallow and raspy. She struggled to lift her arm. "Peter," she called out. "You came back. I thought they would stop you. You came back." Her words were soft and slow and garbled.

Peter faced the doctor, his eyes burning with anger.

The doctor shrank away. "It was only a painkiller," he said, his words edgy and afraid.

Peter continued to stare, a piercing brilliance in his eyes.

"That's all it was—just a painkiller. Rev. Moses ordered it." The doctor withered under Peter's glare. "That's all it was, just extra painkiller. . .that's all." The doctor slunk into a far corner as Peter knelt at his wife's side.

"Linda," he said, whispering into her ear, "I'm back. We're together now. I can take you home with me."

Her hand struggled to find his face, and her fingers grazed his cheek. She spread her palm out full, her hand slipped to his neck, and she pulled him close. "Peter," she gasped, "you do still forgive me? For everything?"

He nodded. "For everything."

"And you love me? You still love me?" Her words sounded as if they were coming from a hundred miles away, slower and more garbled with each second.

"I will always love you, Linda," he said louder, making sure she heard him. "I will love you forever. I will love you as long as I live, Linda. Always and forever." He leaned back up and watched as a smile dawned on her face, marking it with delicate wrinkles born of love and laughter.

"Peter, I will always love you too. Always and forever."

Then the lightness in her eyes faded, and her arm slipped from Peter's neck and fell, limp, to the bed. Her breathing slowed.

Peter knew, yet did not want to admit, that his wife neared the door of heaven as he held her. He knew her death was only heartbeats away. A peace authored by God swept over him. He knew from Linda's beatific smile that she felt the same.

Peter bent down and embraced his wife tightly, calling her name tenderly in her ear.

—◦—

Tom waited just outside the back door to the parsonage, hoping no guards would interfere with their mission.

From across the lawn, he saw a guard marching toward the front of the church. What chilled Tom to his soul was how the guard carefully checked his pistol, pulling it out of his holster as he mounted the steps of the church.

—◦—

Father William stood silently in the hallway, with the nurse only feet away. The priest did not want her to run off and alert anyone of their presence. The nurse would not return to her chair, nor had she tried to walk off. The priest was uncertain what he would do to stop her if she chose to run.

Father William turned at the sound of footsteps clumping up the back staircase leading from the church and not the outside door. The chill returned, filling the hallway with a cold evil.

The priest shut his eyes for a second to pray. *Your will be done, Lord. Your will be done.*

—◦—

A breathless Rev. Moses landed on the last step of the parsonage's rear staircase at the same time Goodboy reached the second-floor landing. "Is he here?" Rev. Moses shouted. "Is Peter here?"

Goodboy, his eyes dull and pained, shrugged. "Didn't see anyone drive up. I was—I was busy."

They turned the corner in the hall and saw Nurse Fox glaring at a stranger.

Rev. Moses's eyes widened. "It's that Catholic heretic!" he

shouted. "That means Peter is probably with him. He's here in the parsonage."

The reverend turned to Goodboy and grabbed him by the shoulders. "They're coming to destroy the Garden. Remember me preaching about the Catholics? How they're aligned with the Antichrist? How they should be punished?"

Goodboy shrugged again.

"Shoot him!" Rev. Moses ordered, his voice high and panicky. "Shoot him before he lets the demons loose! He's a devil!"

Goodboy stared at Rev. Moses. "Shoot a priest? He's not doing nothing except standing there."

"I said shoot him!" Rev. Moses screamed.

Goodboy squared his shoulders and stood still. "Now, Reverend, I don't mind doing things that seem right. But I'm not about to shoot an unarmed priest."

The Reverend Moses drew himself to his full height. His eyes were blazing and wild with fury. "I said shoot him!" he bellowed. "You have to obey me! You have to obey me!"

Goodboy slowly shook his head. "I obey most things. But I'm not shooting a man like this. It looks like murder."

"You are disobeying my order! You are then disobeying the will of God, Goodboy! That gets you sent to hell! You'll go to hell!"

Goodboy shook his head. "Reverend, I'm not shooting any-one—not me. And I'll risk the hell part, if you don't mind."

Without a word, Rev. Moses snatched the gun held loosely in Goodboy's hand. It felt warm and comforting and heavy in his hand. He curled his fingers around it, his finger finding a home around the trigger.

"Be careful," Goodboy cried, "the safety is off."

"You've disobeyed my order!" the reverend shouted, his eyes narrowing to evil slits.

He fought a smile from creeping onto his face. His finger snuggled at the trigger; he blinked once, then tugged. The gun exploded, and Goodboy slammed back into the wall, his blood streaking down the wall behind him. His eyes grew cold and vacant as he slumped to a sitting position, then tilted and fell on his side to the floor.

Elijah puttered to a wobbling stop at the east side of the bridge. His jeans were torn and his knees bloody. He had fallen at least six times and had struggled to restart the vehicle every time. Soaked to the skin, Elijah let the motorcycle fall to the ground, not knowing how to turn it off or where to find the kickstand. He had not taken the motorcycle out of first gear the entire trip.

A dozen guards stood there, huddled under a makeshift shelter out of the chilling rain. None of them spoke; they just gaped in silence at the spectacle before them.

Elijah brushed some water from his face, stood up straight, and walked toward them without saying a word. His eyes were fixed on theirs. When he came within a few feet, they parted and let him pass, with no words spoken by any man. He stepped on the metal grating, did not look back, and kept walking toward the Temple of God's Calling. God was indeed watching over him, he decided.

Megan and Revelations came sprinting over the last rise on the road. She saw the gray clouds and heard a crackle of thunder roll in from the west. She gulped, wiped the rain from her eyes, and ran straight for the bridge.

Nurse Fox screamed as the pistol shot exploded in the hallway. She continued to scream as Rev. Moses slowly turned from the now lifeless body of Goodboy and walked toward her and the priest. She screamed louder and ran toward the back stairway, her arms flailing.

Father William turned squarely to face the reverend. "Go away,

Rev. Moses. Peter has come for Linda. This is no concern of yours."

Father William marveled at the cool polish of his own words in the face of a man holding a gun pointed at his heart. He marveled at his composure after watching a man murdered so close to him.

"You Catholic scum! How dare you darken the doors of a proper Christian church?"

"I have accepted God's gift," the priest returned. "His Son died for me as well as for you."

"You have no right to be here. You have no right to help that heathen escape!"

Father William felt all of destiny pour about him as the reverend stalked closer. He knew that he must do what he could to save Peter. "Rev. Moses," the priest stated, "this is not the way God wants anyone to solve a problem. We can talk this out. There is another way! There must be!"

"Get out of my way, you priest of the devil! Get out of my way!"

Diplomacy having failed, Father William knew there was no alternative. He dove for the gun.

Rev. Moses didn't hesitate even a second. He did not flinch or shirk back from what was before him. He pulled the trigger twice more, the gun roaring.

The pain was sharp in Father William's chest, and the force of the bullets threw him backward. He crumpled against the far wall. His right arm was lifted in mute protest as he lay there, his eyes growing dull.

He tried to call Peter's name, yet only a whispering gurgle came from his lungs. He glimpsed the spreading stain on his chest and closed his eyes. A peace washed over him.

Lord, please take me home. Forgive me for my weaknesses. Please take me home to Paradise.

A cold shaft of fear drove into Tom's gut as he heard the bellowing gunshots. He turned to the door, took a step, and felt the fear tighten his chest. He decided that now was the time to get the rifle stored in the Hummer.

While the guards raced about, lost without a commanding officer, Tom sprinted back to his vehicle and clambered underneath the chassis, ignoring the mud and the rain.

Elijah could only hobble toward the church, his legs and knees battered from his falls. He winced with each step, thinking he may have broken his right ankle in a spill partway to town. The sound of the shots stopped him for a moment. He looked around for a branch or something to use as a crutch.

Megan heard the shots as she came across the bridge. The guards let her cross without a word.

As she turned the corner by the park, she saw Elijah dragging toward the church, his right foot limp and canted at the wrong angle. She ran up to him and slipped under his right arm. "We'll make it, Elijah. We have to make it in time to help."

"Megan"—he winced through the pain, stumbling even with her help—"we'll get there when the time is appointed."

A curious wave of dispassionate emotion rose in the reverend's chest as he watched the priest fall and die. The acrid smell of the gunpowder filled his nose, and the roar of the explosion deafened his ears. His eyes teared from the smoke, not from regret.

She must not be allowed to destroy the Garden! he thought wildly. *Peter must not be allowed to help her spread her lies and perdition. They are devils, and they must be destroyed.*

The doorknob to the room felt as hot as the sun as he grabbed it and threw the door open. Peter was kneeling by his wife's side while the doctor remained cowered in the corner.

"You," Rev. Moses ordered, pointing the gun at the physician, "get out. Now!"

Without a word, the doctor scrambled to his feet and fled the room.

The reverend's smile twisted in perverted pleasure as he pointed the weapon at Peter's heart.

Peter did not flinch, did not turn to face Rev. Moses. He simply held his wife's cold hand in his.

"Now, Peter, your time has come," the reverend's voice boomed. "God will not let you and your ilk destroy the Garden. No, He will not let such evil go unpunished."

Peter lowered his head and touched his forehead to his wife's.

"Peter!" the reverend shouted. "You will listen when I speak to you! You will obey!"

Peter could feel the reverend's glare but ignored it. He moved only his lips, offering a prayer.

"Peter! Get up and look at me!" Rev. Moses bellowed. "Get up!"

Peter remained motionless for a long time. The singing from the church filtered into the room, only barely masking the heaving breathing of the Reverend Moses. Peter closed his eyes and tried not to notice the fetid, decaying smell that pervaded the air.

"I will stand up," Peter said, "but not because you ordered it, Jerry, but because I want to see your eyes. I want to see the evil there and confront it."

The reverend rocked back on his heels as if physically struck. "Evil! You call me evil?! I am not seeking to destroy God's handiwork! You are. Not me. You!"

Peter shook his head. "I expected evil to be smarter, more aware. Yet you are not. You are evil and are so unaware of it. How does that happen, Jerry? Do you get a little bit stupider each day? A little more evil every hour until your mind is so muddled and cursed that you no longer see reality for what it is? Tell me, how is it that evil is so deluded?"

"Silence," the reverend roared, thrusting the pistol closer to

Peter. "You will not speak to me that way."

"Jerry," Peter responded in an even voice, "I am not one of your lackeys. I will speak to you as God directs me."

"God!" the reverend hissed back. "You do not have God on your side. We do." Rev. Moses gestured in a wide circle with the hand holding the gun. "There are more than ten thousand pilgrims here—all because of me! Not you! Me!"

Peter stepped closer. "And you've lied and misled a lot of innocent souls, Jerry. God will not be pleased."

"Not pleased? How could you think that? This is the new Garden! God's holy place is growing again."

Peter's laugh shocked the reverend. "You hoodwinked a bunch of foolish people. You think that pleases God? Some of what you've done is good, but so much is wrong. . .and evil. Did you start out on the right path and go astray, or did evil always flow through you, Jerry? Don't you feel it? Don't you see it? Have you been blinded so totally?"

The veins in Rev. Moses's neck pulsed and stood out like cords. His teeth were clenched, his breath pumping. Slowly he raised the gun and pointed the barrel squarely at Peter's chest.

Peter knew that he should dive for cover or try to knock the gun away, yet he did nothing, save stand erect and square to the Reverend Jerry Moses.

The music and singing from the church continued, but the pitch was wrong, the melody discordant. A hum of voices swirled about, just below understanding. Peter imagined that they were the voices of hell, frantic over their mishandled plans. He imagined that all the demons and devils would howl in pain and loss within the next few minutes. Such thoughts gave him courage.

"Jerry," Peter said calmly, his words bold and clear, "you will have to kill me to stop me from speaking. Yet as you pull that trigger, you must admit to your masters that my death will bring their plans to a close. Jerry, you know if you do not serve the risen Lord, then you serve the forces of evil. There is no middle ground. The Lord will spew out the lukewarm and the lost. You are lost, Jerry, as are the demons about you. Kill me, and my martyrdom will spread like weeds through your Garden. Let me live, and I will expose your evil."

Peter could see the reverend's finger tremble against the cold metal trigger.

"Let me live, and I will destroy your evil," Peter repeated. "Kill me, and I will destroy your evil."

The room grew colder and colder. Peter would have sworn that he could see his breath condense in the air.

"You have lost, Jerry. You have lost," Peter said calmly. His words grew brilliant because of their truth.

"I have not lost!" Rev. Moses screeched. "I have not lost! You will not destroy the Garden."

With no more deliberation, Moses pulled back on the trigger. The hammer rose, caught, then fell with a snap on the shell. A smoking, belching roar ensued, and Peter jerked from the force of the bullet. The reverend pulled the trigger again, then again. Peter staggered, struggling to keep his eyes open and focused. The reverend pulled the trigger one last time, though the firing pin finally fell on an empty chamber. Only a *click* sounded.

Peter stood for awhile, hands braced against the wall. "You've lost, Jerry," he gasped. "God has defeated you."

Slowly he slid to a sitting position. He looked over at his wife, lying peacefully at last, and held out his hand toward her. It trembled in the air. He smiled, his hand dropped to his side, and he closed his eyes for the last time.

The last volley of gunfire echoed to silence as Tom climbed out from under the Hummer. The lock on the compartment with the rifle was dented shut, most likely from hitting a rock as they crossed the river. Tom knew he could not wait any longer. He ran to the house and bounded up the stairs without a weapon.

⎯⎯⎯⎯

As Elijah, Megan, and Revelations arrived at the front of the church, the skies opened and the deluge began. Guards raced about, trying to find the source of the gunshots they had just heard. Some of the congregation ran in panic from the church or embraced in the safety of twos and threes, huddled against the rain.

The back door of the parsonage flew open and Tom, carrying Peter's bloody and limp body, walked blindly into the night. Megan and Elijah gathered about him, their tears mixing with the rain. In a moment Elijah had enough of the facts of the story. He turned from them and hobbled through the front door of the church.

Banging open the doors to the sanctuary, Elijah limped in, dragging his broken ankle. He simply hobbled past the guards, who turned their guns away as if ordered and stood at the back of the sanctuary.

Rev. Moses looked as if he had just returned to the platform. He was trying to calm the stir among the congregation. At Elijah's entrance, he grew white with surprise. "Now, folks," Rev. Moses called out as if nothing was wrong, "we need to continue the service. God has still not spoken—"

"God *has* spoken," Elijah roared. Every head in the church turned to him. "My namesake in the Bible called on the God of Abraham, Isaac, and Jacob to prove that He was the God of Israel. He called on God to prove himself. He called on God to answer him so that the people would know that the Lord is God and that God had brought them back to Himself. I ask you now, God, to once again prove yourself to these people and prove that You are still in control of this world and our lives."

He now stared directly into the eyes of Rev. Moses. "Prove to me, Rev. Moses, that you did not kill Peter Wilson. There is blood on your hands. The blood of Peter Wilson is on your hands! Tell us that what I see is a lie. Tell us that I am not speaking the truth."

431

Hobbling, Elijah dragged himself halfway up the center aisle. "Did you kill him? Did you kill Peter Wilson?"

Rev. Moses's jaw moved, and his lips curled back as if he were about to scream in protest. But no sound other than an evil rasping, boiling up from deep within his gut, appeared. Something inside the man appeared to click to the off position. His bluster and bravado and bullying simply evaporated. Like a balloon pricked with a pin, Rev. Moses began to deflate.

"The silence proves that you are guilty, Rev. Moses!"

Elijah took another step forward, and as he did, Rev. Moses retreated a step. As Elijah moved into the light, the Reverend Moses slipped back into the darkness and shadows at the back of the stage. With every step painful, Elijah climbed behind the platform.

"Everyone in this room! Everyone who hears my voice on the radio! Listen to me!" Elijah called out. He grabbed both sides of the pulpit to steady himself. "You have been lied to. Since the Silence there have been many who would mislead. There is only one voice you must listen to, and that is the voice of God. Pick up your Bible now. Pick it up. Open it to the Gospel of John. Read it. Then read it again. Then yet again. Those are the words you must obey. Those are the only words—God's words!"

The reverend's eyes were hateful as he stared at Elijah. Elijah knew the man wanted to force him from the pulpit. But the reverend's legs no longer seemed able to move on his accord.

Elijah glared out at the audience and let a long silence fill the church. Then slowly, his eyes tight in pain, he climbed down from the platform and hobbled back down the center aisle and back into the rain.

He knelt beside Peter's lifeless body. "Peter, I will miss you. I don't understand why it had to be this way. Maybe it didn't. Maybe we were just muddling through as best we could. If your death brings these people back to God, then perhaps I can begin to understand. . .perhaps."

Tears streaming down his face, he looked up to the heavens. "Please take Your servant home to You, Lord. Please take him into Your arms."

—⟨∙∙∙⟩—

The Reverend Moses slipped out into the rain. He carried with him a second clip of bullets he had tucked into his pocket. He walked as if in a trance into the dense trees, now growing black in advance of the night.

He peered down at the gun in his hand as he inserted the fresh clip. The rain spotted the black metallic finish. He stared down at it, admiring its sleek polish and comforting weight. He lightly caressed the trigger.

And the blackness welcomed him into its chilling embrace.

—⟨∙∙∙⟩—

Riley ripped off his headphones. He had been monitoring Moses's broadcast and had wondered why the singers had been introduced at that unusual point in the service. When he heard the accusations of murder from someone in the congregation, Riley knew trouble had hit. If they were going to act, this was the opportune moment. They now had legitimate reasons for taking the Reverend Moses down. He ordered Dave and Chuck to go back to the Hummer and get it to the church ASAP.

As he and Mark worked their way to the back of the church, he heard a bullet's peal in the woods ahead. From their years of experience, both Riley and Mark knew that could mean only one thing—one part of their assignment was taken care of. Now they needed to make sure chaos did not follow the vacuum of power.

As they continued toward the church, a calm settled over the small town. The storm clouds broke, and the sun's power washed over the land and its people.

october 12

Megan had watched Becca cry for several days after the terrible death of her parents. But Megan also saw in the little girl's eyes something deeper and more real than she had ever seen before. Megan could only describe it as the presence of God. It was as if the child knew why things had happened, and now she had God's peace in her heart. It was as if God had whispered to little Becca that her parents had given themselves for a greater good. The child would not understand it all—not this year, perhaps not ever—but God's soothing words dried her tears and eased the pain in her little heart. Megan knew that the pain was not gone, but she could tell that Becca simply knew, beyond all understanding, that God had her in His powerful hands.

When such loss occurs, God supplies the greater peace, Elijah had told them. And Megan, as well as the Reverend Moses's followers, now felt the breath of freedom and truth in their lungs. It was a definite presence in the air, in the sky, in the very nature of all that surrounded them.

The healing was most evident today, almost two weeks after the shootings. Tom, Megan, and Becca walked down to the stream in the waning daylight. Their hands linked them into a chain, and the dried grasses whisked against their legs. Tom and Megan looked down at the little girl between them. Her eyes were tightly shut. She was now depending solely on their hands for her steps and safety. She walked, without opening her eyes, walking with trust alone.

They stopped at the edge of the field just beyond the barn.

Becca was the first to speak. "I miss my daddy and mommy," she said softly.

"I know you do, Becca," Megan said. "We all do."

"You do?" she asked.

Tom nodded. "Your father was a very special person. He was very brave."

"I know," she replied. "He didn't mind going out in the dark if there was a funny noise and I was scared. And he could spot deer prints in the mud, and he knew how to braid my hair." Becca stopped and cocked her head toward Tom. "Do you know how to do those things?"

"Well, I'm not very good at braiding hair, but I sure could try." He bent down to her. "I bet Megan is a whiz at hair braiding. Aren't you, Megan?"

She nodded.

Becca eyed both of them again. "Are you married?"

Tom nearly blushed. "No, Becca, we're not married."

Her delicate face twisted into a puzzle. "But don't mommies and daddies have to be married?"

"Well, yes they do," Tom replied.

"Aren't you going to be my mommy and daddy now? You have to get married. I need a new mommy and daddy, don't I?"

"Well, Becca, usually I have an agent do my negotiating, but you're doing a good job here. I think that is a very good question, and Megan and I will have to talk about it for a little while."

"But to be a mommy and daddy you *have* to be married," Becca repeated in a tight, pinched voice.

Megan bent to the child. "Sweets, if that's what it takes to be a mommy and daddy, then I think we can do that. I would say yes to being your mommy if Tom said yes to being your daddy."

"And get married," Becca added with finality.

"And get married," Tom replied.

Tom and Megan exchanged a long, lingering look between them. Each knew that this was right, that the three of them—three people from different parts of the land—were now being bonded together into a family.

I will marry this woman, and we will take this child as our own, Tom realized with a start. *This is what God has brought me here for. To be a husband and a father again. To follow Him and to obey Him.*

And in Megan's smile, he knew that this was indeed the truth.

———————

The moon lit the sky as a circle of gold. Megan and Tom sat by the stream. Revelations wouldn't leave Becca's side. He slept beside her on her small bed in the trailer. Her arms were wrapped about his furry neck.

Tom took Megan's hand in his. "You agreed with the little one today."

Megan smiled and nodded. "She knows what she wants."

"And you're all right with this? With everything she wants?"

Megan nodded again.

"I never thought that such things could ever happen again."

"I know. Neither did I. To be happy. To know love."

He hesitated. "There is one other thing, Megan."

She softly answered, "I know."

Tom squeezed her hands and gazed into her eyes. "You know I'm talking about your soul. You have to do this. You have to. Will you give your heart to Christ? Can you do that?"

Tears slipped down Megan's cheeks. "I can, Tom. I can, and I want to. It's the time that Father William told me about. He said I'll know when it's time. And it's time now."

october 16

So how many people are on this farm, Leo?" asked Mary Beth Anderson, a pilgrim to Stonefort who had journeyed on foot from Atlanta.

"Well, a few have come and gone, but at last count we had"— he shut his eyes and tilted his head back; his lips moved slowly, forming the numbers—"thirty-nine. Most from Ann Arbor like me, but Tom's from the West Coast, and Megan's from the East Coast. But I guess now we have thirty-seven, you know, with Peter and Father William being gone."

Mary Beth nodded, then smiled and placed a hand on Leo's arm. He wasn't used to the gesture but liked it all the same. Leo stood a bit taller and smiled.

"Why here and not on one of the Garden farms?" she asked.

"Well, Peter is the one who invited us all to stay and gave us a home when we had nothing but a few ragged tents. He trusted us, man, he trusted us. And we looked like a bunch of beat-up old hippies then."

Mary Beth smiled again. "And now you look less like hippies?"

Leo snapped his head back and forth, and his dreadlocks flew in a circle like a carousel. "Well, no, man, but you know what I mean."

"I do, Leo, and I'm only teasing you."

"I know, but when I think of Peter, my heart hurts. Like he had to do what he did so everyone would listen and see the truth of what was happening."

"I know, Leo. I was in Stonefort for over a month, and I didn't realize a thing about the real truth. Not a thing."

Leo nodded and fingered a small clutch of the beads in his hair. "What's happening to all the farms and stuff now that the reverend's gone? Are people splitting?"

"Some. Maybe a few hundred have gone. But where would the rest of us go? This is our new life. This is what we are now. This is where we live. Those men from Washington said some National Guard units are on their way to help keep the peace and figure out just how to govern the Garden. Mayor Smidgers is enjoying being back in charge in the meantime." She took his hand. "And besides, everybody is saying that Elijah will be preaching to us soon. I'm looking forward to that."

"Mary Beth," Leo stammered, "I need to ask you something real important."

She stared into his eyes. "Yes, Leo."

"Mentioning Peter and Elijah reminded me of what I gotta do."

"Yes, Leo?"

"Mary Beth. . .do you know Jesus?"

———

The sun hung low in the autumn sky, coloring the warm air with gold. Megan and Tom sat at the edge of the stream, holding hands, while Becca walked along the stony banks looking for frogs and crawfish. She would lunge for them and then giggle as they scooted away or hopped into the deeper water.

A comfortable silence fell between Tom and Megan. It was as if they were communicating by the simple touching of flesh to flesh, of hand to hand.

Finally Megan looked away from Tom and up at the reddening sky. "Tom, why did all this happen?" She spoke softly, not wanting Becca to hear her question.

"You mean what happened to the world? Or what happened here in Stonefort?"

"Both," she replied. "I guess I should be satisfied that all of this—all of what happened—sort of came out for the best. But that doesn't answer all my questions."

He nodded. "I know, Megan. Everyone has questions."

"Are there any answers?"

"Well, if you're asking about the world, the dramatist in me says that it was a great way for God to get our attention."

"Wasn't there any other way?"

"I don't know. All the destruction and death were terrible, but I found God because it happened. You did too. I bet thousands of others did. Maybe hundreds of thousands."

"And that justifies it all? Doesn't seem right. Seems like a pretty high price to pay."

"Yes, I guess it is. But. . ."

Megan squeezed his hand, sensing his reluctance to finish his thoughts. "Tell me."

"Well, the world did seem to be spiraling out of control. Maybe this was the only way to get us all to slow down and find the truth. It kept us from destroying the world. And I think we were well on our way to doing that. Maybe God wanted us all to have a little more time to tell others about His truth."

"Do you believe that? Is that why God let it happen?"

Tom shrugged. "I don't know. I'm no theologian."

"And Peter and Father William—why did they have to die? It just doesn't seem fair."

Tom stood up and walked a few paces away. "I don't know. I know that God is in control, but I admit I don't understand it all. Maybe they had to make a sacrifice so we all could live. Maybe that's what offering your bodies as living sacrifices can mean as well. Without them, without their sacrifice, the Garden would have become more and more evil, I guess."

Megan nodded, though she didn't fully agree with or understand his answers. She glanced over at Becca, who had her hands inches from a crawfish. "As she grows up, are you going to tell her that her father was a hero?"

Tom didn't hesitate. "I am, Megan. I am."

—◦—

The Hummer rumbled along the rain-slicked roads just south of Frederick, Virginia. Riley was slumped in the passenger seat, his last cigar clenched in his teeth.

"Good thing we're getting you home, Riley," Macaluso said as he drove. "None of us could tolerate your cigars. I wonder how we might manage without 'em."

Riley reached up and waved at the air, dismissing the other agents' laughter.

Dave, who had been staring out the back window for hours, sat up straight and leaned forward. "I've been wondering about something ever since we left D.C."

"Wondering what?" Riley asked in an uncharacteristically soft voice.

"I know why we went. I know what our mission was. To get control back. To stop the panic. To return Washington to power. But what I don't know—even now—is if any of it is really coming back? Is what we had before the Silence coming back?"

A quiet followed. Riley did not answer. He looked over his shoulder and saw Chuck put down the Bible he had picked up in Stonefort. All four men had spent a few days after the shooting at Peter Wilson's farm, and they had spent some long nights with Elijah.

"It's going to come back," Chuck said with certainty. "It will. The world may come back humbled and changed, maybe more responsive to God, but it will all come back. Anyone who doesn't see God now is deliberately blind to Him."

Riley scratched at his lighter. The smoke filtered up and was gently sucked out the crack in the open window. For once Riley had no caustic response. If the others had looked closely, they might have seen Riley smile briefly and nod.

Tom stood in the bright sunshine, shielding his eyes. "So all the records are gone?"

Mayor Smidgers nodded. "They been buried since the quake. You could dig them up, I guess. Take awhile."

Tom smiled.

"But if you ask me, the boy you're talking about is the boy that Rev. Moses adopted. He's a good boy. Name's Matthew. I think he's twelve, maybe thirteen."

Tom nodded. "And he's with his aunt and uncle?"

"Yep. They're over in Eldorado. Heard Rev. Moses say that everything was fine with them. Those folks are on his mother's side, thank heavens. Salt of the earth, both of them. I hear they love him to death. He's a good boy. They're raising him to be a good Christian boy."

Tom extended his hand to the mayor. "Thanks."

"Say, why you asking? Is that boy a relation of yours?"

"Sort of," Tom replied. "It's a complicated story."

God may have used that boy to get me to Stonefort. I might not have come otherwise, Tom realized. *And now I'll wait for God's timing. Maybe someday I'll take a walk over to Eldorado. Maybe someday.*

october 20

Not only did the original residents of Peter Wilson's farm gather Saturday night to listen to Elijah speak of the Scriptures and how to use them, but nearly one hundred people walked in from Stonefort.

"Who do we listen to now that Rev. Moses is gone?" was the most common question this group asked.

Elijah, his ankle bandaged, spoke briefly, praising the work and words of Peter and encouraging everyone to do as Peter had told them to do: spread the Good News of Christ to everyone and to help others as they could. He spoke of his journey from Milwaukee to Stonefort, from darkness to light, from the cold chill of loneliness to the warm embrace of Christian friends. He told everyone to offer the same warm embrace to the unbelievers and the searchers. "It's our love that shows them how Jesus loves," Elijah concluded.

Afterward Herve Slatters came up to Elijah, hat in hand, and waited until all others had left with their questions answered. "Mr. Elijah," he stammered, "I was the man who was working on the radio and all for Rev. Moses, and now that he's gone. . .well, I was thinking that maybe my sons and me bring the radio out here to this farm. It isn't just me, but the town council said it'd be fine with them. They want you to do the preaching now." Herve kept his eyes averted the entire time he was talking.

"Mr. Slatters," Elijah replied, "being on the radio's not anything I would have sought after. But if the church elders would be willing to listen and offer correcting when my words call for it, then such an arrangement would be satisfactory with me. I'm going to argue with the Holy Spirit since He's been nudging at me to tell others as much as I can tell about Jesus. This would be a fine way to do that, I guess."

Herve nodded and smiled.

epilogue

On the rise at the far edge of the farm, the plot of land bounded by a grove of birch and poplar and oak, stood three small crosses. Each cross, marking a final resting place, faced west into the setting sun. Each cross had been hand-cut from a fallen oak tree and bore a few lines of carving—a date and a name and a promise.

When the wind fell still and the sun hung low in the western sky, groups of two and three would walk there, kneel, and pray. In the quiet of the long shadows, the breeze carried those prayers in a whispering breath from Stonefort to the seas and mountains, to the forests and deserts, like a balm descending on a broken, quiet land.

ABOUT THE AUTHOR

Jim Kraus is an accomplished author and senior vice-president of the Periodical Division at Tyndale House Publishers. He and his wife, Terri, live in the Chicago area with their son, Elliot.

Jim earned his B.A. in English from the University of Pittsburgh in 1969 and also participated in the dramatic arts program at the Paris-American Academy in Paris, France. Jim won several awards while a photographer/reporter on a small-town newspaper in southern Minnesota, as well as several cover and design awards while a magazine editor in Chicago.

OTHER BOOKS BY JIM KRAUS

The Unfolding
The Choosing
  MacKenzie Street Series
  coauthored with wife Terri Kraus

The Price
The Treasure
The Promise
The Quest
  The Circle of Destiny Series
  coauthored with wife Terri Kraus

Pirates of the Heart
Passages of Gold
Journey to the Crimson Sea
  Treasures of the Caribbean Series
  coauthored with wife Terri Kraus

His Father Saw Him Coming

NOTES

i   ("The Lord is my shepherd...") Psalm 23:1

ii   (It's in Romans 5:9) Romans 5:9

iii   (And one of the prophets) Zephaniah 1:15

iv   (And wars will break out) Matthew 24:6–8, 29

v   (As she took her first step) Psalm 23:1

vi   (I will uphold you) Isaiah 41:10

vii   (He is the one) 1 Thessalonians 1:10

viii   (If the Scriptures) Mark 13

ix   (I, the Lord, will) Isaiah 13:6–8, 10–11

x   (But it will be shortened) Matthew 24:19, 21–22

xi   (Since we have been) Romans 5:9

xii   (I know that) 1 Corinthians 13:12

xiii   (But you may ask) Matthew 24–25

xiv   (Matthew records that) Matthew 24:14

xv   (Take, for example) Matthew 24:24

xvi   (Because I say) Matthew 24–25

xvii   (But all this) Mark 13:5–8

xviii   (What I say to you) Mark 13:35–37

xix   (For that day) 2 Thessalonians 2:1–3

xx   (Keep alert!) Mark 13:33

xxi   (And the Good News) Matthew 24:13–14

xxii   (An eye for) Exodus 21:24

xxiii   (But if you give) Mark 8:35

ALSO FROM
BARBOUR PUBLISHING

Chayatocha
ISBN 1-59310-051-5
Discover what happens when an innocent man meets
an ancient evil bent on possessing him—as it has
possessed others throughout history.

The Jewel in the Crown
ISBN 1-58660-774-X
A crack security team, hired to compromise the Tower
of London's defenses by stealing the Queen Mother's
crown, is in for a big surprise.

Marduk's Tablet
ISBN 1-58660-768-5
A mysterious, ancient clay tablet, believed to have
healing powers, has led to the death of a researcher.
Can his daughter, pursuing its secrets,
escape the same fate?

Abduction
ISBN 1-58660-812-6
Where is God when nightmares come true?
Detective J. J. Johnson and Zoë Shefford are desperate
for answers when a number of little girls go missing.

Available wherever Christian books are sold.